WINTERTHORNE'S SHARDS

The Curoria Chronicles

E. A. Almanza

Sarcastic Cat Writing, LLC

Copyright © 2024 by Emily Almanza

First Paperback Edition September 29, 2024.

ISBN —— 979-8-9905197-0-1 (paperback)

Printed by Sarcastic Cat Writing, LLC in the USA.

Cover done by Beautiful Book Covers.

Printed Edges done by Painted Wing Publishing.

Editing done by Finnely Raymond King-Scoular.

Sarcastic Cat Writing, LLC
P.O. Box 1352
Hendersonville, NC 28792

To those who feel too much, so they feel nothing at all.

Rindria
Kratos
Sherril
Weorren City
Freedom Gulf
Tressidil
Frisca
Baymore
Otterlow Reservoir
Hasenfort Ocean
Jassini
Carcalet
Skeletosa
Hirane
Minelle
Lake Navitiva
Dalia City
Milca
Darco
Raeria
Dalia
Ansora
Poigenoux
Cowalenes
Musrove Basin
Cowlany Harbor
Raeria City
Pentaine Ocean

Morroek
HELLA
VALEMONT TUNNELS
RETILISK COVE
LAURELLE
CHAUVI
LAKE HOLMERE
THE FAERIE LANDS
Lierre Fideles
BRACENORA HARBOR
Westerlands
ESCADA S-
MARISOPE
COVE OF GHAGYN
Sauvegarde Corolline
ARCHAMA
AIONSTOWN
Le Golfe Lontaine
Arbres Dorés
Perivina Fluere
RAULLE
RAUDES SEA
CALMEAVIS HARBOR

Rindr
TRESSIDIL
FREEDOM GULF
OTTERLOW RESERVOIR
ASENFORT OCEAN
AVONDRA
LAKE NAVITIVA
MUSROVE BASIN
COWLANY HARBOR
PENTAINE OCEAN

Morroek
RETILISK COVE
BRACENORA HARBOR
ESCADA SEA
COVE OF GHAGYN
LE GOLFE LONTAINE
LAKE HOLIMEDS
THE FAERIE LANDS
Thestitiunia
IERAUDES SEA
CALMEANIS HARBOR

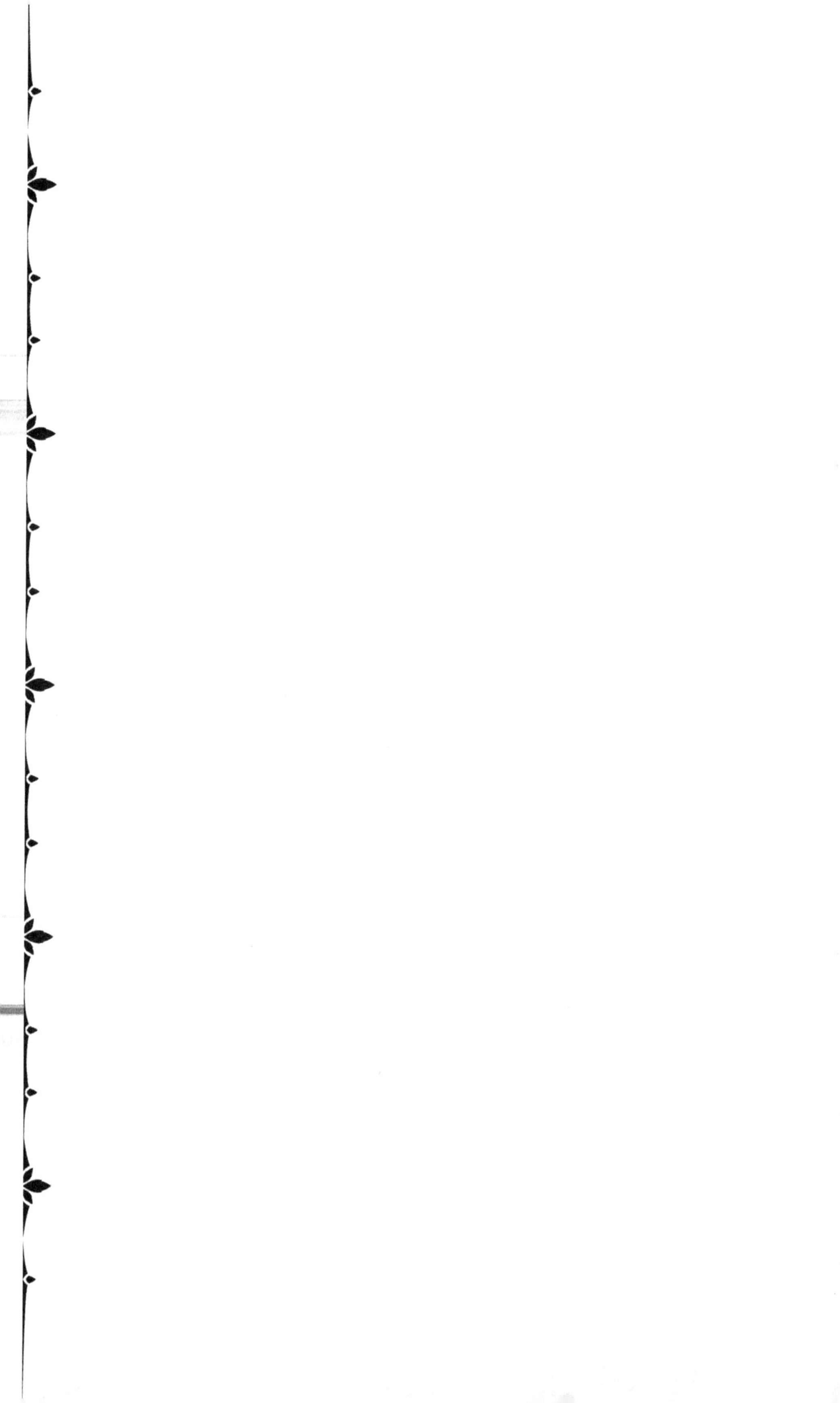

Winterthorne's Shards is a fantasy novel containing adult content such as gratuitous violence, torture, death, grief due to death of loved ones, depictions of post traumatic stress disorder, disabling injuries, mentions of abortion, mentions of suicide, and harsh language. The protagonists in *Winterthorne's Shards* are anti-heroes and as such they will do, say, and think awful things. There are no pillars of virtue in a quest for power.

I n *The Guileful Rose,* Amaria Raulet's friend Delphina died when thieves broke into her home to steal the Raulet Ruby, an ancient magical gem holding dark magic. Shaken with grief, Amaria kills one thief in the Drowning Tombs, a prison in which she has been trained as a torturer by her father, Aaron Raulet.

This unfortunate event occurs on the eve of Amaria's wedding to Theodmon Chauvignon, a powerful lord and warrior from the Westerlands province of Thestitiunia. Theodmon and Amaria marry as planned, and they build a bond of mutual respect and adoration.

In Cesmassia, everybody has an agenda brewing. The Avonnian Queen, Lynette Edrion, plots with dark magic and the Riam government, which is no friend to Thestitiunia. Amaria and Theodmon capture a runaway Riam duchess, Liara Nalaeny, and marry her to Theodmon's brother, Aloysius, to give themselves a foothold in Rindria.

One of the thieves escaped on the night Delphina died, and she managed to get the Raulet Ruby to Princess Clarissa Nalaeny in Rindria. Determined to retrieve the Ruby, Amaria and Theodmon head to Rindria. In the conflict to retake the ruby, Clarissa throws it. The gem shatters and Amaria absorbs the dark magic.

The dark magic starts to overpower Amaria and Lynette unsuccessfully tries to kidnap her.

Durek Svilas, the heir to the Kingdom of Morroek, makes a secret alliance with Theodmon and Amaria, hating Lynette and dark magic more than he hates Thestitiunia.

Theodmon and Amaria make a public alliance with Lynette. All the while, they stage a failed assassination attempt on Clarissa Nalaeny, purposefully implicating themselves. Now, Rindria wants war, and Lynette refuses to help either ally. Morroek and Thestitiunia attack Rindria.

During the attack of Wéorren City, Amaria purposefully gets herself captured. Going mad with the influence of the dark magic, she kills the entire Riam royal family while being tortured in the dungeons below. Once the attack ends and Amaria is ransomed, the Thestitiunians go home. Rindria is heavily weakened with no leadership: the heir to the throne, Tesden Nalaeny has been in exile as so was spared Amaria's massacre. Lucas Bécharil has gone after him. And Tesden's sister, who is second in line for the Riam throne, is none other than Liara Nalaeny.

As the dark magic's influence further impacts Amaria, she and Theodmon meet with the faerie Oberon to destroy the Raulet Ruby. Before destroying the Raulet Ruby, Oberon offers to save Amaria from the dark magic for a price. Amaria agrees and she emerges from the faerie lands around seven months later with wings and more powerful magic. But war against Lynette and dark magic is already underway at the border between Morroek and the Badlands.

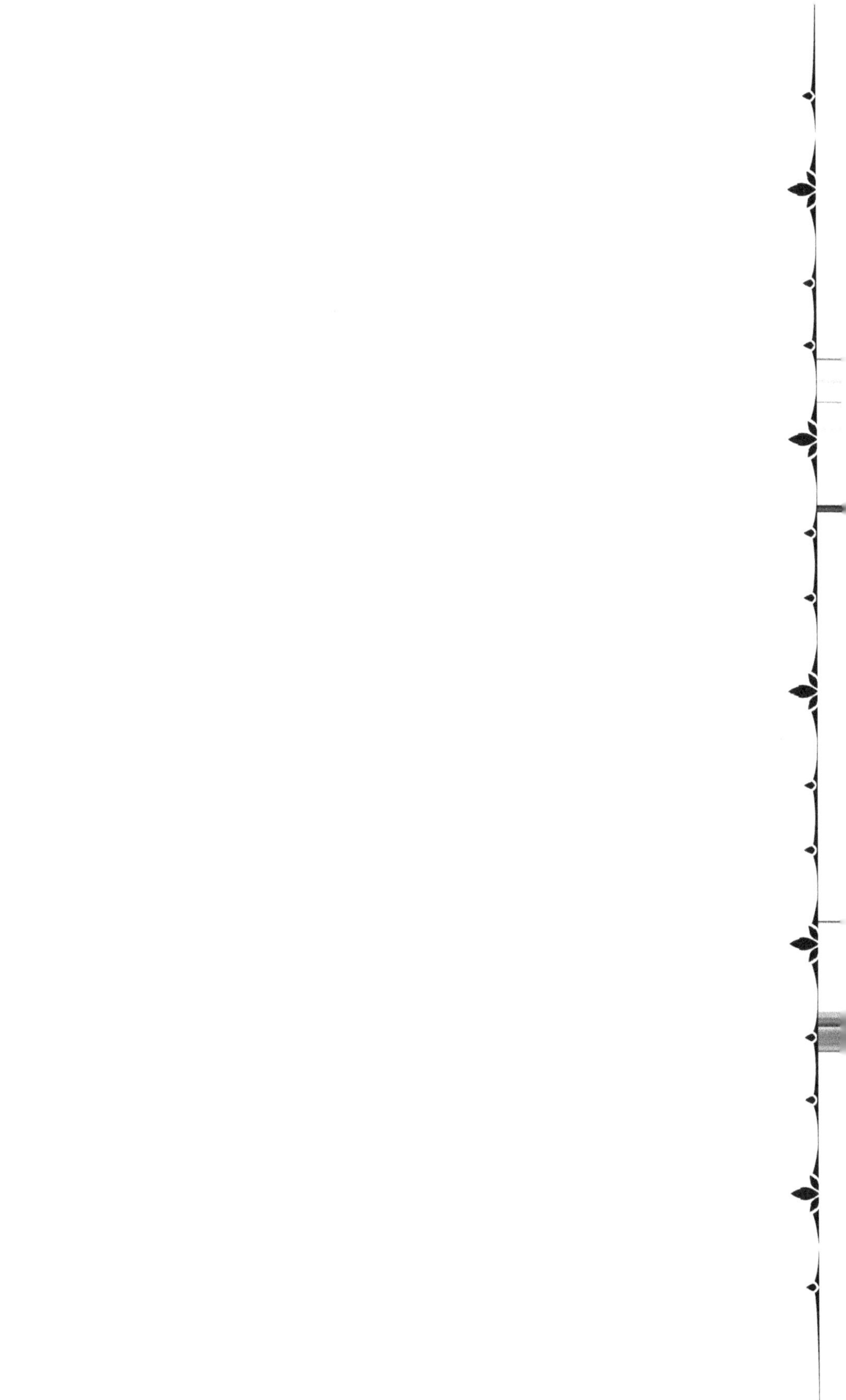

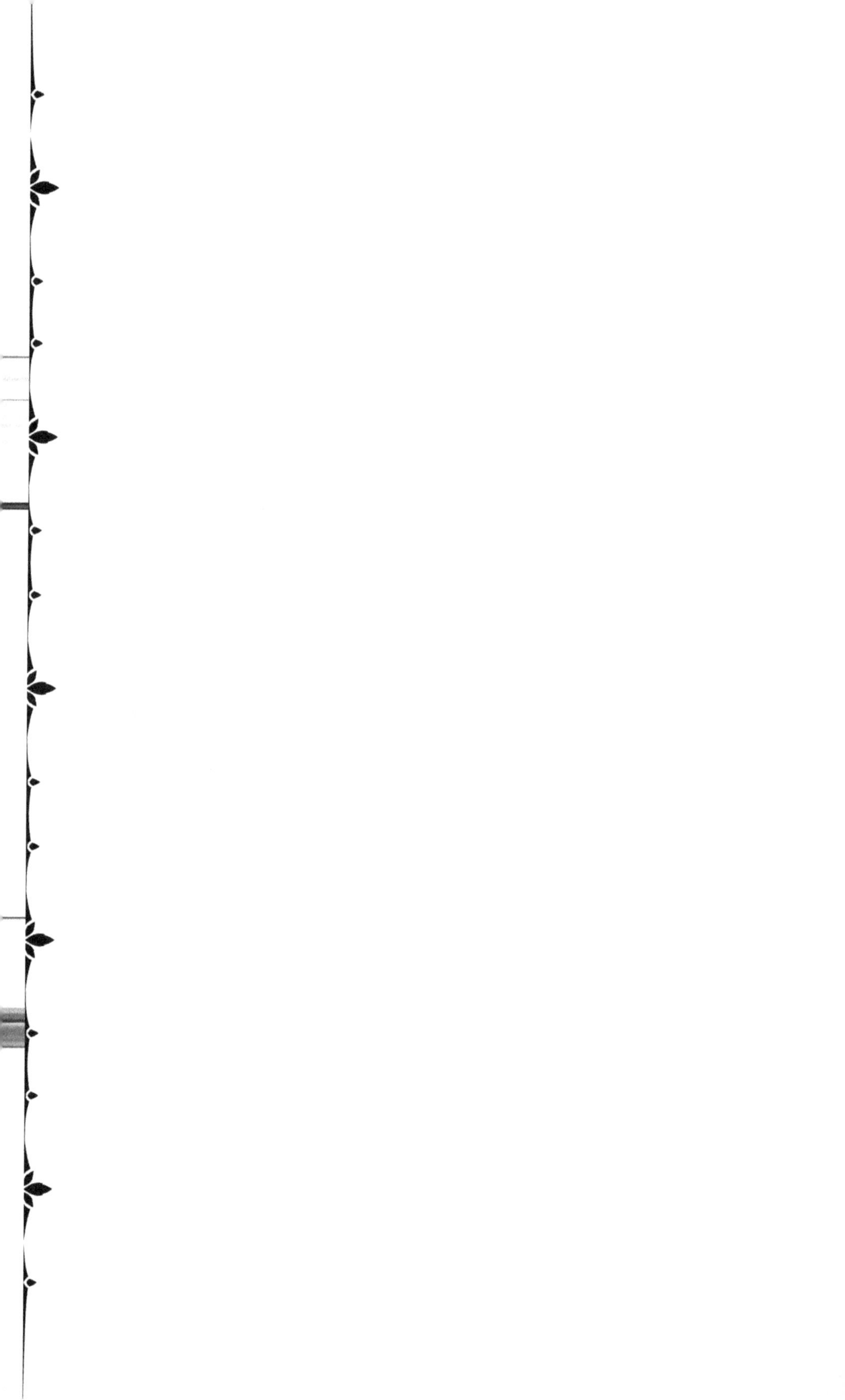

Table of Contents

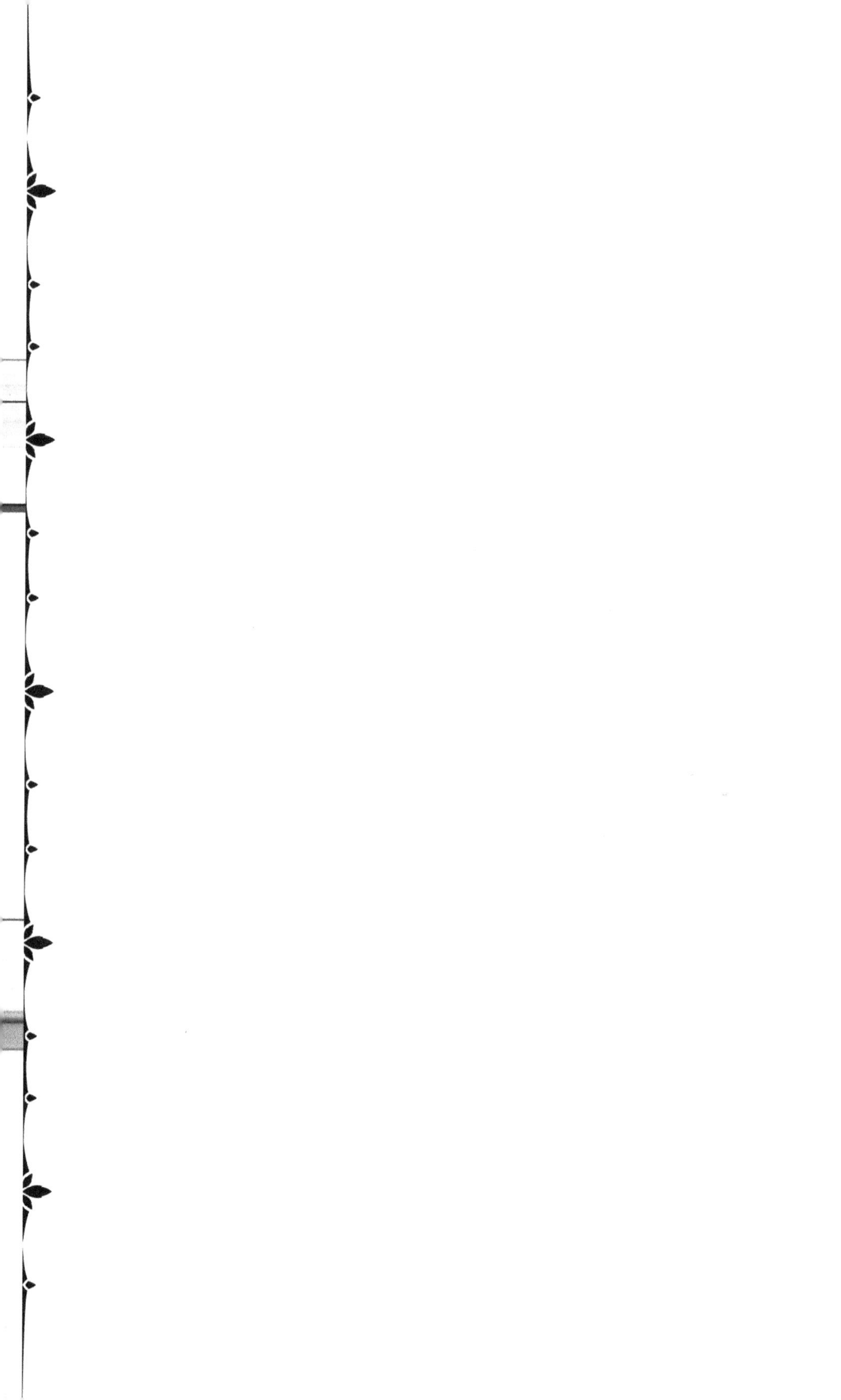

Part One

the queens

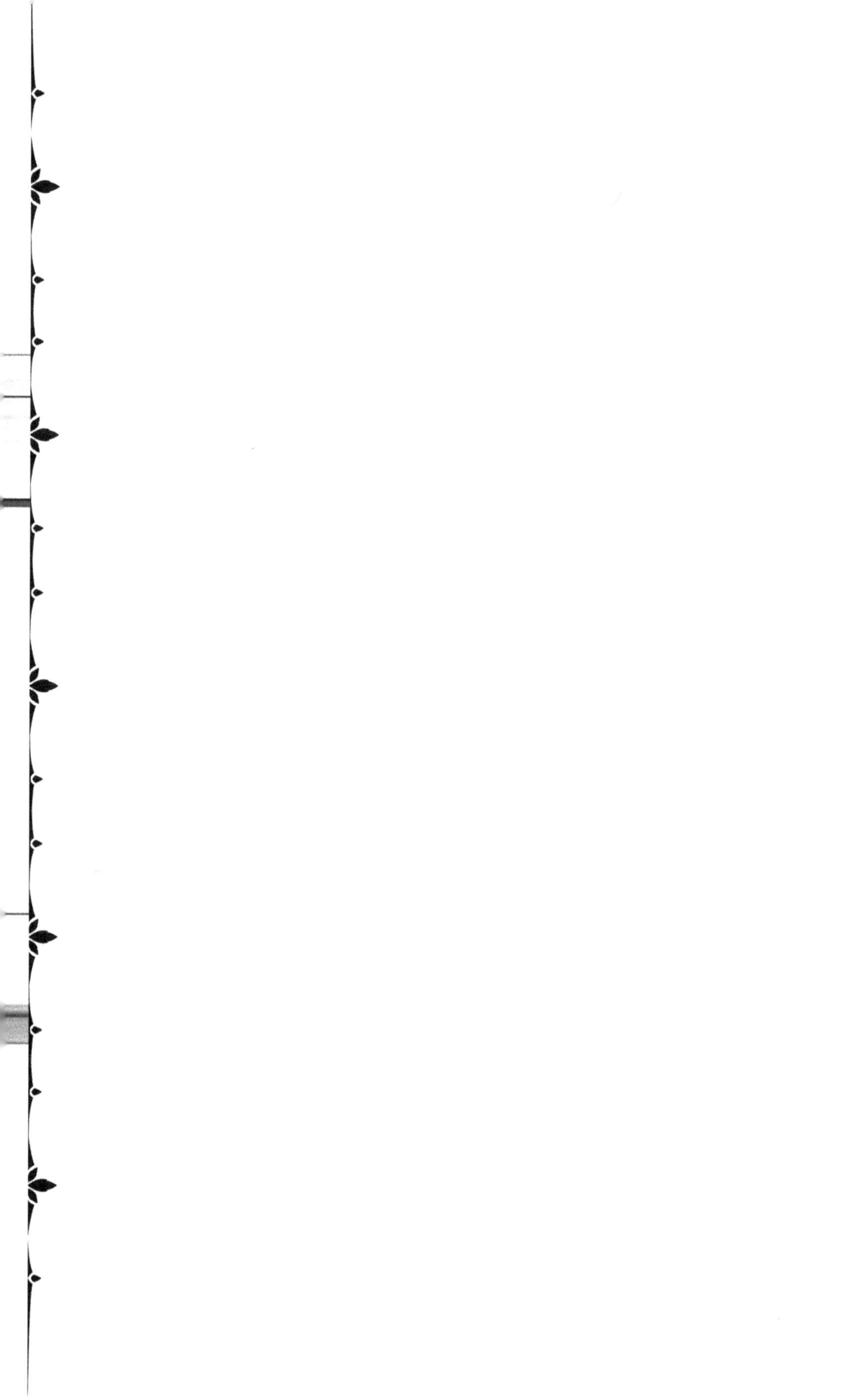

Chapter One

Theodmon held Amaria tight, breathing in the scent of oranges and roses as his hands brushed against feathers. Her wings. The faeries warned them of physical changes, but this was beyond anything he could have ever imagined.

Amaria radiated power, even as a non-mage he felt the magical aura around her pulsating. Her skin now had a silvery glow, her eyes were wider, making her appear younger–but Amaria also seemed older, as if she had seen a thousand years and was jaded from it all. Her hair seemed to be full of life, it didn't hang at her side–rather it seemed as if there was an ever so slight breeze lifting her hair. And the silver eyes glowed a million times brighter than before.

That wasn't even considering the large wings sprouting out of her back. Theodmon sighed. He loved her. But he wasn't sure how to handle what he felt about having a wife who radiated that much power. And before today, he had never been threatened by Amaria.

Theodmon coughed, hiding the choking sound his chest made as he realized he was threatened now. He loved her. She was beautiful. He wouldn't hurt her and she wouldn't hurt him. But how was he supposed to deal with the fact that she had been created to breed for faeries? They claimed she wouldn't have to, that their daughter would be sufficient—whatever the faeries claimed was irrelevant. That was what Amaria was now:

an entity weak enough to not threaten the faeries, but strong enough to birth their kind. He should have never agreed to this. They should have found another way to save her.

"Do you hate them?" Amaria looked upwards at him, her expression fracturing.

Theodmon's hands clenched around her shoulders. He would learn to deal with the wings–love them even. Amaria didn't need him condemning her right now. She was still her. The dark magic left her. Theodmon couldn't explain it, but she felt different. She still had that dangerous edge to her, he loved that about her, but it was more controlled.

She had been erratic with her dark magic. It wasn't the actions Amaria did–burning someone alive, manipulating people, and planning assassinations wasn't abnormal for her. However, how Amaria seemed to have no control over herself, as if she was compelled into insanity by an unknown force instead of choosing to maim, torture, and kill of her own volition. If Theodmon was honest with himself, it scared him. His hand brushed over Amaria's face as he pulled her into a kiss. She was alive and safe, and that was all that mattered.

Theodmon pulled away from their kiss. "I love them. They suit you."

Amaria scoffed and rolled her eyes. "Now you're just coddling me."

"No, I'm not, and I mean it." He brushed the top of her hair with his palm. "I promised you I'd always love you. This changes nothing. Besides, we're going to fight Lynette, I think this can be a morale booster. You look righteous, like an angel from the gods."

She was angelic to him–beautiful, fierce, intelligent. Gods, he was happy she was alive and he wouldn't have to marry one of Durek Svilas's simpering, idiotic daughters. His daughters were nice enough, but bland; they were so unremarkable Theodmon couldn't even remember their names. A Svilas girl would tell him what he wanted to hear, shying away from hard realities. And he was sure they would be disgusted with him as they heard about the things he did.

Amaria never looked at him with disappointment because she understood why he did the things he did. He didn't have to hide the dark part of himself, suppressing it so she wouldn't back away in terror. She knew him and she embraced him all the same.

"Angels haven't done the things I've done," Amaria said.

Theodmon pulled her closer to him. He didn't care what sins Amaria committed, they were necessary. And besides, he'd done worse. She shivered against him, and his eyes softened as he noticed her lips turning blue. She wasn't dressed for this weather–she wore a flimsy silver dress that exposed her arms and back. She looked striking but miserable in the cold, and he wrapped his cloak more firmly around her.

"An angel of death then," he conceded, if only to give her a win. "I've always loved how ruthless you are."

Oberon approached from a distance, the trees seeming to bend away from him as he walked through the woods. He came more into focus, to where Theodmon saw the smug bastard's smirk. Theodmon restrained his scowl; the last thing he wanted to deal with was the faerie who transformed his wife, who laid claim to his unborn daughter in marriage. Oberon did what Theodmon couldn't—Theodmon was supposed to protect his family, not a creature with wings and green skin.

His hands moved towards her, cradling the bump on her belly with his palms. Theodmon cursed the fae, it'd been months since Amaria left with Oberon and Theodmon guessed she was around seven months pregnant.

"They want me to train with them for the war." Amaria appeared pained, as if she were spitting glass out of her mouth with each word.

Theodmon sighed. That would be sensible. He could see how unacclimated she was to her new physiology–she was stumbling like a drunk, the wings dragging behind her with each step. Theodmon knew that Amaria needed the faeries to train her, not that she was training with them. But what good would come of telling her that now? He hadn't seen her since summer, there was no point in fighting.

"I missed you," Theodmon kissed the top of her head as Oberon materialized from the end of his walk. Theodmon tensed, focusing on breathing so as not to flinch away from the faerie.

"Tell me about the war preparation." The faerie haughtily looked over at Theodmon. "How are the final touches?"

Amaria looked between Oberon and Theodmon. "Final touches?"

Theodmon's eyebrows bunched together as he realized that Amaria had no knowledge of what occurred in the human world since she left with Oberon into his realm.

"There's been a large breach in the Badlands near the Morrian border." Theodmon's shoulders slumped, his energy draining. "Dark creatures are escaping, Lynette invaded and Avondra acquired Morrian land. Svilas is worried."

"And what're the final touches?" Amaria crossed her arms, her voice increasing in pitch.

Theodmon was worried too. Not that he was going to admit that around Oberon.

"We have to close the Badlands. The faeries and their power can help us, but...." Theodmon trailed off, the words catching in his throat.

"So we're closing it?" Amaria pressed.

"Not yet," Oberon said. "The humans will have to stall until we arrive."

Stall. Theodmon's nostrils flared. That's all they'd been able to do, stall and hold the line. And humans died and died and died waiting for the promised faerie aid. It hadn't come yet, and it wouldn't come for a while. Theodmon didn't want to go back to the border of the Badlands and fight an unwinnable war, allowing deaths that were preventable if the faeries pulled through their end of the bargain.

"Why aren't we going now?" Amaria glared at Oberon.

"Because you can barely walk," Oberon dismissed. "When you no longer have the upper-body strength of a sickly chicken we'll discuss leaving for war."

Amaria's jaw clenched. "You've changed my physiology—"

"We're gathering supplies and troops," Theodmon interrupted. No matter how much he wanted to fight Oberon, that fighting an ally they needed was unwise. "Some Avonnians are helping us. They despise dark magic and Lynette–your aunt among them." Theodmon tried to keep his voice calm as he referenced Miana Raulet, now the Duchess Alexandre of the Province of Dalia of Avondra. She was a vicious, conniving snake; likely fighting not as an actual aversion to dark magic but as an opportunity to seize the Avonnian throne after Lynette was deposed.

Theodmon understood that Miana had ulterior motives, but as long as they aligned with his, and he could secure his sister, Ophelia, and her husband increased positions in Queen Miana's court, he didn't give a shit how devious she was.

"How fast can you train me?" She looked over at Oberon, the corners of her silver eyes tightening.

Oberon flexed his fingers, his lips becoming thinner. "Months–"

"We don't have months." Amaria scowled at Oberon.

"You need to give birth," Oberon snapped.

"I'll give birth after we take care of the Badlands."

"That's ridiculous," Oberon sputtered.

Theodmon despised agreeing with Oberon on anything, but the faerie had a point. Amaria's wings weighed her down and Theodmon guessed it would take a month or two at minimum to train Amaria, and at that point she would be near her due date. Despite how strong Amaria was, she couldn't stop nature, and her giving birth in the middle of battle was something Theodmon wanted to avoid.

"Train." Theodmon embraced Amaria, looking into her eyes. "Meet us at the front when you're ready. We can hold it until then. You nearly passed out last time you were in labor, imagine if you did that in front of a hoard of unicorns."

He didn't want to imagine those beautiful silver horses tearing Amaria apart, eating her limb by limb. Still, the image flashed in front of him and he clenched his jaw. "Please, deliver here where it's safe. For me."

"I'm not weak because I'm pregnant," Amaria crossed her arms.

"I never said that," Theodmon whispered. "Training will make you more fearsome, and you need to train. You can barely walk with those wings...can you fly with them?"

"Not yet," Amaria said in a flat, emotionless tone, her shoulders slumping.

"Imagine Lynette seeing you coming from the sky to kill her. The terror she'll feel." Theodmon's hands cupped Amaria's face. "Train. Please."

Amaria's chest rose and fell, her expression as harsh and unreadable as stone. Theodmon didn't want to argue with her. Yes, Amaria was capable and her pregnancy didn't change that. However, last time she was at a battle she had gotten herself captured and tortured. And she had just gone through...well, whatever the faeries did to her. She needed to acclimate. He needed Amaria deadly, not dead.

"Alright," Amaria sighed. "I'll train and give birth before going to war. It's only a few months, right?"

Theodmon exhaled. Good. He didn't have to argue with her.

"Go back to the faerie lands," Oberon commanded Amaria. "I need to speak with the liaison."

"Then you can tell me as well." Amaria's eyes flashed.

"The liaison title belongs to your husband, not you. Go back into the forest. I'll–"

"You should respect your future mother-in-law," Amaria challenged.

Theodmon bit on his lower lip, hiding his smirk, as his heart ballooned with pride. "I'll tell her everything anyways."

Oberon cast both of them a dark glance. "Fine." He met Theodmon's eyes. "It may be best to leave the baby with us when she is born."

"No," Amaria said. "She'll join you when she's of marriageable age *for a human*, and not a second before."

"The faerie lands aren't another human kingdom–"

"I'm aware, I've been there," Amaria snarled.

"Then you know how human bodies react to exposure to it," Oberon said. "She should grow up there, gain a tolerance."

"She'll gain a tolerance when she joins you as your wife," Theodmon interjected. "At eighteen." He shouldn't instigate Oberon, but the faerie infuriated him with his sneers and scoffs. Oberon was a necessary evil they had to align themselves with to defeat Lynette, who threatened instability for everyone. And Theodmon, despite everything, preferred Oberon to Lynette. Oberon was a self-satisfied prick but at least he had never tried to tear his marriage apart.

"I'll see you soon." Amaria's body pressed against his. Theodmon didn't want to let her go as he kissed the top of her head, his lips brushing over her hair.

"Try not to kill Lynette until I get there," Amaria chuckled, but the laugh caught in her throat, as if she was trying not to cry.

"Never," Theodmon said, his voice breaking. "You're the angel of death, aren't you?"

"I think we both are." Amaria looked at him pointedly. Theodmon sighed, understanding that she was referencing a nickname he'd received at sixteen: the Archangel of Harréow Field.

"Come home to me." Theodmon's arms tightened around Amaria.

"Only if you promise the same."

He cupped her face in his hands, lifting it upward in a kiss. He was being forceful, but he couldn't bear the thought of losing her once again. This winter had been hell. Every night Amaria wasn't laying next to him had been agony, especially considering he didn't even know if she was still alive.

This time will be different. Theodmon pulled her closer to him, her soft skin brushing against his, inflaming his senses. *She's alive. She's not undergoing life changing–physiology altering–procedures.* He took a deep breath, trying to force back the protruding through.

Childbirth.

Theodmon couldn't think too hard on that–he couldn't afford to spiral right now. Not with Lynette still alive. Not when he had to focus on fighting.

Theodmon and Amaria pulled away from each other.

"I love you." Amaria blinked back tears before she turned on her heel, heading towards the faerie lands, her wings dragging in the dirt behind her.

Theodmon looked over at Oberon. "I'll head out. I have a long ride ahead of me."

"No you don't," Oberon said. Theodmon stopped himself from grinding his teeth. Oberon had the noxious habit of always thinking he had the most important thing to say.

"Where's my horse?" Theodmon stepped closer to Oberon, cracking his knuckles.

"I transported it to Morroek already."

"Then how am I getting to Morroek?" Theodmon's jaw locked as he debated whether punching Oberon was worth the repercussions.

"We're going to transcend."

"That's helpful," Theodmon said dryly. "What's transcending?"

"Hold onto my arm."

"What?"

Oberon lunged at Theodmon. On instinct, Theodmon raised his foot, intending to kick the faerie away from him. Instead, as soon as Oberon touched him, Theodmon was pulled through a tunnel at a speed that made his skin feel as if it was melting from his body. He saw bright flashes of lights and he shut his eyes, trying not to scream as he felt as if every tendon was torn and sewn back together.

And then he was on all fours, his fingers becoming numb from the cold ground. He heard shouts of men and the clanging of metal. Theodmon forced himself to open his eyes, and he saw Thestitiunian, Morrian, Tressi, and some Avonnian flags flying around him, tents set up around them, and a vast field ahead.

Theodmon saw Durek Svilas and Aaron Raulet riding over on their horses towards him as he began to vomit into the snow.

Oberon left the war camp, disappearing into thin air as Aaron and Durek circled Theodmon, asking him questions without giving him time to breathe.

Theodmon forced himself to sit upright on his knees.

"Where'd he go?" Durek's head whipped around as he searched for the faerie.

"Not important." Theodmon pressed his eyes shut. "Svilas, can you help me stand up?"

Durek snorted. "You can't stand up?"

"I was pulled through a magical portal and traveled from the outskirts of the faerie lands to here in a matter of seconds," Theodmon snapped. "No, I cannot fucking stand up."

"Get him to a tent," Aaron directed. "We need to discuss the upcoming battle."

"Another one?" Theodmon questioned. Durek grumbled, but he helped Theodmon to his feet. Theodmon groaned, black spots dotting his vision.

"We need to be on the offensive for once," Durek said. "We're being slaughtered defending the line."

Theodmon, gritting his teeth, leaned against Durek, as they trudged to the tents through the gray slush. He didn't disagree with Durek's sentiment, but he wasn't sure that going on the offensive would fix the issue. Theodmon opened his mouth to critique Durek and instead vomited again.

Chapter Two

A few weeks later, Theodmon surveyed his foot soldiers as they stood in the cold, waiting for the signal to attack. He could feel the nip of frost even through his gloves. Theodmon rubbed his hands together, trying to warm them. The soldiers shivered, the furs of the winter uniforms not enough to keep out the brutal chill.

Phantagero, Theodmon's war stallion, neighed as he tossed his mane. Next to Theodmon, Henri was on his own horse, holding the gold and scarlet Chauvignon banner, a sword hanging from his hip. Usually Lucas would be in this position, but he was gods knew where, hunting for Tesden Nalaeny; and Lucas had been gone since the royal family was slaughtered in Rindria. Haerdnor surveyed the battlefield nearby with his bannerman, Oliver Neremoux, at his side, displaying the Raulet flag.

The black mountains loomed ahead of them, and if Theodmon squinted he could almost make out the silhouettes of dark creatures lining up in their own formations.

"This will likely be a long one," Henri muttered. He appeared nauseated and Theodmon wondered what he heard from the thoughts around them. Theodmon gave him a pained smile in sympathy. He could only imagine the pain Henri felt in being able to read minds but not be able to control what thoughts he heard.

"Have you told the Morrians about Amaria's wings?" Aloysius looked over at the Morrian troops that joined in with the Thestitiunians. The Morrians were deeply superstitious people who hated magic, and Theodmon cringed as he imagined how they would react to Amaria's wings. They already viewed Amaria with extreme suspicion; Amaria helping her father, albeit at the emperor's request, manufacture a famine in Morroek didn't invite likability.

"Are you sure you didn't hallucinate?" Aloysius continued. "It sounds unbelievable."

"I know what I saw," Theodmon said. He knew what he felt, too—the brush of feathers and the flex of bone and tendon. And he didn't need this argument to distract him before battle.

"Have you seen your sister recently?" Henri asked, his eyes drifting between the two brothers. "Ophelia lives in Avondra, right?"

Theodmon curtly nodded. He hadn't spoken with Ophelia in a long while. He sent up a silent prayer to Vathar, promising the god that after this battle, if he survived, he'd write to his sister.

He turned to face the soldiers, his heart thudding.

"Ready for this?" Henri muttered to Theodmon.

"As ready as I'll ever be."

Theodmon nodded towards the heralder, and at his command, the horn signaling the charge blew. Theodmon pulled out his sword, Winterthorne, before he spurred his horse, leading the charge towards the Badlands.

Aloysius, Haerdnor, and Henri followed suit, prompting the rest of the front unit to march forth behind their bannermen.

"Stay close, watch each other's backs." Aloysius nodded affirmatively.

"See you on the other side?" Henri gripped his horse's reins.

"See you on the other side." Theodmon confirmed before he raised his sword to the sky and swung it forward in one smooth stride, pointing the tip straight towards the Avonnian side where they were cozy with the dark creatures. Theodmon squinted, trying to distinguish the creatures, seeing the silvery glow of a herd of unicorns, giant spiders, and wraiths.

His stomach rolled, wondering how anyone could bear to ally themselves with monsters, to fight with the rejects of the gods. It was unnatural, and the fact that Morroek and Thestitiunia were fighting together against it showed the severity of the depravity Lynette was engaging in.

Theodmon's face turned red and he lifted his sword upwards.

The soldiers ran, calvary behind the lines of foot soldiers, meeting the Avonnians aligned with Lynette in the middle of the field. An arrow whooshed past Theodmon. He ducked, rolling off his horse in his attempt to not be pierced to death. Theodmon stood up from the ground as an enemy soldier ran towards him. Theodmon raised his shield blocking the blow of a sword; he swung Winterthorne up and attempted to stab the soldier from below. The soldier blocked Theodmon's blow. Theodmon dropped his shield and pulled a dagger from his side, and he thrusted it upwards. Theodmon rolled from under the soldier, stepping over him as he cut the enemy's chest open with his sword. As Theodmon pulled Winterthorne from the soldier, he fell to the ground, blood splashing from his body as it stained the gray slush further.

"Fuck," Theodmon panted. His horse was nowhere to be found. And he heard the clicking of pinchers approaching from his left. His body tensed, he turned towards the sound, knowing what it was before he saw it.

She had to have fucking spiders. Theodmon blanched as they crawled towards him, their pincers contorting as they scurried down the hill like demons. His breath caught in his chest as he felt his legs tightening, flinching as his knuckles turned white. He didn't like spiders even during the best of times–and giant, man-eating spiders were far from that. His hair raising on his neck, wishing he could flee. Theodmon steadied his sword in front of him as the spiders crawled towards him.

"Fuck!" Aloysius's eyes glowed a dark crimson as his skin turned to bronze.

Ah, Aloysius, the human shield. Theodmon hoped that his brother's magic was strong enough to stop him–well all of them, from being torn apart by the spider's mouth. Theodmon shuddered, bringing his sword up to hack a spider's leg off.

A soldier shrieked as a spider spit on him, his skin melting from his bones, appearing as if wax. The bones deteriorated just as quickly, becoming a pile of goo in a matter of seconds.

"Get back!" Haerdnor commanded, his hands already lit; he threw handfuls of fire, rapidly hitting each spider in turn. The fire wasn't powerful or large enough to destroy the spiders, it was only angering them as they seemed to shake off the flames with their pinchers clicking more rapidly. All the spiders were on fire but the flames didn't spread quickly enough. Theodmon's hands shook, his sword slipping.

"Give me energy you two," Haerdnor directed Henri and Aloysius, sweat beading his forehead. Scrambling towards him, the other two mages placed their hands on Haerdnor, and Theodmon saw Henri's blue aura swirl from his hand to Haerdnor's hand.

"Now," Haerndor gasped, Aloysius and Henri stepped back as Haerdnor launched a series of fireballs. They had to find a way to fight these beasts without getting close to them. Theodmon cursed, wishing one of them was an archer.

The flames engulfing the spiders were brighter, but it still didn't seem to be enough to destroy them. "Retreat," Theodmon commanded, backing away from the spiders, the hairs of his neck standing up on end.

And then the flames exploded at once. Theodmon didn't know spiders could scream but it was high pitched and braying. And although he should be relieved, he was just in pain.

Worse still, Haerdnor fell off his horse and now seemed to be unconscious.

"He burned too much energy." Oliver dismounted to clumsily throw Haerdnor's body over his own horse. "Theodmon, take Haerdnor's horse, just until you find your own. I'm bringing him to the medics."

Theodmon nodded, watching as another wave of enemies seemed to appear from over the hill. These ones were worse than spiders–cheimónas. An otherwise beautiful woman, this evil creature was haunting with the blood pouring from her eyes and down her face. Underneath her, the snow turned black as the air turned even colder and Theodmon's nose upturned as he smelled something putrid. A cheimóna killed the land she touched and caused famine and disease. He hadn't ever seen one. They were supposed to be myths. Legends. But no, cheimónas were as real as he was.

"They can't touch us." Henri's voice shook. "They touch us and we're dead."

Theodmon's heart pounded. They needed archers. And they had lost their fire mage. Theodmon stepped backwards, breathing heavily as he mounted Haerdnor's horse. "We're going to retreat. We need ranged weapons."

"I'm reaching out." Aloysius's eyes glowed with his magic once more. "The mage links are blocked up, it's chaotic."

"I need to get back to camp," Henri added. Theodmon noticed how much he was shaking for the first time. Theodmon's stomach sank. As a mind reader, Henri must be suffering more than most–often Theodmon wondered how he didn't go insane. He knew he likely would have if he had to hear everyone's dying thoughts.

"Three...two...one," Theodmon threw himself on Henri's horse, bursting into a gallop, narrowly missing the lunging grasp of a cheimóna.

"Archers! Cheimónas!" Aloysius shouted as they rode. Perhaps someone would understand what was needed in those panicked two words. Over and over again he screamed this through the battle and he continued to scream it as they reached their war camp.

"What's happened?" Durek Svilas ran from the stone bridge that had been used as an archers tower, a flaming arrow still in hand.

"Cheimónas," Theodmon said. "If they touch you, you die. We need ranged weapons to kill them...it's too risky with swords. Fire mages can help."

"And wind?" Durek asked suspiciously. Theodmon couldn't blame him, last time ranged magic had been used in battle around Durek, Amaria used her wind magic to strangle elephants. And then the entire Riam royal family.

"If they're powerful enough–which if we're using Amaria as a baseline, you'll not find many. Fire is easier as they're approaching now," Theodmon said. "Give me a bow. I'll help."

"Are you an archer?" Durek asked.

"I've hunted." Theodmon followed Durek to the archers tower. Behind him, Aloysius followed. Henri was going to his tent. Theodmon noted that it wasn't a medics tent, but he didn't fault Henri for avoiding that place. Being around injured and dying people was likely the last thing a mind reader needed right now.

Theodmon himself didn't have that option. Not now with the cheimónas rushing towards them. How could the human Avonnians bear to side with Lynette? Wouldn't the cheimónas kill them too after there were no more enemy forces? Surely they realized that.

Of course they do. Theodmon scolded himself as he grabbed a crossbow and arrows. *Lynette likely has leverage over them. They likely are saving their reputation or trying to keep a relative alive. Maybe some are blinded by money.*

He reached the top of the bridge. Next to him, Durek was loading his longbow. On Theodmon's other side, Aloysius was loading up another crossbow.

The cheimónas were approaching.

"Crossbows are more accurate, focus on that," Durek barked. "Longbows, light your arrows on fire and shoot as many as you can. Accuracy is important, but volume is needed more."

Arrows and flames rained down on the battlefield. The cheimónas fell with merciless shrieks, the land turning black around them. Theodmon ground his teeth as he released an arrow from his crossbow. Despite the onslaught, cheimónas still rushed forward, their shrieks causing Theodmon's blood to freeze. Theodmon released his arrows into the ones withering on the ground. Better to kill them before they could recover..

"Keep firing!" Durek commanded.

Arrows flew until the last cheimóna fell to the ground, withering as she shrieked in pain, her scream dying with her.

And then there was a silence over the battlefield. The hairs on the back of Theodmon's neck stood on end, and he frantically surveyed the field for the next threat.

And then, there was a female, *a human*, scream that reverberated from the battlefield. His heart thudding, Theodmon scanned the field, trying to find the noise.

As if the gods cruelly wanted him to see this, Theodmon's head whipped to where the female scream came from. And he saw Ophelia, his sister, chained and being dragged out by Lyseno Vypren.

A muscle jumped in Theodmon's cheek as he stared down at the Avonnian duke. He was Amaria's old fiancé; he had tried to carve out her organs when the engagement was broken. His heart thudded, the lump in his throat bobbing and becoming larger.

Ophelia. Theodmon notched an arrow in his crossbow, releasing it towards Vypren. The arrow missed.

Theodmon cursed the god of war, Vathar, under his breath as his feverish eyes couldn't break away from Ophelia's face. Her lips were moving rapidly, and she tried to pull away from Vypren despite being chained. Theodmon released another arrow. It found Vypren's arm as a mark.

Theodmon clutched his crossbow as he loaded it up with another arrow, scolding himself for focusing so much on sword fighting and not enough on archery. Vypren pulled out his sword as Theodmon released the arrow.

The arrow struck Ophelia in the chest. She screamed out in pain and Theodmon winced, his eyes momentarily shutting. He wasn't an archer. He was making this worse. He couldn't save Ophelia, he could only hurt her further. Theodmon looked at Ophelia, wishing he could tell her how much he regretted his poor aim. How he wished he could have her safely away from that vile manifestation of a man.

Vypren raised his sword as he pushed Ophelia onto the ground. Theodmon loaded his crossbow, bargaining with the gods to save Ophelia as if they cared. In one fell swoop, Vypren cut Ophelia's head off. Theodmon screamed, dragging his nails down his cheeks, as Ophelia's body fell onto the ground. Theodmon pulled an arrow into his crossbow, haphazardly releasing it. He missed. Tears streamed down Theodmon's face as he loaded another arrow as Vypren fled towards the catapults.

Theodmon's blood boiled as the catapult released. He wanted to kill Vypren. He wanted him to suffer ten million deaths, each one worse than what he had done to Ophelia. He wanted the gods to resurrect Vypren so he could do it again. Still, as it raced towards the stone bridge they had been using as an archers stand, Theodmon dove away from the bundle hurtling towards them. It landed on the stone —but it wasn't heavy enough to break the stone and it wasn't on fire.

"Gods!" Durek's face paled as he moved the fabric holding the bundle.

Theodmon stood up, rushing towards the delivery. He almost vomited when he saw what was inside. But he didn't–he decided Vypren would suffer instead. Vypren and the Avonnians sealed their fate when they delivered Ophelia's head, along with her children's and husband's heads, at Theodmon's feet.

Chapter Three

The day after Theodmon left, Amaria woke up to Oberon dumping ice cold water on her. She jumped out of bed, cursing. "Why did you do that?"

"I've slowed time down here so it matches the human realms." Oberon stepped away from her as she shook water from her arms.

"Why did you throw ice water on me?" Amaria glared at him.

"You have to train."

Amaria's stomach hardened. "And throwing freezing water on me was necessary for that?"

"You can warm and dry yourself off." Oberon shrugged. "Try it."

Try it? Amaria's nostrils flared at the faerie's condescending tone. Warming and drying oneself off was a basic wind mage skill, she had this mastered by the time she was six. She summoned the wind, channeling the same focus and energy she always had, bringing the warm air towards her and then a funnel of wind erupted, the gale growing as her magic burst from her. Amaria's hair whipped around her face, and the mattress was blown from the bed frame.

Amaria dropped her hands as she stopped summoning her magic. As she did so, the wind died. "Did I do that?"

"You can't use your magic like you did before," Oberon said.

Amaria's jaw locked as her eyes narrowed. "Thank you for the insight."

"Why can't you use your magic like you did before?" Oberon asked pointedly.

"I'm sure you're going to tell me."

"You have more power," Oberon continued as if Amaria hadn't spoken. "You need less force to do simple things. Don't human mages have a similar concept?"

"You don't have to be condescending," Amaria grumbled.

"Try again," Oberon commanded.

Amaria crossed her arms, puckering her lips. He was infuriating, arrogant, and she wanted to smack the smirk off his mint colored face. *Stop,* she chided herself. *Calm down.* She forced herself to uncross her arms, bringing a small sliver of power to the tips of her finger tips.

"Good," Oberon encouraged. "Dry yourself."

Amaria breathed deeply, the air filled up her diaphragm as she released her magic, drying herself off with a warm breeze. As her dress fluttered around her, she laughed. She was doing it–she was controlling her magic and it took no effort at all.

The brush of summoned air brushed past the perfume bottle near her, shattering. Amaria dropped her hands, looking at her feet, her face flushing with heat.

Her magic took no effort but it now required significantly more self-control.

Oberon scoffed under his breath. "Alright, I'll see you outside."

"For what?"

"Training you how to walk." Oberon narrowed his nose at her as the weight of the wings forced her to hunch and hold onto the bedpost for support. "I've seen newborn kittens with more coordination than you."

"Have some manners," Amaria snapped. She didn't want to train. Training would mean that she accepted this deal she had made with Oberon—she had bargained her life for her daughter's but she couldn't admit that. She was an awful mother, she shouldn't have made this choice.

"Manners for humans?" Oberon scoffed.

"What manners do the fae have?" Amaria impulsively said, regretting the words as soon as they came out of her mouth.

"Since you're ready to fight you shouldn't have an issue with training," Oberon remarked.

Amaria groaned, dragging her feet. She shouldn't be struggling with walking. She had never had issues with it before, in fact she had impeccable posture. She folded her arms in front of each other, forming a barrier between herself and Oberon's ceaseless criticism.

"You're a spoiled child," Oberon tapped his foot as he stood by the door. "Hurry up."

"I've never needed any sort of physical strength before," Amaria snarled, striding faster towards Oberon, forcing herself to maintain eye-contact. "In fact, it'd be highly discouraged."

"You need it now," Oberon dismissed, the two of them walking through his house, carved out of a tree, perhaps still living.

Amaria forced back a lump in her throat, her lips pressing together with a small tremor. She could run from whatever Oberon had in store here, hide away from faeries and magic the rest of her days.

Don't be stupid, Amaria told herself as the hair on her nape stiffened. *I'm not going to let a moment of self-doubt ruin my life.*

I let it ruin my daughter's—-no, I didn't. Amaria felt nauseous as her thoughts raced through her head. *She'd have died if I didn't do this.*

A sob threatened to escape her. "You could have picked any other physical manifestation–"

"No," Oberon interrupted sternly. "That was entirely your magic's fault."

"My fault?" Amaria's eyebrows rose incredulously as she crossed her arms.

"Yes," Oberon rolled his eyes as they stepped into the forest. "Try taking some accountability, won't you?" He pointed at a branch that was perfectly level to two trees, growing from them both. It looked a lot like a pull-up bar.

"No." Amaria stepped away from Oberon, shaking her head. "I can't even stand and you think I can do pull-ups?"

"No." Oberon smirked. "I know you can't, that's why I'm having you do flexed arm hangs."

Amaria didn't even know what that exercise was. She turned her body away from Oberon, staring out at the forest. "I'm going to fail." The admission felt like a knife was being twisted in her heart.

"Yes," Oberon agreed, "but you'll get stronger. Now stop wasting time."

Amaria grumbled under her breath as she followed him to the bars.

"Jump," Oberon directed once she was standing under the bar.

Amaria gritted her teeth together and jumped, barely moving from the ground.

"Use your wings." Oberon summoned an apple from thin air. He leaned against a tree, taking a bite. "Go on."

Amaria's cheeks flushed and she looked upwards at the bar above. She lifted her wings, grunting from the effort. And then she jumped, frantically flapping them as if she were a dying baby bird. But it worked, and gripped the wood with her palms.

And she dropped to the ground, falling on her back, as she was unable to hold her weight. She heard Oberon laughing behind her.

"Aren't you worried that falling from pull-up bars is risky to your future bride?" Amaria whirled her head around to glare at Oberon, her eyes blazing. "What happens to our agreement if my daughter doesn't come out healthy?"

"I guess you'll have to give me another one," Oberon said blandly. "Now run."

"I'm pregnant!" Amaria protested.

"Wasn't it you who said you weren't weak because you're pregnant?" Oberon smirked.

"I meant with magic!"

"If you don't start acting like a powerful magical being instead of a helpless damsel I'm going to make you run by setting my hounds on you," Oberon threatened.

Amaria glared at him, but started jogging, the wings pulling her back and dragging in the ground. She made it one lap around the massive tree that held Oberon's home, her lungs burning as she collapsed on the ground.

"Again." Oberon threw a thorny briar he summoned at her.

Amaria coughed, feeling as if her muscles were being torn apart.

"Get your shit together." Oberon forcefully pulled her to her feet. "I don't want a weakling for a mother-in-law."

Amaria pulled her arm away from Oberon's grasp. "Don't remind me."

"You said it first," Oberon smirked.

And I regret it. Amaria forced herself to start jogging again, feeling as if she was being tortured. *Oberon is enjoying this too much.* She wheezed, stopping and leaning over on her knees.

"Who said you could stop?" Oberon said.

"I feel sick." Amaria felt like crying. She was useless, weak, and she would never get better. She'd spend the rest of her life falling off pull-up bars and running until she vomited, Oberon constantly insulting her.

"Keep running until you faint or vomit," Oberon dismissed.

"What if I faint and fall on the baby?" Amaria snarled.

"As I said, you'll just have to provide me another one."

Amaria cast him another glare as she stood up, forcing herself to run again despite the sharp pain in her side. This was never going to get better.

But over the weeks, it did. The magic was easier than the physical training and she found herself enjoying it. Once, she wove an entire blanket with pure water, using her magic to manipulate and uphold each individual strand.

And while she didn't enjoy running, it grew easier. She could stand up straight without falling due to the weight on her back, and her wings were no longer drooping. Instead, they stood upright, extending to their full glory. She now liked her wings, and in this forest they made sense. She belonged here, the magic all around her embracing her, ensuring she was safe.

She finished her run, panting, sweat dripping from her forehead.

"Good job," Oberon said. "You're stronger."

"I know," Amaria stated.

Oberon's eyebrows raised. "Go do a flex arm hang."

Amaria strode over to the bar, jumping and holding onto it, letting her body weight hang. The muscles on her back tightened and she breathed in steadily.

"That was a minute," Oberon said.

Amaria bit her lip and then pulled herself upwards. Oberon called her weak, and she would show him that she was strong. She did a full pull-up, holding herself above the bar for five seconds before she let go, flapping her wings to let her fly.

Oberon's eyebrows rose. "Good job. Now, go rest." He looked at her bulging stomach. "You'll need to prepare for that. We'll work on flying after you've given birth."

"Right after?" Amaria's jaw dropped as she remembered how sore she was after she'd given birth to Lysander.

"You'll be fine," Oberon dismissed. "It'll be like you were never pregnant."

Amaria's fists clenched. "How can you say–"

"You're ulzania. Do you remember the original purpose of your kind?"

"My kind? I don't know why you are such an insufferable—"

"Your kind," Oberon repeated. "As you're not fully human anymore due to faerie magic changing you. As I was saying before you acted like a hot-head, ulzania existed to breed for faeries. The magic woven through you as part of that process makes your recovery...ah, instantaneous. Don't worry, it doesn't impact breastfeeding."

Amaria felt nauseous. She focused on the last thing Oberon said, finding it more palpable than the rest. "I give my children to a wet nurse."

"You won't with the one promised to me. She needs nutrients from faeries to heighten her chances of surviving her full transition to ulzania. A human wet nurse can't give that to her."

"It's against social norma–"

"Do you actually care?" Oberon retorted. "You obviously love your children. If not for social expectations, what would you prefer?"

Amaria looked down at her bump, cradling it with her hands. She enjoyed the convenience of having others feed Lysander, however, the limited times she did feed him, she enjoyed how close it made her feel to her son.

"I'm still bound by them." Amaria deflected Oberon's question.

"You can boil people in their own blood," Oberon deadpanned. "Who is going to tell you no?"

"They'll gossip—"

"Then let them talk. But if you're focused on social expectations, fine: your husband entered into a marriage alliance. It is your job to raise your daughter well, prepare her for being my wife. Depriving her of nutrients will harm my alliance with your husband."

Heat bubbled in Amaria's chest as she averted her eyes from Oberon. "Fine. I'll breastfeed her after this war ends. I'm dropping her off at Forteresse les Blanche on our way to Morroek."

Oberon surveyed Amaria, his ice blue eyes flickering as he slowly smiled. "Alright," he agreed. "That's reasonable. Now rest."

Oberon and Amaria transcended to the tops of the trees, thousands of feet above the faerie lands. He let go of her arm and she swayed, still not used to the form of transportation. For a week after she had given birth to her daughter, Sylviana, Oberon had been transcending with her in safer locations to prepare her for this. The mode of travel had taken a while to get acclimated to, although Amaria couldn't say she enjoyed it.

She gripped the branch of the tree, clouds several hundred feet underneath her. She wiped her clammy hands on her dress, her teeth chattering. She'd never been afraid of heights, but this made her want to never leave solid ground ever again.

Oberon waved his hand, the trees moving to make an empty path straight down to the ground. "We're going to fly."

"Couldn't we have done flight training anywhere else?" Amaria's head spun as she looked down.

"Being this high up allows you to more easily self-correct," Oberon explained. "So go ahead. Jump down."

Amaria peered over the edge of the trees, her body shaking as she froze in place. Her chest hurt as she imagined her broken and flattened body smeared on the ground.

"You're acting like a coward." Oberon waved his hand, the branches on which Amaria stood jumped away, knocking her feet from under her. She stumbled and fell, screaming.

"You can control the air!" Oberon shouted, wings popping out of his back—he had the convenience of having them out or—well Amaria didn't know where they went. "Fly!" He passed by her, his wings extending to help him glide and navigate the air.

Amaria was going to die. Oberon would have killed her. He had put her through all this pain in the guise of helping her, saving her, just to kill her when he got what he wanted. She tried to clench her fists, but she couldn't, the air around her pushing them open.

She wasn't going to die. She was going to live, fly well, and wipe that self-satisfied smirk off his face. She forced herself to roll over, her face looking down to the ground instead of her back. Still screaming in terror, she opened her eyes, seeing clouds pass by her as she fell. She bared her teeth, grunting as she forced the muscles on her back to constrict then open, her wings extending.

The wind brushed past her feathers, and with her wings now extended, her momentum slowed enough to allow her to control her fall. Her hair whipped past her hair in the wind, and she grinned, laughing. She was flying! Amaria held her arms out, embracing the sky.

"Not bad." Oberon flew beside her. "Let's work on some forms."

"You pushed me!"

"Why do you think I waited until you gave birth?" Oberon smirked. "You can fly, babies can't. Imagine if you've given birth while in a free fall. Now, I'm going to show you a dive with a dead-stop mid-air. Pay attention." And then, without waiting for a response, Oberon curled his wings against his back, propelling downward at impossible speeds until he shot out his wings, laying perpendicular to the ground, almost hovering. He then flew back up to Amaria.

Amaria took a deep breath to steady herself and then dove, closing her eyes as the wind whipped across her face. She laughed, momentarily forgetting everything but this euphoria.

Chapter Four

Theodmon paced in his tent, rubbing his temples–something he often did in the weeks after he had received his sister's decapitated head. The last time he lost a family member in war was nearly twelve years ago, when he was sixteen, in Harréow Field, Rindria, a village on the Riam side of the border of the Westerlands and Rindria.

His father died that day, killed by enemy soldiers, and when Theodmon saw his father stabbed through the heart, he blacked out. He'd come to in a field of dead Riam soldiers. Fifty or sixty at least. There has been so much carnage it has been impossible to property count. He was trying to survive, and it was the Riams or him. It was war, and he was the monster, the angel of death, because of what he did to survive.

That day, Theodmon gained two titles: Marquis Chauvignon and the Archangel of Harréow Field. When he made his way back to the Thestitiunian side of the battlefield he had been greeted with forlorn faces, suppressed tears, and condolences. Theodmon's father, Raphael Chauvignon, had died, leaving his sixteen year old son to lead both a duchy and to conclude a war.

Foreign nations thought he would fail since he had only been sixteen when he assumed his father's title. Unfortunately for them, that was a deadly mistake. Theodmon was competent–no, he was more than that, he was skilled at both war and ruling. In fact, he rather enjoyed them.

But this war was long. Too long. His men and their allies died at alarming rates and for what? They were barely defending the line, and the Badlands creeped further and further into Morroek. And now, Theodmon considered an attempt to negotiate with Lynette to spare his men. Quickly he stifled the idea, dismissing it as impossible. How could he negotiate with a woman hellbent on being the queen of a continental graveyard? Rational people didn't work with dark magic. They didn't employ giant spiders or unicorns or cheimónas.

He didn't know what to do. They couldn't sue for peace. But, as it stood, they couldn't win this war. So they kept fighting.

A commotion outside Theodmon's tent broke through his concentration. People screamed in panic and Theodmon cursed, grabbing his sword and thanking the gods he was already wearing his armor.

"The Avonnians are charging with the unicorns!"

"The injured! Get them out of the way."

Theodmon rushed out of his tent, grabbing his horse. He swung his legs over the horse and once he was saddled, hit his heels against the horse's side to force him into a gallop.

Theodmon's sword, Winterthorne, slashed through flesh and bone; an Avonnian soldier's head fell onto the snow and another Avonnian cut open by Winterthorne, their entrails hanging out of them.

Avonnians, unicorns, and any other enemy fell around Theodmon. Theodmon did not distinguish between the monsters, animals, or humans. He was numb and trite details didn't matter. He did not know how many he killed. It was just him and his sword.

It wasn't Theodmon who left a path of death in his wake. He was no longer a father, husband, brother, hunter, chess player, who liked the color orange and honey with his chicken. He became someone separate.

Theodmon hadn't yet reconciled the two people. He supposed he never would.

Theodmon gave another solider a necklace of blood.

As Winterthorne turned the snow into a canvas of blood and breathing men into chopped limbs, Earl Stephan Belamy—a war mage Extractor, joined the fight, along with Aloysius, Haerdnor, and Oliver Neremoux, among others. Theodmon couldn't distinguish all of the faces in the chaos.

"Aloysius, attack the left flank of their front. Earl Belamy, take their right side. Haerdnor, fall back—use magic! Neremoux, with me." Theodmon barked out orders as he cut down enemy after enemy.

"Follow me!" Cedric Marion, the crown prince of Thestitiunia, charged forward. Theodmon gritted his teeth. Cedric Marion was posturing, he'd never seen battle. He was too soft for it. Just like his idiot father.

To his soldiers' credit, nobody followed the prince–the soldiers listened to their orders they received from Theodmon.

"Get back!" Theodmon barked at Cedric, riding past him. Cedric would cause unnecessary distractions, putting his men at risk. And nobody wanted to be the reason the emperor's son died, so he was a liability to any task being done efficiently.

"We need to find Lynette! Cut it off at its head—"

"Lynette isn't a military leader," Theodmon snarled. It would be as if somebody killed Amaria instead of him to end a war. "We need to find Vypren."

"Lynette is queen–"

"Fucking gods, are all Marions this idiotic?" Burgundy sparks flew from Aloysius's aura. "Get your head out of your ass and listen to someone with military ability."

That might have been the nicest thing Aloysius ever said about Theodmon.

"What will you do?" Cedric paused in the middle of fighting to glare at the Chauvignon brothers.

Oliver Neremoux pointed his sword at Cedric's throat, his green eyes unwavering in fury. "It's a war. Give me a reason."

"It would be treason–"

"It's war. People die." Oliver said.

Cedric raised his sword. Oliver thrusted his into the prince's neck. "And I don't have an issue with treason when it's against idiotic brats." Oliver pulled his blade out of Cedric's neck, blood dripping from the steel.

Oliver looked over at Belamy, Haerdnor, Aloysius, and Theodmon. "He was killed by an enemy. A monster from the Badlands."

"Why are you telling us?" Belamy said.

"We saw it happen," Aloysius agreed. "He didn't see the unicorn until it was too late."

"Tragic," Haerdnor dryly added.

Theodmon gave Oliver a curt nod, before racing into the thick of battle once more. They had to catch Vypren. He was the general behind this. They needed him gone to cripple Lynette—she needed to be crippled to even give them a chance to breathe. Theodmon didn't know how they would win.

He needed the faeries. He needed Amaria. Where was she? When would they arrive? Was Amaria alright?

Theodmon shook his head as if the motion could clear his thoughts. None of this was important now. He had to find Vypren. That was all that mattered.

Theodmon didn't process–*couldn't process*–how many he cut down in the fighting. Vaguely, as if it were a distant memory he couldn't quite remember, Theodmon noticed the blood pouring from the bodies he passed and he realized that the bodies were falling onto the ground as he passed them.

Later he would piece together that he killed many, but for now, he was numb. Feeling the despair of taking another human's life, feeling the panic of almost dying–it wasn't safe. Not in battle. One mistake could cost Theodmon his life.

How did someone choose between their life or their soul? When it came down to it, Theodmon found the choice simple. Theodmon chose his life. His soul could be salvaged later through sacrifices to the gods and alms and prayers. No amount of gold or fasting could bring the dead back to life.

And he survived as he cut through his enemies. Theodmon didn't pause until he was in the middle of their camp, panting as he hid from view behind a tent.

"We need to move," Haerdnor said, his hands resting on his knees, sweat dripping down his brow despite the bitter winter cold.

"Vypren should be near the center of camp–most commander's tents are," Belamy warned.

"Let's go." Oliver stood up, ready to charge into the thick of it.

"Stop," Aloysius thrust his hand out in front of Oliver, causing him to fall back. "We need a better plan."

"Too late," Theodmon said. There was no time for a clever plan. The rage died down. He was chasing after Vypren without a plan. Vypren killed Ophelia like that for a reason, he wanted them to come after him. "We need to retreat *now*. This is a trap."

Retreating would mean they were cowards without honor, but the idea that honor existed in war at all was laughable. War was hell, and to survive hell one had to become a demon themselves. And so, they retreated, running from the enemy war camp, running through the battlefield, the area which the Morrians called Sielvahella–cursed land.

Once they made it away from the enemy's camp, the tents behind them, it became eerily silent, as if the ghosts could not walk on the ground of where they died and where their brothers would die soon enough.

Somehow, the gods smiled upon Theodmon, despite his stupidity. All of them made it out alive despite Theodmon almost leading them into a trap. He needed to wait to kill Vypren, come up with a plan.

Theodmon's lungs burned as they ran, only stopping once they were surrounded by his own banners once more. Theodmon collapsed on the ground, along with Haerdnor, Oliver, Henri, and Belamy as horns went off from the camp, a stampede of people running towards the southernmost corner of the camp.

Around a hundred feet away, Aaron Raulet burst out of his tent, running–as much as he could anyways, it was more a half-run, half dragging his leg behind him–out of another tent, shouting for the archers to stand down.

What....? Theodmon questioned as he forced himself to sit up and despite his fatigue run, his lungs tightening knowing that something had to be serious for Aaron to react in that way; Theodmon almost didn't want to know what the crisis was.

Chapter Five

Amaria's knees locked as she fell forward as the world stopped spinning.

She blinked, adjusting to her surroundings. The skin around her knuckles were pink as she sat in the snow. War tents rose up around her as the ringing in her ears gradually dissipated, she heard the clanging of swords and armor.

Amaria stood up, shivering. Her breath escaped in wispy puffs as she stood up, the snow crunching beneath her boots. Her dress, while much more practical than the one she wore when she last saw Theodmon, still left her back exposed as it was supporting a gap for her wings.

A purple banner with interlocking dragons and hydras flapped in the wind—the banner of Thestitiunia. Nearby was the familiar blue banner with a golden money scale balancing white roses. Closer to it was a red banner with a gold griffin.

Most surprisingly was the Marions orange banner—whipping bright orange in the gray snowy wind with its red sun. Amaria wondered if Aion or Cedric were here themselves or if it was just their banner men. She rubbed her hands together, jogging down the hill to warm herself.

As she neared closer to the camp, horns went off and an arrow flew near her. She raised her hands, summoning her magic to make a shield from air.

"Stop!" Aaron limped out of a tent, as Theodmon sprinted from behind him, barreling towards Amaria. "That's my daughter, you idiots."

Amaria watched Theodmon run down the hill as she maintained her magical shield, only dissipating it when he was within ten feet of her. Did they not tell others about her wings?

"Amaria." Theodmon pulled her into a hug. "Are you alright? Where's the baby?"

Amaria sighed. She had given birth with the faeries as she trained, but she wasn't going to bring an infant into war. But she didn't leave her daughter with the faeries either. "We stopped at Forteresse les Blanche. She's with Lysander and the nannies."

"Healthy?" Theodmon questioned.

Amaria nodded, her jaw clenching from the cold. "I named her Sylviana."

Theodmon kissed her forehead before pulling away and looking up the hill. "They're fighting. We should go help."

"Did you not warn the others about my wings?"

"Morrian archers," Theodmon explained. "I don't think hearing about it is the same as seeing it...."

Amaria hugged herself as she trudged up the hill with Theodmon. She supposed he was right, this was shocking to her and she was accustomed to magic. To a Morrian who only knew magic as indiscriminately evil, she could see why in their ignorance they'd try to protect the camp.

"You should scare the humans on the other side," Theodmon whispered. "You look like a goddess, or at the very least, chosen by them."

Amaria nodded and looked down at her cracking hands, pink dotting her skin from irritation. She needed gloves, more furs–anything. She knew she'd have to make do for now, it wasn't as if there were ample amounts of extra clothing at a war camp. She hated being cold–if not for the need to preserve energy, she would have warmed the air around her.

She exhaled sharply. *What if....?*

Her magic was stronger than ever. Perhaps she could do that now without worrying she'd burn up too much unnecessary energy. Mage fatigue always scared her. If a mage burned up too much energy they could become sick, even die in extreme cases.

Amaria couldn't afford that. She also couldn't risk dropping dead of frostbite.

She warmed the air around her until she stopped shivering.

She flapped her wings, running forward until her feet lifted from the ground. "I'll see you after the battle."

Both of them looked towards the battlefield where war was still occurring, despite Theodmon's retreat.

He squeezed her hand, dropping it as she floated higher. He charged towards the battlefield. Amaria flew higher, wanting to survey the situation as best as she could before rushing in.

The field was littered with corpses and weapons. Red and brown stained the previously white and sage landscaped. The frozen lake was shattered, and its waters dyed blood; this place was a canvas for death and a soundboard for the cries of the dying.

Amaria had more pleasant nightmares.

Adrenaline and rage coursed through Amaria's veins as she looked to see the humans: Thestitiunians, Morrians, and the rest combined with the faeries to fight Lynette's allies.

She despised Lynette and her monstrous allies. And she pitied the humans on Lynette's side, wondering in a fleeting moment whether they had a choice in this war or if they knew why they fought.

Screaming came from below, and Amaria's eyes narrowed as she saw a rushing flood coming from the front ranks of her side; the water rushed towards the enemy. She felt the surge of power. Amaria followed it, she could help this mage.

As she came closer to the surge, she saw Juliette collapse, the flood pausing with her fall as she convulsed on the ground.

Amaria landed next to Juliette, cursing under her breath, as she put her hands on Juliette's chest, forcing magical energy to flow into her. But the energy Amaria gave her was almost instantaneously drained. Amaria's hands shook. No. Not again.

"Stay with me." Amaria clutched Juliette's arm as she threw her arm over her shoulders. Her wings gave a few powerful flaps, lifting her and Juliette momentarily before they crashed back down to earth.

"Help!" Amaria screamed as she looked around wildly. Juliette had over exerted herself and was dying. Amaria didn't care that she was exposed; all she cared about was saving her friend. She wasn't allowing Juliette to die.

"Stay with me," she pleaded, bringing a tidal wave of energy to her hands. Amaria forced the silver energy down into Juliette's chest as the world slowed around them. She knew she was a target, a visible one with her silver wings, but she didn't care.

"Amaria." Michel Valouis, an Extractor, ran up to her. "What the hell? The enemy is swarming with this mag–you have wings?"

"Help," Amaria whispered, still forcing her energy inside Juliette. "Defend me as I save her."

Juliette's eyes fluttered open.

Michel leaned over, watching her. He sighed. "I'll bring her to safety. I hope she isn't scared of bears. I don't think an eagle could support her and a dolphin is just absurd on land."

Michel was a shape-shifter. A powerful one. He could alter his appearance into any human and into three animals. Amaria blinked and he was a white bear, the fur matching his hair. Amaria lifted Juliette onto his back.

"What happened?" Juliette looked around in terror. "I summoned water and–"

"Go!" Amaria's heart thudded as a stampede of unicorns came down the hill. "I'll explain later!"

Amaria beat her wings, flying above the incoming stampede. Some people froze, either in terror of the oncoming white and silver horses, or they were entranced by their magic. Unicorns had an unknowable but palpable call that made those without protection run to them.

Beneath the unicorn's hooves, flowers that appeared as translucent as glass grew.

One unicorn reached a soldier, lowering its head and stabbing the man through the heart with its horn. It threw the soldier over its head onto its back, the horn tearing him in half. The unicorn paused, looking upwards at Amaria as she landed, its mouth bloody.

Her hands shaking, Amaria threw one fireball towards the soldier's body and another one towards the unicorns. As they shrieked around her she launched up into the air once more, throwing more fire down as she did so.

Hundreds of unicorns came from the hills. Amaria's breath racked her body. They had to stop this somehow. Could they trap them in the earth? No, humans would be trapped with them. They'd be condemned to be murdered and eaten.

Amaria crashed down to earth as Marisa Dubois, a war mage Extractor, ran towards her. "Trap them! They'll kill us all."

Amaria reached out and swirled the air, blending swirls of hot and cold air until a small gale whipped in her palms. With deep breaths, she channeled energy until the wild winds became the size of a cat, the size of a horse, then launched into the sky like a tower barreling towards the unicorns.

Soldiers screamed as they were swept away in the torrent, but it was fewer than if Amaria had swallowed the unicorns within the earth.

But more unicorns kept coming.

Amaria's body shook. She couldn't do much more. A tornado wasn't enough. What could she do? Her head rang. Faeries around her fought. Humans around her fought. She couldn't raise her arms.

Amaria was paralyzed. And she hated herself for being so weak. She couldn't be weak. Biting her tongue to feel pain so she could remain in the present, Amaria forced her magic to combine with the faeries, all of them raising the earth with their magic.

As she did so, Marisa pushed a young soldier beyond the raising wall; the last thing Amaria and the saved soldier saw was Marisa being impaled with a horn.

Amaria screamed as the snow turned red.

She closed her eyes and lit the world on fire. The ground burned, somehow, despite the snow.

The stampede came closer. Behind her, she heard the faeries yelling, running and flying to meet them. Adair Cassidae rode with them, he projected his shield magic out, trying to protect as many as he could. With him, Elena Marion rode, she was covered in a lavender glow, she was giving Adair her energy.

Unicorns tried to bite and maul soldiers, but bounced back, Adair's shield protecting against them. The soldiers, invigorated by the chance to live, were able to kill some unicorns; Adair's shield seemed to only work one way.

Around Amaria, the war continued. Elena burst into flames, she had over exerted herself and the mage fatigue taken her in that violent fashion. Amaria heard the stories, the cautionary tales of immediate mage fatigue, she had never believed them. Mage fatigue was usually a slow process–a terminal death, but Elena died quickly.

Behind Amaria, she heard the clicking on pinchers. She gasped, whirling around with her heart pounding. She screamed, dodging the venom of a spider. The venom hit a solider behind her, and he instantaneously melted.

She grunted, summoning frost to her hands, shooting it at the spiders. They twisted and shrieked, the frost slowing them down. One spider's leg fell off. However, the spiders only slowed down–they kept crawling towards them despite their injuries, hell bent on melting everyone with their venom.

"Why in the gods' names are you using ice?" Adair, the head of the Extractors, shouted. "Use fire."

Amaria's hands shook, unable to dissipate the image of Elena being burned alive with her own magic from her head. And the spiders appeared after she used fire. Her head pounded, she felt nauseous.

A wraith came by a knight, engulfing him. The knight fell to the ground, his armor clanking. The helmet fell off, exposing a skeleton, the ligaments, skin, and muscled taken by the wraith. Amaria dry heaved, stepping backwards, clutching her stomach.

"Fire!" Adair shouted. "Are you dumb? Fire, girl!"

Forcing back the lump in her throat, Amaria summoned flames, the fire hugging her arms as it burned from her shoulders to the tips of her fingers. She burned spiders, she threw fire at wraiths, them shrieking as they backed away from her.

The air around the wraiths was cold. Amaria felt the frost seep into her bones despite the fire embracing her, and she wondered if she could ever be warm again.

It wouldn't matter, would it? Amaria blinked back tears as she saw the battlefield, soldiers either turned to nothing from spider venom or stripped down to only their bones after meeting a wraith. And perhaps they were the lucky ones, Adair's shield faltered, and soldiers, not even dead, were torn apart by unicorns.

She'd die in this cold, miserable place. She's never see the sea again. She'd never see Lysander and Sylviana again, and Oberon would take Sylviana for himself.

No. Amaria growled, pushing out the fire in a circle, engulfing as many spiders and wraiths as she could. *He will not.* Ahead of her, a spider stabbed Adair with its pincers, the spider tearing him limb from limb as the venom dissolved Adair.

Amaria closed her eyes, forcing the flames to reach ten, twenty, thirty feet, killing as many spiders and wraiths as she could. Unfortunately, many fighting against them also burned, their screams haunting.

Amaria's chest tightened, her body shaking.

Around her, the sky around the Badlands and Morroek burst into a symphony of colors. A long line of reds, pinks, blues, yellows, and other colors Amaria had never seen before went on for as long as her eyes could see.

"They're resealing it." Amaria gulped, clenching her shaking hands into fists as she ran toward the faeries and the other mages trying to close the Badlands.

A green toned faerie looked over at Amaria, her narrow eyes slanting. "Force out as much energy as you can for us to stitch the energy together."

Amaria's eyebrows rose. She never heard of magic being stitched together. However, the faeries seemed to know what they were talking about and it may be her imagination but perhaps the incision was becoming shorter.

She forced her energy outwards. It may have been years or seconds but she swayed as a litany of colors surrounded her and yet escaped her, rushing towards the Badlands. There were screams. There was laughter. Amaria saw flames and a dead land, the animals skeletal. And woven through it she saw plump angels in a garden.

She experienced deaths in her life again and the births of her two children. She saw Ghagyn both filled with light and then her eyes bleeding with dark magic. Magic, Amaria now understood, wasn't good or evil, but rather an evolving tool. Life could not exist without death, light could not exist without shadows. And while one may be often preferable to the other, it was not equivalent to the downfall of the other to view the contrary as evil.

The light coming from all the mages became blinding, there was only light and no colors or shapes existed. Amaria fell to her knees, screaming in pain. She heard similar screams around her.

And then a breath. The light stopped and the world was dark and silent. Amaria could feel the cold from the snow against her cheek. It was the only thing grounding her to reality.

Her eyes adjusted to the dark. No, it wasn't dark–it was still daytime. Amaria been blinded from the light that could only come from the gods or a godlike power. She blinked, shapes dimly coming into view.

Amaria breathed, looking around the vast mountains and ice around her. The incision in the sky was sewn together—perhaps not that, with sewing you could tell where the stitching occurred. Here, it seemed as if the breakage never existed, as if the Badlands hadn't tried to invade Morroek.

Chapter Six

Theodmon paced around the commander's tent. How had he been so stupid to run right into a trap? If Aloysius hadn't said something, and if Theodmon hadn't been brought to his senses, they'd all be dead. Theodmon didn't know the exact trap, but he didn't need to be brilliant to assume that whatever it was, they would not be leaving Vypren's tent alive.

And he had to strategize on how to fix his mistake while the battle raged on outside. And listen to Aaron call him an idiot.

"Stop pacing and do something useful," Aaron said. "You fell for Lyseno Vypren's trick, but you retreated, and you're calm now. So what are you going to do?"

Before Theodmon could say anything in response, Amaria walked in, her clothes splattered with blood.

Aaron stared at her wings, the silver feathers emanating a soft glow. "How? I heard you had dark magic, that you killed the entire Riam Court with it—and you wanted more, almost killing Lysander. Then you two went to the faeries and she comes back with wings–"

"What's there to explain?" Amaria shrugged. "I got wings from the faeries. I don't have dark magic anymore...it was a process they did to get rid of it and I got wings from it. And dark magic, it has nothing to do with intent–only control."

"What do you mean?" Aaron asked.

"Dark magic controls the user. That's the only difference–how susceptible the mage is to manipulation and if they can control their powers," Amaria said. "That surge from the Raulet Ruby is more powerful than I was."

"Was?" Theodmon said.

"Was," Amaria confirmed. "I'm infinitely more powerful now."

"What did the faeries ask?" Aaron hissed. "What did you promise them?"

"Sylviana," Amaria said. "Father, you have a granddaughter."

Aaron's hands dropped to his side as he stared at Amaria. "When did this happen...it wasn't a Riam soldier's baby was it?" Theodmon noticed that the ground seemed to shake—Aaron's earth magic was causing the ground to respond to his emotions.

"No," Amaria shook her head. "She's Theodmon's...we found out from the faeries that she existed before we even knew I was pregnant. I gave birth with the faeries–"

"And you promised her to them?" Aaron said. "That's what you said, wasn't it?"

"Yes," she croaked. "She'll marry one of them. Oberon."

"A strengthening alliance between humans and faeries or Chauvignons and faeries," Aaron said. Theodmon knew that was supposed to be a question; however, it sounded like an accusation.

"Both," Theodmon said.

"Good," Aaron said. "We may need that soon enough." He turned towards Amaria. "Let's discuss some things. Theodmon made the idiotic decision to run into a trap–"

"Ophelia was murdered by Vypren." Theodmon cracked his knuckles.

Amaria's eyes widened. "What?"

"Vypren killed Ophelia," Theodmon repeated. "He cut off her head and catapulted it—"

"What are you going to do about it?" Aaron interrupted. "The battle is raging, you retreated, so what do you think Vypren expects?"

Theodmon scowled. He didn't need Aaron to be patronizing. He was a capable commander and strategist, not a child in need of a lesson.

Vypren likely was confused at how his trap didn't work. But perhaps, he was boasting about the outcome–he tricked Theodmon, and Theodmon acted like a coward, fleeing before the fight could occur. Someone who fled would likely not come back, or if Theodmon fought again it would be with the main battle, he could still hear the clangs of swords and catapults in the background.

Theodmon's eyes blazed, a fury burning in his heart. "I'll kill him now. While the battle is happening."

Aaron gave a tight lipped smile, looking like a snake. "See? You aren't a half-wit."

"The battle is ending." Amaria's eyebrows bunched together. "We've sealed the Badlands."

Theodmon's blood turned cold. He picked up his sword. He had to go now, before Vypren realized what was happening. Before the battle ended.

"Who's going?" Aaron asked.

"Henri, Aloysius, Stephan Belamy, and Haerdnor," Theodmon answered, right as the named people stepped into the tent.

"Couldn't help but overhear you might need us," Henri said.

"I should go," Amaria said.

"No." Aaron held his hand out towards his daughter. "You will not."

"He tried to kill me—"

"And I can't have you being seen killing more foreign leaders," Aaron interrupted. "We can't change what happened in Rindria, and we can't change that due to Lynette's sheer magical power you'll need to help depose her. But Vypren, that makes you look capricious."

"I am capricious." Amaria crossed her arms.

"Aaron has a point," Theodmon said. "It's fine, I have this handled. I'll bring you back his head."

"Miana will love that," Aaron said under his breath, referencing his sister who was married to likely one of the best contenders for the Avonnian throne other than Vypren himself.

"Miana?" Theodmon questioned.

"She's on her way," Aaron said dismissively.

"I won't wait around." Theodmon already started to move out with Henri, Aloysius, Oliver, and Belamy, having zero desire to be around that conniving snake.

"Give Aunt Miana my best," Haerdnor said, the tent flap closing as he stepped out behind the rest.

Theodmon swallowed the lump in his throat, looking over at the men coming with him to kill Vypren. "We need to remove our armor." The last thing Theodmon needed was for the mission to fail because creaking metal gave them away.

Haerdnor looked over at his tent, his being the closest one to Aaron's. "We can discard it there." All of them moved towards his tent, pulling off their armor once they were inside, their tunics and pants all that remained underneath.

Theodmon felt almost naked going into the enemy camp, without armor.

"I'll go first," Aloysius said, "considering...." he trailed off, his chest heaving.

"That you're a human shield and the only one with protection," Henri said dryly.

Aloysius chuckled, the laughter sounding forced to Theodmon.

"We have a good team," Theodmon said, in part to comfort the others but he too needed reassurance. "Fire mage, two war mages, a mind fuckery mage," Theodmon nodded at each person in turn, realizing for the first time he was the only one without magic. All he had was his sword. "We have to move fast," Theodmon said decisively. "Stay out of sight." He met each of their eyes in turn, a long moment passing between them.

They ran off into the night, using the darkness to hide as they raced across the abandoned battlefield. Above them, the small sliver of the moon shone above them and Theodmon thanked the gods that the moon wasn't full, limiting how illuminated they could be.

As soon as they crossed into the enemy camp, Aloysius pushed Theodmon behind a barrel, drunk soldiers passing, singing off-key. Theodmon held his breath, as if the slight noise would betray him.

"Henri," Theodmon hissed. "Can you sense Vypren's thoughts?"

Henri held up a finger, and Theodmon's muscles tensed. Sure enough, more soldiers passed, as loud as their predecessors.

"He's near the center of camp," Henri said. "There's less thoughts coming from that way, we should—"

"You can only read human thoughts, right?" Belamy interrupted.

Henri gave a tight nod.

"That's where the monsters are," Belamy said. "We aren't going there."

Theodmon's head rang. This was a war camp. There had to be a way in. He paused, sucking in his breath. "Henri," he ventured, knowing what the answer to his question would be. Theodmon also understood that Henri also would despise what Theodmon was about to request. "Is there a path where the thoughts are all about sex?"

Henri cast Theodmon a dark glance. "You know there is and it's vile."

Theodmon shrugged. "They're having sex. They won't be too concerned about anything else."

"I hate you," Henri said, crossing his arms. "But follow me."

Henri and Aloysius led the others through the enemy's camp, dodging behind tents and barrels. Theodmon felt as if his heart was going to burst from his chest. He despised these types of missions. He would rather stab someone through their face than sneak through the shadows.

"We're here," Theodmon whispered, stopping outside an emerald green tent. His throat was dry. He wanted Vypren to feel every blow and ounce of pain that he'd caused Ophelia a million times over.

"Burn him," Theodmon told Haerdnor. "Burn him and then stop before he dies."

A deep blue haze engulfed Henri, his eyes glowing. "Go." Henri's voice was a dull echo. "Vypren is stuck in his worst memories now."

Theodmon stepped away from Henri, shuddering. "Belamy," he directed the Extractor war mage, "protect Henri."

Belamy raised his sword, nodding as his eyes scanned the horizon.

"I'll get the back," Aloysius said, a crimson glow coming over him as his magic melted over him, turning his skin to metal. He clanked away as Theodmon and Haerdnor burst into the tent, Lyseno Vypren convulsing on the floor, weeping and begging for something to stop.

Theodmon's chest rose and fell as breaths came faster, a flush of warmth encompassing his body as his gaze honed in on Vypren, everything else fading away in the background. He ran towards the pathetic creature, lifting up his sword and bringing it down right above Vypren's knees.

Theodmon stepped back, watching the blood pour from Vypren's stubs. "Cauterize it," he told Haerdnor. "Belamy, we don't need Henri's magic!"

Haerdnor placed his fire near the stubs as Vypren stopped convulsing, his eyes rolling the correct way in his head.

"Fucking Vathar!" Vypren cursed, his face pallid.

Theodmon's nostrils flared as he lowered himself towards Vypren, so close he could smell the man's vile breath. "Why?" Theodmon hissed.

Vypren sneered. "Will it change anything?"

No. Theodmon clenched his fists. Ophelia was still dead. Knowing the twisted depths of Vypren's mind could change that.

"You killed her," Theodmon stated. "I think her relatives deserve to know."

"You only deserve what you're willing to take," Vypren said. "I'd thought you'd learned that already, taking the woman I was to marry."

Glowering, Theodmon hit Vypren on the head with the blunt of his blade. They had to leave soon, every second they spent here they risked not coming back alive. And now, outside the tent, there was the clanging of swords and shields. His eyes drifted towards a journal near Vypren's bed. Theodmon quickly grabbed it. Perhaps it would have something useful as far as strategy.

"Burn him," Theodmon commanded, his breath quickening.

"My men will kill you," Vypren grunted.

Theodmon sneered, followed by a bark of laughter as flames leapt up and down Vypren's body. Vypren twisted in agony, sobbing. Haerdnor, after a few seconds, stopped the flames.

"Quickly." Haerdnor's eyes darted towards the entrance. Theodmon followed Haerdnor's gaze, jumping as a sudden spatter of blood appeared on the canvas from outside.

Theodmon wanted to make this last, but as he heard Belamy scream outside he ground his teeth together and swung his sword, decapitating Vypren. As he crouched down, picking up the head, Theodmon felt a rush of power, feeling as if he could be invincible.

"Go," Aloysius burst into the tent. "Get Henri and Belamy and run!"

Theodmon swallowed, his head ringing. He led them into a slaughter again. The room spun. Aloysius' shoulder hit him as he rushed and Theodmon blinked, adrenaline shooting through him. They had to go.

Theodmon, Haerdnor, and Aloysius fled from the tent, seeing Henri surrounded by soldiers who were on the ground, clutching their heads as they convulsed. Nearby, Belamy had a dozen arrows in his back and a sword and spear through his chest.

Henri looked over at them, blinked, and then all of them fled the enemy camp, unable to stop until they were safe, surrounded by their own familiar banners.

Chapter Seven

"Aaron?" A soft voice emerged from the tent flap only a few moments after Theodmon left, revealing a tanned woman with long braided hair. Her long, billowy lavender sleeves engulfed Aaron as she hugged him. Within a few breaths the woman turned towards Amaria, pulling her into an embrace.

"I've missed you," Amaria whispered as if the confession would make Aunt Miana dissipate in front of her.

"I've missed you as well." Miana petted Amaria's hair. "You've matured into a wonderful woman."

"I did awful things–"

"We've all done awful things," Miana interrupted. "And we'll continue to do awful things to survive. Those who act like they'd not cross lines to save themselves and those they loved are one of three things: suicidal, stupid, or self-righteous hypocrites." She pulled away from Amaria, her hands still gripping her niece's shoulders as she sternly, but kindly looked at her. "I adore your wings. We have a lot to catch up on so perhaps your father should leave."

"Mi–" Aaron started to protest.

"How do the wings affect your menstrual cycle?" Miana's eyes warningly drifted towards Aaron's. "Do tell me all the details."

"Your wings are terrifying," Aaron dryly noted as he passed Amaria as moved to leave the tent. "Some say you look blessed by the gods."

"Faeries aren't gods," Amaria said.

"But to be god-blessed," Aaron whispered in her ear. "You should let everyone see you, the wings need to be commonplace to bring a sliver of normalcy to them–if that's possible."

Amaria nodded. She knew what that meant. She was to allow as many people to see her, her magic, and her wings so as to present as an ethereal pillar of strength chosen by the gods. All to further her family's power.

"Of course, Father." Amaria's eyes shone a bright silver. While the idea of rivers of blood sickened her–something she would have delighted in a year ago, Amaria didn't need dark magic to enjoy the mental chess games of manipulating the government. She enjoyed it for twenty-three years, and she would enjoy it for at least twenty-three more. Longer if she lived that long–the games she played tended to be deadly.

"You're probably tired of explaining the wings," Miana said once Aaron left. "And others will make you explain it to them, and you'll have to do it because they won't rest until they've heard the same story a million times. So I won't ask you. You're free to talk about it if you want, but you don't have to."

Amaria forced back a lump in her throat. "It's been so much...these past two, three years–I've lost a whole year with being in the faeries lands–it doesn't feel that long but, it is—I'm being stupid." She brought her wrist up to her face, wiping her wet eyes with the sleeves.

"No," Miana said. "You're not. Is it true you were tortured in a Riam prison?"

Feeling as if she was suddenly tight laced, Amaria saw stars flash in her eyes before she saw the Riam prison in her mind. Her breathing slowed. Amaria couldn't do this–she was *safe*. But her body obviously disagreed with that sentiment. Her hands shaking, Amaria slowly nodded, forcing herself to look at Miana directly.

Amaria hadn't seen her aunt in ages. After Amaria's mother died, her aunt had been one of the only positive adult female relationships she had. And Miana lived hundreds of miles away in a different country. A true tragedy of political marriages was the relationships lost or hindered for the sake of the alliance. When did Amaria last see Miana? Probably at her wedding. But Amaria hadn't been able to spend a lot of time with her, or anyone but Theodmon that day. And she had been so terrified.

Amaria wasn't terrified anymore. She wasn't nervous. Amaria was resigned to the cold neutrality of reality.

I was infected by dark magic. I killed countless people. I don't know which of my actions were influenced by dark magic. I no longer have dark magic. The faeries cleaned my dark magic by making me ulaniza. I bargained my daughter's future in exchange for my life. There's nothing I can do to change these facts. Rindria is a mess. We have to move forward in cleaning up the destruction we–I–caused.

These thoughts were nihilistic, but somehow, they made Amaria feel better. It let her ignore the terror and pain she truly felt.

"Forgive the question." Miana's voice lowered to a barely audible whisper. "But did you...were you actually...did you have dark magic?"

Amaria shook her head as she licked her lips, desperately trying to bring moisture to them. "I did. Not now. The faeries...they disposed of it with this process."

"Do you want to talk about it?"

"No." Amaria said curtly.

Miana pulled her closer into another hug. Amaria focused on the scent of amber, rose, and vanilla floating from her aunt as she stifled her sobs. So much had happened. And Amaria hadn't even had time to process even a fraction of it yet. And it seemed with the Riam conquest and a potential Thestitiunian coup on the horizon, she wouldn't have the ability to pause, breath, and recover.

"It's alright." Miana's hands ran over Amaria's hair, her fingers pulling at a few knots. Amaria's body melted in Miana's arms. Her aunt had always comforted her with her mere presence. Still, Amaria couldn't ignore the truth, glaring obvious as the sun in summer: that this situation was not alright by any means, but regardless, Amaria had to appear unbroken and unphased. Her own gods forsaken stability depended on that façade.

"You don't have to do anything right now," Miana shushed Amaria. "I want to talk to you about some things."

"What things?"

Miana sighed heavily. "Laurents is in line for the throne, there's just a few roadblocks...Vypren hasn't had son's–only daughters–marrying them off to foreign nations and also our unmarried sons will help solve that."

"And Vypren?" Amaria asked. She knew that Theodmon left to kill him, but she wanted to know what Miana had to say about the situation.

"You know already," Miana said with a knowing smile. "I'll see you soon," Miana said before leaving the tent.

Amaria sighed, stretching out her wings. She hadn't even realized how tense they were, as if she had been clutching them to her body defensively. Although Amaria trained with the faeries and could manage her new anatomy, she still sometimes felt as if she weren't truly in her own body, rather as if she were a visitor in some stranger's body. Amaria had wings, and if she admitted it, she liked the soft silver feathers brushed against her arms and how it made her seem ethereal–as if she were above petty human emotions and desires. Amaria looked like she never knew pain, grief, anger, or despair.

And in that, she didn't recognize the girl in the mirror who looked more faerie than human. But she was human. Amaria's hands involuntarily moved to her ears to make sure. The tips were still rounded–human. Fae had pointed ears, humans had rounded. She was human. Wings. Ulzania. More powerful magic. Despite those things, Amaria was human. She grieved too much in her life. She felt anger; she felt pain, humiliation, sadness—and despite her outer appearance she was deeply human.

And nobody would ever understand that. Amaria sank to her knees, curling them up to her chest as her eyes welled. She hadn't realized how different she was until she was around other humans. They stared at her, and drifted their eyes when they noticed her looking back at them.

They'd done that when she was an ordinary human–well perhaps not ordinary. She was a Raulet and an Extractor. And although the difference in how people looked at her now was subtle, Amaria heard the difference in the whispers as loud as if the sun exploded.

She mourned what she hadn't even known she lost until she was staring down the muzzle of the wolf. Sniffing, Amaria wiped the annoying tears out of her eyes with her sleeve before they could fall down her face. She didn't need to cry–not now, not here. And it was stupid to cry over being extraordinary. How many people would kill to be where she was at in having powerful magic–likely the most powerful magic a human had in centuries? How many people would kill to be ethereally beautiful? How many would kill to be feared?

Amaria found being feared was an exhausting endeavor. A necessary one, but exhausting all the same. And she would continue to weaponize that fear, despite any personal objections she may now have about it. With all of the plans she, Theodmon, and her father had on the horizon, Amaria couldn't afford to not weaponize the memories of the destruction she caused.

Rindria. The thought was an intrusive worm. Amaria scowled, forcing herself to think of the sea. Of sunflowers. Of swans. Any small, unimportant thing she could visualize perfectly in her mind. She could see the black, slightly curved beak of a swan. She could see their dark gray flippers propelling them as they floated serenely on top of a pond. The pond had a fountain. The swan ruffled its feathers.

She couldn't stay here anymore with only her mind for company. Amaria stood up, determining she would see Juliette to ensure that she was alright. Juliette almost burnt herself out with magic on the battlefield and Amaria hadn't the chance to see her. Or perhaps Amaria avoided seeing her—she didn't like seeing Juliette in pain, and moreso, Amaria despised having the inability to help Juliette. Amaria was good at causing pain, however, she didn't know how to alleviate it.

Amaria found Juliette laying on a cot in a tent with another mage, Brigitte Belamy.

"Juliette," Amaria breathed, feeling as if a weight lifted off her shoulders as Juliette gave her a bright smile, her face pale and her body covered in bandages. "I should've seen you sooner–"

"You were busy," Juliette said.

"No," Amaria shook her head, tears welling in her eyes as she nearly flung herself onto Juliette, hugging her fiercely. "I should have seen you. Are you doing alright?"

"I'm recovering," Juliette gave a side glance towards her arm in a sling. "How about you? You have wings."

Amaria nodded, her throat feeling tight. "I...the faeries helped me. I'm changed, better, in more ways than one."

She wanted to tell Juliette that the dark magic was gone, but she didn't trust Brigitte enough to disclose that part of herself. While Brigitte might have suspicions on what occurred, it was one thing to suspect, and an entirely different thing to hear a confession.

Juliette's eyes briefly drifted towards Brigitte. "We'll talk later. You'll have to tell me about your year with the faeries."

"It didn't feel like a year," Amaria muttered. "It felt like a month at most."

Juliette's eyebrows lifted but she didn't say more, instead beginning to fill in Amaria on the drama she missed this past year between Rindria's succession crises, Lysander terrorizing the castle, her missing Lucas, Aloysius and Liara allegedly had a spat in which he cursed her in front of the whole Chauvignon court.

"Really?" Amaria laughed.

"It was hilarious," Brigitte said. "He called her a miserable shrew."

Amaria's mouth dropped as she laughed. "No."

"Yes!" Juliette insisted. "He said she was a miserable shrew and that she couldn't run away from her problems forever because she was the problem in every situation she found herself in."

"He had been nothing but kind and generous to her," Brigitte twirled a strand of hair in her fingers. "He was always kind to me–not many were. I was too weird, too boyish."

"You're a war mage," Amaria said softly. Female war mages were given grace with many things–they were allowed to fight, to train in physical activities, and to hold a variety of weapons without becoming a social pariah. Magic was integral to who a mage was, and to suppress their magic often ended up with catastrophic results; especially with war mages who had one of the more destructive branches of magic.

"Doesn't mean the court had to like it at social events," Brigitte replied. "Anyways, Aloysius is tired of his wife scorning him after all his efforts to make her comfortable. And once she tried to climb over the walls to escape–well, he kinda exploded on her."

Amaria wished she could be as simple-minded as Liara. Perhaps then she would have been happier. If Amaria wasn't clever then she couldn't scheme, and if she couldn't scheme, well life would have been simpler and less painful for her. Amaria's fingers traced over her wrists–although the faeries took away the physical scars from her body, Amaria still felt the phantoms of the shackles from her imprisonment.

She'd been stupid then. Her cleverness almost got her killed. From now on, Amaria would have to be more than clever–she would have to properly hone her sense of self-preservation.

But sometimes self-preservation required confrontation.

Chapter Eight

Theodmon leaned against a post, breathing heavily with the burlap bag holding Vypren's bloodied head under his cloak. Henri, Aloysius, and Haerdnor had already left back to their tents, but Theodmon needed a moment alone, the cold numbing his senses. Slowly, Theodmon rubbed his hands together, watching his breath puff in the air as he composed himself, the heat of killing Vypren still rushing in his ears.

Miana Alexandre approached him, her skirts dragging in the snow. Once she reached his side, she lowered her head, a hood pulled over her hair to protect herself from the chilly wind.

Theodmon scowled, turning his body away from Miana, as to shield the burlap bag away from her view.

"You can't promise support?" Miana asked, her lips hidden from how she tilted her head. "After they killed your sister?"

Theodmon resisted a groan. He should have known she would dig her claws in to try and convince him to do what she wanted. Of course Miana would see this as an opportunity to get herself on the Avonnian throne, and of course she would try and manipulate relationships to get there.

"We just fought in a war," Theodmon said, taking a step away from Miana. "And it's not even over yet."

"And you are about to fight in another," Miana gave a harsh laugh. "Do you think your men will appreciate that?"

His shoulders tensing, Theodmon's eyes narrowed as he whipped his head to look directly at Miana. "Keep your mouth shut."

"Or what?" Miana smirked at him, her eyes flashing in ill-gotten triumph.

Theodmon cast a fugitive glance around him, ensuring that nobody was watching. When assured he was adequately alone, he pulled out the bag, opening it slightly so Miana could see.

"Gods," Miana said with a gag. "What's that?"

"Lyseno Vypren," Theodmon said coolly.

"And why are you showing me this?"

"Who has the most to lose from killing Vypren?" Theodmon asked. "You're a Raulet, you're not above murder to gain power."

"Neither are you," Miana said.

"But your countrymen likely don't want another queen with that amount of bloodlust. It won't be hard to convince the nobles that you and Laurents made questionable decisions."

"You have reason too," Miana said, "He killed your sister."

"And that is a much more acceptable reason to kill someone," Theodmon said. "But who knows who actually killed him? People love gossip; which scenario is more interesting?"

Miana's face paled slightly. "You wouldn't."

"If you keep your mouth shut, I won't," Theodmon agreed. "Don't bring Ophelia into this again."

Silently, they stood there. Theodmon had his own issues and judgments with Aaron, but Miana–Miana Raulet was a million times worse than her brother. Laurents Alexandre was also her fourth fiancée before she actually married–the other three had allegedly mysteriously died on the eve of their wedding day. And Miana Raulet, beautiful, rich, and now tragic, became even more desirable. If a man died for her, well, there were worse deaths. And if he survived to marry her, he was now favored by the gods.

Laurents was clearly infatuated with Miana. Theodmon wondered about the nature of their relationship–the reality of it at least. Was Laurents acting? Or would he truly let Miana do whatever she so wished because she was beautiful?

"Goodbye." Theodmon turned on his heel to leave, walking through the camp until he reached his and Amaria's tent.

"Are we alone?" Theodmon asked as soon as he stepped inside the tent. Amaria stood up, making her way towards him, her neck and face flushing.

"Yes," she said.

Theodmon pulled the journal from his cloak, tossing it onto the ground as he pulled the burlap bag out from underneath the flaps of his cloak. He opened the bag, dumping the head near the journal.

Amaria crouched down, picking up the head, staring it dead in its face. She was expressionless, crouching there for what felt like an infinity.

"How do you feel?" Theodmon gingerly ventured.

Amaria dropped Vypren's head, it rolling away from her as blood dripped onto the ground. "Nothing. I thought I'd feel relieved that he's gone, but nothing has changed. He couldn't hurt me this whole time. I don't know why I ever feared him."

She looked over at the journal. "What's that?" She shook her head. "Wait, no. Before we start on that, tell me what happened when I was away. Did anything happen that I need to know about?"

"Like what?" Theodmon asked.

"Important events, things that I need to know in order to conduct intelligence," Amaria said. "I'm missing a year of information."

Theodmon sighed, sitting down on the bed. "Cedric Marion is dead. Officially it was from enemy forces."

"And unofficially?"

"Oliver Neremoux killed him." Theodmon lowered his voice. Even here, seemingly alone, they had to be careful. "Aion hasn't fought."

"Of course not," Amaria said sharply. "Tell me some actual news."

Theodmon felt a sinking pit in his stomach. Amaria deserved to know. She would be involved with intelligence and had set up the groundwork–however rash and violence the methods were–for Thestitiunia to have the chance of conquest. But he hadn't seen her in so long and Rindria had always been a sensitive topic. "Rindria."

Amaria raised her eyebrows in question, as if she were compelling Theodmon to continue talking.

"Liara is a problem." Theodmon placed his head in his hands. "Tesden too—Lucas has been missing for a while, I'm hoping he finds him soon and eliminates him. Last I heard from Lucas he was in Tressidil, and killing an exiled prince on the land of our closest allies is not often seen as appropriate," Theodmon shook his head, redirecting his thoughts to be more focused.

"She does realize the only use she has to anybody is to produce heirs?" Amaria questioned crudely. "Nobody is keeping her around for her charming personality and as for her political connections, well, I killed them all didn't I?"

There was something about that Riam girl that brought out the worst in Amaria. Theodmon squeezed her hands, calmly looking at her. She met his eyes and after a few moments of looking at him with a sharp hatred in her eyes, it melted away and she collapsed in his arms.

"What do we do?" Amaria asked.

"Celestine has been spiking Liara's food with fertility herbs at home," Theodmon said. "I believe the last time Celestine sent a letter she said Liara was vomiting. She gives birth, and then we let the doctors neglect her in the afterbirth. She should die of an infection." Theodmon kissed the top of Amaria's head. "And with Lucas soon killing Tesden, we'd have the sole heir to the Riam throne in our control–an infant, needing to have a regent rule in their stead."

"Aloysius." Amaria stated the name of who they knew the regent would be. "Is he okay with murdering his wife? He seemed defensive of her."

"He caught her trying to carve her womb out of herself," Theodmon said. "She refuses to share his marriage bed but threatens to throw herself out of the highest tower if he takes a mistress. She told him she wished he would die in this war." Theodmon felt his voice starting to shake. Aloysius did nothing but be kind to Liara–yes, he, Amaria, and even Celestine had been awful to her, but Aloysius did nothing but try to make her comfortable.

"Aloysius is okay with being rid of her," Theodmon said. "He's ready to take random women to bed without worrying about the scandal of a suicide. And when he's done with the whores, he's ready for a compliant wife."

Theodmon didn't dislike women who would challenge their spouse–Amaria did it often. However, there was a level of stoicism he expected. Some tasks and duties must be done, and sometimes gritting your teeth was the only way to endure.

"What a year," Amaria remarked.

You've no idea. Theodmon thought. There was no amount of briefs that could get Amaria to comprehend the chaos and pain he felt all that time–the pain he felt with her absence. None of this was her fault, and saying this would be needlessly blaming her for something outside her control. Amaria too, had a life changing year. And it felt like weeks to her apparently. Theodmon remembered that she seemed shocked that when she emerged from the faerie lands the first time that it was winter. It had been almost six months since the faeries took her and she believed it had been a few days.

"You've missed a lot when you were with the faeries," Theodmon replied.

"I wish I had been here." Amaria snuggled up tighter in his arms. Theodmon pulled her closer to him, kissing the top of her hair.

"It's not your fault." His breath moved over the top of her head, a few flyaway hairs shifting upwards. "And I'm glad you weren't."

War wasn't a place for a lady, even one like Amaria. Theodmon sighed. *No*, he corrected himself. *War isn't a place for anybody. War is chaos–it is dirty, dishonorable, and agonizing. Only ostentatious idiots would presume to write ballads that said otherwise.*

Unfortunately, people were more apt to believe a beautiful story than the grimy truth.

Amaria twirled her fingers over his chest hair, smiling at him as she laid her head on his shoulders. "I love you. I'm glad you still love me...despite...."

His heart twisting with longing, Theodmon brushed a strand of hair from Amaria's face, his rough calluses rubbing against her smooth cheek. "You're my forever," he whispered. "Now and always."

"Even with wings?"

"The wings don't change anything other than I think we'll need a larger bed."

Amaria burrowed further in his arms, her hair tickling Theodmon's nose. "What's next?"

Theodmon looked over at the bound journal laying on the ground. Perhaps there was something about Ophelia in there; it couldn't help her, but perhaps he could find closure. His hands brushed over the binding, but he couldn't make himself open it.

"It's alright." Amaria placed her hands over his. "I can read it. What are we looking for?"

A bulge bobbed in Theodmon's throat as he looked at Amaria with glassy eyes. The gods blessed him with her. "Ophelia."

Amaria kissed him on the forehead before standing up, moving towards the table. "I'll let you know what I find."

Chapter Nine

Amaria flipped through the journal, looking for Ophelia's name. Vypren's handwriting was large and messy, making it difficult to read. And she couldn't read Avonnian, making finding closure for Theodmon in Vypren's writings near impossible.

Amaria yawned, her eyes swimming with the unfamiliar words she couldn't comprehend. She wished she was literate in this gods' forsaken language. She learned the Avonnian alphabet, but any attempts to further build upon that skill ended in failure.

"Would he have referred to Ophelia in any way other than 'Ophelia', 'Belegines', or 'Chauvignon?'" Amaria asked. "And if there's something else how do you spell it?"

Theodmon shook his head. "I don't know. Have you been able to find anything?"

"No," Amaria's voice cracked. "But I'll keep looking."

Theodmon gave her a small nod, placing his head back in his hands. Amaria bit her lip, reaching out towards Theodmon. "I'll find something," she said softly, promising something she wasn't positive she could deliver. But Theodmon needed her. "There has to be something in here."

"Thank you," Theodmon said, his voice raw.

Amaria directed her attention back to the journal, searching for an iteration of those three names as she flipped through the pages, slowly scanning the pages. And then she saw her father's name, the letters stark against the page.

"Theodmon," she hissed. "Can you read this?"

"Did you find Ophelia's name?" Theodmon's head rose sharply.

"No." Amaria's mouth turned dry. "My father's."

Theodmon stood up from the bed, groaning. "It's probably just Vypren insulting him." He took the journal from her hands, Amaria watching him as he read.

"When were you engaged to Vypren?" Theodmon asked. "What age?"

"Eight," Amaria said. "By the emperor's command. Why?"

Theodmon's chest heaved. "It's better if I just read it. *Aaron Raulet approached me today asking if I'd marry his daughter when she turns of age. Child is three. I laughed in his face, that's a long time to not–*"

"That's impossible." Amaria forced herself to swallow, her head spinning. Her father rescued her from that horrible marriage before it could go forward. Her father always protested against Aion wanting to marry her to Vypren.

"There's some pretty detailed accounts of how excited he was for your dowry." Theodmon flipped through the book. "And listen to this one: *Engagement is public now, and–*" He stopped.

"What?" Amaria's heart thudded as loud as a galloping horse.

"It's a bunch of crude words about a child," Theodmon said. "But the point is, that was written in the year 3212, you were born in 3204, right? Your engagement became public when you were eight."

"No," Amaria said angrily. "That's when I was engaged. There was no prior secret engagement; Aion forced my father to do it when I was eight. Father never wanted to marry me to that–" Amaria clenched her fists together, shaking. "My father loves me. He saved me from that marriage."

"Amaria," Theodmon said softly, "I think he's the reason you were in that engagement in the first place. I'm not denying he loves you, it's probably why he broke it off at the last minute–"

"My father wouldn't do this to me," Amaria insisted. "It's Aion's fault. The emperor told my father–"

"Was it Aion?" Theodmon hugged her. "When your father is as powerful, truly more powerful, than that bumbling idiot? We all know who the true power behind the empire's throne is."

Amaria's head spun as her mind raced, attempting to process the implications of what she just heard. The room seemed to close in on her, the fabric walls of the tent suddenly too confining, as if the very air thickened with the weight of the deception. Her father wouldn't have let her be abused for years, it was Aion's fault.

"No." Amaria's chin shook. The lie, once hidden in the shadows, now stood starkly in the harsh light of truth. Amaria would not, could not acknowledge it, and so she would turn away from the light and look for an answer in the shadows.

"Marriage is traditionally left within the sole discretion of a woman's closest male relative," Theodmon whispered. "Wouldn't that be your father?"

Amaria's palms felt clammy, and her heart pounded in her chest as if trying to escape the reality crashing down around her. She looked at the journal, Vypren somehow hurting her beyond the grave. It was just words, it shouldn't hurt. But she couldn't strangle a dead man's words.

Her father loved her. And while Aaron could do underhanded things, he would never hurt her. Aaron did what was best for the family and Amaria was part of that family. Aaron Raulet was a conniving man, with little remorse in harming those against him but Amaria had never been opposed to him—she was his daughter. Their interests had always been aligned.

"What did he say about the end of the engagement?"

"Amaria," Theodmon's eyes furrowed together. "I don't think it's healthy–"

"I need to know. He has to be lying," Amaria said. She felt Theodmon press his hand against her back, steadying her.

He sighed, and she heard him flipping through the journal, pausing after a few minutes, reading over the page. "Are you sure you want to hear this?"

"I need to," Amaria said.

"He talks about how he should have *pre-consummated* the marriage earlier." Theodmon's voice tightened. "A lot of crude remarks on what he'd do to you, and an incoherent paragraph on—I'll read that one, there's no other way. He says 'angry vengeful shrew, should have disciplined it out of her' and then goes into methods, then after all that says 'perhaps not–a mother with fire births strong sons' and then more crude remarks about his visualizations of you in bed. And then he calls your father a liar and rants about losing your dowry."

Amaria felt as if she couldn't breathe. Vypren was lying. He was vengeful. He wanted to hurt her.

Why would he lie in his private journal?

She looked back at Theodmon, her eyes watering. "I'll need your help."

"Always," Theodmon responded.

"Can you tell Henri...." Amaria gulped the tears falling down her face. "Can you ask him if he can find that memory in my father's mind?" She stood up, wiping her nose with her sleeve. "I need some air."

"Of course," Theodmon said softly. "Do you need me to come with you?"

Amaria shook her head, pushing her way out of the tent. Her chest was tight, she couldn't take a breath without shaking. Vypren was lying. He was vengeful. He wanted to hurt her.

She doubled over on herself, screaming in agony. She was making a scene, someone would surely come and find her, gossip about her. But Amaria couldn't find it in herself to care. What does it matter now?

Vypren told the truth. Her father lied to her, he lied to her her entire life.

Amaria collapsed in the snow, clutching her knees to her chest as she sobbed. Her father hurt her and never once admitted to it. The frost bit her skin, but the physical pain couldn't numb the storm that was tearing her apart inside.

"Lady Chauvignon," one of the sentries that guarded her and Theodmon's tent ran towards her.

"Leave," Amaria sobbed, clutching her knees to her chest.

"Let's get you inside–"

"Leave!" Amaria screamed at him.

"It's alright," Theodmon's voice floated from behind her. "I have this handled. Thank you for your concern."

Theodmon crouched down in the snow with her, silently wrapping his arms around her as she sobbed.

"He lied to me," Amaria's voice cracked.

Theodmon kissed the top of her head, allowing her to sob openly in the snow, the pain of the cold and the warmth of Theodmon's arms the only things grounding her. Everything hurt, her world was collapsing. And she would never calm down from this, she would never not feel this intense pain.

Slowly, the tears dissipated. And eventually Amaria calmed down enough to stand up from where she hugging herself.

"I'll be fine," she whispered to Theodmon.

"Amaria," he protested.

"I need a moment alone," she pleaded, her eyes wide. "Just give me ten minutes and I'll be back in the tent. Please."

Theodmon looked at her sadly, his hazel eyes unblinking as his gloved hand brushed over her cheek. "Alright," he sighed. "But only for ten minutes."

Amaria kissed him on the cheek. "Thank you," she said, before the two of them drifted away, Theodmon heading inside to his tent and Amaria to wander around the camp. She didn't even feel the chill of the snow anymore.

"Amaria," a familiar male voice called out.

Amaria paused in her walk and turned to see her father leaning against a post. Despite relying on a cane, Aaron Raulet held himself as if he were invincible. Perhaps he was invincible in what his craft was and that was why he perfected it to a hyper focused amount, neglecting all of his shortcomings to where they became more poignant, as the rust on a dull and neglected blade.

As her father said her name, Theodmon's translation of Vypren's written words slithered into her mind. Involuntarily, Amaria stepped away from her father, crossing her arms.

"We need to talk," Aaron said. "Uncross your arms, you know to have better posture than that."

"I'm not sure you're aware of what I know." Amaria's nostrils flared. "But I agree, let's talk."

You know. The intrusive thought barreled through the fragile, glass door barrier of her mind. *You just don't want to admit it. That's why you're asking him, to give him the opportunity to rationalize his way out of accountability.*

Amaria bit her lip, shaking her head as to push the thoughts out of her head. He was her father. Aaron Raulet wouldn't hurt her. Amaria wasn't sure she knew the status of many things anymore, even things that had once been as familiar as breathing–but she knew her father wouldn't do anything to jeopardize the family's position, and a weakened, hurt, and vulnerable family member did exactly that. Aaron Raulet wouldn't weaken, hurt, or make Amaria vulnerable—she was integral to the family and she needed to be strong to maintain their power. Her father always had her best interests at heart, despite everything.

"Behave." Aaron looked at her sternly as Amaria unblinkingly met his eyes. She would not let him intimidate her in this. As silver and brown challenged each other, Amaria felt the pressure of her father's magic press against her mind, as if it was a creeping, thorny, yet still flowering vine. Sighing, Amaria lowered her magical barriers, allowing her father to enter her mage link.

"*Yes?*" Amaria said.

"*It's safer to talk this way,*" Aaron said. Amaria resisted rolling her eyes. She knew it was safer–nobody could enter a mage link without the mage's consent–well except for mind reader's.

"*It's all about safety, isn't it? That's why I do your dirty work.*"

Aaron winced, and immediately, Amaria wanted to reach out to him. She wanted to help him, after all he was her father and she didn't even know if Vypren's accusations were true.

"*Amaria,*" Aaron said. "*I never had you do anything I wouldn't do.*"

"*Except marry Vypren.*"

Aaron arched an eyebrow, scoffing under his breath. "*That was Aion–*"

Amaria's fists clenched around her skirts. "*Aion does whatever you ask, and marriage is usually the father's initiative. Why did you lie to me?*"

"*It was easier to let you think someone else was sending you to the lion's den–*"

"*I'd have done it!*" Amaria mentally screamed. "*I'd have done anything to advance our family. But why, why did you let me think Aion was sending me there?*"

"*Would it have been easier if you knew I sent you when you were being beaten?*" Aaron challenged. "*I was giving you someone to blame.*"

"*You thought I'd blame you,*" Amaria corrected. "*You wanted a scapegoat. But it would have helped me to know–I'm as ambitious as you. I can handle a few beatings for power. I couldn't tolerate being beaten because of somebody else's incompetence.*"

Amaria withdrew her magic from the link, her hands gripping her skirts so tightly her knuckles were white. She blinked fiercely, the winter chill stopping the tears in her eyes as a gust of wind brushed past her face. If only the frost could stop the pain in her chest—her heart was breaking, and Amaria wasn't sure how to handle the revelation that her father had always lied to her.

"You should get inside." Aaron spoke outside of the mage-link. "You'll get frost-bite."

"I'm fine." Amaria summoned her magic, warming the air around her. The snow, falling gently overhead, melted as it neared the bubble around Amaria as she walked away from her father. She gritted her teeth–cold splashes of water weren't better than snow before she moved more of her magic upwards, making the air directly over her comfortable bubble hot enough to evaporate the snow before it turned to slush or rain and hit Amaria's skin.

She pushed her way through the camp, moving so fast she was almost jogging, pulling her cloak tight against her. She couldn't breath, she couldn't think. Around her, the wind picked up, the air rapidly turning turbulent.

Amaria extended her magic, small wispy tendrils reaching out to sense her brother's magic. She needed him. He was the only one who could understand what it was like to live with their father.

Her magic collided with the barriers of Haerdnor's mind; the presence wild like a deep forest in which unicorns roamed, but stifling as if a wildfire was about to destroy the forest and the lands around it. Almost immediately, Haerdnor's mage link opened to Amaria.

"What's wrong?" Haerdnor asked quickly.

"I need you," Amaria said, feeling as if her lungs were deflating.

"What's wrong?" Haerdnor repeated.

"Father lied to me about Vypren, who knows what else." Amaria couldn't feel the cold around her; she was separated from her body. She didn't care what happened next, she just needed some control. Her life had been planned out for her and the person she thought had been honest with her raised her like a lamb for slaughter.

She had to do something that she, and only she, could do. Something that nobody could claim they manufactured later. Amaria was going to do something impulsive, without time for planning.

"We're going to kill Lynette," Amaria snarled, realizing she was being irrational but not knowing how to stop herself.

"Are you sure–"

"Where are you?" Amaria's hands clenched into fists. *"We're leaving now. I'm going with or without you."*

Haerdnor's presence melted away slightly but then after a few moments returned. *"Oliver and I will meet you near the armory closest to our tents."*

Amaria nodded, as if Haerdnor could see her, unfolding her wings and launching herself into the sky, flying towards the armory. She stood there, in the dark, waiting for Oliver and Haerdnor to join.

It took too long, but finally they arrived. Amaria felt her eyes getting heavy as her heartbeat slowed. Perhaps this decision was rash.

"How'd you find out he lied to you? What was the lie?" Haerdnor pulled her into a hug. Amaria closed her eyes, her ribs pinching.

"I'd been engaged since I was three," Amaria whispered. "It was never Aion."

"This is a bad idea," Haerdnor said. "You're in no state–"

Amaria felt heat rising to her face. "Are you going with me or not?"

Haerdnor sighed, his fingers tapping against his leg. "Of course I am."

"Then let's go."

"Wait," Oliver called out, pulling his cloak out. "Your wings are still poking out from your cloak, wear this. The wings–it's a giant beacon."

Amaria stiffly turned towards Oliver, her muscles tense as she took the cloak from him, adjusting the cloaks around herself.

"Better," Oliver affirmed once she was standing still. "Let's go."

And under the cover of darkness, they ran across no-man's land, rushing into enemy territory.

They infiltrated Lynette's camp.

"Where is she?" Oliver questioned.

"Perhaps the middle," Haerdnor said. "It's generally where higher ranks are."

Amaria imagined blood pouring out from Lynette onto the snow. Lynette killed Amaria's friend, Delphina, when she directed people to break into Provincia Palencia. She brought cannibalistic animals into this damn world–being eaten by a unicorn or spider was a death even Amaria cringed at. And Lynette tried to destroy her marriage.

Lynette's throat would be sliced open, perhaps with steel or perhaps with ice. Or maybe she wouldn't be cut with hand-held weapons, perhaps Amaria would boil her blood.

"We need to go," Oliver said. "It's risky waiting here."

The three of them moved through the camp, using the shadows as protection.

"Should we beacon Amaria out to Lynette?" Haerdnor crouched behind a tent. "Then we can attack while she's focused on how my sister somehow grew feathers."

"It's a shame you think that plan is clever," a female voice sneered.

All three of them turned towards the feminine laugh, their weapons raised. Lynette stepped from behind a tree. "Don't look so shocked; I'm a seer after all."

Amaria bared her teeth slightly. "Then you've seen your own death."

"I've seen yours," Lynette said. "You could have been great, it's not too late to joi—"

Amaria pulled a weed out of the ground, enlarging it into a whip. She lashed out at Lynette, trying to wrap her in the magic, wanting to trap Lynette so she could hurt her. Lynette must feel a portion of the pain she caused Amaria before she died.

Haerdnor charged at Lynette, his flaming sword a beckon in the night. Lynette let him come, dodging out of his way at the last moment, touching him on the face with her palm. Immediately, Haerdnor fell to the ground, convulsing.

Amaria held out her hand, choking Lynette, the cloaks falling from her shoulders, her wings unfurling. She let all of her power go through her, slowly taking away Lynette's life.

"Kill me and you risk darkness again," Lynnette sputtered.

"The darkness was always there," Amaria said. She was not a helpless spring rose. She was a flower cultivated in the winter, she stared at death before, she caused death, and she was as poisonous as nightshade.

"I'm sure my allies in Rindria would love to hear that," Lynette said as Amaria's hands shook, her grip on Lynette becoming unsteady.

"Former allies," Amaria said, her limbs feeling heavy.

"Amaria, don't be stupid!" Oliver screamed. He looked at her, saw her flickering eyes, and ran towards Lynette sword drawn. Lynette rolled her eyes, waving her hands so that smoky black tendrils came out of her. She turned to face Haerdnor, a burst of black light surrounding her.

Immediately, Haerdnor fell to the ground, screaming in agony. Amaria's heart raced. *You're not taking anyone else from me.* Spittle built up at the corners of her mouth as she attacked, sending a large wave of energy, hoping to drown Lynette's power with her own.

A wave of silver light rushed towards Lynette; The black tendrils hardened and stabbed Oliver. He fell, screaming but managed to slash her shins. She stumbled, blood pouring from her legs as she knelt on the ground, the silver encompassing the black.

Amaria met Haerdnor's eyes as he stood from the ground, shaking. Haerdnor cursed in pain, lighting his sword, Eternal Flame, on fire, running his hands over the blade in one smooth sweep, his fire magic embracing the steel.

Amaria summoned a cloud of snow flurries, holding them close to her chest, as she focused on making them intensify. She had a miniature blizzard in her hands. Her magic was stronger, she grudgingly had to admit that Oberon helped her there.

Amaria met Haerdnor's eyes and they nodded, as she released the blizzard, frost and snow barreling towards Lynette. At the last second, Amaria redirected the blizzard, forcing all of the snow to turn into icicles and hurl towards Lynette.

As the icicles stabbed Lynette, the queen howling as she was pierced. Rage boiled beneath Amaria's skin, but she suppressed it, forcing herself to focus on the coldness around her. Impulsive rage was for children, not powerful magical beings. Amaria was controlled, and she had a part to play in this.

As Amaria maintained the icicles, Haerdnor rushed towards Lynette, bringing his flaming sword down upon the queen's neck. And as soon as he dealt the blow, blood, fire, and ice swirled together blackening Lynette's body. The queen screamed, and Haerdnor lifted his sword once more, hacking it against her neck once, twice, and finally a third time, her head severing from the rest of her body.

"Haerdnor," Amaria gasped, looking at the head in the snow. However, as soon as Lynette's body fell, Haerdnor ran over to Oliver, clutching his hand, ignoring the sudden thundering of a thousand horses, men, and inhuman monsters rang in the distance, likely having heard and seen the fight. Amaria turned to see the entirety of Lynette's army stampeding towards them. Towards the Badlands. Amaria didn't know. She didn't care.

"Run!" Oliver commanded.

"No," Haerdnor said. "You'll die if we leave you."

"They can't get reinforcements or go back." Haerdnor clutched Oliver's hands. "We'll hunt the rest down here."

"Haerdnor," Oliver's breath was pained and Amaria noted that he was paler than the snow.

"No," Haerdnor said sharply, his hand lightly brushing over Oliver's face. "Shut up."

"You know what I'm going to say," Oliver gave a pained chuckle.

"Only because it's stupid. So forget it."

"Kill me. Please," Oliver begged, gripping Haerdnor's hand. "Give me an easier death."

"Fuck no," Haerdnor said under his breath, forcing back sobs as he clutched Oliver's hands.

Amaria gulped, feeling tears well in her eyes, remembering how she'd been in a similar position once, begging Delphinia to not die in a hopeless situation. But here, it would be worse for Haerdnor–losing Oliver would be the same as losing Theodmon.

"Haerdnor," Amaria said softly, the army quickly approaching. "We have to go."

"I've been giving him my magic…I don't think Lynette infected him, I think it was just knives…I've never seen anything like that," Haerdnor blubbered. He was pale. Both of them were.

"Move," Amaria commanded. "Tell Faelyn to be ready to heal him when we get back to camp. You'll burn up your energy."

"He's cold!"

"You're not the only fire mage here," Amaria countered. "I'm more powerful here, get him help. Oliver needs you to get Faelyn, not risk mage fatigue."

She scooped up Oliver in her arms, using her magic to create a cradle of warm air to help support his weight, as she grudgingly admitted Oberon's lessons were helpful.

She breathed heavily, her eyes unbreaking from Haerdnor's as she flew up towards the sky, hovering over him slightly, telling him the one thing she could to get him to flee. "You should get the honor of announcing Lynette's death. You're a Queen Slayer."

Chapter Ten

"Oliver!" Haerdnor pushed through the healing tent, frantically looking over the heads of the injured. "Oliver!"

Amaria trailed behind him, trying to not flinch as people stared at her slack jawed. A few tried to touch her wings, as if they were trying to convince themselves they were real. She moved away from them when she saw a hand reaching for her. She wasn't fully comfortable with them yet, she didn't need complete strangers touching her.

"Amaria," Theodmon walked from behind her, stopping once he reached her side. He slipped his hand in hers.

"Haerdnor killed Lynette," Amaria whispered under her breath as she watched Haerdnor embrace a stitched-up Oliver.

"I'm surprised," Theodmon said.

Amaria turned towards him, her eyes widening. Haerdnor was capable...why would he be surprised?

"It's...it's weird," Theodmon continued, his speech slowing as he seemed to be searching for words. "We were being slaughtered until you and the faeries arrived—and we won quickly once you arrived. It feels almost, it's going to sound ridiculous, but it feels anticlimactic. I'm glad more didn't die–don't get me wrong–but it's weird. And I expected a faerie to kill Lynette, not Haerdnor."

"If the results of war could be predicted nobody would go fight," Amaria sighed.

"The other side is in disarray," Aaron entered the tent, stopping next to Amaria and Haerdnor. However, Aaron's voice carried. "Does anybody have an explanation as to why?"

"Haerdnor," Amaria said. "He killed Lynette Edrion."

"So what now?" Theodmon asked sardonically. "Do we help your sister claim the throne of Avondra?"

"She can handle her country. If she wants to rule Avondra, she will have to conquer it with her own blood." Aaron said coolly. "But you ask an apt question as a commander on this side. What do we do now?"

"I'm sure you have a suggestion." Theodmon rubbed his temples with the tips of his fingertips, and Amaria noticed the dark circles around his eyes, making him seem gaunt--as if her husband was tempting death and would soon join Sadthos's silent kingdom.

"Offer amnesty to the humans on that side—as long as they aren't actively practicing dark magic," Aaron said.

"Is that a suggestion or a command?" Theodmon said.

"Neither." Aaron said. "It's the best choice of strategy you have. I'm sure you've seen the benefits in it as I have."

"I've considered it," Theodmon popped his jaw, the noise reverberating in his ears. "Unfortunately, seeing my sister have her head cut off as she was in chains on the battlefield has currently made me less than amenable to that side."

"It's Aunt Miana and Uncle Laurents country," Amaria glared at her father. "They can decide what to do with the Avonnians on the other side. We've won, there's no more war. Theodmon won't make an unpopular decision to shield them from accountability."

Faelyn came over, his hands stained with blood. "Out. My patients don't need to hear about murder or who died and they especially don't need to listen to your political schemes." He looked directly at Amaria, his eyes drifting from her eyes to her wings. "You're going to tell me later about how you got those."

The three of them stepped outside the tent, and Oberon was there waiting for them. Amaria crossed her arms, glaring. She wouldn't be surprised if he had been outside this tent the whole time, waiting to ambush them.

"You two," Oberon directed Amaria and Theodmon, "let's talk."

Without waiting for a response, Oberon strode off towards the direction of the forest. Amaria and Theodmon met each other's eyes, worry creasing the corners of their eyes. Both of their chests heaved slightly as they followed Oberon, a sinking pit appearing in Amaria's stomach.

"We're leaving." Oberon stopped on the outskirts of the forest. "Since the Badlands are closed there's no reason for the fae to stay."

"You pulled us away just to tell us you're leaving?" Theodmon crossed his arms. Did Oberon want a thank you?

"No," Oberon said. "I'm warning both of you that I'll be watching you and Sylviana to ensure that my investment pays off."

Chapter Eleven

After Oberon vanished, Amaria and Theodmon hiked back to the camp, burrowing themselves in furs and blankets as they curled up together. The cold finally caught up with Amaria and she was shivering, despite her fourth cup of wine.

Amaria burrowed closer against Theodmon, her teeth chattering. "This isn't warming me up."

"It's wine," Theodmon laughed. "You need something stronger for up here."

"Mhmm, perhaps." She leaned her head against his shoulders. "But I don't like the taste of those."

"Can you believe Oberon made us hike to the edge of the forest for that?"

Amaria rolled her eyes. "He threatened to set his hounds on me if I didn't run to his liking and pushed me down from thousands of feet to teach me how to fly."

Theodmon sat up sharply. "What?"

Amaria rubbed his arm soothingly. "I'm alright. My point was, making us hike a few hundred feet is mild for him."

"Fucking faeries," Theodmon cursed, laying back to where he was before.

Amaria laughed, kissing Theodmon on the lips lightly. "They're the worst," she agreed. "But we don't need to worry about Oberon, not for a while."

"Oh?" Theodmon pushed back a lock of her hair, his hand cupping her face.

Amaria sighed, her skin tingling. "We'll be home soon. And we will—"

Someone coughed from the tent's entrance, causing her to stop mid-sentence, whirling around to see the intruder, wind swirling in her palm.

"Easy." Henri stepped forward with his hands outstretched. Behind him were Faelyn Laurellanza, Michel Valouis, Samuel Beaulane–the other living Extractors.

Amaria's intestines knotted themselves into a million different tangles as a bead of sweat appeared on her forehead, despite the chill of the winter air. Nothing good could be happening if all the remaining Extractors were together so soon after the faeries left.

Her hands shook. She folded them together to hide them. Amaria felt as if she would vomit. "What is this about?" Amaria forced the bile down as she directly looked at each remaining Extractor in turn.

"Theodmon," Faelyn said gently, his gray eyes drooping as he suppressed a yawn. "Please leave, just momentarily."

Theodmon squeezed Amaria's hand. Her eyes widened as she looked at him, her stomach fluttering. Amaria didn't care that the Extractors were a secret order, she wanted Theodmon to stay with her. However, he removed his hands from hers, kissed the top of her forehead, and departed leaving her alone with the other four Extractors.

"What is this about?" Amaria repeated.

"Adair died," Henri said gently. "We need to choose a new leader."

Amaria sighed, her shoulders leaning forward. That did make sense. And Elena Marion, who could control magical energies of others and regularly talk to the gods, and who had been the anticipated successor of Adair was dead. Amaria met Faelyn Laurellanza's eyes. Duke Laurellanza would be a good choice—he was respected. He was a powerful healing mage. He had solid political connections as the leader of the Lirere Fideles province. "I'd vote for Faelyn."

"I'm not the candidate," Faelyn said. Amaria blinked, looking over the remaining options. Henri wasn't the choice, he was too much of a risk of needing to withdraw when they needed him most—mind readers could often go insane if they couldn't retreat when they became overwhelmed. Samuel Beaulane, while a powerful metal-working mage, was a commoner. He did not have the political connections needed to be successful. Perhaps it was Michel–an untitled lord was still a lord, although lacking as much wealth and power as those with title's. But Michel's transfiguration magic was powerful and often worth as much in court politics as land was.

Amaria noticed Henri was looking at her wings. She blinked, processing that they were all looking at her, almost with anticipation. "Me?" Her voice cracked. "I've been missing for a year, I went insane in Rindria–"

"You have the political connections," Faelyn interrupted. "And you have the most powerful magic of any of us," he inclined his head towards her glowing silver wings. "You look the part—there's no other choice. We've all voted in favor of you if you accept."

Amaria's chest tightened. She had never seen herself as the head of the Extractors. *No human can compete with my magic.* Amaria bit down on her tongue, flinching. *Of course with the old head dead they'd look at me now.*

Amaria wet her lips, her tongue brushing over the rough flesh caused by the cool winter air. "I accept. On one condition."

Faelyn could cause the most issues of the three Extractors Amaria if he resisted her when–*if*–she made a bid for the Thestitiunian throne. Bringing Faelyn into the fold was essential for the future as she needed his loyalty, or at least a way to divide his loyalty enough, to win. Besides, Faelyn was competent, her father always spoken highly of the mild mannered duke.

"Which is?" Faelyn asked. Behind Faelyn, Amaria saw Henri unsuccessfully hiding his smirk. She resisted an eyeroll. *Mind readers, what could you do with them?*

Amaria cleared her throat to center herself to the present situation.

"I get to choose my successor. And they'll accept without protest. And you'll all accept who I chose." Amaria's silver eyes flashed as she met each other the Extractors's gazes in turn.

"I'm alright with that," Samuel said.

"Seconded," Henri said, almost too quickly. Amaria resisted glaring at him, he knew what she was doing but he didn't have to appear so overly eager.

Faelyn, his eyes narrowing slightly as he looked over Amaria, slowly nodded. "I'll agree to those terms."

They all looked over to Michel. "The successor is an Extractor?"

Obviously, Amaria thought irately. However, she kept her face neutral as she politely nodded towards Michel.

Michel scanned her face suspiciously. Amaria observed his jaw twitching, keeping her own jaw locked. She wondered if he would refuse to accept the condition. She wondered how he even voted for her, as he obviously didn't trust her.

A soft wave of energy lapped against her mind and she suddenly smelled old books. Amaria opened her mind, lowering her barriers as she avoided looking at Henri.

"He didn't want to," Henri told her in the mage link. *"But it was fairly obvious that three people wanted you and he wouldn't get their support for another candidate."*

"Faelyn and Samuel were that insistent?"

"Sam is from Perivina Fluere," Henri chuckled in her mind. *"From Raulle specifically. He's one of the strongest allies you have."*

Now that Henri bluntly stated it, Amaria supposed that was true. She closed her eyes momentarily, breathing as she calmed her mind. She turned to look at Michel. "Do you agree?"

Michel's eyes narrowed, huffing as he scowled. "I suppose I must. Whose second in command?"

As the ghost of a smirk appeared on her face, Amaria felt taller. "Faelyn."

Michel's chest fell but the worry lines on his forehead disappeared. Amaria didn't bother to further analyze his reaction, turning towards Faelyn. "You'll be my second in command?"

Chuckling, Faelyn held up his hands as if in defeat. "I suppose I agreed to the terms. So you accept your nomination as Head of the Extractors?"

"I supposed I agreed to that." Amaria's face was rosy.

"Then let's start the ceremonies," Henri said. "I believe it's the second sworn in first?"

"No," Michel corrected, pulling out a bag from under his cloak. "It's the Head, then the second." He pulled out a heavy golden chain, laden with inscriptions and jewels on each piece of the jewelry. A soft orange glowed from around the jewelry as Michel held it. It kept its glow as it was handed to Henri, a deep blue merging over the orange. Then Faelyn's mint green joined, and last was Samuel's rust colored magical aura.

"Amaria Chauvignon, born to the House Raulet," Faelyn stated, his usual soft voice booming in the tent. "Step forward."

Locking her jaw and forcing herself to focus on breathing steadily, Amaria stepped forward, her wings extending slightly.

"Do you vow to uphold the honors and traditions of the Extractors?" Faelyn asked.

"I do." Amaria hated how dry her voice sounded.

"Do you vow to keep our secrets?"

"I do."

"Do you vow to keep the independent integrity of this order?"

Amaria paused. *Independent integrity?* It almost sounded as if the Extractors were not supposed to take direction from outsiders—like the emperor. Amaria swallowed her spit, trying to bring moisture back to her mouth.

"I do," she said.

Faelyn suppressed a yawn, his body slumping forward. Amaria realized how fatigued he must be from constantly healing injured soldiers for what had to be months of this war. "Do you vow to protect the Extractors from those who would seek to destroy us?"

"I do."

"Add your magic to the emblems," Faelyn directed. Amaria held out her hands, letting Samuel slide the heavy gold jewelry into her hands. They were hot to the touch—Amaria supposed that's why the metal crafting mage was holding it through this ceremony. She summoned a sliver of her energy, bright silver light encompassing the necklace. Through the light she saw designs of the hydras and dragons, designs of the gods, and smaller designs that represented the current Extractor's magic abilities.

Sure enough, Amaria saw a picture of a vine and water stream becoming perfectly entwined around a flame as wings spread out behind them in the center empty golden oval of the chained necklace. Her magical representation. As the silver died down, the necklace appearing ordinary now, Faelyn took it from her.

"Do you accept to be the Head of the Order of Extractors?"

"I do," Amaria repeated once more.

"Then kneel," Faelyn directed, already lifting the necklace. Amaria obliged, lowering her head as she lowered herself into a curtsy. She felt the necklace slip over her head, pulling at her hair.

"Rise," Faelyn continued, "Marchioness Amaria Chauvignon, Princepsia Magia Exia of Thestitiunia and the Order of the Extractors."

Leader of the Mages. Amaria's beamed, slowly standing upright.

"Do you, Samuel Beaulane, swear fealty to Amaria Chauvignon as Princepsia Magia Exia of Thestitiunia and the Order of the Extractors? Do you, Michel Valoius, swear fealty to Amaria Chauvignon as Princepsia Magia Exia of Thestitiunia and the Order of the Extractors? Do you, Henri Delaluna, swear fealty to Amaria Chauvignon as Princepsia Magia Exia of Thestitiunia and the Order of the Extractors?" Faelyn kneeled before Amaria, the other three following suit.

"I swear fealty to you as Princepsia Magia Exia of Thestitiunia and the Order of the Extractors," Faelyn swore. Amaria's eyebrows flashed up and stayed raised as her chin lifted and her lips twisted into a small smile.

Henri, Samuel, and Michel repeated the same oath Faelyn said. Amaria surveyed them, her heart thudding as if it would burst out of her chest. She was exalted. She could conquer the world.

Beaming, Amaria spoke to the other four Extractors. "Rise," she commanded, her wings giving a few powerful flaps in stretching out the tendons that extended from them. The silver from her wings danced in the candlelight. She was infinite, a million and one exalted breaths dancing towards the sky, as if she were moonlight reaching to be in the stars embrace.

She couldn't suppress the horrible thought of what this sworn fealty could do when it conflicted with all of their sworn fealty towards the emperor and Thestitiunia. Could she ask them to make a choice that in whatever they choose they'd be breaking faith and their honor. If she did what her father asked, and if she was being truthful, something she too wanted. If she did that, she'd be making all four of them traitors.

Amaria breathed in the crisp air through her nose. She wouldn't think of this, not now. Numbly, she made her way through the similar ceremony making Faelyn the second in command. And as Faelyn rose, and the ceremony ended, Amaria beamed at Henri, reaching her arms out to hug him. And when they hugged, he whispered in her ear: "it's not breaking faith if we also want to do it."

But did every Extractor wish that? Amaria doubted it. However, perhaps one day she would be forced to hedge all her bets on that assumption.

Theodmon, welcomed back into the tent by Faelyn, stood in front of the flap, shivering. Amaria turned her head to see him, her face turning rosy once more as she smiled at him. She would have to hedge her bets one day, but today there were other things at stake.

After all, why consider treason when the overthrow of a foreign nation was an easier and more imminent game to play?

Chapter Twelve

T he next day, Amaria stood outside Aion's tent with Faelyn, rubbing her hands together as she saw her breath puff in front of her. Her heart thudded and her mouth felt dry as she waited to be let into the tent.

"He could let us wait inside," Faelyn grumbled. Amaria forced her hands under her armpits, biting her lip.

"I'm going to warm the air," she said. She knew displays of magic were inappropriate before a Princepsia Magia Exia and the second-in-command swore fealty, but it was entirely too cold to be subjected to waiting like this.

"Are you sure?"

Amaria shrugged, already swirling her magic around them. "What can he do to me?"

"It's a faux pas–"

"So is making your Extractors get frostbite," Amaria said cooly. "I'm not letting either of us lose fingers due to his incompetence."

"You may enter," a guard said, stepping out of the tent, interrupting them. "His Imperial Majesty is ready for you."

"What prudent timing." Amaria cast a look towards Faelyn as she kept the warm air around them both. As she stepped inside she saw the tent littered with empty wine and ale bottles, and she scrunched up her nose, biting her tongue.

"He's drunk," Faelyn muttered.

What for? Amaria felt a rush of heat rush to her chest as she heard a roaring in her ears. *Aion didn't fight, he didn't make strategies, he didn't collect or develop intelligence—what possible reason could he have to be drunk?*

Amaria's fists clenched, and their air around them became scorchingly hot.

"Amaria," Faelyn warned.

She forced down a lump in her throat and she nodded, stilling her magic. It was best when meeting Aion if she didn't open herself up to the risk of burning him alive in the middle of a war camp.

"It's a simple, almost informal swearing," Faelyn told her as they approached Aion. "His guards will likely be the witnesses needed."

Amaria gave a curt nod, and the two of them were silent until they were standing in front of Aion and he staggered to his feet, reeking of alcohol. "Why are you here?" Aion asked.

"You summoned us," Amaria said. "We are here to swear fealty as the new head and lieutenant of the Extractors."

"In costume?" Aion lunged towards Amaria, grabbing a fistful of her wings.

Amaria screamed in pain, pushing Aion off of her.

He stumbled backwards, landing on his butt, sputtering. "How dare you? I am the emperor–"

"Apologies," Amaria said curtly. "But you attacked me."

"I am your emperor–"

"And what grounds do you have to mutilate me? What crime have I committed?"

"I am sure Marchioness Chauvignon has deep regrets for touching Your Imperial Majesty," Faelyn interjected diplomatically. "But due to the novelty of her new physiology–"

Aion waved his hand, sitting back on the chair he positioned to seem like a throne. "No mind," he said, interrupting Faelyn. "Why are you here?"

"You summoned us," Faelyn said calmly. "We will swear fealty as Machioness Chauvignon is the new Princepsia Magia Exia and I am her lieutenant."

Aion cast a glance at both of them, his eyes narrowing. "Amaria? Faelyn? Where is Adair and Elena?"

"They died," Faelyn said. "The Extractors have voted us to lead the Order."

"Alright," Aion slumped in his seat. "Have you seen Cedric?"

Amaria stared cooly ahead, keeping her face neutral. Bless the gods for Oliver and killing that problem. "Last I heard he was still missing. I am sure he will be found now that the war has been won. May we go ahead and swear fealty? Duke Laurellanza has been busy tending the injured."

Aion blinked, as if he were in a fog. "Yes, yes," he muttered. "Go ahead. I'm sure you know the words."

Amaria did not, and usually with oaths of fealty there was a call and response between the two parties. Gritting her teeth, she kneeled in front of Aion, racking her brain for the words–for what the Princepsia Magia Exia would swear. She took a deep breath, her mouth dry. "I, Amaria Chauvignon, born of the House Raulet, swear as Princepsia Magia Exia that my magic and influence will always go to the preservation and best interests of the Thestitiunian Empire and her citizens."

Amaria stayed kneeling, waiting for Aion to say something. Behind her Faelyn coughed.

"Very well." Aion's words slurred. "Faelyn?"

Faelyn made the same oath Amaria made and they departed. Once they were both outside the tent, Faelyn stopped and whispered into Amaria's ear. "You didn't swear fealty to the emperor."

Neither did you, Amaria thought. She smiled at Faelyn, tilting her head. "I thought I did?"

Faelyn's eyebrows rose. "Amaria."

"I was expecting a call and response," Amaria shrugged. "I never thought I'd be the Princepsia Magia Exia, the proper words slipped my mind. I am sure you relate as you made the same oath."

"I have no idea what you are talking about," Faelyn said. "Excuse me, I have patients to heal."

Amaria bowed her head, stepping out of Faelyn's way, deciding to fly before she was contained in a carriage for the next few weeks.

Once Faelyn departed, she leapt into the sky, flying above the war-torn landscape. The gentle breeze, although frigid, cradled Amaria through the clouds. Amaria dove, curling her wings to her back as she dove downwards, accelerating towards the earth. She screamed in elation, beaming as the wind ran through her hair. Perhaps she loved her wings, if only for moments like this.

Amaria spent these last moments before their departure swooping and diving, avoiding the thought of how painful her wings would cramp on this journey. Unfortunately, it couldn't last forever, and Amaria steadied herself as she landed on the icy ground, her knees ringing with the impact.

And her feet fell out from under her, and she slipped, landing on her hands. She winced, she felt the ice cut her hands.

"Amaria!" Aloysius ran from ten feet away from where he been directing someone on where to move the packed food in the Chauvignons' carriages. "Are you alright?"

"Fine." Amaria forced herself to her feet as she felt the blood dripping down her wrist, red streaking her dress.

"Less force," Amaria muttered under her breath as she tore off a strand of her dress, wrapping it around her hand before she marched off towards the carriages. "Less force to do simple things."

Amaria curled up against Theodmon, breathing softly as her head rested against his chest, the occasional bumps in the road causing her to jolt. Her wings stretched out over both of them, as if a blanket.

She turned her body slightly, adjusting her arms under herself. As she did so, the sunlight, pouring in from the windows, bounced off the small golden plate sitting upon her chest, the griffin that was etched in the necklace illuminated.

"Does it ever seem odd to consider how much has changed?" Amaria asked, the words dripping almost lazily from her mouth in her relaxation.

"What do you mean?" Theodmon easily replied.

"Almost three years ago we didn't know each other, and I was terrified of you as my husband. Now, we've killed the reason why I viewed any new husband with suspicion, we've fought battles together, and I have wings. Would you have guessed back then on our wedding night?"

"Not the wings," Theodmon chuckled. "But I always suspected, or perhaps just hoped, we would work well together." He kissed the top of her head. "I'm glad I wasn't wrong."

Amaria closed her eyes, snuggling closer to him. He radiated body heat, warming her. Her hands brushed over his muscled abs, making their way up to his broad shoulders. "I don't think anybody could have predicted the wings."

"Perhaps that High Priestess." Theodmon's hands rubbed her hair, his strokes momentarily pausing. "What did she say?"

"She said a lot of things," Amaria sighed. "A lot of it was to take my blood–which she used to save me–and you gave her leverage later to save me with it...I can't remember."

"No, you told me one prophecy she gave you—if we can call it that. You'd be a queen among mortals."

"And I'd be despised for it," Amaria finished. She remembered how absurd that line felt at the time–she basically called the High Priestess a charlatan because she believed any fool could tell a Raulet that. Amaria's wings fluttered slightly as she inhaled deeply. Perhaps this High Priestess saw more than she understood. It was definitely more than Amaria understood at least.

"Do you think Celestine is doing alright?" Amaria asked, changing the topic. "She's been running Forteresse les Blanche and the Westerlands for a while now."

Theodmon nodded. "She's doing great. From what I heard she's more conniving than you are in some areas."

Amaria laughed. "Good. Celestine is smart, she should use it."

Theodmon joined in her laughter, pausing momentarily to kiss the top of her head. "We'll see how much she uses it soon. Are you ready to be back home?"

Amaria nodded. "I've missed being home with you. It's so peaceful and perfect with you at Forteresse les Blanche. And I've missed Chauvi too–it feels just as much as home as Raulle did, more sometimes if I'm being honest." Amaria sighed. "I've made a lot of mistakes recently."

"They're fixable," Theodmon said immediately, gripping her tighter in his arms.

"How can you so easily say that?" Amaria questioned.

"You're perfect," Theodmon answered, causing Amaria to lightly snort in disbelief.

"I mean it," Theodmon said gravely. "You're perfect to me. No mistake you could ever make will change that. And we have each other and both of our extensive resources–I love you and we both can fix any mistake either one of us ever makes."

Amaria's palms cupped Theodmon's jaw, as she gave a broken smile up at him. Amaria heard his steady heartbeat thumping through his chest and she wondered if he could hear hers too. "Thank you," she told him. "Thank you for always being there, unconditionally."

Theodmon placed one of his hands above hers. "Always, my love."

Part Two

the griffins

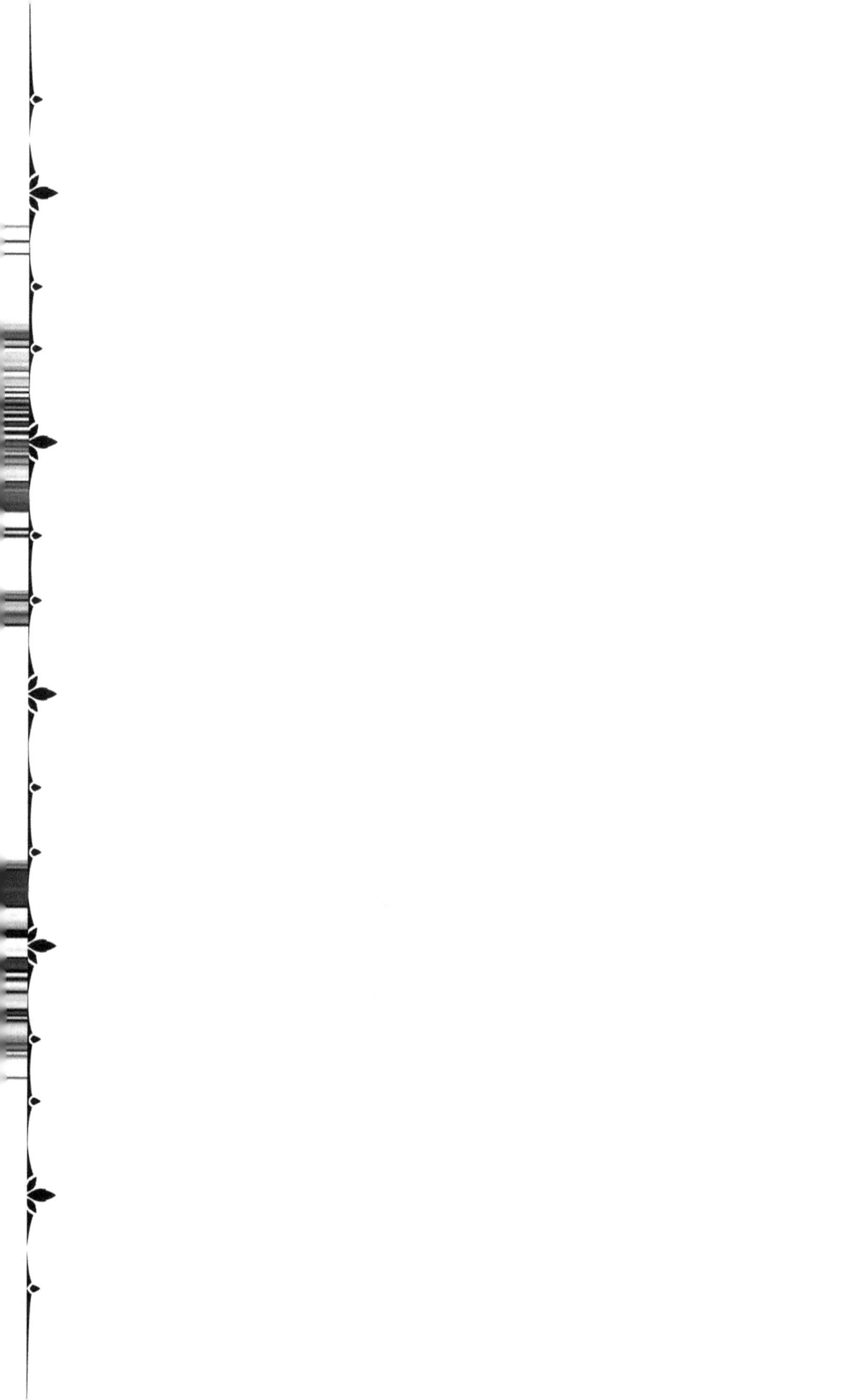

Chapter Thirteen

After numbing weeks of travel, Theodmon finally saw the familiar smokestacks puffing from Chauvi. The snow thickly coated the ground, with small icicles hanging from the cliffs of the mountainous path.

"Is it safe?" Amaria asked.

Theodmon took a deep breath, wondering how he was going to proceed. It would be a special type of cruel irony to survive the war to die by falling off a mountain.

"If it's melted, will it be safer?" Amaria looked outside the carriage window.

"Yes," Theodmon said. "As long as it doesn't freeze again before we make it up."

Amaria gathered her skirts, kissing him on the cheek before she pounded her fist on the roof of the carriage. "I'll take care of it."

"Be safe." Theodmon held her hand in his.

"I can fly," Amaria laughed as the carriage pulled to a stop. She gathered her skirts once more, stepping out of the carriage. With the door still open, Theodmon watched her launch herself into the sky, her wings spreading with a powerful flap.

She was beautiful and terrifying. And she was his.

"My Lord," the guards pulled open the gates as Theodmon, Henri, Juliette, Haerdnor, and Aaron finished their trudge up the mountain. Their luggage would arrive soon with the pulley system. Usually Theodmon had zero complaints about Forteresse les Blanche's location but after war, he cursed whichever ancestor of his decided that this much geographic protection was necessary.

"Your wife arrived already," the guard continued. "She's taking a bath now before the court is heard."

"Already?" Theodmon questioned.

"Your sister had matters planned for today. We could ask Lady Celestine if she needs to reschedule?" The guard's voice shook, as if he didn't know the proper procedure for handing off the proxy head of court when the true one arrived. Or perhaps he didn't want to challenge Theodmon.

Theodmon waved his hand dismissively. "No need. Have court ready in a few hours."

"Yes, Marquis." The guard bowed deeply. Theodmon walked past him. He was somehow both frozen and sweaty from hiking up the mountain, and he needed a warm bath because of how grody he felt. The moisture in his boots alone made him internally cringe.

He tried not to focus on how his socks squished every time he took a step, instead focusing on how beautiful the red rugs were against the white stone hallways. It didn't work, instead he just heard the squish against the carpet.

"Theo!" Celestine ran from around a corridor, her face bright as she launched herself in Theodmon's arms. "You're back. You're safe. Is Aloysius...?"

Theodmon felt as if he had been punched in the gut. Celestine didn't know about Ophelia yet. Theodmon's jaw popped as he tried to open his mouth, his airways feeling obstructed by an invisible force–a cruel trick of the gods.

Theodmon licked his lips to gain moisture back into them. "Aloysius is fine."

"What's wrong?" Celestine asked. "What happened? Why did you say it like that?"

"Like what?"

"Like you're delivering a eulogy. What happened to Aloysius?"

"Nothing. But Ophelia...." A sob racketed in his chest, escaping with the tears from his eyes. "Ophelia was murdered."

Celestine sunk to the ground, wrapping her arms around herself. "Where? How? By who?" Tears welled in her eyes as she stared blankly ahead of her.

"She was dragged to the battle front." Theodmon tried to force the vivid reminder away from his memory. He could almost smell the blood and shit now in the pristine halls of Forteresse les Blanche. "Probably by Lynette, she was an Avonnian citizen. Vypren...," Theodmon paused, debating on telling Celestine the details of how Ophelia died. She had a right to know how her sister died, but still, it almost felt needlessly cruel to give the details. Theodmon wished he didn't know all of the details–a part of him too died with Ophelia on that field.

"Vypren?" Celestine prompted.

"...he killed her," Theodmon forced out.

"How?" Celestine's voice was a chilly calm.

"It's not neces–"

"I've a right to know," Celestine interrupted. "Tell me."

"Not now." Theodmon cast a glance around the corridor. Ophelia was gone and he had to acknowledge he'd never see her again. Gods, she hadn't even gotten a proper funeral. And now he had to tell Celestine, remain strong for her in his grief, when he hadn't even processed his own. And the suppressed sobs threatened to burst.

"I have a right–"

"In private. Not where people can see us." He moved briskly down the corridor, pushing to where he knew there would be an empty room.

"How did Ophelia die?" Celestine asked as soon as the door shut behind them.

"He cut off her head and her children's heads before he catapulted it towards our side," Theodmon forced out, feeling his throat close up. He sank to his knees, the tears flowing freely down his face.

Celestine knelt next to him, hugging him. He felt the wet spot on her face as they embraced. "She's gone?"

Theodmon couldn't speak, he just nodded, fearing his voice would crack, or worse, he would scream.

"Are Lynette and Vypren dead?"

Theodmon gave a short nod, the lump appearing in his throat making it impossible to speak.

"By you?" Celestine asked.

Theodmon nodded. "I killed Vypren."

Celestine sniffed, wiping her tears away with her sleeve. "Good." She breathed in deeply. "And Lynette?"

Theodmon shook his head. "Haerdnor killed Lynette."

Celestine nodded, slowly standing up. "Will you be alright?"

"Will you?" Theodmon countered her question, looking at her in concern as he stood up.

"No," Celestine said as they moved out of the room and back into the corridor. "Not now anyways, not ever maybe. But I'll recover enough to where it's not as painful. Just like with Father."

Again, Theodmon felt a thorn in his heart. He hadn't processed Father's death, not really. Theodmon merely buried the pain—he buried it so well that he could ignore it until the ghosts of the past dug up the grave.

Not now. He told himself. He already cried once today. Generals didn't cry. Marquis's didn't cry. And Chauvignons didn't cry—not the men anyways. He would be judged for any breaches in decorum and Theodmon wouldn't invite speculation of the weakness of his rule. Ever since he became Marquis Theodmon Chauvignon of the Westerlands of Thestitiunia other foreign heads speculated how long it would take for him to fail. Not to his face, but it didn't take a genius to know that the world was speculating that a sixteen year old head of state would fail miserably. Theodmon should have failed, but instead he thrived.

"You don't have to go to court today," Theodmon told Celestine. He needed control of the situation before he lost control of himself.

Celestine smiled at him sadly. "I do," she said as they stopped in front of his chambers' doors, the guards slightly inclining their heads as they opened them to reveal Theodmon's chambers. His sister gently squeezed his arm. "We'll both be passable by then. Talk to Amaria, she'll help."

"And who will you speak to?" Theodmon asked.

A small smile briefly appeared across Celestine's face. "I have friends as well. And Aloysius. I know he won't talk to Liara. I have to talk to you all about her—she trusts me."

Theodmon stepped into his chambers, Celestine following him as the door shut.

"Are we still moving forward with the plan?" Celestine whispered.

"Are you soft on her?" Theodmon snorted.

"No," Celestine said coolly. "She's petulant and tiresome and I want jewels for my efforts. But this plan is complex and we need to be on the same page."

"Go ahead," Theodmon told her. "As soon as we have news from Lucas about Tesden Nalaeny you're free to proceed."

"Good." Celestine's blueish-greenish eyes sparkled. "I want amethyst. I think it brings out the color in my eyes."

Theodmon rolled his eyes. "Get the job done, then we'll talk about the designs of your necklace."

"Necklaces," Celestine emphasized. "It's been hard work running your province and befriending that girl, all while nudging her to do what we wanted without her even knowing. And I'm so sweet, I could never be this conniving–"

"Get out before I throw a pillow at you," Theodmon laughed.

Celestine stuck out her tongue, laughing as she opened the oak doors, leaving Theodmon's chambers.

For a few moments, Theodmon breathed in and out, taking in the peace. He saw the bed, he'd missed his comfortable bed. He saw the tapestry hanging near the fireplace that was embroidered with roses, griffins, money, and a sword with a man and a woman embracing in the center—the union tapestry Amaria made. Their union was stronger than anything her embroidery could have predicted.

His chest rising, Theodmon closed his eyes. He was home, safe from war if only for a moment. As his eyes shut, he heard droplets of water from another room–or perhaps he imagined it knowing, wishing perhaps, that Amaria was already in the washroom. Standing up, he strode towards the washroom, his hands on the golden handle as he swung the magnificent doors open to an almost ostentatiously gold lined marble room.

Chapter Fourteen

As Theodmon entered the washroom, he saw Amaria lift her head up from the water where she been floating. "Theodmon!" She beamed warmly at him, her hair sticking to her body as she waded over to him.

Theodmon gave her a half-hearted smile back.

"What's wrong?" Amaria's grin immediately disappeared as she swam to the edge of the basin. "What happened?"

Theodmon shook his head as he crouched by the edge of the basin, sliding his legs into the water. "Nothing happened, not like how you're thinking anyways." He dunked his head under the water, staying under there as long as he could hold his breath, letting the water's pressure cradle him. As the bubbles escaped his nose, he stood up, breaking the surface of the water.

"I told Celestine about Ophelia," Theodmon informed Amaria, acutely aware that she was carefully watching him, as he wiped the water out of his eyes.

"How'd she take it?" Amaria hugged his shoulders from behind. "How are you handling it?"

"As well as I did." Theodmon's shoulders relaxed beneath her touch. "I didn't expect her to die. It was...." He trailed off wanting to say that it was senseless, that Ophelia should not have ever been killed like that. But he couldn't, because the more he thought of how Ophelia died, it made perfect sense.

"It's all my fault," Theodmon whispered.

Amaria's hands tightened around his shoulders. "It's not–"

"No," Theodmon interrupted. "It is." Vypren's attack on Ophelia would have never happened if she wasn't his sister. Killing her served no purpose except for severely disturbing him–and Vypren almost succeeded with capturing and likely killing Theodmon. He was a major commander of their side. If he was taken hostage or killed it would have been detrimental.

"She died because of me." Theodmon slumped down into the bath, engulfing his face so he could hide his tears. His sister, nieces, and nephews deaths were all his fault, collateral damage in the psychological warfare meant for him.

"She died because of Vypren," Amaria said hotly. "He's the one who killed her—"

"And she only died because she's my sister," Theodmon shot back.

"I know it's hard." Amaria wrapped her arms around him. "And there's nothing I can say to make it better. But Ophelia is with the gods now, and her killers are dead."

Theodmon sank down, his shoulders soaking in the warm water. Tears escaped his eyes once more.

"I can start court for you." Amaria rubbed his shoulders. "Give you some time before you have to put on a brave face....It hurts, I know. Give yourself as much time as you can."

Theodmon didn't need to be reminded of how acutely Amaria must know how he was feeling. She had to be married in front of an international audience weeks after her friend been murdered in front of her. And, if he was being honest, Theodmon suspected that she never properly grieved– he could see why it was a part of why she was so volatile when seeking revenge for Delphina Ginsery's death.

Would Theodmon go that far in avenging Ophelia? He would like to believe that his rage had limits, but Theodmon also strove to be honest with himself. He honestly couldn't say what his limit may be. He once blacked out in battle and killed nearly a hundred men. What else may he be capable of?

"I need a distraction," Theodmon sighed. "I want to enjoy this time together."

"I know a way," Amaria began, but Theodmon shook his head, knowing what she was implying.

"Not yet. Not first," he amended. "I'll still be in my thoughts, I need to have another way...at least at first."

Amaria pecked him on the lips before pulling away, kicking her feet to float away from him. "I can still help," she said lazily. Theodmon didn't fully hear what he said, he was watching her float on her back—her wings seemed to drag in the water under her body, but it didn't seem to slow her down. How did that work anyways? Magic—it had always been a mystery to Theodmon.

"What are you planning?"

Amaria gave him a wry smirk. "Remember last Summer Solstice...I suppose it was two Solstices ago...." Amaria cringed and Theodmon moved to hug her, understanding that she too was dealing with something. Theodmon felt similarly—he felt as if he was a stranger in his own home because of it. And his passage of time had been consistent.

"What about it?" Theodmon asked.

"Remember when I said I could craft a better dolphin from the water with my magic than the Imperial Court mages could?"

Theodmon didn't remember that, but still, he nodded.

Amaria smiled softly, her white teeth flashing as she raised her hands, a blob of clear water rising from the tub. The water seemed to resist her and Amaria moved her hands, the water slowly conforming into the shape of a dolphin. "Watch," she said as she forced the "dolphin" to flip in the air. Laughing, Amaria made the dolphin dive into the water before it exploded from the water, doing yet another flip.

Although he felt numb, seemingly as if somebody else was controlling his body, Theodmon smiled as Amaria summoned more dolphins, water stitching together their translucent bodies.

The water seemed to ripple as the dolphins did tricks, as if the water made muscles and tendons with the magic it was woven from. Two dolphins rose, twisting together as they jumped through the air, his eyes locked on the water show. As the dolphins jumped higher and higher, nearly touching the ceiling, they merged together. The dolphins became a dolphin and then a multitude of butterflies that showered down on them.

The water was warm, as if it were summer rain and Theodmon laid back in the water. "Impressive," he complimented Amaria.

She swam over to him, kissing him gently on the lips in response. "It's alright to feel this way," she told him softly as she broke away.

"I'm supposed to be strong–"

"You're strong," Amaria interrupted firmly. "You're not weak for grieving." Her voice cracked as she wrapped her arms around herself. "It's a lesson I wish I learned earlier."

Tears glistened in her eyes as she took a deep breath. "Unfortunately, the rest of the world sees it as weakness, and so, we must hide it. But don't feel ashamed for feeling these feelings, especially here where you are safe."

Theodmon heavily sighed. "How is it not weakness when we have to hide it to appear strong?"

"Think of it as chess." Amaria laid on her back to float with him. "We can't change what is without consequences. We aren't pawns–you don't sacrifice your queen or king to make a point."

Theodmon closed his eyes, trying to reconcile what she was saying. He was never as clever or as slippery as Amaria was. Her logic was impenetrable and yet it was inconsequential, changing with however she believed the winds would blow. He half believed that if anybody let her talk long enough she could convince the gods the inverse of their creations.

Amaria believed truth was absolutely relative. Theodmon could never fully accept that belief. But that belief–one of them having that belief–served them well. And besides, Amaria had a point and he didn't want to argue. Not now.

"Alright." Theodmon forced himself to relax, allowing the water to cradle his muscles.

They floated in silence for a few more blissful moments before Amaria stood up and waded to the edge of the pool, stepping onto the stairs and finding a towel.

As Theodmon watched, Amaria dried herself off, the warm wind ruffling her hair and the feathers in her wings. "I'll be at court. Take as much time as you need. I'll stall business as long as I can."

She ran her fingers through her hair as she watched him intensely. Theodmon knew the unspoken promise that lingered in the air, she would also conduct court business if needed, if he needed more time.

He nodded, forcing back tears once more. He hated to admit this, as it felt as if he were admitting his own weakness, but Amaria was right—he wasn't in any state to conduct matters of state. She strode over to him, leaning down to kiss him. "I love you," she breathed, her lips hovering over his.

"I love you." His hand cupped the soft cusp of her cheek. Their eyes met, and her silver eyes seemed to soften, as if she were melting steel on a blacksmith's anvil.

"It's alright to not feel alright," Amaria whispered. "I'll help you through it all."

Theodmon's eyes softened, and he brought her cupped face closer to his. "I know," he affirmed. "And I'll do the same for you."

"You already have," Amaria said before their lips connected.

Theodmon wasn't sure who pulled the other one into each other, and he wasn't sure on whether or not Amaria meant to fall back into the pool. But they were together and they were one. And together, there wasn't any challenge they couldn't overcome.

Including the problem of not seeming weak to the public when Theodmon had never felt so small and broken inside.

Theodmon caught sight of Amaria's bare hands, and with a jolt, remembered that he had a ring, a replacement of her wedding ring she had taken from her in a Riam dungeon, stored in a chest in their chambers.

Theodmon gently pulled away from her. "Amaria."

"What?" Amaria followed him as he waded out of the pool. "Stay," she said, her voice sounding almost as if she were begging him.

"Come," Theodmon pleaded in return. "I know you lost your ring and then you went to the faeries before the replacement I commissioned was completed...."

"You got me a replacement?" Her cheeks were wet. "We thought I was going to die."

And that's why I didn't replace the dagger yet. Theodmon nodded. "I wanted you to die as my wife if you had to die at all."

"We won't die." Amaria embraced Theodmon. "We'll give gifts to the Silent God and his kingdom but we will not be delivered to him until we determine it is time."

Theodmon shook his head. "You can't stop mortality."

"But we can gain power." Amaria's eyes blazed. "We all must die eventually and I'd rather have a short, extraordinary life with power, wealth, and influence than a long, mediocre life."

Chapter Fifteen

Freshly clothed and bathed, a good cry behind him, Theodmon now was as impassive as a statue, the very image of a stoic warrior, as he strode into the great hall. As he entered, the crowds of the great hall stood up, tilting their heads towards him in acknowledgment. Amaria too, who was at the head of the great table, stood and watched Theodmon as he strode through the hall, the people slinking out of his way for him to have a clear pathway to his spot.

He breathed in, focusing on the red banners on the walls with griffins and the Chauvignon family motto embroidered in gold–*vires exputatum esse sanguinas*–strength tested by blood. Theodmon chanted this motto in his mind as he made his way towards the front. Soon, he reached the table, and nodded his head, permitting the hall to stand at ease.

Wooden chairs scrapped across stone as those near the front–Amaria, Celestine, Henri, Aloysius, and Theodmon included–sat down. Shifting in his seat slightly, Theodmon made himself comfortable as he adjusted himself in the largest chair in the hall, his elbows on the table in front of him. Behind him, the great fireplace roared and he felt the comforting heat across his back. Next to him, Amaria squeezed his hand reassuringly, despite her otherwise cold demeanor. She stared straight ahead, her expression emotionless, her wings slightly spread out. She had been made for this. She belonged here, at the head of this table.

Theodmon wondered how much he still truly belonged, despite the title he held over this place. He was finally home, but felt like a stranger. Daily activities went on without his presence. His children were growing up without him. And Theodmon knew that he would soon be absent for longer. Would he be absent from here more than he would be home?

Did Father feel this way? Theodmon shoved the intrusive thought away like a gardener yanking out a weed and focused on the now. "Who's next?"

"We're working through the Peasant's Petitions." Amaria's fingers drummed on the table. "Would you like to take over?"

Not particularly, Theodmon thought. However he nodded at Amaria, squeezing her hand briefly, knowing that he should take over. "Thank you," he whispered to her gratefully.

She smiled softly. "Up next is citizen Gerald Nixou." She turned towards the crowd and repeated Gerald Nixou's name, indicating that he should come forward with his issues.

Gerald, an elderly man, shakily made his way towards the front staring at Theodmon and Amaria–well more Amaria's wings, in clear apprehension. "Marquis," he wheezily said, giving a clumsy bow.

"What is your petition?" Theodmon numbly asked the traditional question that came with these sorts of things.

"My goats." Gerald's voice lowered. "They're dying. Not enough grain for them."

"Won't goats eat anything?" Aloysius questioned.

Theodmon glared at him from the side of his eyes. This wasn't Aloysius's place. "What my brother said," Theodmon directed the man, smoothing over his facial features.

"Yes," Gerald stuttered. "That's why...I'm wondering if I could allow the goats to eat bark and leaves from the hunting lands—nothing more, just to allow them to eat. My Lords, forgive me–"

Theodmon curtly held up a hand, directing the man to stop his blubbering while he stroked his chin and thought the problem over. "You are free to use the leaves and bark on my lands for your goats' food in exchange for sixty percent of the production of wool to be used for the soldiers in the army and thirty percent of the cheese and milk from the goats for five years."

Amaria's head snapped over to look at Theodmon, her eyebrows raised with her mouth slightly ajar. However, Theodmon saw her look of surprise quickly turn into a satisfied smile, the slight uptick of her lips bringing him pride.

"Address the specifics of the economics of this with my wife. Amaria, could you hand the roster to Aloysius?"

"Of course, my Lord Husband," Amaria answered, the pinnacle of courtly formality. She gingerly slid the parchment across the table, passing Theodmon to arrive in front of Aloysius.

"Fiona Nofiana," Aloysius read out as Amaria beckoned for Gerald to come closer to her. As Gerald and Amaria discussed a rough idea of the specifics of the arrangement, a young woman, her face aged beyond her years due to the worry-lines etched into her skin, stepped forward to address her concerns with Theodmon.

Slowly, Theodmon made his way through the Peasant's Petitions, then to the petitions from the servants and guards who resided in his court, then to the petitions to those Westanni nobles that were not in his court but still his citizens. By the time he reached the petitions of nobles that resided at Forteresse les Blanche, Theodmon's mind felt as if it were bleeding; these things were painstakingly mind numbing.

"I've got it," Amaria whispered to him. Turning to the court at large, she addressed the court nobles. "I'll be hearing your petitions. First on the roster is Baroness Evelyn Limonoux?"

A red haired woman stepped forward, addressing Amaria with her concerns. Slowly, Theodmon exhaled, letting his mind wander as Amaria began the process of wrapping up court. Miraculously, in seemingly no time, they were nearing the end.

A knock on the door pounded, but Theodmon could have imagined it—castle's had a weird echo to them sometimes. However, he noticed a guard stepped outside the great hall, and when he returned he was whispering to the heralder, who then picked up his horn, giving it a singular blow, the melody catching Theodmon and the rest of the remaining people's attention.

"Yes?" Theodmon questioned.

"Do you have time for one more petitioner? He's a lord in your court," the heralder said.

Did this lord in my court not know the time of the petitions? Theodmon scowled. *If he lives here, this mysterious lord should know better.*

"Whose the lord?"

"Lord Lucas Bécharil. He said he comes with important news for you."

Immediately, like sunlight on a cloudy day, Theodmon's annoyance dissipated. "Bring him in."

The guards and heralder followed his instructions. Lucas stepped through the door, grimy and caked in mud with his cloak torn. His beard was long and raggedy, his hair limp and heavy with grease.In his hand, Lucas held a brown tweed bag. Judging by the state of him, Theodmon guested that he had just arrived at Forteresse les Blanche.

As Lucas neared the great table, Theodmon smelled the foul scent wafting from Lucas's body, further confirming his suspicions. Involuntarily, Theodmon coughed, hiding his true desire to gag.

Lucas bowed his head slightly, his eyes unbreaking from Theodmon's. "My Lord," Lucas dryly said, a smirk crossing his features.

"Lord Bécharil." Theodmon wanted to smile, to greet Lucas warmly without the regards for social niceties—Theodmon hadn't seen Lucas in so long. At times, he had worried that Lucas had died. But he sat still and proper, resisting the urge to tackle the bearish blond man in front of him. "Do you have a matter to address to the court?"

Lucas lifted the burlap sack above the surface of the table. "With your leave."

Theodmon looked around the hall at the court. Most of the courtiers departed. All of the peasants left. It was only a few of the trusted members of his inner circle, Haerdnor and Aaron Raulet, servants, and a few courtiers that straggled behind. Enough people to spread rumors, but not enough to give it any sort of solid credibility–rumors spread like wildfire, and Amaria, Henri, Celestine, Aloysius, Juliette, Haerdnor, Aaron, and Nicoletta could further spread conflicting stories against the servants and low ranking courtiers if needed. Theodmon gave Lucas a curt nod, signaling him to proceed.

"I present to you, Tesden Nalaeny." Lucas opened the bag, dumping its contents onto the ground, revealing the heir to the Riam throne's detached head. There was no blood, and the flesh seemed gray. The eyes seemed dried out–as if Tesden Nalaeny was a prune.

A few seats away from Amaria, her friend, Nicoletta, screamed, almost drowning out the gasps coming from the others in the hall.

"My Lord." Lucas stepped away from the head, allowing the members of the Chauvignons' court to bask in the full gory glory of the decapitated Riam heir.

"It seems as if my wife is the sole heir to Rindria," Aloysius muttered sourly, sitting directly on Theodmon's right. Theodmon's eyes briefly darted to see Aloysius slumping in his chair, his eyes rolling slightly.

"Long live the queen," Theodmon dryly replied.

Chapter Sixteen

"My Lord." Aaron stepped closer to Theodmon. "We need to handle this."

Obviously. Theodmon sourly thought. He nodded, his face impassive. *I wish Lucas picked any other way to announce Tesden Nalaeny's death other than depositing his head in the middle of court.*

"Attention," he bellowed. He tried to ignore Nicoletta's sobbing behind him as he motioned to a nearby guard. "Get them out of here," Theodmon commanded, nodding to the servants and straggling courtiers.

At least he knew Lucas completed the mission Theodmon assigned him over a year ago.

"Stay with Nicoletta," Amaria whispered to Juliette. "Be with her in her rooms; you were always more comforting."

"You'll let me know what was said," Juliette said.

"Of course," Amaria assured her.

Juliette squeezed Amaria's hand before rushing towards Nicoletta, wrapping her arms around her shoulders. Theodmon noticed that Nicoletta momentarily tensed before he turned to see Amaria beside him.

"Will they be okay?" Amaria hesitantly looked behind her towards her friends.

"They'll be okay," Haerdnor said. "Lucas, the Chauvignons, and Raulets–due to family reputation or actually carrying a severed head into court–are the escalating people, she'll be fine once we aren't there."

"She's married to Lucas–" Amaria began as Theodmon gently pushed her into the passageway. Haerdnor was correct, they couldn't stay there much longer.

"And nobody would believe she would sever a head," Theodmon said truthfully. Juliette was kind, soft-spoken–the exact type of person nobody would believe could be capable of cruelty. But she had been an invaluable asset to their intelligence networks, and Theodmon seen her react unflinchingly to situations that made his skin crawl. Gods, she cleaned up the blood of those Lucas tortured from him without saying a word.

"Am," Haerdnor said, "let's go. You're one that others would believe severs heads–you aren't helping them."

As Theodmon looked down at his wine, feeling sick as he looked at the deep red liquid.

"Lucas, what in the gods' names was this?" Theodmon said. "I wanted to have lunch after this." He looked at the others. "My offices, now."

Lucas shrugged, picking up the head and throwing it in the bag. "You wanted to see me as soon as I arrived back once the mission was complete. That was what you told me last anyways."

"Why did it take over a year?" Aloysius asked as they moved out of the hall, moving into the corridors.

"He was hard to find and harder to kill." Lucas cast a dark look at Aloysius.

"I'm trying to not make Liara Nalaeny despise me," Celestine intervened. "How are we supposed to hide this from her?"

"Keep her locked in her rooms, threaten servants with execution if they speak to her," Amaria said. "How long does this need to stay secret for?"

Celestine crossed her arms. "It'll only be secret for a week, and you know it–"

"I'll bury the memory in others' minds," Henri interrupted. "It'll be like it never happened."

"And how long will that last?"

Henri shrugged. "Weeks? Months? Maybe years? It depends on the mental fortitude of the person."

"Helpful," Celestine said sarcastically.

"Let's discuss this once we get to my offices," Theodmon intervened. "Alright?"

"Tesden Nalaeny is dead." Aloysius stated the obvious once they were all comfortably seated in Theodmon's offices and the doors were shut and barred. "And my wife is the sole heir."

"Has she provided you with an heir yet?" Lucas asked Aloysius.

Aloysius looked over towards Celestine, shrugging.

"No," Celestine scoffed. "She's been caught multiple times using birth control methods, we've tried to stop her but it's nearly impossible to watch her all the time unless we actually throw her in a dungeon."

"So our goal now isn't an heir," Lucas deduced.

Sighing, Theodmon nodded. "We will take the only heir that's left so they have nobody to rally behind—the Riams have martyrs, yes, but martyrs cannot lead a country or raise funds to direct an army."

"We're limiting her martyrdom." Celestine cast a glance towards Aloysius.

Theodmon looked between his two siblings and Henri laughed, his eyes unbreaking from Aloysius. "You're going to send her to war." Henri announced Aloysius's thoughts to the group. "But you want to let her think she's running away."

"She'll die," Aloysius shrugged. "I've tried everything to make her comfortable. She's done everything to make my life a living hell." He sighed. "I'm not comfortable killing an innocent woman who had the misfortune to be a petulant Riam noble, so don't ask any more of me."

"We won't," Henri assured him.

"We're going to attack Rindria," Theodmon looked at all of the people in the room in turn. "We cannot expect any foreign help outside Thestitiunia. The Tressi are notoriously non-interventionist, Avondra has their own civil war and Morroek–" Theodmon paused. Would Morroek join in defending their former ally against imperialism? Likely so, as the Morrians knew that if Rindria fell that they were next.

"I'll work with Morroek." Amaria's hands rubbed over his. "If we continue to maintain our formal promise of no more forced famines, as well as a promise to not attack for a set number of years, as well as marriage promises–both present and future–Morroek will likely remain neutral."

"Marry me off," Henri spoke up. "I'm unmarried, once my father dies I'll be a Marquis, I'm close to the Heads of State in the Westerlands. I'm a good match, and if needed–I can alter my new wife's memories and thoughts with my magic. I'll also always know what she'll be thinking–it makes sense for all sides for me to be on the table."

As long as the other side just doesn't know how good for us. Theodmon smirked, nodding slightly at Henri. Henri's magic wasn't actually mind reading, it was a passive manifestation of it just in how Amaria could comfortably sit in boiling water was a passive manifestation of her magic. Henri's actual magic, as Theodmon had just been reminded, was infinitely more terrifying than just reading minds. Not for the first time, Theodmon was glad for Henri's intense loyalty.

"Durek has a daughter I was supposed to marry if Amaria–" Theodmon choked up, unable to finish the sentence. "I'll write a letter and seal it. Can you negotiate?"

"I'll need sealed approval from Marquis Delaluna," Amaria said. "But with that, I'm sure I can come together with something. Marquis Delaluna can also participate–would your father be able to do that?"

"My father is bedridden," Henri slumped in his chair. "I've been conducting his affairs for years. He's been unable to distinguish reality from fiction for a while and he's not eating....I'll draft the letter for you. Actually, it may be best if I negotiate with you."

"I've no issue," Theodmon agreed readily. Henri would be better suited in a court setting–Theodmon remembered all too well how poorly Henri reacted to war in hearing the thoughts of all the dying men around him.

"Thank you," Amaria told Henri warmly.

"We need to plan quickly to attack the Riam front," Aaron said.

Amaria stood up as she brushed down her skirts. "I should go comfort Nicoletta. I'm not much help with war formations anyways." She lightly pecked Theodmon on the cheek before she departed from the room.

"I'm not either," Celestine said. "I'll continue my friendship with Liara, and make sure she doesn't find out about Tesden just yet."

And she too departed the room, leaving only the men behind.

For the next few hours, Theodmon made war plans, Aloysius, Haerdnor, and Lucas giving heavy opinions on fighting strategies, and Aaron and Henri giving advice on political maneuvering and intelligence operations–and it was decided that Aaron and Amaria would be directing most of the operations from Forteresse les Blanche or Provinica Palencia and Lucas and Henri would deal with intel at the front. Theodmon felt slight guilt at deciding for Amaria, but only momentarily. It was what made logical sense, and besides, Amaria was good at intelligence. Theodmon doubted she would mind this role. Gods, she'd probably be more angry if he didn't give her a role in this war.

Once planning was completed, Theodmon slumped in his chair, exhausted. He wanted to relax with his family. He had no idea where Amaria was, but perhaps he would see Sylviana and Lysander. But it was late, his children would surely be asleep.

Sighing, Theodmon picked up his quill. He could draft a few more letters, including the one to Durek Svilas.

Chapter Seventeen

Amaria exhaled as the office door shut behind her with a small snap, leaning against the door momentarily. She'd been continuously moving, dealing with the crises that Tesden Nalaeny's severed head caused that she hadn't time to breathe.

Amaria stood up straight, trying to ignore the continuous shaking in her hands and she breathed, her chest feeling as if something was racketing inside of it. She needed to find Nicoletta and Juliette.

Amaria thanked the gods that Juliette was a mage. Clasping her hands together and forcing herself to take long inhales and exhales, Amaria reached her magic out. She searched for the calming presence of Juliette's magic, wishing to feel the comforting embrace of her lilac aura.

Soon, Amaria felt her magic entwine with Juliette's, silver and lilac braiding together as their minds opened to allow each other in.

"Amaria?" Juliette's voice was a steady as a tree, but as flexible as the water's currents. *"Is everything alright?"*

"Yes," Amaria said in the mage link. *"I'll explain later in more detail. Where are you and Nicoletta? Are you alright?"*

"We're fine," Juliette sighed. *"We're in her chambers, she seems to be in a bit of shock."*

Amaria swallowed the lump in her throat. Of course Nicoletta would be in some form of shock—any sane person would be witnessing what occurred.

"I'm on my way," Amaria told Juliette, withdrawing from the mage link. Hurriedly, Amaria made her way through the winding stone halls, pulling her wings close to her, trying to force her muscles to flatten across her back so as to not have the tips scrape along the walls or the floor. Forteresse les Blanche had wide hallways where Amaria wouldn't have to worry about this, but many corridors were narrow, made for a fortified defense and nothing more.

Amaria knew her way around Forteresse les Blanche, and soon she reached Nicoletta's rooms, easily stepping inside Nicoletta's chambers to see the two women sitting close to each other on the bed, speaking in hushed tones.

"Nicoletta?" Amaria gingerly moving towards her.

Nicoletta looked towards Amaria, her eyes and nose red. She wiped her face with her sleeve. "What?"

"Are you alright?" Amaria asked, already knowing the answer.

"What do you think?"

"There's no need to be hostile," Juliette said as Amaria sat on the bench at the end of the bed.

"I'm not hostile," Nicoletta protested. "I'm just processing all of this shit. Tesden Nalaeny's head. Liara Nalaeny was in this castle when this occurred—she doesn't even know, does she? And you appear with wings and a baby—when were you pregnant?"

Amaria's nostrils flared. "I didn't know I was pregnant when I visited the faeries."

"What happened there?" Nicoletta asked. "Are you a faerie?" Amaria noticed Nicoletta's gaze did not break from her wings.

"We went to destroy the Raulet Ruby." Amaria slouched forward so her elbows rested on her thighs. "And they saved me–I'm not a faerie."

"Are you human?"

Yes. Amaria bit her lip. "Not entirely," she said slowly. "But I'm still me."

"What happened?" Juliette asked.

Slowly, Amaria began to explain what she knew happened to her in the faerie lands. In doing so, Amaria noticed a shift in Nicoletta's demeanor—a quiet withdrawal and a subtle sadness lingering in her eyes. Amaria wrapped her arms around herself. "It's been a year, hasn't it?"

Nicoletta hesitated for a moment, but seeing the warmth and concern in Amaria's eyes, she sighed softly. "It's been a lot. Nothing is the same anymore, and I don't like the changes."

Nicoletta seemed deathly pale at seeing the violent result of Lucas's journeys. Amaria had never seen her friend as having a weak constitution for blood–Nicoletta had always seemed practical to her. Perhaps Amaria misjudged Nicoletta, blinded by their childhood friendship and shared grief over Delphina's untimely death.

Perhaps she'd been uncomfortable with the violent situations she circled around. Now that Amaria thought about it, Nicoletta seemed horrified at the torture of the man who killed Delphina. It seemed ridiculous. He deserved it. Being kind to him wouldn't bring Delphina back. Torture and murder wouldn't heal the past either, but it would help bring a sense of justice—if you killed others you would have to watch over your shoulder or risk being killed yourself.

It was how Amaria operated. It's what made sense. Violence wasn't senseless, it was what was needed to survive.

There were many courts that would be elated to see her severed head delivered to them.

Amaria had done everything not only to protect herself, but also her loved ones. Nicoletta was included in that number. Did Nicoletta know this or was she just disgusted? Was Amaria erroneously imputing her beliefs of Nicoletta's feelings onto her when Nicoletta didn't actually feel that way?

"Things change." Juliette rubbed Nicoletta's arms.

"That doesn't mean I have to cheerily accept the changes," Nicoletta said icily, pulling her arm away. "I hate most of the changes, actually. And I know where're heading with all this scheming you, and Theodmon, and your father are doing."

"Nicoletta," Juliette said softly, however, Nicoletta ignored her, her fists clenching.

"I *hate* war," Nicoletta exploded.

"Me too," Amaria said quickly.

Nicoletta snorted, rolling her eyes. "You know how to lie better than that. We both know that you love war."

Heat flushed through Amaria's body as her eyes hardened. Who was Nicoletta to say what she did and didn't like? Nicoletta had never seen war. She could barely handle Delphina's death, fracturing under the weight of it. Who was she to lecture Amaria about an event she'd never experienced but Amaria endured a million times over.

"No," Amaria protested, her voice rising slightly.

"Forgive me, you don't like the battlefield," Nicoletta scoffed. "But the intelligence part of it–can you tell me you dislike the mind games. That you dislike whatever you do in dungeons?"

"I–" Amaria paused, the words catching in her throat. She wanted to assure Nicoletta that she didn't enjoy those things, that it was a horrible chore she wished she could avoid. But she couldn't, not honestly. And blatantly lying to Nicoletta wouldn't help the situation–it would only make it worse, validating the horrible things Nicoletta must be thinking right now.

Perhaps she could give a half truth? A half truth wasn't a lie–at least not a blatant one. "I think I'll struggle with dungeons after my time in Rindria."

"Because you feel empathy for these poor prisoners? Or because you'll be so stuck in your own opinions you can't conceptualize that they may be innocent?"

"I wasn't innocent, nor did I ever believe myself to be," Amaria said. "If that's what you're insinuating."

"Why do I have to insinuate anything?" Nicoletta challenged, her lips narrowing. "I'm not like you. Not everything I say is a political web of doublespeak."

"Don't be difficult," Amaria hissed. "You've lived in court your entire life, you know the risks in this life–how it is a hard fact of kill or be killed—"

"And who decided that?" Nicoletta stood up, her eyes flashing. "People like your father. Power-hungry, conniving, and cut-throat men have made decent people's life hell."

"Nicoletta," Juliette warned. "Let's be–"

"You're just as bad," Nicoletta shot. "Doesn't it bother you what your husband does?"

"Does it matter?" Juliette challenged. "If it bothered me, what would I do? I already, as you pointed out, don't participate. Lucas is my husband, and I have to tolerate that for the rest of my life–being abrasive isn't helpful."

Amaria admired the fluidity of Juliette's conflict management. She focused on that to keep her face pleasant, as she felt her lip beginning to curl as Nicoletta honestly believed that Juliette was a passive bystander. Nicoletta was the most passive bystander in the Chauvignons inner-circle, and it seemed that now she would be soon departing from the innermost and dirtiest secrets the circle partook in.

Amaria couldn't trust Nicoletta anymore. Not as much as she once had. Tears welled to her eyes as she felt the sting of her longest friend moving away from her.

"Tolerate?" Nicoletta scoffed. "You love Lucas."

"I don't want to be miserable." Juliette stood up as well, glaring at Nicoletta. "You've been doing that enough for everyone here."

"I hate him," Nicoletta snarled. "I hate how my husband touches me, looks at me—."

"You don't hate him," Juliette said. "You hate being tied to any man. If only society–"

"Blame society won't you?" Nicoletta scoffed.

"Give up your titles and wealth then," Amaria snapped.

"Maybe Liara had a point about you," Nicoletta cruelly said.

"I was trying to comfort you!" Amaria shouted, exasperated. "I just arrived, I've in the faerie lands for months! I didn't know where Lucas was, and I didn't know he'd be arriving today. I didn't know he'd showcase Tesden Nalaeny's severed head!"

"But it didn't bother you," Nicoletta insisted.

"Of course it bothered me!" Amaria's fists clenched. "Do you truly believe I'm so devoid of emotion that seeing a severed and decaying head wouldn't bother me?"

"You want to tell me you wouldn't have killed Tesden Nalaeny yourself if you had to?" Nicoletta spat.

"Listen to yourself," Amaria hissed. "*If I had to.*" Her wings rustled behind her and her heart thudded in her chest. "Just because I do something doesn't mean I like doing it." Tears fell from Amaria's face. "Nicoletta...what happened to us?"

Tears shone on Nicoletta's face. "We grew up. And we changed."

"Is there still...are we still?" Amaria didn't know how to phrase the question.

Nicoletta pulled her into a hug. "Always."

Amaria pressed her face into Nicoletta's shoulder as they hugged. Nicoletta did the same, their individual tears soaking the other's dress. She hadn't lost a friendship– it was just changing.

Once they stopped crying and hugging, the three talked, played cards, and caught up on what they missed from each other's lives. Wine and spirits were brought up to the rooms and they flowed easily in between the pastries they ate. In the past year, it turned out that Juliette started trying to garden without her earth magic but found it frustrating and gave up relatively quickly. Nicoletta started to play cricket and was fairly talented according to her and Juliette. It was late at night when Amaria and Juliette departed from Nicoletta's rooms and made their way to their own.

Amaria, groggy with exhaustion, stumbled into her own chambers, collapsing on the bed fully clothed. The small benefit of the clothes she got from the faeries was that they were so flimsy they were as comfortable to sleep in as a nightgown. She would have to schedule fittings and meetings with the seamstresses to make something more appropriate–both for court and the weather itself.

Groaning, Amaria forced herself to get up and throw back the blankets and furs on the bed so she could climb in. She wished Theodmon was here, and she wondered where he may be; was the meeting with Lucas and the rest taking that long? Amaria debated staying up for Theodmon, missing him and wanting to ensure everything was alright. However, her body, angry with the filibuster, ended the debate as her eyes became heavier and heavier and she drifted off to sleep.

Chapter Eighteen

The first light of dawn painted the room in soft hues of gold and the tranquil silence of the morning enveloped Theodmon and Amaria's chambers. Theodmon, nestled at the edge of the bed, gazed at his wife as he traced the contours of her face with the tips of his fingers.

Amaria lay there, embraced by the warmth of the blankets, her chest rising and falling in a serene cadence. Strands of dark hair spilled across her pillow, framing her face like a soft halo in the morning light. Theodmon could not ignore the irony, or perhaps the perfection, of that imagery as his hand lightly brushed against her wings as he moved to cup her face with his palm.

Amaria's eyes gently fluttered open, a sleepy smile tugging at the corners of her lips. "Theo?" She rubbed her eyes. "When did you come in?"

"After war plans were made." He gently kissed the top of her hair. "It was late."

Amaria yawned. "I wish you'd woke me." She motioned her hand out for Theodmon to join her in bed. Laughing, he obliged, snuggling with her under the warm blankets. The comfort of the bed seemed to cocoon them, the rays of sunlight peeking through the stained glass.

"What time is it?" Amaria asked.

"Not too early," Theodmon reassured her, the creases of his eyes crinkling at the corners as he gave her a tender smile. "You can rest a bit more."

Amaria laughed gently, sitting up to stretch. Her wings popped out, almost hitting Theodmon in the face. "Oh gods! I'm sorry," she said, scooting towards him as she angled her body away from him, her wings facing outward from them.

"It's alright," Theodmon said. "It didn't hurt."

Amaria exhaled, leaning forward and collapsing in his arms. "Thank you."

Theodmon pulled her closer into his embrace, he enveloped her in his arms, cherishing the warmth of her presence. "For what?"

"For always being here for me." Amaria snuggled her face deeper into his chest.

"Always," Theodmon replied. They were a pair, an unwavering partnership. In more ways than one. People tried to destroy their relationship–Lynette Edrion was a bad memory of that occurrence. And more people would surely try with the wars on the horizon.

Amaria laughed as they lingered in each other's embrace. Breathing softly, Theodmon heard her heartbeat against his and he pulled her closer against him. "Should we?" He looked over her body, noticing her breasts pressing against her gown.

"Later." Amaria sweetly kissed him, pulling away with a smile. "Have you met your daughter yet?"

Theodmon felt a pang of guilt. "Not yet."

"Send for breakfast and a seamstress," Amaria commanded him gently. "And then we'll see our children."

"Seamstress?" Theodmon's eyebrows rose at the sudden, and seemingly random request.

Amaria's lip curled. "I despise the clothes I have and I need new ones that accommodate my wings without making me feel as if I'm a step away from dressing like a prostitute."

Theodmon chuckled slightly as he sat up in the bed, shaking his head humorously as he moved to the dresser. "How about bacon for breakfast?" He pulled out a shirt. "Also, let me tell you about the meeting last night—you're going to be running the intelligence from Raulle with your father...."

The color drained from Amaria's face.

"Are you alright?" Theodmon reached out towards her.

"It'll be difficult to work with my father." Amaria's chest heaved. "Considering everything I learned...."

"Can you handle it?" Theodmon squeezed her hand.

Amaria gave a curt nod. "I'll have to."

Theodmon crouched near a crib in the nursery. His son clung to his leg, showing off each of his brightly-painted wooden horses to both his parents. Lysander had shyly looked at Amaria's wings for a few minutes before he asked for a feather. Amaria told him no, but she didn't stop him from running his hands against her wings.

Theodmon tried not to laugh when Lysander plucked a feather. Amaria scolded him, but she was forcing down her smile in an attempt to be stern. She couldn't stop herself from cooing over him and how big he had gotten. Lysander seemed to thrive in the attention, perhaps that was why he was clinging to his father's leg, demanding more attention as Theodmon looked down at Lysander's sister.

Sylviana had her blanket tightly in her fist as she slept. She was so small, and Theodmon brushed his fingers over her few wispy locks of hair.

"Apparently she hates tummy time," Amaria said behind him. "You should hold her."

"I don't want to wake her," Theodmon said quietly.

Amaria chuckled before moving to pick Lysander up. "You're so big and strong," she complimented him.

"Blue!" Lysander gleefully thrust a blue painted horse in front of Amaria's face.

"Yes, blue," Amaria validated as she set Lysander down on the ground. Lysander beamed before running off to find another horse.

"Yellow!" He picked up a horse painted with yellow suns.

"What would we do without him teaching us the colors," Amaria joked.

Theodmon chuckled in response, finally tearing his eyes away from his daughter. He could hardly believe she was real. He hadn't seen the pregnancy or the labor, it seemed as if Sylviana were a dream and if he looked too far away she would vanish like a phantom in the wind.

For hours, they played with Lysander, reading his books and letting him show off all his toys and their colors. Sylviana woke up, and once Amaria fed her–she'd been bizarrely adamant on feeding the child herself–Theodmon held her for the first time.

Unfortunately they couldn't stay, and they departed once Lysander was laid down for his nap. There was work to be done, however, Theodmon could not bring himself to do it. He may later regret this decision, but what was one day of relaxation? They just arrived home after all.

"Let's go to the gardens," he told Amaria.

"In winter?"

"Don't pretend you don't know how the magic works," Theodmon snorted.

"Better than you." Amaria smirked as they walked through the interior passageways of the castle.

"Of course," Theodmon jokingly conceded. "So why the 'in winter?' question?"

Amaria rolled her eyes, her mouth breaking into a grudging smile as they entered the labyrinthine paths of the gardens.

Although it was winter, they paused by a cluster of roses, their petals in various shades of red, pink, and ivory. Thank the gods for earth mages and their magic. Theodmon plucked a single red rose, its velvety petals a stark contrast against his strong, calloused hand. With a graceful gesture, he offered it to Amaria.

Amaria accepted the rose with a smile, holding it in her hand, her fingers carefully avoiding the prick of the flower's thorns.

"We'll have to go to Provincia Palencia soon," Theodmon said softly.

Amaria inquisitively looked at him and Theodmon almost winced. He had forgotten that she would have missed the wedding announcements. Still, it was a surprise that Aaron or Haerdnor hadn't mentioned it to her.

"Your brother's engagement," Theodmon began.

"Is he finally getting married?"

Theodmon nodded.

Amaria sighed, laughing slightly. "It's about time. I've been the only one carrying on the damn bloodline. It's time Haer pulls his weight in the preservation of the family legacy."

Theodmon gave a barking laugh. "It might be harder for him."

"Yes," Amaria dismissed. "He's a notorious pillow biter. His wife-to-be is the same. Still, he is a Raulet and she will be married to one. They'll do what Raulets do and provide heirs as is their duty. Haerdnor knows the stakes of providing heirs with the family name. He'll do what is required, one way or the other."

Theodmon's eyebrows rose slightly at the blaze dismissal Amaria had of what other people may consider a base obstacle. But she was so confident in her family's ability to preserve regardless.

"Spare me the stubbornness of the Raulets," Theodmon joked.

"That's a family trait now?" Amaria rose a singular eyebrow, her mouth tilting in a smirk.

Theodmon laughed as he wrapped her in his cloak, hugging her tightly. He noticed she was shivering and her lips seemed to be a brighter pink than they been when they were inside. "Ammy?"

"Mhhm?"

"Will you warm the air for us?" He brushed back a lock of her hair, looking at her in concern. She never restrained from using her magic before, not unless she had to conserve her magical energy. "What's wrong?"

"Wrong?" Amaria questioned. Still, Theodmon felt the air warming around him, quickly becoming a sauna as they walked through the stone pathways of the garden.

"Your magic," Theodmon pressed. "Why the restraint?"

Amaria slowly inhaled, her chest staying inflated for a long time. "It feels different." She shook her head, her long hair moving over her back as they walked.

"What is it?" Theodmon asked as they reached a marble gazebo nestled amidst a grove of trees. Theodmon drew Amaria closer, his arm wrapping protectively around her waist as they stood in the warm air, the chill circulating around them but not touching them through the barrier of Amaria's magic.

"I don't know how much of my earlier actions, after I absorbed the Ruby's energy, were dark magic. I don't want to go crazy again," Amaria whispered. "I enjoy power. I need to know I'm in control."

Theodmon hugged her tightly. Silently, they stood there, embracing each other in the garden. Theodmon wished they could stay here forever, but the weight of his responsibilities gradually pushed itself to the forefront of his mind until he could no longer ignore it.

"I have to train." Theodmon's lips brushing over her hair as he kissed the top of it.

"I have to meet my father," Amaria responded. Still, neither one of them moved away from each other. Theodmon didn't want to leave her. They both had responsibilities—what would it be like to let Marquis and Marchioness Chauvignon die and have Theodmon and Amaria live?

Chapter Nineteen

Amaria made her way back inside, sighing at how familiar this all felt. Amaria turned to a guard, inquiring if any knew where her father and brother may have gone too. The guard informed her that he saw them heading upstairs towards the west wing.

She moved towards the staircase, leaning against its railing as she forced small slivers of her magic outwards, searching for Haerdnor or her father. Slowly, her silver threads of magic snaked out through the estate.

Her magic collided with the strong, and ever expanding magical aura of her father. He was like an old oak tree. Sighing, she pressed her magic against his, requesting entry. And after a few moments, Aaron Raulet let her in.

"Father," Amaria greeted in the mage link.

"Amaria," her father replied in acknowledgement.

"Where are you?" She asked.

"We're in the guest offices on the third floor," her father informed her.

"I'll be there shortly," Amaria promised before she disconnected the mage link. Sighing, she lifted her skirts and began the journey up the stairs. She longed to fly up the stairs, but she wasn't sure if the flapping of her wings would cause damage to the interior of Forteresse les Blanche, and if so, the extent of it. They would be funding yet another war soon enough, the last thing they needed to spend money on was cosmetic repairs.

And so, Amaria made her way to the third floor, finding the offices her family were in with grace.

"I hope we didn't cause you too much inconvenience," Haerdnor lazily said as Amaria stepped inside the warm office. As he reclined on the plush cushion couch, Amaria noticed that his warm brown eyes sparkled with mischief. "I can leave bread crumbs behind us next time if you want."

Laughing, Amaria rubbed his arm warmly, her eyes creasing. "No need, but thank you." She turned to look at her father. "We've all had a long journey and a long night afterwards, so please, rest. We'll have a formal, non-eventful dinner together tonight." She saw Aaron holding Sylviana, examining her closely. "I see you found your granddaughter. Did you see your grandson as well?"

"Lysander was taking a nap," Aaron replied. "His nanny thought it best that he not be awakened."

"Of course." Amaria reached out for Sylviana, and Aaron, to his credit, quickly handed her to Amaria. Cooing softly, Amaria bounced Sylviana in her arms and the baby looked over her mother's shoulder, bright-eyed and curious.

"Motherhood suits you," Aaron nodded approvingly.

"I would hope so," Amaria could not control the sour creeping in her tone. "I have been specifically groomed to be a wife and mother since I was a child. I believe I was expressly told that the highest compliments I should aspire for were about my beauty, obedience, passivity, and future as a wife when I was six. I was six, wasn't I?"

"We all have expectations," Aaron coolly lowered his tone, warning his daughter to not go further and embarrass him. Aaron grabbed her arm, his nails painfully digging into her skin, causing her to flinch slightly. "Be quiet," he hissed, spit hitting her ear. "You *know* better."

Amaria bit her lip, avoiding looking at her father's face as she held onto her daughter a little more firmly. She hadn't forgiven him for what she learned from Vypren.

"I gave you assignments outside of the traditional expectations of her gender." Aaron jerked Amaria's arm so she would have to face him. "You received your assignments because I *trust* you."

Could've fooled me. Everything seems to be a critique with you. However, she did not voice her thoughts. She hated that her decorum shattered, if only momentarily.

"Are there any requests you have for dinner tonight? I am going to the kitchens anyway after I depart from you all." Amaria asked in a forced cheery tone.

"If you have duck, that'll be great, but anything is fine," Haerdnor said hastily. "We're all tired from traveling, I'm sure any well cooked meal will be satisfactory. Until then, I'll be in my rooms; I need a nap."

"Nap?" Amaria suppressed her smirk as she reached into her and Haerdnor's shared mage link. *"Is it with Oliver?"*

Haerdnor shot her a withering look. Amaria bit her lip, composing herself before turning to her father and Haerdnor once more. Before she could speak, Aaron sternly looked at the two of them.

"Sit," he commanded his children. "We've a lot to discuss."

"About what?" Haerdnor challenged. "We had a long meeting last night. What more could you possibly have to discuss?"

"Your sister wasn't there–"

"I'm sure she's aware of what's happening," Haerdnor said emotionlessly. "We're taking Rindria. Whoo."

"It isn't about the meeting," Aaron snapped. "It's about your wedding and upcoming marriage. Amaria, there's not a woman to help with the wedding at Provincia Palencia. Not a Raulet woman anyways."

"And whose fault is that?" Haerdnor muttered under his breath.

"What was that?" Aaron chillingly questioned.

"The wedding?" Amaria said loudly, a fake smile plastered on her face.

"I said," Haerdnor ignored Amaria's attempt for peace, "whose fault was it that Amaria is the only Raulet woman? You could've remarried and provided more heirs–something you are quick to remind us we need to do for the family legacy. Why didn't you? Any young bride would have her parents throwing her at you for the chance to become Duchess Raulet."

"I loved your mother," Aaron sibilated. "I couldn't remarry–"

"But I love Oliver and can't be with him. Amaria was terrified of Lyseno Vypren, and she didn't protest her planned union with him. Where's your expected sacrifice?.."

"Haer," Amaria softly warned, watching her father clench his fists. "It's alright, I don't mind–"

"Well, I do," Haerdnor dismissed. "Father, we deserve answers if you want us to uphold your legacy."

"I was selfish." Aaron's eyes flashed. "Is that what you wanted to hear?"

"What sacrifice will you make if I can't have children?" Haerdnor pressed. "I don't find women attractive, and unfortunately for men, attraction is somewhat necessary in doing our duties."

Amaria closed her eyes, trying to burn the crude image of her brother in that setting from her mind.

"We can't be the only one furthering the Raulet legacy," Haerdnor said. "What will you do, Father?"

"I may know a candidate," Amaria sighed, exhausted from the idea that formed in her mind before she even shared it, yet she knew it was the solution they've been looking for ever since she survived her encounter with dark magic and Theodmon was no longer available to marry Durek Svilas' daughter. "Duke Raulet will be a better match for Durek Svilas's daughter than Henri Delaluna."

"What?" Aaron sharply questioned as Haerdnor's jaw dropped. "What are you talking about?"

"We need someone to marry Durek Svilas' daughter—the Morrian king is dying and he's the heir presumptive. And Morroek must be appeased if we're to successfully attack Rindria," Amaria said. "I'm no military strategist, but even I can see a two-front war is inefficient."

"She's seventeen," Aaron protested.

"You're younger than my last fiancé," Amaria said brightly, hiding her lack of sympathy behind a cheery facade. "I believe that means she should be extra-fertile, wasn't that what you told me when I was distressed over my engagement?"

"Marry her," Haerdnor said coldly, standing next to Amaria in solidarity. "Or I promise you, I'll be the last one to have the name Raulet."

"What will you do?" Aaron's hands gripped the wooden armrest, his lips pulling back as he bared his teeth. "You are my son, you do not have the authority to make decisions like this for me."

Haerdnor crossed his arms. "It's my family too."

"And you're not Duke Raulet yet," Aaron snarled.

"And if you don't do this, then I never will be."

A vein in Aaron's forehead bulged. "What do you mean?"

"I'll join the imperial guard," Haerdnor said. "They can't marry or hold titles. Will you give your titles and lands to a Chauvignon child or perhaps a distant cousin? Either way, it sounds as if there would be a nasty succession crisis brewing."

"You cannot join the imperial guard," Aaron derided.

"Why?" Amaria brushed against her father's and twin's mage links. *"Does it ruin our future treason?"*

"You know it does," Aaron shot back in the mage link. *"And Haerdnor, Oliver killed the crown prince–*

Aaron paused, turning away from Amaria and Haerdnor. She stopped herself from beaming at Haerdnor. Their father only mentioned overthrowing the emperor in passing, a very casual consideration between family members–if treason could ever be defined as such. But Amaria knew how much her father craved power, and to overthrow the emperor, well, that would raise his influence to new heights. And Haerdnor threatened to cut their father's ambitions off at its knees.

"I don't know what you're talking about," Haerdnor said.

Cutting off the mage link between them, Haerdnor looked solemnly at Aaron. "All we're asking is for you to help in upholding the family legacy. I have concerns about my ability and I can't have you fuck my wife can I? Marry, get a second Raulet son. It's why multiple children exist–to prevent a succession crisis."

Amaria understood the sentiment of wanting to uphold the family legacy in spite of personal objections within the family–all of their power, wealth, and status came from the continued strength of the Raulet name.

Amaria looked over at her father, forcing herself to soften her gaze. "It's admirable how much you loved our mother," she said diplomatically, "but marriage is a tool. Theodmon would have married the Svilas girl if I died."

Aaron looked at them silently, before placing his head in his hands. "I think I may have trained you two too well."

Amaria tended to agree. She gave Haerdnor a soft smile, thankful for him in standing up to their father and staying steady in the challenge.

"I'll let Henri and Theodmon know that there will be a new groom, one Durek Svilas can't refuse," Amaria said softly. "Thank you, Father. Our family means everything to me."

"Enough that you are willing to have a Svilas as a stepmother," Aaron said dryly.

"It's what must be done," Amaria said. "And naturally, I'll help with Haerdnor's wedding, and when the time comes, I'll help with the planning of yours. When are we leaving for Raulle?"

"In the next few days," Aaron said.

Amaria nodded her head, using the incline and her hair to shield her smirk as she kissed the top of Sylviana's head. She and Haerdnor won something against their father–and it was a big win too–by using his own words and logic against him. They didn't plan it, and the victory came at the cost of Haerdnor threatening to abandon the family, but Amaria couldn't recall when they'd ever been able to negotiate with their father like this.

"We'll leave you to it," Amaria said politely. "Haer, do you want to walk with me?"

"Gods, yes," Haerdnor exhaled as they stepped into the hall away from the critical eyes of their father. Silently, they walked through the corridors, Amaria, adjusting Sylviana's blankets as she did so, as to protect her from the bitter temperatures nipping her nose. Amaria's shoulders were bare, the fabric dipping off of them to expose her collarbone. And although she had a makeshift cape covering her back, the dress she wore still exposed her so her wings could escape. She would need to figure out this outfit conundrum sooner or later.

Sighing, Amaria summoned a gust of warm air to circle her, Haerdnor, and her daughter. The temperatures were fine inside individual rooms, the fireplaces were efficient at keeping smaller rooms lined with furs and furniture warm; however, the stone corridors were iceboxes.

"How are you feeling?" Amaria asked Haerdnor. "About the wedding?"

"It was bound to happen," Haerdnor dismissed, his jaw tensing as he turned his face slightly away from Amaria. "It's not a big deal."

Amaria scoffed, Haerdnor was a terrible liar. "It was going to happen, but you're still allowed to have feelings about it. Haer, it's okay."

"I'm sure she's a nice girl, my bride, Lady Naomi Brassir of Tressidil," Haerdnor said. Amaria noticed the formality in the titles, as if he was trying to distance himself from the emotional realities of the union—that if he made her formalized she was more distant, as if she didn't really exist. Amaria had once tried that same method.

"It must be difficult," Amaria whispered, "hiding who you truly are."

Haerdnor's shoulders rose and fell. "It's a specific torture," he admitted. "I am the perfect heir on the surface—but, I can't do it. The main thing, I don't think I can continue the family line...." Haerdnor trailed off, his shoulders slumping. "Until today, I thought the main line would die with me, and then...I didn't want to know that when I died our House would erupt into a mini civil war on whether you and your children, or a male cousin with the name Raulet would inherit."

"I know," Amaria said, "I wouldn't want that either."

"I'm surprised Father agreed," Haerdnor said.

Amaria lightly chuckled. "Me too. That was brave of you–stupid–but brave. Where did it come from?"

"You," Haerdnor said.

Amaria's eyebrows rose disbelievingly.

"Its true," Haerdnor insisted. "I saw you spiral leading up to your little murder spree in Rindria, and while it was slightly frightening, it was also somewhat of a relief to see somebody acting, saying some of the things we all knew to be true but we kept quiet about."

"So I inspired you?" Amaria snorted, rolling her eyes as they neared the nursery.

"I wouldn't call it inspiration." Haerdnor shrugged. "More of a realization. See, I was thinking *'oh shit...maybe we should go crazy like she did. It'll be fine, right? Maybe I'll get wings.'*"

"I despise you," Amaria told him as he laughed boisterously, causing Sylviana to wake. "I want you to know how much I hate you."

"You love me," Haerdnor said between laughs. "Admit it."

Amaria rolled her eyes, knocking on the nursery door, and waiting for the nannies to come and retrieve Sylviana. Haerdnor hadn't stopped laughing and when the nanny appeared, her eyes briefly darted towards Haerdnor before she composed herself to be the epitome of professionalism.

"Thank you," Amaria told the nanny, waiting until she stepped back inside the nursery, the door softly thudding behind her to turn towards Haerdnor.

"Have some decorum, won't you?" Amaria said.

"Wow, you sound like Father now," Haerdnor smirked.

"Shut up," Amaria snapped.

Haerdnor snickered. "You should have some decorum."

Chapter Twenty

Rolling her eyes, Amaria bid her twin goodbye. She realized as they walked away that she missed their twenty-second birthday when she was in the faerie lands. It was their twenty-second, right? Amaria counted in her head, she had been twenty when Lysander was born, she was twenty-one when she entered the faerie lands...gods, she had missed so much.

Forcing back the urge to cry, Amaria turned around, hoping that Haerdnor was still around, that they could plan something for their birthday. It was six months away but Amaria didn't think that was relevant–it gave them more time for planning. But by the gods, Haerndor was being married–and not to the man he wanted to be with–near his birthday.

She wished the world weren't so cruel and restrictive. Still, as Amaria moved downstairs, moving around the wall of the circular staircase in the foyer, she admitted that it was better to be a part of that cruelty and to reap benefits from working inside the restrictions they were given. She enjoyed having nice clothes, enough food, power, money, and furs. She loved her white furs. And the reality was that she couldn't have any of these without cruelty and without restrictions.

Perhaps she'd been too cruel at times–the admission hurt Amaria even to think about. And perhaps she, too, longed for freedom. But she only was cruel for her protection–for stability. And so she wouldn't regret her actions because showing mercy damned herself.

As Amaria stepped into the kitchens, she spotted three people gathered around a small wooden table--none of whom she had expected to see.

"What're you doing here?" Amaria approached Liara, Celestine and Aloysius, picking up the hem of her skirt with one hand to step over a pile of dirt.

Liara froze, Celestine squeezing her hand.

Aloysius leaned back against the table from where he was sitting on a stool, throwing back a bottle of whiskey. "Booze," he said casually, as if he were a farmer instead of a lord. "It's too cold to be sober."

"Good," Amaria smirked. "You'll be warm enough to visit the griffins with me."

"Griffins?" Liara questioned.

"How long have you been here?" Amaria barked, immediately irate. "Griffins are bred and live here, or are you as blind as you're daft?"

"Maybe if you didn't keep me locked up–"

"You mean your role in society," Amaria interrupted, exasperated with Liara. "Believe me, if I had my way you'd be joining your brother."

"What?" Liara stepped backwards, blinking rapidly. "What do you mean? What happened to Tesden?"

"Oh you didn't know?" Amaria didn't bother to hide the smirk creeping across her expression. This was unnecessary, Amaria knew that she was being senselessly cruel. But she couldn't stop herself.

"Amaria," Celestine warned. "It's not prudent. Remember that time the gardener pruned the roses with Theodmon's consent but you didn't know and screamed at him?"

No such incident ever occurred, at least not to Amaria's knowledge. Which meant that Celestine was telling her something. Amaria looked over at her quizzically, and Celestine's eyebrows rose momentarily as she met Amaria's eyes, her lips twitching slightly. *Theodmon knows what she's doing.* Amaria realized, piecing together the puzzle Celestine gave her. *Which means she's not actually helping Liara. And Aloysius is tired of her–he's told Theodmon as much from what he told me. Celestine wants us to keep pushing, to not be prudent in Liara's eyes.*

"Oh?" Amaria said, primarily to adjust her thoughts without a delay that would cause suspicion.

"She should know." Aloysius's words slurred more than Amaria thought was possible for a man with his alcohol tolerance as he looked at Liara with a level of disdain even Amaria couldn't muster towards Liara. Amaria made a mental note to ask Aloysius what truly occurred to cause this much hatred, as whatever Theodmon told her didn't seem enough to inspire this. "Tell her," Aloysius continued, "as a warning to my wife of how my brother handles stupidity."

"What?" Liara's voice shook.

"I don't think she needs to hear it." Amaria's voice was as smooth as silk as she turned to look at Celestine and Liara. "Bring her to the walls."

"Is that necessary?" Celestine protested.

Amaria looked at Liara coldly. "Does her husband have any objection?"

Aloysius shrugged, his hand slipping off the table as he stumbled to a standing position. "Do what you have to do."

Liara frantically looked around the kitchen, searching for an escape. Amaria grabbed her by the arm–immediately Liara started thrashing, trying to push Amaria off of her. "Get away, you winged freak!"

"Behave," Amaria pulled air from Liara's lungs, the Riam gasping for air as a look of horror exploded across her features. When her eyes bulged just enough, Amaria released her magic, allowing the air flow to go back into her lungs.

Liara fell to the ground, gasping as she clutched her throat. Behind Amaria, Celestine scolded her, rushing to Liara's side, comforting her.

"Try anything else," Amaria crouched next to Liara, "and I will not stop my magic before you die."

"It's true," Liara's eyes watered as she leaned backwards from Amaria. "You killed my family in Rindria..."

"It doesn't matter if it's true," Amaria dismissed.

"Of course it matters!"

Amaria's eyebrow rose scoffingly. "Does it?" She pulled Liara up off the ground. "Truth is what the victors make it. Nobody cares about the semantics or even morality of the story as long as they can root for a winner. Now, behave."

She let the silent threat of *or else* linger in the air for a moment before she unceremoniously dragged Liara out of the kitchen.

"I can walk." Liara attempted to pull her arm out of Amaria's grasp.

Amaria tightened her grip. "Remember what happens if you run."

Liara jutted her chin out defiantly. "I'll scream that you're murdering me."

"And who'll care?" Amaria laughed. If Liara cooperated, swallowed the bile and had children–she'd be alive; killing her wouldn't even be a true consideration–it would open the Chauvignons up to questions they didn't want to, or couldn't, reasonably answer. Liara could have even influenced her children, carefully and in secret, and reclaim her country within a generation or two. That's what Amaria would have done. Not have whined, wishing for something to change against all odds.

Nothing was ever going to change: daughters were married off and used as pawns, and any power any of them acquired was clawed for. Aloysius wasn't even a bad husband, if Liara had half a brain, she could have had a decent life.

Being difficult for the sake of being difficult would only get you killed. Amaria learned that lesson, she had it beaten and waterboarded into her as a child. She was being cruel, she knew, but she couldn't be sympathetic to an adult who couldn't act as such.

"Celestine," Liara said. "The servants like me."

"The servants we pay and rely on their continued job here? The servants that may be spies?" Amaria snorted. "Now, act happy, people will talk; you may discover you're not as well liked as you believe if they think you're ill mannered to the point of abrasive insanity."

Liara glared at her with a look that could make flowers wither, but thankfully, she remained silent allowing them to pass through the halls to step outside on the walkways of the curtain walls, where the heads of enemies and executed prisoners were displayed for the birds to scavenge and eat until the flesh was so rotted that it repulsed the vultures.

"Look." Amaria pointed towards Tesden's skewered head.

Liara's eyes followed Amaria's finger. Immediately, as her eyes drifted towards her brother's head, she stumbled backwards, cursing under her breath. "How could you!" Liara moved her head into her arms, sobbing, turning her back away from Tesden's head so as to not look at it.

"If you don't do what you're told, that will be you." Amaria walked away from Liara without a second glance. "Choose wisely."

"I'm the last heir to Rindria." Liara shouted. "Doesn't that bother you? Shouldn't it scare you that the last heir despises you and your country?"

Amaria paused in her departure, turning to look at Liara. "You're a Thestitiunian by marriage. And I don't feel anything for you—in fact, I barely consider you."

Chapter Twenty-One

Liara's eyes welled up with tears and Amaria momentarily felt a twinge of pain in her chest—was this empathy? No, it couldn't be. Still, as Liara ran away and Celestine ran after her, shouting false comforts, Amaria imagined if she saw one of her siblings' head on a stick. And the very thought of it sickened her.

The difference was she would do more than just cry. She would kill the executioner herself. Amaria did her share of sitting–preening, simpering, appearing as a useless ornamental piece–but she had never been that. Her preening was a pretense, one that would let her be underestimated so when she simpered and sat through parties and political events nobody would suspect she was secretly gathering information from them to use against them later.

This method gradually lost the majority of its effectiveness as her notoriety grew, still, idiotic men loved a beautiful woman flattering their ego. If Amaria could do that, she could still be effective against many.

Amaria stretched her wings outwards, enjoying the pull of her muscles allowing her to do so. *Those methods won't work now.* She reminded herself. She expected to feel some sort of loss, a mourning of an effective strategy that was almost a part of her—Amaria felt nothing. Perhaps that wasn't true, no, Amaria felt relieved. She was tired of pretending to be stupider, weaker, *lesser* than she actually was. And the wings, these things that made her *other*, that made her terrifying because nobody could easily define her or her presumed roles anymore, they freed her from the continuing obligations of that pretense. Oberon, although crass, made a good point, and Amaria was appreciating it more daily.

She wasn't weaker—she had never been weak, but it was now impossible for anybody to deny or dismiss her magical powers. And she couldn't be lesser, how could she when there was nobody like her–nobody living and human at least. She wouldn't hide her intelligence anymore. If she was too much, she was too much and those who dared stand in the direct sunlight had no reason to complain once they were burned.

"Let's go," she said to Aloysius, who too, silently watched Celestine run after Liara. "Are you alright?"

"Do you want the polite answer or the honest answer?" Aloysius shoved his hands under his cloak.

"Whichever you prefer," Amaria shrugged. "I can infer what the honest answer is though."

Aloysius sighed, looking around to see if anybody was in earshot as they made their way down from the battlement to the courtyard below. "It's been a miserable year and a half. I tried, I really did with her—is it me? Am I that intolerable?"

"No," Amaria quickly reassured him. "Not in the slightest. Any girl with sense would have been tripping over herself to marry you."

"Including you?" Aloysius teased, stepping away from her as she glared at him. "It's a joke," he said, his hands raised. "You were obviously tripping over yourself to get to my brother."

Amaria suppressed a small smile. "You aren't nearly as funny as you think you are."

"Most people tend to disagree," Aloysius laughed as they departed the courtyard, walking through the grounds. "Where are we headed?"

"Are you just blindly accompanying me?" Amaria said.

"I have to make sure you're protected. What if a bird came and tried to run off with you?"

Amaria's eyebrows rose. "You're worried I'll be kidnapped by a bird."

"Well the feathers could be confusing you know. And while it would be entertaining to see how Theodmon would react," Aloysius shrugged, "I don't want to see what your father would do–I have a healthy dose of self-preservation."

"Do you?" Amaria laughed.

"It comes out occasionally." Aloysius smirked. "In all seriousness, where are you going?"

"The griffin pens," Amaria said. "Theodmon said he'd be there today."

Aloysius gave an over-emphasized eye roll. "Gross."

"Speaking of marriage, I have news," Amaria whispered under her breath to Aloysius.

Aloysius leaned in closer, waiting for her to continue.

"Henri is no longer a candidate for Durek Svilas' daughter," Amaria said.

"Do you know her name?"

Amaria didn't–she had never paid much attention to the girl before now and while she knew the name was noted in a written record somewhere, Amaria never found it pressing information worthy of memorization.

Amaria ignored Aloysius's knowing and insufferable smirking. "We've found a better candidate to mitigate that situation."

"Does the candidate know?"

"Oh yes," Amaria laughed, remembering how Haerdnor backed their father into a corner. "He's aware and he's consented–under duress but still, he's willing to marry her."

"Will Duke Svilas find this marriage profitable?"

"I'd be shocked if anybody refused this match," Amaria said as she saw the griffin pens ahead of her, Theodmon feeding the griffins from his hand.

"Do Henri and Theodmon know yet? Who is the candidate?" Aloysius's eyebrows knit together.

"Not yet, but I'm sure they'll have zero issue with the changes of plans. And the groom is my father."

As Aloysius's jaw dropped, Amaria sped up, taking longer strides to reach Theodmon faster as the grayish-blue feathered animal tossed its head back proudly, his hooved claws raising into the air as he roared when Theodmon threw a chunk of raw meat into the air. Amaria knew this was Bluequill, one of Theodmon's favorites.

"Theo!" She exclaimed gleefully as if she hadn't just left Aloysius gapping like a dumbfounded goldfish a few feet behind her.

Theodmon looked over, beaming. As soon as she reached her husband's side, he pulled her tightly into a hug. "You must be cold."

"You too," Amaria replied. "How long have you been out here?"

"Long enough to induce their warm-up laps and feed them a snack," Theodmon nodded approvingly at Bluequill and the rest.

"Are we using them with Rindria?" Aloysius asked.

Theodmon gave a curt nod as a golden and red griffin butted its beak against his shoulder, lifting its face upwards with a croaking noise as it exposed its feathered neck for a pet. When Theodmon obliged, the griffin croaked even louder.

"Lightcrest," Theodmon lightly chastised, unable to stop his laughter.

"Is he prepared for the conflict?" Aloysius asked.

Amaria tried to focus on what was being said instead of the fact that the griffins seemed to be nearing closer to her, some coming so close from the nearby pen that their breath moved her hair slightly.

Slowly, Amaria unlatched the pen to the female cage close to her.

"Careful," Theodmon warned as she stepped inside. Amaria didn't need the warning–griffins, while they were loyal, were also territorial and fierce, willing and able to tear apart any they viewed as a threat.

She outstretched her hands towards a silver and white winged griffin, exposing her body towards the animal. A large smile broke across Amaria's face as she stopped herself from running to this griffin. "Snowy," Amaria said the griffin's name softly. "How are you?"

Theodmon given her this griffin six months into their marriage. Amaria remembered she feared that Snowy wouldn't like her, as if a griffin rejecting her was symbolic of the potentiality of a failed marriage with Theodmon.

But Snowy easily accepted her, and if Amaria catastrophized the worst case scenario in her imagined symbolism, perhaps Snowy's easy acceptance showed that Amaria would easily integrate into the Chauvignon family.

Snowy stood on her hind legs, tossing her head, before charging towards Amaria. Amaria chuckled, not making an effort to move. Snowy halted in front of her, nudging Amaria with her head. Immediately, Amaria petted the griffin's feathers, hugging her around her neck, the white of her dress and the white of Snowy's body becoming indistinguishable.

"Theo," Amaria said as she petted Snowy. "Henri isn't getting married anymore."

"Her father likes to ruin plans," Aloysius interjected.

"Aaron?" Theodmon said disbelievingly. "What did he do?"

"He's marrying the Svilas girl instead," Amaria said brightly.

Theodmon made a choking sound. "How in the gods' names did you get him to agree to this?"

"Haerdnor." Amaria shrugged. "Turns out when all you care about is family legacy it is easy for your children to blackmail you."

Theodmon blinked, his eyes seemingly glazing over.

"Care to explain?" Aloysius prompted.

"This goes without saying," Amaria whispered, Theodmon and Aloysius leaning in closer to hear her, "but this can't be shared."

"Obviously," Aloysius snorted, Theodmon hitting him on the arm with a stern look. For a few moments in the chilly grounds, Amaria relayed what happened between her father and Haerdnor. She tried to ignore the incredulous expressions as she told her story—perhaps she was still crazy and hallucinated this. It sounded ridiculous—how could Aaron be bested by his son? By anyone? However, his son was a sort of perfect irony–the prodigy he trained, the one to inherit everything he built–the student outwitted the master.

A twig snapped behind them. Amaria's shoulders tensed as she whirled around, raising the snow banks with her magic around her.

"Relax." Lucas held his hands up in front of him. "It's just us." Behind Lucas stood Henri, who didn't look alarmed, rather he was smirking, lazily cracking his neck with a head roll.

"I heard my engagement ended before it even began," Henri said. "I only wish the new groom's thoughts were as elated as mine are."

Amaria resisted a snort, instead choking on her own breath and saliva.

"What's he thinking?" Theodmon looked over at Amaria momentarily, his eyebrows creasing in concern. Amaria shook her head, giving him a small smile, indicating that she was fine.

"He is somehow both infuriated and proud," Henri replied. "I'm trying to block out his thoughts to be perfectly frank with you. But, when's the wedding? Am I invited?"

Amaria rolled her eyes. "With the timing of the wedding, we have to get through Haerdnor's wedding and also get Svilas's approval."

"When is Haerdnor's wedding?" Lucas's mouth dropped slightly. "Is it finally happening?"

"It's in six months," Amaria informed him. "I'm leaving for Raulle soon to help direct preparations for it."

"I wish you weren't." Theodmon held her arm firmly. Amaria moved her hand over his arm, holding it gently. She wished she wasn't leaving either. They had barely been together for a few months before they had to be separated once more.

By the gods, Amaria despised war. What she would do, who she wouldn't kill, to remain in the security of a castle with its high walls and roaring fireplaces, safely wrapped in warm blankets and cuddled in Theodmon's arms. Instead, she settled for burrowing her face deeper into his chest as she hugged him.

Closing her eyes, Amaria tried to ignore the distant shouts she heard. It was likely a training exercise, the men could be loud.

"Let me through!"

Amaria tried to ignore that the voice was coming closer as Theodmon's arms uncurled themselves from around her, leaving her exposed to the cold.

"Celestine?" Theodmon asked.

Amaria's eyes snapped open as her stomach sank. Whatever this was, it couldn't be a training accident. Celestine was not one who bothered with those sorts of things. Swallowing the lump in her throat, she turned to face the noises behind her, her hands shaking.

"What's wrong?" Theodmon asked Celestine who was pale, her lip quivering.

"She's dead," Celestine whispered. "She did it in front of me, she made sure I saw it."

"What?" Theodmon gently questioned.

"She jumped off the eastern bridge...she fell down the cavern...I had to go down there to remove the body so townspeople didn't see..." Celestine didn't blink, almost seeming hollow. Amaria's blood chilled as she realized why: Celestine saw her first dead body...and it was likely mutilated after falling down the cavern.

"Who is she?" Theodmon said.

"You know," Celestine whispered. "She made sure I saw it as her final revenge."

Amaria breath caught in her mouth. Liara. This had to be Liara. She had to have known her death wouldn't have affected them other than a celebration and she wanted to have them suffer. So that bitch killed herself in front of Celestine.

"Liara," Amaria growled. That girl was lucky she was already dead.

Celestine sobbed, forcing her face into her hands. Amaria's head tilted slightly, her eyes narrowing. Celestine was made of more steel than this. Yes, Celestine was sweet and kind, but she was still a Chauvignon.

"Let's get you inside," Aloysius picked up his shaking sister in his arms. "Is it necessary to interrogate her in the snow?"

"Sorry," Theodmon told Celestine.

Amaria used her magic to raise the temperature slowly, watching Celestine closely to ensure the temperature change didn't harm her more. "Just tell us where the body is, and go to your chambers. We'll handle it from here."

Celestine gulped, her eyes hazy. "Alright," she said in a small voice.

"It was selfish of her to kill herself in front of you." Aloysius cursed loudly. "By all the gods, she hated us all and for what reason? I did everything to make her welcome! To make her damn fucking comfortable and she decides to kill herself in front of my sister."

Celestine sobbed, her wails breaking into the winter sky. In her peripheral vision, Amaria noticed Henri's eyes narrowed and widened as he looked at Celestine, his mouth opening slightly.

"Not now," Amaria whispered to Aloysius. "Vent to me or Theodmon later."

She's not telling us something. And Henri knows what. She's obviously distressed, let's leave her alone and find out from Henri. Amaria wished Aloysius could read her thoughts without opening a mage link. She wished she could communicate with Theodmon with a mage link—sometimes him not having magic could be terribly inconvenient.

Amaria clenched her jaw as they hurried into the castle. Once, Amaria thought she would celebrate the day they were free of Liara–in fact, she was sure of it. She may have fantasized about the food at the feast of mourning that they would hold to maintain social customs. Instead, Amaria had a million questions and her heart thudded against her chest as she felt a deepening concern for Celestine.

What happened on the eastern bridge?

Chapter Twenty-Two

For a moment, Theodmon's head rang. Vaguely, as if muffled and distant, he heard Aloysius say: "By the gods, she hated me and for what reason? I did everything to make her welcome! To make her damn fucking comfortable and she decides to kill herself in front of my sister."

Celestine was sobbing.

"Get her to her chambers." Theodmon felt as if he floated out of his body. He was here, handling the situation, but not truly processing it. "Call Katerina to attend to her. Tell the guards and servants to give Katerina anything she needs, no questions." Theodmon didn't know why he added that–Katerina always received anything she needed, a perk of being the resident healing mage of the Chauvignons.

"Bring me to the body," Theodmon told a guard who ran up with Celestine earlier.

Gulping, the guard nodded.

"We have to plan a funeral," Lucas said under his breath.

"Good thing she can be burnt on a pyre wrapped in a shroud," Amaria said. "Jumping from that distance must have made her ugly in death."

"Be nice," Lucas said.

"I'm not saying it to be mean," Amaria said. "How beautiful is someone who likely shattered every bone in their body?"

"We'll have to mourn her," Theodmon muttered. "As much as we can without it being overkill."

"Should I wear yellow to a funeral?" Amaria smirked. "I doubt anybody would believe it if I showed sorrow."

"They'd expect you to at least keep up appearances, however unconvincingly," Lucas said. "Who'd have thought the remaining heirs to the Riam throne would die so soon?"

"I'd believe you planned this," Theodmon said as they descended into the dungeons, following the guard through the metal gates. Immediately, on instinct, Theodmon forced himself to take shallow breaths through his mouth, trying to avoid smelling the stench around him. Even without stepping down the stairs he could already smell the sweat, urine, feces, and decomposing flesh—it would only get worse the deeper they descended into the prison. The dungeons were built into the mountain, the only light came from torches and the specks of daylight that escaped in its one entrance.

Next to him, a raspy sound escaped Amaria and she seemed to be shaking. Theodmon squeezed her arm, nodding to her in encouragement.

"Oh gods!" Amaria brought her hands to cover her nose, forcing back a gag.

Theodmon turned his head to see what she saw. From the shadows of her flickering flames he saw maggots eating a man's flesh; and the prisoner didn't scream, accepting his punishment and death within the mountain.

Amaria almost seemed more pale-faced than the prisoner.

"You don't have to be in the dungeons if you don't want to be," Theodmon whispered. She must be remembering Rindria—how hard must it be for her to step down here?

"No," Amaria said firmly. "This is what I'm good at, I'm not going to let a few bad weeks change the rest of my life. I'll get over it."

Theodmon's eyebrows rose slightly. He didn't believe that was the truth. Perhaps Amaria was trying to delude herself. However, he wasn't going to make her confront her suppressed emotions and memories of a prison inside a prison.

"Amaria," Theodmon breathed softly. "I love you." It was all he could say at that moment.

"I love you too," Amaria sighed. "Let's get this over with."

Beside them, the guard lit the pillars on the outside of the doorframe. "She's in here," he informed them before stepping away from the door.

"Thank you," Lucas said, politely but unequivocally dismissing the guard.

"Give me the key," Theodmon directed. "I'll lock up this. You may go." He didn't need a gawker as they saw the body. Without waiting for a response, Theodmon stepped into the cell, Amaria and Lucas close behind.

"Oh gods," Lucas cursed as the light flickered in the cell, illuminating Liara's bruised and bloodied body, more blue than flesh colored. Her limbs were bent in ways a human body shouldn't be able to bend in, and half of Liara's face was caved in.

"Wrapped entirely in a shroud for the funeral," Amaria noted.

"She didn't seem like the type to jump," Lucas said, the three of them stepping out of the cell and making their way out of the prison.

I'm surprised she had the nerve. Theodmon thought in agreement. *Suicide–it seemed like a lot of self resolve would be needed for an act like that. Perhaps she tripped over her own face and fell off the bridge?*

Theodmon immediately dismissed the idea. No, Celestine's behavior made that unlikely. Celestine saw worse than a clumsy idiot tripping to their death. Celestine had seen death and while she always had an obvious discomfort with it, she never blubbered. Sweetness aside, Celestine was a Chauvignon and she developed the stoicism they all had.

Theodmon's eyes widened as if he were shocked by electricity. Perhaps Celestine hadn't witnessed a suicide.

"I'll go help prepare for the funeral," Amaria said dully, unaware of the thoughts roaring through Theodmon's mind, causing him to internally reel.

"I'll spread misinformation," Lucas said, oblivious to the realizations that were hitting Theodmon as if they were a million blunted swords.

Theodmon nodded, a lump forming in his throat. He had his own important task at hand. The light was becoming brighter; soon they would be free from the rotting bodies–both dead and living, and be able to breathe without feeling as if their lungs were collapsing from the stress. Soon, they would be alright.

The light was so close it could almost be touched. The guards saw them approaching and prepared to lift the gates. They almost exited the Mortsenia Labyrinths, and Theodmon felt as much relief as he presumed a prisoner would feel to be released from here.

As Theodmon stepped into his sister's chambers, he saw Katerina slowly soothing Celestine, glowing a soft green with her magic. Celestine was still pale faced, but she was no longer shaking. Instead she seemed as if she were empty, her eyes staring numbly ahead of her–focusing intently on one point of the wall and yet unable to focus on anything at all.

"Leave," Theodmon instructed Celestine's ladies. He turned towards Katerina. "Will she be okay if you leave for a moment? We need privacy. If she still needs your care, it can wait."

"I'll be outside." Katerina gathered her supplies in her skirts. Silently, Theodmon and Celestine watched her go, their chests raising and falling in unison.

For infinity, nothing happened. Nothing happened until a loud sobbing noise escaped Celestine and she buried her face in her blankets.

"Celestine," Theodmon said soothingly, rushing to her bedside. "It's alright."

This, unfortunately, only made her cry harder. "You don't understand," she wailed.

"What?" Theodmon kept his voice low, as if she were a wounded deer before the kill. Except, he wouldn't harm Celestine.

"Theodmon...she didn't...Liara didn't jump. I...I was tired of hearing her whine and demand respect while not showing it to anybody else. And how she talked about you. How she talked about Aloysius...." Celestine gulped, shaking beneath her blankets. "I pushed her."

Theodmon sighed. He had never expected Celestine to kill someone–he tried his best to protect her from those horrors. And somehow, despite his best efforts, he failed. Even worse, the failure happened in their own home.

He wasn't sure how to comfort her in this moment—he couldn't acknowledge the truth, could he? Would his blunt acceptance of harsh realities, the attitude he took with everyone else, cause her to spiral? Would it be better to deny that it hadn't happened?

Theodmon decided to take the gentlest route with Celestine. "It was icy and you were trying to stop her from jumping–"

"It's not my reputation I'm concerned with," Celestine interrupted. Theodmon looked at her unblinkingly, waiting for her to continue. Painfully silent moments passed. "Okay, I am worried in part but...I've never killed anyone." Celestine whispered this last part, her eyes welling. "I wasn't bothered by you, Amaria, Aloysius, Lucas, and all the rest killing people but I never thought I could–would–do it."

How could somebody come to terms with the fact that they took a life? Over time, each life became less painful—sadly, Theodmon was ashamed to admit, some of the lives blurred together, becoming indistinguishable with the passage of time. However, your first kill, that changed you, it harmed the soul. And for that reason, it was impossible to forget.

Part Three

the roses

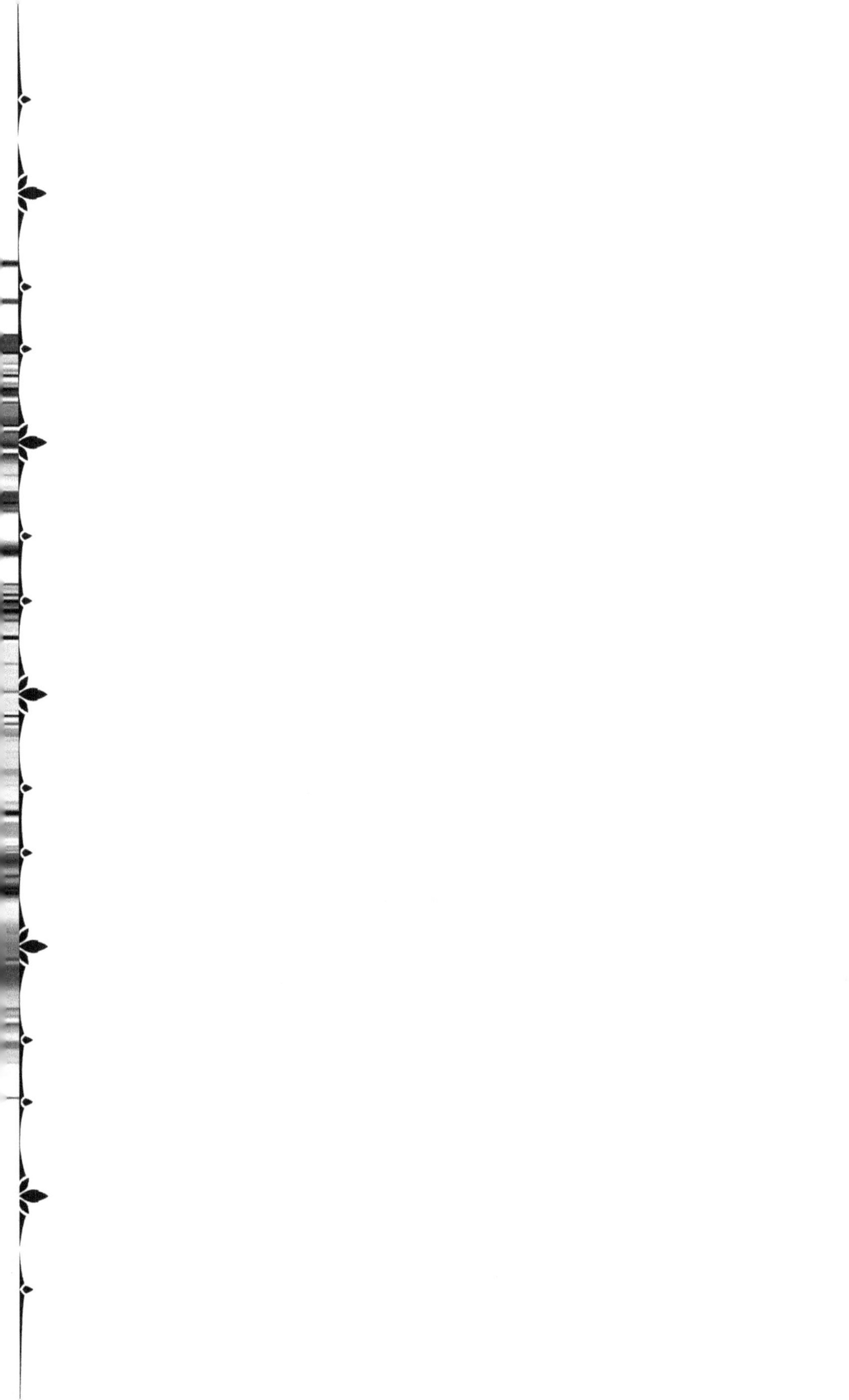

Chapter Twenty-Three

A bolt of lightning illuminated Theo and Amaria's rooms through the stained glass windows. Theodmon scowled at the storm. It showed that everything was outside of his control, even here. He couldn't predict the storm, he couldn't predict what was to come in the future, he didn't even have hegemony over the events in his own home––and that Celestine of all people would have done it. Theodmon desperately wanted to close the curtains, to hide the reminder of how powerless he truly was.

But he couldn't. Sitting on the balcony, a smile on her face, Amaria sat in the storm, the water running down her face, her magical aura cracking with energy. Once, Theodmon had worried that she would be struck by lightning. But the bolts always seemed to go around her, as if power recognized power and chose to stay away from each other.

Sighing, Theodmon went to the wardrobe, pulled out his cloak and threw it on, securing the clasps over his neck. He momentarily looked at his fur-lined leather gloves, knowing it would be cold outside. He turned to see Amaria sitting in the rain once more and he abandoned the gloves as he strode across the room to the glass doors, stepping outside onto the balcony.

As he shut the door behind him, Amaria turned her head to momentarily smile at Theodmon, her wet hair sticking to the edges of her face.

"Hey," she breathily said. Theodmon noticed her wet dress clung to her body, leaving very little to the imagination. He could see every level of her curves–only shielded by a soaking piece of fabric.

"Why do you sit out here anyways?" Theodmon sat down beside her, his hands momentarily slipping on the stone railing.

"It's calming," Amaria said.

"Sitting in a storm?" Theodmon's eyebrow arched in disbelief.

"I like the water. The wind, the energy that's as chaotic as fire—it feels...it feels safe." She gave a harsh laugh. "I must sound insane to you."

Theodmon paused. "We all have things that make us seem insane."

Amaria looked at him, the ceases around her eyes deepening. She scooted over towards him, the drenched fabric of her dress clinging to her skin and to the ground. Amaria placed her head on his shoulders, the wet strands of hair tickling his face.

"It's cold," Amaria said after a few moments. "We should go inside."

"Yes," Theodmon muttered the agreement into her hair. The rain felt like ice as it whipped across his face. He unwrapped his arms from around her as he stood up, shivering and trying not to slip on the wet stone. He noticed that the front of his left boot was missing some of its grip, Theodmon supposed it was to be expected from the amount of use his boots had recently experienced—fighting non-stop in the Northern Morrian wilderness hadn't been kind to many people. Many had lost limbs or fingers from frostbite, had died, or were shells of themselves now. Theodmon had gotten off easy with only needing new boots.

And seeing Ophelia die.

Closing his eyes, he tried to burn that memory from his mind. Amaria was leaving tomorrow. He shouldn't have been focusing on Ophelia right now. Theodmon opened his eyes, blinking away the rain caught in his eyelashes, as he held out his hand for her to take.

Amaria took his hand, her small palm slipping momentarily in his as she stood up. She looked at him, her eyes stopping momentarily as she gazed over his wet cloak. "I'll dry us off inside."

"No." Theodmon pushed open the door, holding it open with his hand as he led Amaria in with the other, watching carefully as she stepped through the doorway, the water dripping off her dress to make a pool of water at her feet on the marble floor.

"No?" Amaria asked.

"It's our last night together for a while." Theodmon shivered as he took off his drenched cloak, unceremoniously dropping it on the floor, kicking the dripping pile away with his foot. "Let's have a hot bath, a nice dinner–savor it."

"I don't want to—please don't say it's the last night." Amaria wrung her hair out with shaking hands, large water droplets dripping onto the floor.

"It's only a few months," Theodmon embraced her. "I'll see you at the wedding."

"And then what?" Amaria said. "You go to war and I stay behind doing intelligence?"

Theodmon's shoulders heaved. He didn't want to admit she was right. He also didn't want to spend this far away from her and was numbing himself to reality. "It's not forever."

Unless I die. Theodmon's jaw locked. He couldn't afford to think like that. Reality was ugly and Amaria was beautiful. And in his chambers, Theodmon much preferred beauty.

"You can't promise me that." Amaria pulled off her dress as she turned her back to him. "Only the gods can."

"Amaria," Theodmon sighed. "Please, let's just enjoy this night. Nobody will be dying before this wedding, it's just pre-war planning."

Amaria kept her back turned towards him, her shoulders rising and falling. "Alright," she eventually said in a small voice. "Alright."

Theodmon felt as if a weight had been lifted off his shoulders, thankful she didn't argue further. "I'll write to you," he promised. "I'll write every day."

Amaria laughed softly, moving to the wardrobe and pulling out a fluffy light blue robe. "To receive letters every day, none of them a response to the one I sent out before."

"It could be a fun exercise." Theodmon embraced her from behind. "Matching which of my letters answers the ones you've sent."

Rolling her eyes, Amaria leaned into his arms, her wings rubbing against his bare chest. "I can think of better intellectual exercises." She turned her face upwards to face him, her eyes shining brightly. "I can't wear this robe."

"Do you know how much longer it'll take for the seamstresses to finish your new wardrobe?" Theodmon asked. "We can cut silts—"

"No," Amaria said hastily. "It'll ruin them. I don't—they should be done tonight I think."

"I'm sure the seamstresses can adapt this robe for your wings," Theodmon said gently, noticing the golden roses embroidered across its sleeves.

"I'll have the ones at Provincia Palencia do it," Amaria shook her head. "It doesn't make sense to delay this trip. A lot needs to be done in Raulle for Haerdnor's wedding." She took a deep breath, wrapping her arms around herself. "I'm going to dry myself off, hide under the covers while you have someone draw us a bath."

"I can draw us a bath," Theodmon said. "So can you, if you want to use your magic."

"I thought you wanted us to enjoy—"

"Yes," Theodmon chuckled softly. "Alone. The only disruption I want from anyone tonight is when our food is brought to our rooms."

Amaria lightly rolled her eyes, chuckling. But still, she made her way to the double doors to the bathing hall, turning her head to see if Theodmon was behind her. "Well? Are you ready?"

Without waiting for a further response, Amaria ran into the room, a silver glow coming from her hands and Theodmon followed. As he stepped inside the bathhouse, the stained glass windows darkened from the storm outside, he saw water rise in the tub rapidly. Miraculously, steam rose with the water.

"I'll get the soaps," Amaria said.

"I'll get the towels," Theodmon replied, walking closer to the edge of the basin. He looked at the steaming water and he dipped his toes in, only to be greeted by searing pain. He yelped and jumped back, trying to shake away the burning that had seeped beneath his skin.

"What?" Amaria looked over at him in concern.

"It's too hot," Theodmon shrugged, trying to keep his composure as if he hadn't just burned his foot on bath water. Gods, out of all the things to be defeated by, that would be the most unexpected and embarrassing one.

Amaria turned red, her eyes widening. "I'm sorry! I didn't know–I'll make the water cooler." She raised her hands, and almost instantaneously, the water turned to ice.

"Gods!" Amaria cursed.

"What's wrong?" Theodmon asked softly.

"I can't do simple things!" Amaria's hands reached up to her head as she pulled on her hair. "Big things are easier, but since the faeries–since they changed me, I have difficulties channeling my power. I use too much and it's stupid. I should be able to lower the water temperature without freezing the whole basin!"

"Why don't you just heat it back up and we'll wait for it to cool down," Theodmon said. "We can wrap ourselves in robes and blankets to stay warm, you can even dry our hair. And then we'll just play a round of chess or talk while we wait."

Amaria gave a small nod. "Alright," she agreed, reaching out her hands and causing the ice to blister and crack before it reached a heavy boiling. She stepped backwards, further away from Theodmon, as she pointed a gust of wind near her feet, the warm air circulating around the room. "Less heat?"

"Less force," Theodmon said. "It doesn't feel too warm."

Amaria gritted her teeth, her eyebrows weaving together as her brow scrunched. She bit her lip as she looked at the ground, her hands steady in front of her. For a long moment, the air didn't change. Theodmon felt his legs were already dry, although he had to lock his knees to prevent himself from falling over. He was about to say Amaria could maintain whatever she was doing and they could just lay on the floor and let the air cool them that way, when the air seemed to still slightly.

A breeze still was circling them, but it was peaceful—not about to knock them off their feet.

"I'm bringing the air up to our faces," Amaria said, and Theodmon felt a gust going from his feet up his body, staying around his hair until it was dried. Amaria met his eyes, worry creasing her brow.

Theodmon decided to not question her until the wind died down.

"There's blankets out there," Theodmon said, once the wind dissipated, moving over to Amaria's side. He held her waist, kissing the top of her head. "Go wrap yourself up in the bed, I'll get the chessboard."

Amaria's eyes twinkled as she pulled his hand, both of them walking into their bedchambers. "I guess this is one way to enjoy the night."

"And once we bath," Theodmon continued, "what should we have for dinner? I should probably ring for a servant and let them know."

"Soup." Amaria looked towards the storm outside. "We've the weather for it."

"After you sat outside in that," Theodmon shook his head humorously.

"But being inside makes me appreciate the soup more," Amaria protested, her mouth dropping open. Still, she was unable to hide her smile. Theodmon burst into laughter and she joined in.

He held up his hands in a false surrender. "I concede." Theodmon pulled a robe around himself to shelter his privates before he went to speak to the guards standing post outside the chamber, telling them orders of what to tell a maid to tell the kitchen to make. Castles were like a many headed hydra, and often Theodmon didn't know how the heads communicated to each other but everything somehow still ran smoothly.

Once that order of business was done, he came back to the bed, where Amaria was already laying out the pieces.

"Black or white?" Theodmon asked, already knowing the answer. If given the choice, Amaria always chose black.

"Black," Amaria said.

"Why do you always choose black?" Theodmon moved one of the white pawns forward on the board.

"I prefer to not go in blind." Amaria moved a pawn mirror to Theodmon's forward. "Defensive positions are easier."

Theodmon's eyebrows rose. He preferred white for the opposite reason. Offensive positions let him set the stage for his strategy, and offense gave him substantially more control than defensive.

"Why is offensive 'going in blind?'" Theodmon moved another pawn.

"Because you don't know how your opponent will react. It's risky to take action without having some shard of knowledge of your opponent's methods." Amaria moved the knight on her left hand side.

Theodmon chuckled. This is where they differed–both of them liked control, perhaps more than what was necessary and what was healthy. However, Theodmon was a soldier. He felt most in control when he was fighting. Amaria excelled in intelligence; she couldn't control others actions directly and so she manipulated others into taking actions they believed were their own.

He moved another pawn.

Amaria's knight took it.

Chapter Twenty-Four

Theodmon's knuckles cracked as he gripped the war table, the miniature figurines shaking slightly from the force. The air was thick with the scent of burning candles, the smoke lingering as if it were a premonition. Maps and battle plans covered every inch of the walls, although Theodmon didn't see what good could come from this amount of clutter.

Stone animals and castles, representing the war's key players and their battlements, sat strewn across the map of Rindria. Thedmon's chest heaved as he studied the Riam territories that lined the mountainous border along the Westerlands. Theodmon's chest heaved heavily as he looked at the Riam lords and battlements stacked against the border. It would be a bloodbath to get into Rindria now that they were expecting something. News of Liara and Tesden Nalaenys' deaths would spread, and after the last massacre they'd have to be idiots not to arm their borders.

Across from him, Lucas surveyed the map, his eyes sharp and focused, his fingers tapping the table.

"What are you thinking?" Theodmon asked. Lucas had a brilliant tactical mind, and Theodmon was brilliant enough to not let talent go to waste.

"Attack after the wedding," Lucas muttered. "The Riams will be watching Haerdnor Raulet get married along with the rest of the world. If we got them to stay a week or two longer, we would have an opening." Most of their leadership will be absent, and it'll be disorganized."

"We likely won't win right away," Henri stated.

Theodmon grinned at Lucas. "But it might give us the advantage we need so we can win more easily."

"Do you think the Raulets can do this?" One of Theodmon's lieutenants asked.

Pushing over a stag, the symbol of the Riam royal family, Aloysius snorted. "Is that actually a question, Lord Desmond?"

"It's a risky strategy," Lord Desmond said. "We need to make sure that everyone in the plan is well-aware of the plan, and is capable of enacting it. I see that Marchioness Chauvignon has already left, and I am sure we don't want to send this via letter right now considering the wedding? I trust the Raulets capabilities, you would be a fool not to, however, the timing is unfortunate."

Theodmon's brow furrowed as his eyes pored over the map. He hated to admit it, but Lord Desmond had made an amble point.

"It's a risky move, but it could prove to be a decisive victory. We'll need to move quickly and make sure our troops are prepared," Henri agreed. "I believe that Duke Raulet and Marchioness Chauvignon are more than capable."

"And if they aren't, I'm sure the lady wouldn't mind killing them at the dinner table," a man snickered under his breath.

Theodmon's fists clenched. However, aside from a slight flaring of his nostrils, he kept his face neutral. Everyone knew that Amaria had killed several Riams—but they couldn't officially confirm it. And becoming angry at snide remarks such as that essentially did confirm the rumors. However, this man proved he couldn't be trusted and Theodmon made a note to watch to see if he did suspicious activities—perhaps he was a spy.

"Aloysius." Theodmon turned to face his brother. "Can you ride out for Raulle tonight?"

"Tonight?" Aloysius looked towards the darkening windows. "It's going to storm, isn't it?"

"Badly," Juliette said. "I can feel the water brewing."

Theodmon closed his eyes, trying hard to suppress his growing migraine. He didn't understand mages, not fully. And forget trying to understand how their magic actually worked. Amaria, Aloysius, and Henri had tried to explain it to him many times, but it was so abstract he never could fully grasp it.

"Tomorrow morning then," Theodmon amended, deciding it was best to postpone Aloysius leaving for a few hours. If Juliette was right, well what was a few hours to Aloysius' safety? And if she was wrong, well how would Theodmon know? He wasn't an elemental mage and he wasn't about to argue with one over a storm.

As if on cue, the windows lit up, the lightning illuminating itself through the stained glass.

"This discussion is senseless!" Lord Desmond shouted, and Theodmon turned his attention to him, wondering where this outburst came from. Henri sighed, moving away from the table to stand by the windows, his back to everyone else as he leaned against the stained glass.

"What's senseless?" Lucas asked chillingly.

"We should be making direct attacks, not this dishonorable backstabbing."

"Is it honorable to lead your men into an avoidable slaughter?" Theodmon's eyes sparked as he glowed at Desmond. "Do I need to remind you of the casualties your incompetence caused in Morroek? You lost five thousand men with a reckless attack–if it wasn't for the faeries we'd all be dead."

"That was–"

"A mistake," Theodmon finished dismissively. "Yes. I suggest you learn from it or resign yourself to your command in a lesser position."

"You need lesser lords," Desmond said.

Theodmon didn't disagree. "However," he said, "I don't need lesser lieutenants."

Lucas crossed his arms. "Didn't you suggest this?"

"No," Desmond quickly said. "I only suggested that we obtain the Raulets' assistance–"

"Same difference. If you wanted an honorable plan, Aaron Raulet is the last man I'd ask," Aloysius snorted. "He's effective, ruthless, intelligent—but honorable, you'd have to be an idiot to ever believe that."

"You suggested using the wedding as an attack diversion Lord Bécharil," Desmond snarled at Lucas. "Did you forget that?"

Lucas's hand rested on his knife. "I don't have an aversion to dishonorable acts."

"Clearly," Desmond snarled. Behind him, Henri turned from the window, his eyes glowing a brilliant blue momentarily. "Did you fight Tesden Nalaeny like a man or did you act like a *Prison Butcher, my Lord*? You and Aaron Raulet are cut from the same cloth.
"

Theodmon heard Aloysius suck in his breath. Theodmon bit the inside of his cheek debating on whether to step in or to let Lucas handle his own battles. Lucas however, shrugged. "There's worse insults, Lord Desmond. I would rather be like Aaron Raulet than to be like you—at least Duke Raulet had never killed hundreds with sheer incompetence."

Desmond gave off a scream that almost sounded like a growl as he charged at Lucas. Lucas side-stepped him as he pulled his knife from his sheath, raising it towards Desmond's throat. "Come closer, and I swear, I'll do it. Give me a reason."

"Lucas." Juliette stepped closer to Lucas. "He's not worth it."

"He's not," Lucas agreed. "But the men he killed, and then men he will kill, are. We are about to be in one of the bloodiest wars in recent history, don't try to deny it. Does Thestitiunia need a man like him leading us?"

Desmond laughed crudely. "This is insubordination, boy. You may be the Marquis's bannerman and do his dirty work but you don't lead armies."

"It's only insubordination if the stories say it is," Lucas pushed his knife further into Desmond's jugular. "And the victors write the stories."

Desmond's eyes bulged, and he tried to side step away from Lucas. Lucas however, grabbed the back of Desmond's head and forced his dagger into his throat, a geyser of red erupting. Desmond gasped, pulling his hands to his throat as Lucas pulled his dagger out. Desmond fell to the floor gagging, the stream of red unending.

"You wouldn't know anything about being a victor. There's no victory in complacency, and no honor in incompetence." Lucas kicked Desmond's body. "And by the gods, nobody will mourn you, everyone in this room will swear you were a spy and I did what was necessary."

Momentarily, Theodmon's eyebrows rose. However his face quickly became neutral. Lucas was correct, they would protect Lucas, and while Desmond might not have been a spy, Theodmon doubted he was smart enough to pull something like that off, his death was what was necessary. Lucas had saved lives with killing this one, and nobody would fault him for it if Theodmon had any say on it.

Silently, as the storm raged on outside, they all watched Desmond die. And once the sputtering and gasping came to a halt, and Desmond's lifeless eyes gazed emptily in front of him, Theodmon cleared his throat, looking at each person in the room sternly. "Desmond was a spy."

Nobody argued.

Theodmon paced in the westernmost guard tower, desperately trying to get his thoughts in order. It was cold and wet, and he was fiercely rubbing his hands together as they were cold even within his gloves. However, it was unlikely anybody would think to look for him here. Theodmon needed time alone.

He hadn't quite processed that Amaria had left and that Celestine had killed someone, and now he was having to deal with Aloysius leaving and Lucas killing a fellow Westanni in the middle of a war council. Theodmon didn't like Desmond either, but killing him in that manner was shocking. Desmond wasn't incorrect in saying that Lucas and Aaron were cut from the same cloth, both of them were careful to hide their actions, keeping his true nature carefully hidden behind a polite facade. So what had caused this change? What had Lucas endured when hunting for Tesden Nalaeny?

Theodmon's teeth chattered. He started jogging around the tower, quickly moving into a full sprint. After several minutes of this he stopped, cardio wouldn't do much more to warm him up in this storm. Besides, he was trying to outrun his thoughts and they raced much faster than he ever could.

He was better at fighting instead of running. Theodmon drew his sword out of his sheath, moving into a side sweep, lunging slightly as to give him better reach against the imaginary opponent.

Theodmon swung the sword in his hands, turning and hitting another training pose. He held his sword up for the extended period of time, only dropping it after a few minutes of his arms shaking. Taking a deep breath, he moved to the training pose. He knew he should go inside, but he couldn't force himself to do it.

If he stopped, he'd have to acknowledge Aloysius was leaving in the morning. Theodmon hadn't always been the best towards his brother—he had resented him for a while after their father's death. Theodmon wasn't proud of it, and he would staunchly deny it if it was ever brought up, but in the safety of his own self-reflection he had been forced to confront the fact he had despised his brother all from sheer jealousy—Theodmon had to keep not only his family together, but an entire province running, suppressing any grieving he might have done. And Aloysius, well, he got to grieve in whatever way he wanted–brothels, drugs, dangerous activities only a war mage could survive–Aloysius got to do them all as a second son.

Theodmon and Aloysius had gotten over their anger towards each other years ago, but still, Theodmon felt the remnants of guilt from the rift in their relationship. And he didn't want Aloysius to leave into danger. There were spies here, and Theodmon wasn't sure who people really were anymore. He needed Henri to help more–perhaps Theodmon had been pushing more and more people away in trying to take on all the burdens of responsibility himself.

Theodmon moved to another training pose, holding his sword eye level in a deep lunge. As he did so, the door to the tower opened. Immediately, Theodmon dropped the lunge, rolled away from the door and when he sprung up, moved his sword into a jab.

Too late he saw Aloysius' face and Theodmon moved to stop his swing. In a moment, a red aura glowed around Aloysius' body and he turned as hard as steel–a human shield preventing Theodmon's sword from hurting him.

"Shit," Theodmon cursed.

"Trying to kill me?" Aloysius grinned. "You can't inherit my charm, you know."

Theodmon sheathed his sword, glowering at Aloysius. "You should have announced yourself."

"My magic protected me." Aloysius nonchalantly shrugged. "Besides, I liked watching the horror on your face. You were terrified for a split second."

Theodmon scowled. Leave it to Aloysius to be nonchalant about almost being stabbed through the chest. "Why are you here?"

"Checking up on you." Aloysius made room for Henri and Lucas to step into the room. "It's freezing."

"I barely notice it," Theodmon lied, clenching his jaw to prevent his teeth from chattering.

"That's called frostbite," Lucas said. "Do you not want to keep all your fingers and toes?" He looked at Theodmon directly, his gray eyes as turbulent as the storm outside. "Admit it's cold."

"I never said it wasn't," Theodmon grumbled.

"Come inside," Aloysius said. "Now. If you die, I have to lead the Westerlands and who wants that?"

Theodmon resisted rolling his eyes. He and his brother both knew the succession would go to Lysander, with Amaria acting as regent until he was of age. Aloysius was being an ass. "Fine," he told Aloysius, "but it's not for you."

"It's for the people, yes," Aloysius said, not bothering to suppress his own eye roll. "How disgustingly noble of you." He stepped aside, allowing Theodmon to walk past him. The wind outside howled, and Theodmon walked face-first into the brunt force of it without the protection of the towers.

"Gods," he muttered, his teeth chattering.

"Gods," Henri agreed. "Why do you think we pulled you from that tower?"

"Speak for yourself," Aloysius yelled from behind.

Theodmon chuckled, despite his shivering. As they made their way back inside the castle, his body fully processed the cold, and it felt as if a million swords were cutting his skin. He would need to change his clothes *immediately*–perhaps Lucas had a point about the dangers of the cold.

They stepped inside the castle, and Theodmon turned to his brother and friends. "Change clothes. Then come to my chambers."

"Are we having a party?" Aloysius dodged Theodmon's hand as he moved to slap his shoulder.

Behind him, Lucas snickered.

"Are you sure it's wise to party before you travel hundreds of miles?" The corners of Henri's lips tilted upwards. "Are you sure it's wise to party before you travel hundreds of miles?"

Aloysius shrugged, as if there wasn't a worry in his empty head. "I'm not the wise one."

"Obviously," Theodmon said.

"You were about to give yourself hypothermia," Henri said. "You're not the wise one either."

Theodmon shook his head with a laugh. *Henri,* he thought pointedly. *Walk with me. I need to speak to you.*

Henri turned to Theodmon, his expression carefully neutral, as he gave a quick, short nod of understanding. As Lucas and Aloysius departed, Theodmon and Henri slowed their pace to lag behind. When the other two were gone, Theodmon looked around, searching for a private place in the corridors. Between all the servants, guards, and courtiers milling about, he couldn't find anywhere satisfactory. Sighing, Theodmon decided he would have to communicate as best as he could with Henri's expressions from reading his thoughts.

I'm not mad, but keep your face neutral–there's always spies. We're going to go to my rooms if you need to speak in a way other than blinking at me. Theodmon thought. *But you manipulated Lucas's mind to get him to kill Desmond.*

Theodmon meant it as a question, as he wasn't completely positive he was correct. However as Henri's eyes momentarily widened, Theodmon admitted perhaps wording it as a statement was more accurate.

We needed Desmond gone. I'm not mad. Theodmon restated. *But you should let Lucas know.*

Henri leaned in close to Theodmon, whispering so low Theodmon had to strain to hear him. "I didn't cause him to do something he didn't want to do, I can't conjure new thoughts. The desire and thoughts were already there, I just brought them to the forefront of his mind."

Encouragement in that way is still manipulation. Although Theodmon didn't want Henri to hear this, he was unable to stop his thoughts. *How many times have you manipulated our thoughts, feelings, and actions by rearranging our minds?*

Henri's eyes welled with tears before hardening. "You should know better than that," Henri spat. "I could count on my hands the number of times I've done that to anybody outside training or battle."

"Henri," Theodmon sighed, the pang in his chest intensifying.

"No." Henri stepped away from Theodmon. "I'll see you in a bit. For...I want to see Lucas and Aloysius."

Theodmon felt as if he had been slapped. How could Henri hold him to his thoughts? Theodmon would never say it out loud, and he didn't truly believe it either. He could control his actions, his words but to control his thoughts felt as if it were an impossible and unreasonable expectation.

Theodmon curtly turned on his heel to walk away from his friend.

Chapter Twenty-Five

Amaria sat on the beach, the muggy warm spring air hugging the moisture around her body–it had just rained, a normal occurrence in Raulle in April, so the humid droplets seemed to cling to her dress.

It had rained her last night at Forteresse les Blanche too.

Storms felt so different here. She had arrived at Provincia Palencia over a fortnight and a half ago and had immediately been thrust into wedding planning. And considering the bride hadn't arrived yet and Haerdnor would shut down or catch on fire anytime anything wedding related was asked of him, Amaria was having to do this wedding essentially blindfolded.

She could, of course, do the wedding however she wanted to–however, she did have some consideration for the bride and groom. Although, her consideration and patience for the groom was quickly eroding.

Her wings had also recently caused the destruction of a priceless vase that had been in her family for centuries. For some reason that was enough to make her feel trapped in her childhood home.

But in the rain, sitting on the sand with the waves of the ocean lapping her feet, Amaria felt as if she could breathe safely. The storm was chaos, but so was she. And she felt a peace, some sort of order in knowing that she could brave the destruction around her, and that she too were a force.

But she would still be finding craftsman mages to see if they could salvage some of the damage. She wished there was a way to salvage the damage done to her. Suddenly she could smell decaying bodies and blood. Amaria's throat was constricting, she wanted to scream, her vision was turning to black.

And then she passed out on the sand.

Amaria's eyes gently fluttered open as the waves gently lapped against her legs. She stood up gingerly, noticing that she didn't have wings, and that her hair was loosely braided against her back–it had been disheveled and falling pinned curls in the storm.

Where are my wings? She wondered, slowly turning around and processing the beautiful golden and pink sky. *Where did everyone go?*

"Amaria," a rich female voice called out. Amaria craned her head, looking for the source of the voice, when a hand was placed on her shoulder. Amaria turned, seeing a woman with golden hair flowing around her and her silver eyes sparkling. Her simple white dress blew in the wind.

"Child," the woman said. Her voice sounded as full and melodic as a symphony of violins. "Do you not recognize me?"

Amaria had nightmares of the goddesses' dark side. She recognized her. "Lady Ghagyn," she said with a swallow. "I am honored to be in your presence."

"You're in more than my presence, child," Ghagyn corrected. "You're in my realm." There was no malice or offense in her voice--She stated the fact as if she were noting that the sand had a million grains.

"It's beautiful," Amaria complimented.

Ghagyn hummed as if in agreement. Silently, for the gods knew how long, Amaria and the goddess walked side-by-side.

"You must be wondering why you're here," Ghagyn said as they approached the flickering blue-ish fire of a driftwood bonfire. Ghagyn sat down next to the fire with her legs curled underneath her. "Join me, child," she directed. "We've much to talk about."

Amaria's hands shook as she sat down across from Ghagyn, the goddesses' face flicking eerily in the flames. What could be so awful that Ghagyn would bring her from the world to this one?

"You have questions," Ghagyn said as if she had read Amaria's mind. Perhaps she had.

"Yes." Amaria's mouth was still as dry as the desert. "I was wondering why I don't have wings here."

It wasn't exactly what she was concerned about–Amaria had a million more questions, however it was a minor enough concern that she could ask without hopefully offending the goddess.

Ghagyn chuckled. "In my realm, you take your most comfortable physical form. It seems as if you preferred being without the faeries blessing."

"I preferred not having wings," Amaria answered honestly. "I used my appearance as a weapon–to seem innocuous. And that weapon is gone."

"But you prefer the magical power you have now from the faeries," Ghagyn noted.

"I enjoy the power, but I miss the subtlety of my magic before."

Ghagyn slowly blinked, taking in Amaria. "Interesting," she mused.

Amaria wasn't sure she liked having a goddess determine she was interesting.

"I've a few things to discuss," Ghagyn said, as if she hadn't just dissected Amaria emotionally. "Aloysius Chauvignon will be appearing at Provincia Palencia tonight. He will be on death's door. You will need all of your healers to prevent his fate from happening for just a while longer."

"Aloysius," Amaria gasped, her mind turbulent as a hurricane.

"Yes," Ghagyn dismissed. "The next thing I will tell you is more important. Are you listening?"

Amaria blinked back tears. Aloysius might die soon? How would she tell Theodmon?

"Amaria," Ghagyn said sternly.

"Yes, my lady," Amaria croaked.

"Dear child," Ghagyn said softly. "You're thirsty aren't you?" She waved her hand and a diamond goblet filled with golden liquid appeared. "Drink."

Amaria eyed the cup apprehensively. "What's this?"

"Nectar."

"As in the drink of the gods?" Amaria almost dropped the cup.

"You can safely drink it here–it's my land and you're under my protection," Ghagyn stated.

Amaria still looked at the nectar suspiciously, unconvinced she wouldn't burst into flames or otherwise be hurt by the elixir. Still, unwilling to be rude, she tentatively took a sip.

It tasted like cream and honey as it soothed her throat. She hadn't even realized how raw and scalding her throat had been until the nectar soothed it. "Thank you," she told Ghagyn graciously, setting the diamond goblet next to her.

Ghagyn nodded approvingly. "You're starting a war with Rindria."

Amaria blinked, unsure of how to reply. Yes, she was planning on it but should she try to deny it to a goddess? Was Ghagyn horrified? Proud? It was impossible to gauge a goddesses' emotions.

"I approve. They don't worship me, they kill my worshipers, and the country is a shithole because of it."

Amaria silently waited, unsure of how to respond to Ghagyn. The gods were temperamental and this goddess was in the middle of a rant–Amaria knew enough and had enough self-preservation to stay as far away from that as she could.

"When you go to war, you must trust one of my servants. You helped her when you were last in the country. Without this peasant girl, Rindria will stand."

"Are you saying the entire conquest depends on a singular peasant?" Amaria asked incredulously.

Ghagyn gave a cryptic smile, the light not quite reaching her eyes. "Your husband is more peasant to me than she is."

Amaria blinked, unsure of what Ghagyn was insinuating. The Chauvignons were one of the eldest families–even older than the Raulets. How could Theodmon be closer to a peasant than an actual peasant?

"Is she secret royalty? Someone from the Riam royalty we missed?"

Ghagyn burst into laughter. "No. That would be a twist for the ballads though wouldn't it be?" Ghagyn took the diamond goblet from its spot next to Amaria and drained it whole. "I base my versions of nobility on magical talent, not whatever you mortals believe in. If we are talking about her ties to a king, this servant of mine is a peasant."

Amaria's head throbbed. Ghagyn made no sense. "Alright, my Lady," Amaria said politely, trying to quickly gather her thoughts. "Does she knowingly serve you? I thought Rindria doesn't have temples for you–she does it in secret?"

"She doesn't actively serve me," Ghagyn said. "Not yet anyways. In fact, she won't know she's in my service until much later." She stood up, the fire swirling up to cloak her. "She's a good mage though, and is essential to your success. And you've already met her and she owes you a life debt."

Amaria had no idea what Ghagyn met. Nobody in Rindria owed her a life debt. Sighing, she rose to her feet. She needed to move to do something other than sit numbly, and besides, it felt rude to be this way while a goddess was standing.

"You'll be awakened soon." The lines around Ghagyn's eyes creased as if a goddess could show any signs of age. "It's best if I leave you now so your spirit won't be trapped in between two worlds."

"Trapped?" Amaria asked sharply.

"Nothing for you to be concerned about." Ghagyn's ghostly hand brushing against Amaria's cheek as she began to disintegrate in a soft golden light. "Magic seeks to connect with magic–walking between worlds is something you should take caution in. You're mortal, your body will seek to run to the mortal land. But your magic, your life force—it'll want to abandon your mortal body and stay in my realm."

Amaria wasn't sure that wasn't something she shouldn't be concerned about. In fact, that sounded like several things she should be concerned about.

"My Lady," Amaria began weakly.

"Sleep." Ghagyn said forcefully, exploding into a shimmer of pure light as Amaria's eyes forcefully snapped shut.

Someone was shaking her. There was shouting around her. She was cold.

"Amaria!" A male voice screamed above her. "You're awake."

Groaning, Amaria pushed her eyelids more forcefully together. What was going on? It was loud, and she was cold. She tried to sit up, blinking open her eyes.

"Not yet," the voice above her said authoritatively. "Not until Galen comes back."

"Galen?" Amaria groggily questioned. Galen Chironia was the resident healing mage of the Raulets and Provinica Palacina.

She forced herself up into a sitting position. She could see the outlines of people running around but it was still too bright to see the features of them.

"Are you alright?" His voice sounded familiar.

Shaking her head forcefully, as to clear the confusion, Amaria blinked. She slowly began to fully process her surroundings and she saw the hazy outline of her brother's face come into focus around her.

"Fine," she grumbled.

"You were convulsing–"

"Ghagyn seems to have a theatrical side when communicating with us mortals," Amaria dryly snapped.

"Ghagyn spoke with you? The *goddess*?" Haerdnor questioned.

"No need to be so surprised." Amaria was immediately defensive. "She's done it before."

Haerdnor crossed his arms. "What?"

"She's communicated with me, brought me to her realm before. I don't know why, but she talks to me. It's always cryptic, but its not malicious, it's almost how Father—"

"Just because they call mages children of Ghagyn," Haerdnor interrupted hotly, "doesn't mean it's true. Are you sure you aren't sick?"

"These visions started after a high priestess of Dandar, the god of seers, took my blood as payment, so probably not," Amaria said cooly. She forced herself onto her knees, the soaking folds of her dress clinging to her skin. "Let's go speak to Father."

"Shouldn't you rest?" Haerdnor held her arm in concern as he helped her to her feet. "You should really wait for Galen to treat you."

"Galen should save his energy," Amaria said, the words feeling like ash in her mouth. "Aloysius will be arriving tonight gravely injured."

Haerdnor tensed up next to her. "What do you mean?"

Amaria shook her head. "I don't know. Ghagyn didn't tell me more than that and he will require all the healers here to postpone his fate."

Haerdnor cursed. "The gods are cryptic."

"Trust me," Amaria grumbled darkly, "I know."

Haerdnor lowered his voice to a whisper. "What did Ghagyn tell you?"

Amaria shook her head. "Not now."

"We can use a mage link–"

"I'd rather explain it once to you and Father—it's confusing," Amaria said. "Please, just wait for a few more minutes."

Haerdnor scowled, but he didn't press further on the issue. Together, the twins steadied themselves in silence as they embarked down a long window-filled corridor to the offices of their father.

The offices of misery, Amaria had heard it referred to in jest once. Others called it the offices of death–it was a place to be feared as it was where Aaron Raulet, with the stroke of a quill, decided who lived or died with an indifferent disdain. Amaria thought of it as the offices of lectures—a reminder that she may never be good enough.. However, in a way, her father's offices were comforting to her. Amaria had learned many things from her father there, he had expressed pride in her there, and he had given her authority to act as an extension of him in those offices.

At the end of the corridor there was a large double door made of dark wood, possibly cherry, with engravings of the Creation on it. From Ides creation, to the marriage of Rhaerus, to the tumultuous creations of Iston, and Ghagyn's creations and gifts being given, and humans being formed with the animals, and Ghagyn gifting certain animals with magic, the beginning was there. Iena and Iesus with life and death stood at the very top of the arch, and a few minor gods and goddesses were carved in.

"In case we ever wanted to forget the faith," Haerdnor muttered darkly under his breath.

"Be respectful!" Amaria said.

"You always revered the gods more than–"

"What?" Amaria hissed, daring her brother to finish his foolhardy sentence.

"Ah, more than me," Haerdnor said. Amaria knew that was not what he was originally going to say. At least the fire Haerdnor summoned hadn't burned away all of his sensibilities and self-preservation instincts.

They finally reached the door. "We need to speak with our father," Amaria told the armed guard.

"Does he know you are here?" The guard asked.

"Nope," Haerdnor said, popping the 'p'. "Tell him we're here."

"Duke Raulet told me he doesn't wish to be disturbed–"

"I understand," Haerdnor said. "You can tell him you turned away his children. Did my father tell you he gave us permission to speak to him regarding family affairs whenever? There's a wedding coming up. You know what, you're probably right, it's not important."

He turned on his heel, walking away from the guard. He could no longer hide his smirk, and Amaria was struggling to hide hers. She turned away from the guard, walking down the hall.

"My Lord. My Lady." The guard's voice raised a half octave. "Please wait. I will let your father know. One moment please." He knocked on the door and stepped into the chambers.

"I didn't know you had an ounce of subtlety in you," Amaria said sarcastically.

"I was told I can't light all my issues on fire," Haerdnor said. "Shame, it's more effective."

"I'll pay you five gold dragons if you burn down Father's door."

"Make it fifty and I'll consider it."

"Twenty," Amaria countered.

"Forty-five," Haerdnor said.

"Lord Raulet, Marchioness Chauvignon," the guard called out, interrupting them. "Your father is ready to see you."

"Thank you." Haerdnor strode towards the door, Amaria quickly lifting the hem of her skirt and following him. As they passed the guard, she gave him a short nod in acknowledgement.

As they passed the threshold of the office, Haerdnor immediately moved towards the plush, navy chair, upheld by dark mahogany wood, across from Aaron's desk, not waiting for an invitation to sit down.

"Father," Amaria lowered her head upon entering the office. "Pleasure."

Aaron nodded at Amaria, as he finished writing something, dripping his quill back into the lapis lazuli inkwell. Amaria sat down, slowly smoothing down her skirts. "I hope this is important."

"She's having visions apparently," Haerdnor said. "From Ghagyn."

"I know it sounds insane," Amaria quickly interjected. "I've been having them since the High Priestess of Dandar took my blood...and...I know it's her."

Aaron sighed. "Alright," he said.

"You believe me?" Amaria asked.

"You've always been a powerful mage. I don't have reason to doubt that the goddess of magic would talk to you. Gods have been known to communicate with their favored," Aaron said simply. "What did the goddess say?"

"She said that we would need a Riam peasant's help or else we'd never conquer Rindria. This Riam is a mage and apparently she owes me a life debt."

"Who is she?" Haerdnor asked.

"I don't know."

"Why does she owe you a life debt?" Aaron asked.

"I don't know," Amaria repeated, her face starting to burn.

"Do you have any idea on what this person's magic is?" Aaron pressed.

"No," Amaria said. "It's not much, but it's important–"

"I have records of known or suspected mages in all the countries," Aaron interrupted. "I'll give you a list of Riam ones and see if you can work from there."

"Thank you." Amaria looked out the window to see the twinkling stars. In the distance, bells began ringing.

"Anything else?" Aaron prompted.

Amaria's blood chilled. "Aloysius," she muttered. "Oh gods, Aloysius is going to come here gravely injured."

"When?" Aaron asked.

"I think...I think he's here now," Amaria whispered, the horrible realization of why the bells started ringing hitting her. "Ghagyn said he needs all of our healers to survive."

Chapter Twenty-Six

The last time the bells rang at Provincia Palencia, Delphina died.

As Amaria ran out of her father's office and down the polished corridors she scowled–the intrusive thought kept appearing. *What if Aloysius dies now?*

No. She told herself. *We can save him. Ghagyn said so.*

With a jolt, she remembered that she didn't need to run down the corridors. "Open those windows!"

The guard she commanded turned towards her. "My Lady?"

It was night, and they were on the fifth floor. She understood why the guard was looking at her as if she was insane. However, it wasn't it his job to question her or her sanity. "Open it."

"My Lady," the guard conceded.

"Amaria," Haerdnor shouted behind her. "What in all the gods' names?"

"Good, you can help," Amaria turned towards him. "Get the healers. Have them set the hall on the first floor as a healing center."

"It can't be that dire...." Haerdnor said, sounding as if he was trying to convince himself.

"Close that window in a few moments," Amaria commanded the guard, before jumping out the window, extending her wings. As she began to fly, she heard Haerdnor cursing her name behind her.

The wind and rain whirled around her while the sea raged below. Perhaps the gods had sent them a warning--hurricanes were bad omens. She would go and sacrifice to every god and goddess with a shrine in the city as soon as Aloysius was safe.

In the distance she saw a horse with the limp form of a person on its back.

Gracefully, she landed next to the guards stationed on the north gate of the estate, protecting them from the rest of the city.

"Open the gates," Amaria commanded.

"The bells!"

"That's Aloysius Chauvignon," Amaria said. "If he dies because of your failure to obey a direct order, I'll have your head."

The guards looked at each other for an impossibly long ten, twenty, thirty seconds. And then they shrugged, and bowed their heads towards Amaria. "My Lady," they conceded, moving the mechanisms to allow the gates to open.

Amaria flew upwards to the top of the battement, her entire body lighting itself with the heavenly glow of her silver aura. She saw the horses chasing after Aloysius through the city. Amaria breathed, moving her energy to the plants growing around them. She couldn't use fire without burning the city and her citizens. Water and wind were risky with a tropical storm brewing–she didn't need to help it grow. So, earth it was. She willed the branches to life, and through her command, every branch around the archers and horses stabbed them and strangled them.

Cover them. Amaria moved her magic to force the vines to submerge all of the dead bodies as she flew back down to stand near the guards.

"The attackers are dead," Amaria told the guard. "Covered in plants. Bring the horses to the butchers in the slums as a gift. And bring the humans to the Drowning Tombs."

"They're dead?" The guard asked as if he didn't realize the reason why Amaria wanted their bodies in the Drowning Tombs was for their limbs to be chopped up so it was easier to hide what had occurred.

Amaria nodded curtly, already turning her attention to the man bleeding out on the horse. She ran towards him, her heels loudly thumping against the stone pathway. "Aloysius," she breathed before she even saw the man's features. "Get Lord Chauvignon inside. Healers will be waiting in the main hall."

"He's bleeding too much," the guard said.

Amaria looked at Aloysius, her blood freezing in fear. The guard was right, moving Aloysius would be a death sentence now. The horse's back, previously gray, was covered in rust and red. Aloysius's skin seemed to be so pale it was gray, his eyes shut, and his chest still. The healers were inside and to leave Aloysius without healing was also a death sentence, especially since he was still bleeding heavily.

Amaria shut her eyes. *Oh Ignoia,* she prayed to the healing goddess. *Please allow Aloysius to survive this.* Shaking, she stepped over towards Aloysius, frost appearing at her fingertips. She gently moved her hands over his whole body, freezing him. The bleeding slowed, but Amaria knew this was a temporary solution, and a risky one at that.

She looked at the horse. She was never a good rider and the horse could likely sense her nerves. "Drive him to the estate," Amaria commanded a guard.

The guard, without argument, mounted the horse, spurring the animal to ride towards the palace. Amaria heavily sighed, watching them depart for a moment before turning back to the other guards. "Remember the bodies," she told them before she flew off towards the building once more.

Amaria was barking orders as soon as she landed at the front doors of the palace, ensuring that the healers were ready for when Aloysius arrived.

Within minutes, the front doors flung open, two guards carrying Aloysius's limp body. "I've made a station," Galen Chironia said, directing the guards to set his patient on a table covered with white cloth. Aloysius, while he had looked bad outside, looked as if he were a man touched by death himself in the light of the candles and lanterns.

Galen placed his hands upon Aloysius' body, his hands glowing green. The color dulled as it mixed with a rusty hue and Galen's face paled. "His magic is leaking."

"What does that mean?" Amaria questioned, her voice rising in pitch.

"His magic is repelling mine," Galen explained, the wrinkles around his forehead becoming more profound. "His magic will have to be contained before I can do anything."

"Then contain it," Amaria said.

"My Lady," Galen said, "the best way to contain magic is le seda amagia fin. Is there some around, my Lady Extractor?"

Internally, Amaria recoiled, although her exterior remained unruffled. She understood Galen's point, and it was apt. Le seda amagia fin was a carefully guarded secret of the Extractors, and as the only Extractor in residence–actually, the head of the Order, Amaria would be the only one to have some. She didn't however, and while she was privy to the recipe, she wasn't a healer or potion master and the recipe was complex. And she usually only used it for Extractions. She hadn't ever considered a healer would use the substance–but it made sense that a drug made to suppress magic could be used for something like this.

"No." Amaria brought her head to her hands. Aloysius couldn't die. There was a way to save him–Ghagyn had insinuated as much. She paused, lifting her face to look at Galen. "Best way?" She questioned, remembering what he said. "There's other ways?"

"A more powerful mage could redirect his magic away from mine while I worked," Galen said. "Once he is somewhat healed, I predict his magic will stop leaking enough for me to finish without other mages intervention. War magic," Galen shook his head somberly, "it's fickle–it can't handle its wielder being weak and it'll seek to expand as to save itself."

Amaria gritted her teeth. She knew what Galen meant, she didn't need to quibble about his diction and semantics. "I'll do it," she said, moving towards Galen and Aloysius. "Where are you healing first?"

"Direct his magic away from his chest and arms," Galen directed.

Amaria nodded, placing her hands on Aloysius's stomach. She closed her eyes, sending up a quick prayer to the gods.

"Ready." Amaria's eyes jolted open, her magic humming around her. Brilliant silver leaked from her eyes, as if her magic was escaping, yet her fear was more palpable than her aura. She forced her magic to form a wall around Aloysius's, containing it, separating it from Galen's magic. Her fists shook, her skin becoming a sickly yellow color, as she pressed them harder into Aloysius's stomach.

As she did so, Galen worked over Aloysius's wounds, pulling bacteria from them, closing the wounds, dressing them with antibacterial disinfectant, and a million other steps Amaria didn't know or pay attention to. She was too focused on containing Aloysius's magic.

"My Lady," Galen said once Aloysius's chest no longer had multiple stab wounds, instead having multiple scars and stitches. "Stop blocking his magic."

Her hands shaking, Amaria stopped her flow of magic, sitting back on her heels. As she placed her hands down, the room began to spin, thanks to the adrenaline leaving her body. Galen, his magic pulsating around him, touched Aloysius's head.

He closed his eyes, breathing deeply. "Good," Galen announced. "His magic isn't fighting me." Galen placed his two fingers on the side of Aloysius's neck. "There's a pulse.

It's weak but it's consistent. Lord Chauvignon might survive the night yet." Galen looked over at Amaria, her hands covered in blood. "Thank you, Marchioness. You were most helpful. Why don't you clean up and allow the healing mages to finish our work?"

Amaria nodded numbly as she stood up, preparing to depart. "Excuse me." Amaria brushed past the healers, her worry concerning Aloysius's situation quickly escalating to merge with her guilt of the last death that occurred in these halls. The room seemed too small, the walls seemed to be constricting against her, her fear and instability was growing as rapidly as a vine, choking her as ivy choked stone walls.

She had to leave. Now. The estate was suddenly unbearably hot, but she couldn't leave still covered in blood. She couldn't leave without alms, money, sacrifices to the gods, money, and guards—this last part was so her father wouldn't yell. After all, who in Raulle would seek to harm her? She was being cocky perhaps, many would love to harm her—but in truth, who could harm her? Especially now with the increase in power in her magic and the sheer intimidation of her appearance.

She would make herself presentable, gather her tools, and then depart into the city to conduct her business. Amaria picked up her skirt and maintained as much decorum as she could, quickly rushing upstairs to her rooms, walking faster and faster until she broke out into a sprint, stopping only once the door was shut behind her and she could cry within the privacy of her own chambers.

Amaria departed Provincia Palencia for Raulle nearly an hour later, two guards closely tailing her. Her father had wanted a carriage, and Amaria had come to a compromise that he could send a carriage to pick her up—the temple district was almost pressing against the north gate of the estate; she wouldn't be going far. Besides, Amaria needed to clear her head.

The lanterns sparkled in the night, and sweet smelling smoke puffed nearby. People had already begun to celebrate the wedding of the Raulet heir with alms for the poor and bustling markets preparing for the influx of visitors. Amaria noted the paper lanterns and streamers hanging from almost every window and doorway. While the decorations were not as lavish as they were at Provincia Palencia, they were equally as colorful—perhaps even more. While Provincia Palencia tended to stick with whites, golds, silvers, pinks, and oranges—the colors of the gods of marriage, the Raulets, and the Brassirs; the decorations here were every color in the rainbow. Amaria pushed her way past dancing in the streets and vendors shouting about their wares, hoping for a sale.

However, she couldn't celebrate right now. Amaria clutched her hands together, the gesture hiding the visible gestation of how unnerved she had become. She had to remain the appearance of aloofness—she was unshakable, unobtainable, otherworldly.

And shaking hands destroys that image when you have wings? Amaria told herself, knowing she was stupid. Still, shaking hands was a sign of imperfection, and while nobody else may notice, Amaria knew this and would hold herself to her own high standards.

Amaria walked through the city, distributing food and alms to those less fortunate, who hung around the temple district hoping for such gifts. She blocked out the "gods bless you," "many thanks, My Lady," and "good fortunes," preferring to distance herself from the performative nature of alms—from both giver and recipient.

After several blocks, the crowds died down, and Amaria was left in a circular rotunda, several stone buildings facing each other. This was the heart of the temple district, where the most powerful gods and goddesses reside away from the bustle of the city and the temples of less powerful, less terrifying gods. Breathing heavily, Amaria felt a sense of peace envelop her, thankful to be away from the excessive noise and livery of the parties. She glanced around, and walked towards her left to a smaller, gray stone building that had two bronze statues, their toes shiny, adorning its doors.

The female statue to Amaria's left had her hands outstretched. The goddess's face was warm as if she would wrap you in a blanket and hug you near the fireplace after a storm; there also was a deer wrapped near her feet and butterflies settled upon the folds of her dress. The statue on Amaria's right had her arms closer towards her body, and she held a ring of keys. Her face was sterner, as if she had a responsibility to fulfill and she could not be deterred from it, and a serpent sat curled at her feet.

The Twin Goddesses, Thoxlena and Oxmera, Amaria thought. *I suppose this is fitting for the first temple I go to.* Oxmera is the goddess of secrecy and duty and Thoxlena is the goddess of forgiveness, mercy, and miracles.

Bowing her head respectfully, Amaria pushed open the large cherry double doors as she stepped into the chapel. Amaria's dress dragged along the blue stone floor as she paused, taking in the beauty. The ceiling above her was entirely stained glass, the sunlight pouring through and causing colored lights to dance across the walls, floor, and furniture.

We honor the gods in everything. And the beauty in our world is a reflection of that.

Amaria couldn't stop the sour thought that entered her head next: *if beauty is a reflection of the gods being honored, what is the depravity and horror in this world a reflection of?*

Directly to the right of the door sat a jeweled stone basin of water. Beyond it were stone shrines decorated with a mirage of items--cousins, jewels, dolls, food, seashells, rugs, bottles of win, and flowers sat piled high. A few lit candles illuminated the table.

Pausing at the basin, Amaria dipped her hands within it, sprinkling some water upon her forehead and drying her hands on the nearby towel. "Allow me to be cleansed from my wrongdoings in your temple, great goddess."

Amaria, pulling out one of the bags of money she had packed, brought it to the shrines, and lightly placed the pouch upon the altar. Inside the bag there were two hundred gold dragons. Amaria kept her head lowered, moving behind the altar to the circular stone tables behind them—lit and unlit candles resting upon them.

Directly across from these candles there were prayer benches and a statue of the stern-looking goddess, Oxmera, upon the wall. Her heart sinking to her stomach, Amaria kneeled in front of the goddess.

"Lady of secrecy and duty, hear my prayer." Amaria picked up an incense stick, placing it in the flames of a candle to light it. Amaria resisted the urge to cough as the smoke engulfed her, feeling as if her nose was burning due to the overpowering scent of frankincense and cedar. "I beg you, Goddess Oxmera, to understand and alleviate the burden of duty and secrets."

Amaria, having said the traditional opening, silently bowed her head in prayer. She wasn't quite sure what to say to the goddess, so instead she reflected on her duties, on her secrets. She had accumulated many in her life, and she would accumulate more, only being freed from her burden when she died.

"Please," Amaria ended up saying, "let me handle my burden with grace." She bowed her head, kissed the altar, and stood up–her time with Oxmera, thankfully, was over.

Amaria averted her gaze from Oxmera's altar to look to her left, seeing a brazier lit with soft, orange flames. Behind that stood a long, polished wooden altar, adorned with a heavy book, wine, two jeweled goblets, and more candles in front of a statue of the kinder-looking goddess–Thoxlena.

Amaria gingerly moved towards the shrine, bowing her head as she silently lit a candle and knelt on the prayer bench in front of the goddess. The smoky scent of incense listed from the candle and the stick, its end red before Amaria blew the stick out, setting it down before bringing her hands together, her wide sleeves nearly engulfing her wrists. "Oh goddess of mercy and forgiveness, Lady Thoxlena, I beg you to hear my thanks."

Thank you for Aloysius being alive. Thank you for my family. Thank you for a husband that loves me. My magic. My children. My health. My security. My wealth. Amaria took a deep breath. *I'm glad I'm alive.*

Forgive me for the lives I've taken. And forgive me for the lives I've failed to save. Amaria felt a tear run down her face. She wiped her eyes with her sleeve before she blew out the incense, the smoke trailing downwards as she set the stick back upon the golden plate near the foot of the shrine. *And forgive me for all the lives I'm about to take.*

Chapter Twenty-Seven

When Amaria woke in the morning, she rubbed her bloodshot eyes, her body still heavy. She hadn't come back home until around two in the morning, something the assigned guards had relentlessly complained about. One tried to make the argument of propriety, and while there was a point to be made there, Amaria had shot back that she wasn't going to businesses that ran in the night but to honor the gods. If anybody wanted to bring up impropriety for her honoring every god in gratitude for saving her brother-in-law's life she would be delighted to hear what their idea of proprietary was.

Still, she groaned when the maids opened the curtains and scurried around her room.

"Go away," Amaria grumbled into her pillows.

"Good morning, Marchioness Chauvignon," said one maid good-naturedly. "I hope you slept well."

"Leave," Amaria said.

"Unfortunately, you must get ready," said another. "His Grace has instructed us to have you prepared to greet the bride."

Amaria groaned. Of course she couldn't have a day to relax and recover. She had to represent her House, show the bride marrying in as the new lady of the estate how a proper Raulet woman was. Rich dresses, heavy jewels, intricately styled hair, and perfect makeup was what was required for the appearance function of today at least.

"Draw a bath," Amaria rubbed her eyes. "Jasmine and rose soap."

"Yes, my Lady." The first maid curtsied before she scurried off.

"Prepare my stockings and corset," Amaria told the other as she sat up in bed. "You'll need to tightlace me for today and it'll have to accommodate my wings." Amaria swung her feet out of her bed, stretching as her feet hit the floor. "Do also inform my brother that he and his fiancée will be accompanying me to the temples to pray today, and to distribute alms if there's time."

"Yes, My Lady," the girl said. "Forgive me, but are you sure tight lacing—"

Amaria scowled. "What's your name?"

"Dela," the maid answered.

"Dela, the whole point of greeting the new, soon-to-be-Lady Raulet is to show her the pinnacle of being a Lady with the surname of Raulet. It's not supposed to be prudent or sustainable."

"My Lady," Dela said, clearly aghast.

"Spare me," Amaria dismissed as she pulled her silk robe over her nightgown. It didn't fit over her wings but it was too late to pull it off of her–how undignified. She would deal with her mistake until she reached her bath. "Go tell me if the bath is ready."

Dela departed and Amaria laid upon her bed again, breathing in deeply as she stared up at the canopy. She felt her chest rising and sinking, her hands clasped over her stomach, her back sinking into the plush mattress.

These had been her chambers for eighteen years. Yet she felt almost like a stranger in them now, as if she wasn't fully home anymore. Something seemed to be missing. She sighed heavily. With all this wedding planning, she hadn't been able to see her children fully. Perhaps she would change that today and have them sleep in her chambers.

Sighing, Amaria forced herself out of bed, moving towards her wardrobe to see several dresses in varying shades of blue. Amaria rummaged through them, trying to decide which to wear. One color washed her out, another was too close to white it would feel disrespectful, another was too plain, one was too gaudy. Amaria groaned, looking at her other dresses, shades of red, silver, and gold. Her hands, however, stopped at a purple dress–almost eggplant. It was heavy, with broad sleeves and delicate stitching. However, the back was open—perfect to accommodate her wings so they could give the appearance of a further impossible standard.

She smiled, pulling the dress out and draping it over the chair by the vanity. On her vanity she saw a red velvet box, a note affixed to it. She moved towards it, recognizing the handwriting of her father.

Barely able to breathe, Amaria broke open the seal.

A Rose is a Rose no matter where it is planted.

A.R.

I trust you'll bring me pride.

As I've been told. Amaria slowly popped open the lid to the red velvet box. As she did so, she saw a dainty gold chain supporting a ruby rose, emerald leaves laying on the flower's left side. Casting a look behind her, Amaria bit her lip and moved over to the bed, setting the velvet box on top of the blankets, keeping the lid propped open.

She didn't want this to be on the vanity where anyone could easily see it. It felt intimate–personal–as if Aaron was stating his pride in her. And while she would soon wear that pride as a sword, she needed to bask in its comfort first.

The doors to her rooms opened, the maids entering to let her know her bath was ready.

After her bath, Amaria stood in her chambers, silently letting her maids dress her in an eggplant and gray colored gown sewn with silver thread, making forth designs of leaves, birds, and roses. The underdress' thin, silver sleeves hung off her shoulders, leaving her collarbone exposed.

"Hand me the silver belt and leave." Amaria looked at herself critically in the mirror as one of the maids finished pinning her hair, stepping down from the stool.

The maids looked uneasily at each other and Amaria crossly scowled. She didn't need a nanny, whatever her father thought.

"You can tell my father you did your job," Amaria said tersely.

"My Lady–" A maid gasped as the door opened.

"You can leave now or take an extended nap in my chambers," Amaria threatened, summoning her magic to her chest. The maids gave each other an uneasy look, as if debating which Raulet was worse to disobey.

"I'd listen to her," Catalina Raulet said with a small laugh, leaning against the doorframe.

Amaria's head whirled around. "Catalina!" She beamed at her younger sister from across the room. "You've arrived early." She looked at the maids, wind pushing through the chambers in a gushing burst.

"We'll be in the corridor," one maid said, the rest curtseying hastily before departing.

"I figured you might need help," Catalina laughed, removing her habit, her long dark hair falling down her back, the ripples in it like a cascading waterfall. "I know how Father is."

"Thank you," Amaria said, her shoulders sinking as she felt the tension in her back leave.

Catalina shrugged. "Besides, the temple can be stuffy."

"So can court," Amaria pointed out.

"At least the court has parties." Catalina moved over towards Amaria's wardrobe. "Can I borrow a dress?"

"I'm sure you have dresses here," Amaria said.

"I want to wear yours."

Amaria shrugged. "I'm not wearing it anyways."

Catalina already had her hands on a golden gown. Amaria couldn't help but notice Catalina had kept a wide berth away from the blue dresses, as if she was publicly shielding herself away from the acknowledgment of being a Raulet.

"Has the bride arrived yet?" Catalina asked.

Amaria shook her head. "No. I believe she's supposed to arrive today."

"I heard she's a wind-mage," Catalina remarked, perching herself on the edge of the bed. "What's this?" She held up the necklace, dangling the gold chain in between her two fingers.

"A gift from Father." Amaria hoped Catalina wouldn't press further, or worse, see the note on the bed.

Catalina huffed, placing the necklace back in the box.

"You should dress," Amaria told her.

Catalina held up the piece of parchment. "Nice try. What was this a present for? Father rewarding his favorite psychopath for her actions in the Drowning Tombs? Oh, was it for getting wings? That has to be his new favorite novelty–"

"Catalina," Amaria warned. "Don't."

Catalina met her eyes in the mirror, a few silent seconds passing between them before Catalina shrugged, hopping down from off the bed, moving to take her clothes off. "Don't you dare summon the maids."

Amaria smirked. "Are you sure you don't want help looking presentable? Father–"

"You're enjoying this too much for someone who looks like they can barely breathe," Catalina grumbled. Amaria grinned, laughing as she moved towards Catalina, helping her with the laces in her dress.

Nearly an hour later, Amaria and Catalina were fully dressed, with their hair and faces done, a veil pinned into Amaria's curls and a shawl draped over her shoulders, and both girls with jewels hanging from their neck and ears. And it was just in time because the maids came to announce the bride had arrived at the estate.

"What do you think Naomi Brassir is like?" Catalina asked as they descended the grand staircase.

"Probably exhausted and terrified." Amaria remembered how she felt when she was delivered to Forteresse les Blanche before her wedding. Unfortunately for Naomi Brassir, she would never be able to have what Amaria had with Theodmon with her groom. Haerdnor's proclivities would make that impossible.

However, Haerdnor wasn't cruel. Amaria, for Naomi's sake, prayed that she and Haerdnor could develop a friendship. She didn't have much time to tell Catalina this, as they reached the great hall and were stepping inside, beaming to welcome their guests and their new sister-in-law.

"Lady Brassir," Amaria said warmly as she approached a woman with curly straw-colored hair. Naomi turned towards Amaria, her green eyes widened in apprehension. Naomi, however, seemed determined to look Amaria in the eyes–and only in the eyes.

"Marchioness Chauvignon," Naomi said softly, momentarily lowering her head respectfully as she stood.

"There's no need for that," Amaria said. "You're marrying my brother, you can call me Amaria. I apologize for the delay. You came earlier than expected." She turned towards Naomi's father. "Marquis Brassir, I hope your journey went well."

"As well as a sea journey can go," he replied diplomatically.

"I'm glad," Amaria said politely. "Please, do not hesitate to let me know if there is anything the Raulets can do to make your stay more comfortable." She looked over at Naomi. "If there is no objection, I would be delighted to show Lady Brassir around her future home."

Marquis Brassir nodded, waving his hand dismissively. "Have fun, Naomi."

Naomi's eyes widened slightly, before she composed herself. "Yes, my Lad–Amaria, that will be very nice. Thank you for your hospitality."

She's terrified of me. Amaria realized. She couldn't explain why, but it hurt that Naomi Brassir reacted this way to her. She wanted Haerdnor to be happy. She wanted Naomi to integrate well.

She didn't want Naomi to be like Liara.

The realization made Amaria feel as if she was drowning, and she, along with Naomi, both were silent–deep in their own thoughts, until they reached the gardens. Catalina trailed behind them, humming.

"The wings can be a bit much," Amaria said lightheartedly. "At least I always have spare feathers for my pillows."

Naomi chuckled. "It's a bit much," she agreed slowly. "They're beautiful—just like your home."

"My home, *your home,* is a bit much as well," Amaria stated.

"Father is frustrating that way," Catalina pitched in. "If it's not ostentatious, it's a waste of money spent."

Naomi turned slightly to survey Catalina. "Father?"

"Catalina Raulet," Catalina said with a small smirk.

"I was told you were a priestess."

"I am. I just ditched the habit today. I get a lot more privacy in my ancestral home without it," Catalina said. "But let's show you the hidden parts of the garden–you'll need privacy as the future Duchess Raulet, no?"

Naomi gave a shaky laugh. "Yes, I suppose...uh, thanks."

"It's overwhelming," Amaria said sympathetically. "And I'm sure you have questions about your future husband, rumors you want confirmed or denied."

"Yes." Naomi looked petrified in admitting the truth to Catalina and Amaria.

"You can ask us anything you wish about Haerdnor," Catalina said. "We'll answer honestly."

Naomi paused in her tracks, the birds chipping behind her in the garden. "How do I know this isn't a trick?"

Amaria and Catalina met each other's eyes. It was a wise question from Naomi. Already, Amaria found herself liking this girl, and she wanted Naomi to like her. Better yet, Amaria found herself wanting Naomi to be happy, protected, and loved by Haerndor–although it may not be in the traditional sense.

"You can't," Amaria said. "We can only give you our word that we mean no harm, and the knowledge that you'll be a Raulet and that Raulet's are protective of each other." She plucked a flower from a bush, handing the yellow and pink blooms to Naomi. "But this is your chance to get information–you don't have to trust all of it, but you'll have information."

"Information is power," Naomi said. "Do you truly want me to believe that you are handing me a weapon against your brother?"

"Power is power," Catalina corrected. "And fire and wind are a mix that can be destructive. You're looking for ulterior motives? Fine. I don't want your magic and my hot head brother's magic burning down my ancestral home–it barely survived his and Amaria's childhood."

For a moment, only the birds and the pittering of water from the decorative fountains in the garden could be heard as all three women stared at each other. And then, as the sun peeked through the clouds, the three of them burst into laughter.

"How many times did Amaria and Lord Raulet almost burn down the estate?" Naomi said.

"Countless times," Catalina said. "I believe the first time was when they were seven. Haer cut Amaria's dolls hair–"

"Oh it wasn't for that reason," Amaria protested, feeling as if a weight had lifted from her chest as she saw Catalina and Naomi giggling together. Her family would survive this marriage.

She hadn't even realized she had that fear until it had dissipated.

Chapter Twenty-Eight

After a few hours of talking in the garden, the girls departed from each other. Catalina took Naomi to see her rooms while Amaria did none of the things she should have done--checking on Aloysius, preliminary intelligence work, dismembering bodies in the Drowning tombs. Instead, she walked through the gardens, basking in the late-afternoon sun.

The tips of Amaria's wings brushed against the white petals of the flowering trees as she breathed deeply, trying to find peace in this moment. She needed a moment to herself–a moment with no responsibilities. She closed her eyes, tilting her face up towards the sky to let the setting sun warm her.

For a moment, her worries melted away, as she listened to the bush crickets in the flowers and the trickling water from the fountains. And then, in the distance, Amaria heard two male voices arguing. She paused in her tracks, the voices becoming louder.

"Oliver!"

Amaria took a deep breath and let it out through her nose with her teeth clenched. So much for her moment.

"Oliver, wait. I didn't want this."

That was her brother's voice. Amaria peeked over the expertly trimmed hedges, then crouched behind the bush, laying down to ensure her wings did not poke out through the shrubbery and betray her hiding spot.

"I didn't want to be married," Haerdnor said as Amaria slowed her breath, keeping her hands folded over her chest. "Oliver, you've to understand that."

"I do," Oliver said. "I'm not an idiot, whatever you might think."

"I've never thought you were an idiot—"

"Save it," Oliver snapped.

"Oliver," Haerdnor pleaded, his voice breaking. "We can work through this. Nothing has to change."

"You don't get it, do you? We could never last–"

"Because we're men?" Haerdnor said.

"Because I'm an untitled Lord, and that's all I'll ever be," Oliver said, his voice shaking. "I don't have obligations like Duke Raulet will."

"I'm not Duke Raulet," Haerdnor said quickly.

"But you will be. And you will have obligations to fulfill–obligations I can't help with."

"I'm not asking you to." Haerdnor's voice cracked.

"I'm sorry, Haerdnor."

Amaria heard the departing footsteps and a loud thump upon the ground, the sobs growing louder and more intense. She felt pains in her chest as her heart broke alongside her brother's. Amaria groaned. She would be embarrassed and horrified if Haerdnor had witnessed her wallowing the same way, but she couldn't leave him like this, sobbing in the garden, alone in his own despair.

"Haerdnor," she said, stepping from behind the hedges.

"Amaria." Haerdnor scrambled to his feet and wiped his eyes. "I– how are you?"

Amaria moved forward to hug her twin. "I heard what happened."

Haerdnor tensed up in her arms before he relaxed. And then he sobbed. "I hate it. I didn't ask for this."

"I know," Amaria said softly.

"I hate that he's acting like I want this. I'd give it all up to be with him!"

Amaria knew this was a lie. Her brother, much like her, was too accustomed to power and wealth to give it up. The Raulets would cling to their status, wealth, and methods of political, economic, and military power until it was stolen from their dead hands.

However, she knew Haerdnor's love for Oliver wasn't a lie, and that her brother was truly, deeply in pain.

"I know," she repeated. "Let's get you inside."

His eyes glazing over, Haerdnor let her guide him from the gardens. As they made their way inside the estate, Amaria couldn't help but note what a beautiful prison the garden could be. Perhaps it was more beautiful than the glamorous, yet cold castle they lived in. The castle was easily imaginable as being restrictive, but the garden seemed to have freedom. The idea of freedom was dangerous when it was a facade.

Silently, the twins wandered up to Haerdnor's chambers, deep in their own thoughts. Amaria didn't even notice they crossed Naomi's path until they were face to face.

"Lady Brassir," Amaria said politely. "Excuse us."

"Lord Raulet?" Naomi asked.

Amaria curtly nodded, her body tensing, hoping her brother wouldn't speak. "Yes, but it seems as if he's been drinking in preparation for the festivities," she said quickly.

"Festivities?" Haerdnor's lip curled. "Why would I celebrate? I'd be happy if she left."

Naomi stepped back, her eyes watering.

"He doesn't mean that," Amaria said hastily, pushing Haerdnor down the hall away from Naomi. "It's the alcohol–"

"I'm sober," Haerdnor said.

"As a dead man," Amaria hissed in his ear. "Which you'll be if you don't keep your mouth shut."

Haerdnor glared, but stayed silent until they rounded a corner. Once out of site, Amaria pushed her twin against the wall, glowering at him as she crossed her arms.

"Do you really have to treat her like that?" Amaria crossly asked.

"Like what?" Haerdnor challenged.

"Like you despise her. Like you rather her not be here–"

"But I *would* rather her not be here," Haerdnor said.

"Get over yourself! You're home, nothing in your life really changes while this girl has had her entire life overturned. She doesn't want to marry you either. Be a gentleman."

"I'll be polite–"

"I don't mean chillingly cold and distant. You're going to be tied to her for the rest of your life, the very least you can do is be friendly." Amaria scowled. "Go apologize to her."

"I don't see–"

"Stop acting like Father, and have some accountability and care for the people around you." Amaria grabbed Haerdnor's arm, digging her nails in to draw blood.

"Oh that's rich, coming from you," Haerdnor retorted, pulling his arm out of her grasp. "How many people have you murdered recently?"

"None actually," Amaria said. "I've not harmed a single soul since we returned to Thestitiunia."

"Oh, give it up," Haerdnor snorted. "I know about Liara. How'd you do it?"

"I didn't." Amaria's expression turned flat as she lowered her voice to a barely audible hiss. "I can't deny that I wish it could have been me, but my methods would've been very different."

"And what would your methods have been?" Haerdnor asked lazily.

"Simple," Amaria smiled breezily. "I'd wait for war to break out, nudge her into making an escape while she believed it was her idea, plant intelligence on her, and then when she's escaping in the night, she's mistakenly killed as an intruder. We find the intelligence on her and well, there's no tears over a traitor now is there?"

Haerdnor snorted. "And I'm the one who acts like Father? Gods, do you realize that you're essentially him?"

Amaria glared. "It's not my fault I got the worst of him--he turned me into a weapon while you got to be the heir."

"Oh, yes. I've clearly had it *so much easier* than you. I got to be the heir because the laws dictate it, but he values you more." Haerdnor's voice reverberated down the halls. "You're better than me in the things that he values. You can't tell me that you weren't amazing in the Drowning Tombs–you were all he talked about when you were learning. I was constantly compared to you."

Amaria shook her head. "That was a motivating technique, it means nothing."

Haerdnor looked at Amaria, his brown eyes staring directly into her silver. "I think I'll get drunk after all."

Haerdnor left her standing alone in the cavernous hallway, wondering where she went wrong and if everything was truly and finally falling apart, tearing at the fragile seams of a tapestry that lacked the quality thread needed to preserve its woven bonds.

Chapter Twenty-Nine

Over the next few days, Amaria finalized the preparations for the wedding. In the foyer, it seemed as if a garden suddenly bloomed, with at least thirty vases filled with greenery, white, red, and pink roses, and blue delphiniums. The vases, much like the walls and floor, were made of white stone and the flowers brought a vibrant splash of color to the area under the vast dome—only the dome itself had color with intricate geometric and floral designs etched in blue and gold.

Sighing, Amaria rubbed her hand on the pillar of the double staircase, where a golden scale with roses balancing upon it was embedded in the stone, breathing heavily when the stone felt freezing cold beneath her fingers. She was proud of her work, and also glad that Naomi would be alleviating this burden from her soon.

Except for Father's wedding. He'd never allow anyone other than a Raulet to plan that.

Amaria clenched her fists together. *I'll go to the Drowning Tombs after the wedding.* She could no longer afford to be weak. What happened in the dungeons of Bria Hall happened, however she needed to get over her fear of dungeons—she was a trained torturer. She was useless in a skill she had previously been unrivaled in if she couldn't step in a prison without drowning in her own panicked thoughts.

And we will all need my skills soon. Amaria politely nodded at a woman dressed in a stiff dress with puffed sleeves, the fashion of the Riam nobility. The noblewoman stiffened, stopping her features just before they morphed into a glare. "Congratulations to your family."

"Thank you," Amaria said, just as rigid as the noblewoman. "I don't believe I know your name, my Lady."

The woman forced a stiff, fake smile on her face. "No surprise there."

"I hope you have an enjoyable stay at my ancestral home," Amaria said politely, wanting nothing more than for the conversation to end. "Excuse me, my Lady." She moved over to one of the stewards who was moving luggage. "Who is that?"

"Countess Elisa Redwayne," the steward informed her. "She was the principal lady-in-waiting to Princess Karissa Riarl before her death."

Her breath caught. Earl Redwayne had gone bankrupt a few years ago and Countess Redwayne had been entirely reliant on her royal income from being a courtier. She had come on hard times, more than most of the Riam nobles. Rumors were that she was selling herself for coin now–a noblewoman in name and nothing else.

And if she believed the popular rumor that Amaria killed Karissa, then, Elisa Redwayne had a reason for vengeance and nothing to lose in her pursuits.

Her jaw locking, Amaria moved over to a guard. "I want Elisa Redwayne tailed at all times. Search her luggage. If you find poison, weapons, anything suspicious, confiscate it and confine her to her chambers."

Amaria turned her attention back to the guests milling into the foyer, politely greeting those who passed her. Her smile felt frozen on her face, and she wished to be anywhere but here–she'd even take the Drowning Tombs. Amaria felt numb. Theodmon would arrive in a few days, but in truth, she needed him there now.

A trumpet blared. Amaria turned towards the door, forcing herself to be cheery. This was either someone directly related to the bride, the Emperor, or someone directly related to her. She had to be at her best for this greeting. "Duchess Miana Alexandre of Dalia, Avondra, formerly of the House Raulet," the herald announced. "Duke Laurents Alexandre of Dalia, Avondra and their children the lords and ladies...."

The heralds words a dull ache in her ears, so much that she was tuning him out, Amaria exhaled, her shoulders momentarily slumping. "Aunt Miana," she said in relief, briskly walking over to her aunt who pulled her into a hug. "Thank the gods."

"Expecting someone else?" Miana teased.

Amaria didn't say anything, taking this moment in this hug to compose herself.

"Has Theodmon arrived yet?" Miana asked as they pulled away.

"No," Amaria said. "Soon."

"I'm surprised he's not already here," Miana said with a wry smirk.

"He had business at home and traveling through the Westerlands can be treacherous," Amaria smoothly replied.

Miana chuckled under her breath. "Would someone attack a Chauvignon on Chauvignon lands?"

"You laugh, but it's happened before." Amaria scanned the crowd of guests for her brother. "You should find Haerdnor." She lowered her voice as she leaned into her aunt. "Put the fear of the gods back in him so he's not a total ass to his wife." She lowered her voice at this part, imagining the gossip if someone heard her cursing.

Miana laughed. "Understood. I'll do that after we settle in. Oh, I thought you should know," Miana lowered her voice, her lips brushing over Amaria's ears. "We've made our claim on the Avonnian throne–most of the nobles support us, but Aaron lent us his Navy and men in case there's any discontent. We figured it would be best to settle that before your whole Riam issue."

"I know," Amaria whispered back. "Father's been handling it. It's been going well from what I heard."

"My coronation should be in three months," Miana said. "I do hope you can make it."

"Might be difficult," Amaria admitted. "But I truly am happy for you and wish I could be there." She smiled brightly at her aunt. "What do you want for a coronation present?"

"Money," Miana said. "Lynette's war ruined the coffers." Miana shook her head sharply. "This is a happy day, let's stay away from these conversations." Miana sounded almost pained. "Look, I think the Chauvignons arrived. I don't see Aloysius and his wife though."

"Aloysius is already here." Amaria's eyes were glued to the intricately carved double doors that lead outside. She saw Theodmon step through the door and her heart fluttered. From here she could see he was tired from travel, while he maintained the appropriate posture for court, his shoulders sagged in between conversations and he had dark circles etched under his eyes. A lock of hair brushed over his forehead, and his hand hovered near the hilt of his sword. Nobody asked him to disarm, however, the guards knew better than to ask that of Aaron Raulet's son-in-law.

Theodmon turned to look towards her, pausing and giving her a small, almost lopsided smile, when their eyes met. Amaria felt herself breaking into a genuine smile– one that wasn't forced or contrived by social obligation.

"I'll catch up with Aaron and Haerdnor." Miana moved away from Amaria, nodding towards Theodmon. "Go be with him."

Amaria didn't need the encouragement. She had already broken into a brisk walk in Theo's direction. The room had never felt so wide, so cavernous, before. It felt as if time was spanning across the entire night sky, and they were two stars about to crash to cause a mediator shower. Amaria and Theodmon crossed the room and were engulfed in each other's arms.

The hug was too brief. Amaria wanted to throw all caution to the wind, who cared about proprietary right now? She had missed him and he was here with her now. She smelled the scent of cedarwood and amber coming from him and briefly closed her eyes, inhaling the scent.

"I missed you," she said softly.

A smile laced Theodmon's normally stern features as his hand slipped into hers. "I missed you too."

Amaria beamed, looking down at her feet momentarily for privacy. "Will you come to dinner with me tonight?"

"Of course," Theodmon said. "Whose it with? Naomi Brassir and her family?"

"My father and Durek Svilas," Amaria sighed. "He should be arriving soon. Once he arrives, let's go see Aloysius and the children. The courtiers can greet the rest of the guests, everyone of true importance has already arrived."

"Aion isn't late?" Theodmon lightly chuckled.

"I said true importance," Amaria said darkly. "You should know something about Aloysius." She swallowed the lump in her throat. "He was bleeding out, severely injured, leaking magic. He's healing now."

Theodmon's face paled. "Vathar." The god of war, destruction, strategy, and duty's name came out as if it were a curse. "I shouldn't have had him come early."

"Why did you send him?"

"Not here." Theodmon glanced around the hall. "We need to speak to your father, immediately."

Amaria took a look at his face, seeing his dilated eyes and pale face and knew that whatever Aloysius was supposed to deliver was important. "Go. I'll meet you after I greet Duke Svilas."

"He's there," Theodmon nodded towards a red-bearded man who had just walked in the foyer. "Let's address him and go together."

Amaria smiled at Theodmon gratefully, the two of them moving towards Durek Svilas.

"Your Grace." Amaria gave him a small curtsy. "Welcome to Raulle and Provinica Palancia."

"Marquis and Marchioness Chauvignon," Durek responded politely, giving each a small nod.

"I trust you received my father's proposal?" Amaria said. "If you're amenable to it, my father would like to have a private dinner to discuss."

Durek smiled wryly. "Of course. Perhaps my daughter, Natalya, may join us."

"We will see you later, Duke Svilas." Theodmon guided Amaria away by her waist. "I'm sure Duke Raulet will send a formal invitation confirming the time of the dinner tonight."

"Please settle into your rooms," Amaria told Durek. He had stayed here before on business, but now that marriage was on the table, his rooms had been upgraded from the nicer guest ones to the ones family or the emperor stayed in. In fact, Amaria believed that Durek was staying in the same rooms that Theo had when he and her father were having the same conversation.

As they walked away from Durek, Amaria breathed heavily. "My father might not be in his office."

"Can you get in and we wait for him?"

Amaria bit her lip, knowing how strict her father was, but also remembering how she used to sew in his office as he worked. "Perhaps," she said. "How serious is this?"

"How many days until the wedding?" Theodmon asked.

"A week," Amaria said.

"We have a week to make war plans," Theodmon said.

Amaria paled, her heart stopping. It was an impossible task. She wished Aloysius hadn't been harmed, and that he wasn't on so many medications and magical enchantments to ease his pain—he had been sleeping and the few times he was awake he was incoherent.

Amaria's shoulders slumped as fatigue washed over her. "Then we should start as soon as we can."

Aaron Raulet took a long sip of tea, staring down at his daughter, son, and son-in-law who were waiting for him in his office. "This isn't great timing. Haerdnor, are you prepared for the wedding?"

"Father," Amaria interceded. "This is serious."

Aaron waited for them to continue. Amaria's hands shook and she was thankful when Theodmon spoke.

"Aloysius was supposed to deliver a message," Theodmon said. "Unfortunately, he was unable to. We have been making plans to attack Rindria, and the attack starts the day after Haerdnor's wedding. Aloysius was supposed to tell you to get the Riams to stay a week, maybe two, longer—"

"Making them more disorganized and allowing the country more easily to fall," Aaron finished. "Yes, that's smart. But it's late notice."

"Spike the drinks," Haerdnor said. "Not enough to hurt them. Just enough to make them think they have the worst hangover in history. Maybe ensure the festivities go extra late so they can't even remember how much they've had to drink."

"Father," Amaria added, "if Durek Svilas and you sign an engagement contract–"

"Extra parties and celebrations for me and Natalya Svilas," Aaron said. "Yes, that's an ample distraction. We'll spike their food, too. I'll instruct the spies in the kitchen and waitstaff."

"Distract them with sex," Amaria added with an internal cringe. "Have our spies, both man and woman, sleep with any Riam they can. Perhaps with all the alcohol and drugs in their system they'll be able to give valuable information for us to use later."

"What are they looking for?" Haerdnor questioned.

"Anything," Theodmon said. "Any intel can be crucial. After they have slept with a Riam, they'll make a written report to be kept safe with Amaria or Aaron."

"Are your troops ready?" Aaron asked Theodmon.

"They're at the border of Rindria and the Westerlands now."

A knock came at the door.

"Enter," Aaron barked. The door opened, revealing the guard Amaria had given rapid fire commands to earlier regarding a Riam noblewoman.

The guard inclined his head in a shallow bow. "My Lady," the guard addressed Amaria first before turning to Aaron, lowering his head further. "Apologies, Your Grace, your daughter gave specific instructions to come to her immediately if poison or weapons were found on Elisa Redwayne's person."

Aaron arched a questioning eyebrow at Amaria. She met her father's eyes, deliberately letting him see her dart her gaze towards the guard as if to say *not now, I'll explain later*. Her father, thankfully, did not say anything further.

"Yes?" Amaria addressed the guard. "What was found?"

"Poison in her luggage. Galen Chironia inspected it and believed it to be from the venom of a rhabdophis keelback snake, mixed in with foxglove leaves."

Involuntarily, Amaria sucked in her breath. That was no small concoction. "How much poison did she have?"

"Ten vials, all around sixty-five milliliters."

"You're dismissed," Amaria told the guard and he departed.

Aaron looked sternly at Amaria once the guard was gone "That's enough poison to kill at least eighty people. Do you want to explain?"

"Elisa Redwayne is Riam noble–"

"Yes, the great whore with no fortune or prospects," Haerdnor snorted.

"Because your sister killed the princess she worked for," Aaron said coldly. "Have some understanding of your enemy or you will be a very poor Lord." He turned back to Amaria and Theodmon. "Continue."

"She has reason to hate us. I suspected she might act on it, so I had her tailed, and her items secretly searched."

"What next?" Aaron asked her.

"I'll talk to her," Amaria said. "Here." Amaria's stomach knotted at the prospect of dragging Elisa down into the dungeons, but shook it off as quickly as she could, disgusted with herself. Her time in the dungeons of Bria Hall was not a memory she could afford to keep tangled in her mind. "Not the Drowning Tombs. Not yet."

"And why?" Theodmon said. Amaria realized he wasn't actually questioning her, he was letting her think through the strategy, the process she needed to follow to neutralize this threat.

"She likely doesn't like being the great whore, as Haer so kindly put it." Amaria rolled her eyes at her brother. "She has a motive to turn sides, and if she doesn't then that amount of poison indicates she knows something, or knows someone who knows something. Kindness can get you further than torture in some instances."

Aaron folded his hands, his thin lips hidden behind them as he his eyes bore into Amaria's, his gaze shewed and calculating. "And if kindness doesn't work?"

A shiver bolted down Amaria's spine as the ice in her father's voice chilled her very soul. It didn't matter how small her hesitation had been--Aaron Raulet had sensed it and decided it needed to be weeded out.

She swallowed hard and squared her shoulders. "Then I take her to the Drowning Tombs."

Aaron said nothing for a while. Finally, he turned to the papers on his desk, picking up a quill. "Do make sure one of you is in control when that occurs. I trust you to not disappoint me."

Chapter Thirty

Amaria strode towards Elisa Redwayne's guest chambers, trying to not seem bothered. The last thing she needed was to seem worried or frazzled with the entire world in her ancestral home.

Amaria paused by a maid. "Bring tea to Countess Elisa Redwayne's chambers. Knock, but don't come in, I'll retrieve it from you."

If the maid thought this was a strange request, she didn't showcase it, dipping her heels into a curtsy before hurrying off. Amaria sighed. *I'm being hospitable. That's all.*

I'm not interrogating her about the large amounts of poison. I'm being hospitable to a guest in my ancestral home. Amaria forced her facial features to remain cheery, as if the lie she was telling herself was true. It had to be true though, not for her, but for everyone else. Intelligence and court was an enigma: there was the constant faking a lie to cover the truth she knew, and so she could uncover deeper truths that could not be discovered without the false pretense.

She made her way to Elisa's chambers, telling the guards on post to stand guard and to expect a maid with tea. The doors to Elisa's chambers creaked open. Amaria cringed, they needed to oil the hinges of the doors for some of the unused chambers more.

"Countess Redwayne," Amaria greeted stiffly from the doorway.

"Marchioness," Elisa replied just as cooly. "Or is it the Head of the Extractors? Or Faerie blessed? God blessed? Executioner of the Riam Royals? I find it difficult to keep up with your titles. You always seem to have a new one."

Amaria forced herself to remain calm as she stepped inside the chambers, shutting the door behind her. "Countess Redwayne, is there a title or name you would prefer to be called?"

"Must we deal with this trifling politeness?" Elisa said. "You are here to question me about the poison found in my luggage. While we're at it, I prefer Elisa Yearwood, as my idiot husband is the one who gambled away his fortune and died while drinking, leaving me in this position. All my father did was marry me to the fool."

Amaria's eyebrows rose. "Lady Yearwood, what position do you mean?"

"Whoring myself for food and shelter," Elisa said. Amaria's eyebrows rose further, momentarily shocked at the crudeness.

"We can't all pretend to deal in niceties." Contempt dripped from Elisa's words. "The Raulets aren't a struggling noble family, they could support you if you had to come running back to them. The Chauvignons would never go bankrupt. How could they? They'd just conquer something else and steal their money." Elisa's nose scrunched up and her mouth twisted into a sneer. "I'm not even whoring myself for a coin–you're aware the only property Riam women are allowed to own are silverware, dining ware, clothes, and jewelry?"

Amaria's heart thudded against her chest. She knew what Elisa was alluding to, and hearing it laid out in front of her, she was seeing how drastic the situation had to have been for her. Still she flinched as Elisa dealt the final blow of her story.

"When you killed Karissa Riarl, the money she held for me in a palace trust was confiscated. I had nothing but my pretty clothes and jewels. I had nowhere to go, and jewels couldn't pay rent in the village forever–plus with all the unrest in Riam, the peasants would tear a noblewoman apart wouldn't they?"

"My Lady–" Amaria began.

"With the respect you deserve, Marchioness, be quiet." Elisa looked at Amaria fiercely, as if daring her to interrupt again. "Now, since I can't have coin, trying to buy anything without a husband would land me in the same position I was in already. But I was pretty, I was well mannered, and I was desperate. I'd sleep with noblemen, diplomats, even guards for the low price of a meal, a bath, and a bed. I'd get gifted with jewels and dresses too, as if they were trying to make themselves seem more generous. As if they weren't having sex with someone who couldn't say no and despised them."

"And they knew you hated them?" Amaria asked doubtfully.

"Of course not," Elisa said, rolling her eyes. "They're men."

If I hadn't found her with poison, and if she didn't despise me, I think I'd rather like Elisa. I think I still might like her regardless.

"Your position is damning," Amaria said. "And I see why you would want to kill me and as many of us here as you could. Liara Nalaeny insinuated more than a few times that Thestitiunians were heartless—"

"Liara Nalaeny is an idiot," Elisa said.

Amaria's eyebrows raised once more. For someone so devoted to one member of the Riam royal family, it seemed shocking she would denounce another so harshly. Privately, of course she may have her own thoughts, but to publicly voice that was asinine.

This isn't a public denouncement. Amaria bit her lip surveying Elisa.

"She's a naive girl, with ill-founded beliefs on how the world should work," Elisa said. "Anybody could've told her running away was pointless, and look what she did. Her stupidity gave Thestitiunia a weapon and Rindria is dead because of her."

"Rindria is still a country," Amaria said cautiously. "Perhaps we meant Riams–"

"My Thestitiunian is good enough to know the difference of what I said," Elisa said shortly. "I meant my country, not my countrymen. Rindria, as you noted, is still a country. It is weakened. How long will it last? How long until you and your damned empire make Rindria a colony, or a province if we're lucky?"

Amaria silently surveyed Elisa, watching the sweat beads on her forehead, how her wheat color hair seemed limp, how her eyes almost bulged. That didn't cumulate into distress though--what Amaria saw before her was pure, unadulterated rage.

"You wanted us to find the poison." Amaria stood up, moving towards the doors.

"I'm not planning to harm anyone here." Elisa folded her arms and scowled, as if annoyed that it had taken Amaria this long to figure it out. "I wanted you to find it so we could speak."

The hairs on the back of her neck rose. "Do not lie to me in my own home." Amaria would kill her now if it prevented another death in a place she was supposed to be safe. But she would listen to Elisa. She couldn't calculate her true intentions now, but she was intrigued by the potential alliance, despite how uneasy it may be.

Elisa's nostrils flared. "It's not a lie. I knew you'd question me, and I want to privately offer my services—but I have conditions."

Amaria's shoulders relaxed slightly. Bargaining with an enemy, this she understood well. "Naturally."

The door rapped. "Excuse me." Amaria extinguished her flames. She opened the door, taking the tea tray from the maid, the door quickly shutting.

"What's that?" Elisa's eyes narrowed into calculating slits as Amaria set the tray down near the table by Elisa's bed.

"Tea." Amaria poured herself a cup. "It's not poison, if that's what you're wondering." To prove her point, she took a sip. "Anyways, you were telling me your conditions for committing treason against Rindria."

"It's not treas–"

"Elisa, you're intelligent," Amaria interrupted. "Let's call a spade a spade if we're to duel our wits."

Elisa's hazel eyes watched Amaria, now surveying her instead of the other way around. "Alright, *Amaria*," she said, straining out the name with a pained level of emphasis. "I have conditions for becoming a traitor for Rindria for you. You'll need inside help to take the country."

"Yes," Amaria said impatiently. "What're the terms?"

"I get Thestitiunian citizenship," Elisa said. "I get land. I get a title. I get money—an income of at least five thousand per annum. You find me a respectable husband–I don't care who he is, as long as he shields me from being called a whore." Elisa's pitch and voice rose at this last part and Amaria saw the tears watering in her eyes.

"You'll get Thestitunian citizenship," Amaria agreed. "You'll gain land, you'll be married to the new governor of the Riam colonies, and your son from your new husband will be the first Duke of the Riam province. Your title will go from Lady Governor to Dowager Duchess. And as for your income–I'm sure that if our plans work out, five thousand per annum. That's a nominal amount for a Thestitiunian Duchess."

Elisa eyed her suspiciously, turning her body slightly away from Amaria. "Why did you agree so easily?"

Amaria shrugged. "You're right that we need you. Besides, call it empathy, kindred spirits, whatever you wish to call it, but I feel for your situation. Besides, if we can both benefit it's an easy alliance to make."

"I don't trust you," Elisa warned.

Amaria smiled, giving a small laugh. "The feeling is mutual." She brushed down the folds of her dress. "We'll have to give you some training, after the wedding of course. Though, this wedding should last more than a few days. Are you up to having sex with your countrymen for the next few weeks?"

Elisa looked at Amaria scathingly. "I told you that I don't want to whore myself–"

"And you won't," Amaria said. "Once we win. However, until then, I'm not wasting someone with access to the Riam leadership and military who can gain information and distract them without suspicion. If you can do this, then we have a deal. If you can't, you'll go back to whoring. Permanently."

Amaria turned towards the door, a smirk coming up her face as she left the chambers. Elisa was trapped more than Amaria was. There was the risk she would betray them, but it was unlikely that any warning Elisa may give would be taken seriously until it was too late, especially with all the wine and the drugs slipped into the drinks and food. And if Elisa betrayed them, she doomed herself to whoring for a bed until she died.

As the door shut behind her, and after Amaria whispered instructions to the guards to not let Elisa go anywhere tonight and to have food brought to her room, she walked through the halls, hoping that Elisa was as good as a whore as the rumors said.

Chapter Thirty-One

While Amaria was tormenting a Riam noblewoman, Theodmon was enduring his own hell sitting at Aloysius's bedside.

"He's gotten better," Galen Chironia told him as he changed Aloysius's bandages, carefully discarding the bloodied ones. "He was leaking magic when he arrived."

Theodmon blankly looked at Galen. "I assume that's bad."

"Apologies, my Lord." Galen adjusted his glasses that had slipped down his nose. "It's difficult to explain in a conceptual way to non-mages. How we, as humans, need blood, and bleeding out is serious, if magic is leaking it can kill you if enough leaves."

"Taking magic doesn't kill. Extractions—"

"Are different," Galen sighed. "Cutting someone open with a sword will kill them, but cutting them with a scalpel in surgery won't."

"So it's the method of how magic is lost?"

"More like the preparation," Galen said. "He's healing though. His magic is strong, and it's helping the rest of him heal. War mages tend to suffer a double-edged sword with their magic in that their magic is much more intimately tied to their physical health than any other mage." He placed an herb in Aloysius's mouth. "The more physically adept they are, the more powerful the magic—a healing mage for instance couldn't increase our magical powers by running a mile every day," Galen chuckled. "However, our magic doesn't weaken with injury or illness."

Theodmon made a non-committal *'mhmm'* in response to Galen's words. *Aloysius always did tend to have illnesses in worse severity than us, but he recovered quicker,* Theodmon remembered, gripping his brother's hand. He looked so much like their father.

Aloysius gave a shallow breath, and Theodmon's hand tightened over his.

"Has he been eating? Drinking?" Theodmon asked Galen.

"In a way," Galen said. "That herb I've put in his mouth dissolves and will give him minimal nutrition–just enough to keep him alive and not fall into starvation." The healer pulled out a tube, bag, and needle. "This is saline, we have been injecting it into his bloodstream to hydrate him, excuse me, My Lord."

Theodmon moved away from the bed, allowing Galen to insert the needle into Aloysius's arm. "He should be waking soon. He'll likely only be awake for thirty minutes, an hour at most if you're lucky."

"Thank you," Theodmon said, his voice cracking slightly.

"I'll give you some privacy." Galen nodded kindly, before he moved out of the room. "Would you mind calling for me once he falls asleep, Marquis?"

Theodmon gave Galen a curt nod, turning to focus on Aloysius once more. Father. Ophelia. Aloysius had almost joined them in Sadthos' Kingdom. And it would have been Theodmon's fault for ordering Aloysius to ride to deliver a message.

What had happened? Theodmon placed his head in his hands. *And how did one leak magic anyways?* Galen had tried to explain the concept to Theodmon, but he couldn't understand it.

He understood the physicality of training--the honing of reflexes and muscles--and the mental sharpening of the mind with books and puzzles.

But magic.... How could magic be physical, mental, and something else entirely all at once?

I'm glad I'm not a mage. Theodmon hated admitting this to himself. It almost felt sacrilegious in Thestitiunian society, but when push came to shove, he was more than comfortable with his sword and trickery.

On the bed, Aloysius groaned. Theodmon, quickly jolted out of his thoughts, looked down at him. "Aloysius," he said.

"Am I dead?" Aloysius muttered. "It feels like I'm dead."

"Sounds like you were close." Theodmon blinked rapidly to stop his eyes from welling up. "Gods, I'm glad to see you." He squeezed Aloysius's hand tightly.

Aloysius winced. "Ouch."

"What happened?" Theodmon let go of Aloysius's hand. "Do you remember?"

Aloysius's eyes glazed over. "It...it felt like bandits but it couldn't be...they were too organized....they...." he trailed off.

"They...?" Theodmon prompted.

"They knew I had a message," Aloysius said, his eyes drooping. "One said 'good luck getting the Raulets a message when you're dead' and....how—" He cut himself off with a grunt, wincing in pain.

"The plans are underway," Theodmon told Aloysius. "Heal."

"Twenty-three puncture wounds," Aloysius bragged.

Theodmon chuckled, shaking his head. "It's not a competition."

"It's always a competition—"

Aloysius was cut off by the door opening, and Celestine stepped inside the room. "Oh gods," she gasped, her hands flying to her mouth. "Aloysius!"

"Dashing, isn't it?" Aloysius said to Celestine, his eyes twinkling.

Celestine rushed to Aloysius' side, hugging him softly. "Oh my gods, you were almost dead—Aloysius...." Celestine was crying. "Don't do that to me!"

"I'll give you two some time." Theodmon excused himself. "Celestine, find Master Chironia once Aloysius is asleep again, will you?"

Celestine, fully sobbing now, only managed to give a silent nod in between hiccups. Taking that as confirmation, Theodmon left the room, his heart hammering against his chest. In his conversation with Aloysius, one thing became clear that hadn't even been known before: there was a spy in the innermost folds of Theodmon's household.

And he didn't have the slightest idea who it was.

Chapter Thirty-Two

Amaria's stomach tied itself into knots as she stepped into the intimate dining area on the second floor of Provincia Palancia. She barely processed walking in, her father standing near the stained glass windows, his arms crossed as he scowled at the glass mosaic of a garden.

In the center of the room was a long table, covered with white linen and lined with chairs: two at the head and foot, and four lining either side. A golden vase, holding red roses with white babies' breath, stood in the center. Golden plates and silverware lined the table with crystalline goblets marking each seat.

"What's the sitting arrangement?" Amaria walked across the room, her feet sinking into the plush blue carpeting.

Aaron turned to a servant and snapped his fingers, giving a command to remove chairs from around the table, leaving only the ones at head and foot, and two on each side of the table. "That should answer your question. Where's your brother and husband?"

"I wasn't aware I was in charge of their itinerary," Amaria said cooly. Her heart hadn't stopped thudding against her chest and it took all of her willpower not to avert her eyes away from her father.

"What language are we speaking tonight?" She asked, hoping to change the subject.

"Morrian," Aaron said curtly. The door opened behind him. "Kind of you to join us, Haerdnor." He switched languages with as little effort as blinking. "I believe I taught you the virtue of punctuality–"

Haerdnor's jaw locked. "Spare me the lecture or I might be late to my own wedding out of spite."

Amaria shut her eyes, cringing.

"Am I entertaining the Svilas girl?" Haerdnor nodded towards the chairs. "I sit closest to you and she sits closer to her father?"

"That was the idea," Aaron said. "Don't embarrass—"

Haerdnor stared at their father with hatred. "Yes, how embarrassing I am. Tell me, when did you realize how indifferent you were to your only son?"

"Stop," Amaria stepped in between the two. "They'll be here soon and–"

The door opened again and Amaria's breath hitched, only to relax when Theodmon stepped through. "Duke and Lady Svilas are down the hallway," he announced. "Perhaps we should go ahead and sit?"

Her father curtly nodded towards Theodmon, moving towards his chair at the head of the table. Haerdnor moved to sit on Aaron's right-hand side, but Aaron placed his hand on the chair, blocking his son. "You're on my left," Aaron said coolly. "The right-hand is for your sister."

Haerdnor stared at his father, hurt creeping into his brown eyes.

Amaria tried to not meet his eyes as she sat in her seat. Was she honored to be placed at Aaron's right hand, despite not being heir? She couldn't deny it, the swelling in her chest was so prominent she felt tears beginning to well in her eyes. But Amaria and Haerdnor had taken some level of control from Aaron in forcing him into a political marriage, so he was taking back control the only way he knew how--by lashing out. Amaria was all too familiar with the tactic--she saw it in herself.

Like father, like daughter, she thought, biting back a sigh.

Thankfully, the door opened, revealing Durek Svilas, his wife, and their daughter, leaving Amaria no further time for reflection.

They all stood up. "Your Grace," Theodmon greeted in perfect, unaccented Morrian, his face a façade of peace as Amaria lowered her head respectfully, hiding her expression.

"Please sit," Aaron said, already sitting back down. "We've much to discuss."

Durek's green eyes narrowed as if they were snake silts. "We do. I'd like you to meet Natalya." Durek motioned to the young girl beside him. "If I accept your proposal, she will be your bride and step-mother."

Amaria's eyes drifted towards Natalya. The girl was young. Amaria guessed she was around sixteen. Natalya stood behind her father, silently, her eyes dropped low. She had her father's flaming red hair, tightly pinned and coiled with emeralds woven through the strands and hair nets. She wore a pale blue dress, light enough that it almost seemed white.

White was a Thestitiunian bridal color–easier to showcase the two houses that were to be joined colors without their house colors clashing. With a jolt, Amaria remembered the Svilas's color was green.

"For a Morrian, she seems a bit old to be without a betrothal," Haerdnor said.

Durek turned to look towards Haerdnor, his lips parting into a pained smile as he sat down at the end of the table. "Lord Raulet." Durek motioned for Natalya to sit in between him and Haerdnor at the remaining seat.

"Why haven't you been engaged?" Aaron directed towards Natalya. "Your Grace, if there is something defective about her—"

Amaria's throat began to burn. She wanted to beat all of the men with her shoe--or maybe set them on fire--and whisk poor Natyala Svilas away from all of it.

"Earlier betrothal means earlier marriage for Morrian ladies," Durek said smoothly. "Fourteen year old brides tend to be more hassle then they are worth. It's much better to wait until they're sixteen and can more successfully bear children. Suitors can also see what they'll be getting now, and as the grandchild of our king, she is in a position for many suitors to ask for her hand." He looked over at his daughter, who still kept her eyes down. "Speak girl."

"It is a pleasure to meet you, and I look forward to being your wife and bearing you children if that is what my father commands," Natalya said.

Tears burned in Amaria's eyes, then melted into molten rage. Why invite this girl to a dinner in which she couldn't speak, would be spoken about as if she wasn't there–as if she wasn't a human being.

"Father," Amaria said abruptly. "With your permission, I would wish for me and Lady Natayla to be excused so I may show her around the estate so she can get a sense of what she'll be doing as Duchess Raulet?"

Durek's smirk widened. "Your lips move, and yet your father speaks." He turned to Aaron. "Well done on molding a woman outside her nature." He waved his hand towards Natalya, "go girl."

Aaron turned towards Amaria. "You may leave. Show her around the gardens and come back up in an hour. The first course should be ready and gods willing, Duke Svilas and I should have an agreement ready."

Exhaling, Amaria stood up. Next to her, Theodmon also rose. "Your Graces, Lord Raulet, I was only here to accompany my wife. I am not a Raulet nor a Svilas, and I've no place at this table."

"Will you supervise the ladies together?" Durek asked.

"It'd be my pleasure to keep your daughter from harm's way," Theodmon replied politely as Amaria, Theodmon, and Natalya moved towards the exit.

With the door shut and a bit of distance between them and the dining room, Amaria leaned in and whispered to Theodmon, "Stay back a bit. She likely won't be comfortable if you're too close."

Theodmon gave her a peck on the cheek before pulling away, standing in place as Amaria moved towards Natalya and guided her gently forward. "It's nice to meet you," Amaria said.

Natalya gave her a shaky smile. "Thank you," she whispered. Amaria noticed she had tear stains on the corners of her eyes.

"They shouldn't talk about us as if we aren't there," Amaria said.

"There's no harm in it," Natalya said, almost too quickly. "We talk about men's sword fighting ability, titles, and wealth in front of them. Talking about women's childbearing ability and morality is the same." Natalya's voice sounded dull, almost as if she were reciting a poem for a tutor.

"The same?" Amaria questioned gently.

"I'd not marry a poor man who couldn't protect me," Natayla said. "Why should a man marry a wife who cannot bring him children and peace?"

"Stations are important for marriage," Amaria conceded, "But sword fighting is an ability that can be honed."

It's dehumanizing how they talk about you. About us. Amaria bit back a glare.

Natalya was silent. It wasn't until they reached the outside gardens that she spoke.

"I wish to marry your father," she said.

"Do you?" Amaria scoffed. "Or are you also a mouthpiece for your father? All of this is very intentional, your dress is a nice touch. It's ingenious really to show the illusion of how you would be as a bride without fully committing–that light blue color is divine on you."

Natalya's eyes widened. "It's just a color! My father told me to wear it–"

"It's alright." Amaria fought the urge to hug the girl. "May I call you Natalya?"

She gulped, nodding. "Yes, Marchioness–"

"Amaria," Amaria corrected. "I don't wish you harm. I want us to be close–assuming that both our father's get their way, and I doubt they won't, we will be in each other's lives for a very long time."

Natalya's blue eyes widened. "You knew my father was posturing?"

"Aaron Raulet is the richest man in the world," Amaria said gently. "It's a fair guess that nobody would deny an alliance." Amaria's hand touched her necklace–the one her father gave her. Every gift came with strings here, even if those strings were an expectation of excellence.

Amaria didn't want to be bound by that, if only for a moment. "Natalya," she gripped her hands. "This won't change anything, and I'm sorry but please answer this for me. Honestly. Do you want to marry my father?"

Natalya stepped back from Amaria, looking over her shoulder as if she were a hunted deer. Amaria noticed her gaze stopped on Theodmon, who was standing nearly twenty feet away.

"Of course," she said dully.

Amaria sighed. "Theodmon," she called out. "Please leave. We will rejoin you in a second." Warmth flooded in Amaria's gaze as she watched her husband depart. Her father would never respect Natalya, he would never treat her how Theodmon treated her.

"I need you to tell me," Amaria whispered. "I can't stop this marriage, but I can try and make your life bearable as Duchess Raulet. But I need you to be honest with me."

Natalya cast one more frantic look around the garden before she stepped closer to Amaria. "No," she whispered.

Amaria pulled Natalya into a hug. "Let me know if you need anything," Amaria said as she pulled away from her. "Even things, *especially* things, you don't want to ask my father about."

A flicker of relief washed over Natalya's eyes. "Thank you," she said, her voice breaking. She turned and looked at the flowering trees. "This is a beautiful garden."

Amaria gave her a soft smile. "It is," she agreed. "Do you want to go back inside and see if they are ready for us to join them?"

Natayla's stomach growled, but she still made no move to head back inside. "Give me a moment longer." She leaned in to smell a blooming flower. "I've never been allowed outside for so long before."

"The future Duchess Raulet," Aaron raised a glass in Natalya's honor. "We will announce it at Haerdnor's wedding. After the wedding we will have our engagement party, seeing as everyone is already here."

An absurdly large engagement party. Amaria sipped her wine, eyes distance as she tried to calculate how much poison each Riam would need over the course of the two celebrations.

"We can hold the wedding within the year," Durek said enthusiastically. "Marchioness Chauvignon, I presume you are helping your father with the planning of this wedding?"

Amaria swallowed a bite of salmon. "Perhaps my brother's new bride will help instead."

Aaron drowned another glass of champagne. "My daughter will help."

Amaria's jaw clenched, and she smiled, forcing herself to soften it. "Of course."

Throughout the rest of dinner and dessert, Aaron and Durek talked about their plans for the wedding. A few times, Amaria intervened, asking Natalya about what dress she would wish to wear. Haerdnor and Theodmon also attempted to change the subject, bringing up hunting multiple times.

As the desert dishes were cleared, Haerdnor, Theodmon, Amaria, and Natalya all met each other's eyes, a flicker of collective relief passing through them.

"Thank you, Your Grace," Durek said to Aaron as he stood up. "I look forward to joining our houses. Natayla, let's go."

"Amaria," Aaron said as Durek and Natayla left the dining room, "stay behind for a moment, will you?"

Amaria looked at Theodmon, the two of them exchanging a concerned glance. Amaria shook her head at Theodmon, giving him a soft smile.

"I'll be in our chambers," he whispered, squeezing her hand before he departed with Haerdnor.

Silently, Amaria stood there as her father grabbed his cane and limped over towards her.

"Have you been to the Drowning Tombs yet?" Aaron asked as he neared closer. "I have a list of prisoners for you to interrogate."

Amaria knew that—she had seen the list on her dresser. She bowed her head. "No, Father."

Aaron gave a small hmph. "I want you to go tomorrow. If you can't get over that fear, you're a liability to me."

Amaria felt heat rise in her chest. "Fear?" She had been tortured and imprisoned for weeks; how cruel was her father to negate that experience to her being unjustly fearful?

"Fear," Aaron affirmed. "You were trained to be tortured too, Amaria." He looked at her sternly. "You've rarely disappointed me, I'd hate for you to start now."

"And if I do start disappointing you?" Amaria shot out, the words like venom in her mouth.

Aaron looked her up and down, his eyes pausing at her abdomen and her wings. "Then you can do what is expected for a woman of your station—either with Theodmon or the faeries—you can stay in a castle and breed until you die. Ask your new stepmother for advice on how to act in that proper way, if it's not too late. Proper women don't kill rulers of other countries."

"You made me this way!" Amaria yelled, her face flushing.

"A failed experiment," Aaron said dismissively. "Go and tell Theodmon that you'll no longer be a liaison between our two families and he'll have to do it himself or propose a suitable male candidate. Don't worry, I'm sure he'll give you a necklace as a consolation."

Amaria's eyes narrowed and turned cold. "I never said I wasn't going."

Aaron met her gaze, his face unreadable. "I don't give second chances. You have until tomorrow morning to do your job."

Chapter Thirty-Three

Amaria pushed through the corridors, arriving at her room in a rage. She went to her vanity, where a bundle of papers were and she picked up one with her father's seal.

"Amaria?" Theodmon said.

She read over the parchment, confirming there were five names upon it—each with a brief description of their alleged crimes. She threw the parchment down again, moving towards her dresser, ransacking it for a dark dress.

"What's wrong?" Theodmon asked as her hands flew to the back of her dress, shakily undoing the buttons and strings.

"I'm going to the Drowning Tombs–"

"Are you alright?" Theodmon interrupted.

"Fine," Amaria said.

"I thought we agreed to never lie to each other," Theodmon's hands laid on top of hers as he gently guided them away from her buttons and towards her sides. She sighed as his hands lingered to her strings and he unlaced her. "Why are you going to the Drowning Tombs?"

Hot angry tears welled up in Amaria's eyes. "I have to."

"Why?" Theodmon asked. He said it simply, without judgment.

"Because my father will hate me if I don't." Amaria stared at her feet as the tears fell, twirling the rose recklessly in her hand, her thumb pressing against the emerald leaves.

"He won't hate you–"

"Only be disappointed," Amaria said. "Which for him is the same as hatred. Disappointment comes from incompetence and to have a child of his show that trait–he hates it."

"Hating a trait is different than hating the person," Theodmon said gently, finishing unlacing her dress.

Amaria shook her head fiercely as she pulled the dress off. "In my father's opinion, incompetence isn't a singular trait, it is a flaw that encompasses the whole person—it's your character, or for Father, a lack of it. He's killed people for it before."

"He won't kill you. You're his daughter."

"He'll just exclude me," Amaria agreed. "I'm his blood, which gives me protection, but there's worse punishment than death."

"He can't really expect you to go into the prisons so soon—we all saw you in Rindria."

"He doesn't care," Amaria said hotly, picking up her dark dress. "So I either get over it or lose the privileges of being his daughter–you'll have to be a liaison between our families or pick a suitable male candidate."

"Aaron said that?" Theodmon's brows furrowed. "Are you doing this right now because it needs to be done or because your father has gotten under your skin?"

Amaria bit her lip so hard blood appeared. "He seemed serious," she said, pulling on her dress. "Lace me up, please."

Theodmon sighed, but still complied. "I think Aaron is being more harsh than what's appropriate."

Amaria didn't disagree, but that didn't mean she didn't believe her father would follow through with the threats. "I have to get over this. I'm known for certain things–magic, my family, and my skills in dungeons–"

"Make yourself a new reputation," Theodmon said. "Lean into your magic and religion with the wings."

"We're planning wars," Amaria said, turning around to face him. "We need my reputation as a heartless killer." She kissed him softly on the lips. "We've reached a tipping point in this game. Even the gods can't pull us back now."

Theodmon clenched and unclenched his fits as he watched Amaria, seeming unsure of himself. "I can come with you."

Amaria shook her head. Aaron wanted her to do this by herself. Bringing Theodmon with her would only be seen as a crutch, a move which would anger her father. "I have to go alone." She moved away from Theodmon, sitting on the bed as she exchanged her heels for laced boots.

"Take care of yourself," Theodmon said. "I don't care what Aaron wants."

Amaria hugged her arms tightly around herself. Despite everything, Amaria still heavily relied on her father's goodwill. She needed him to trust her. She needed to be involved in his plans. "I will," she told Theodmon before she moved towards their balcony.

"What are you doing?" He asked as she climbed onto the ledge.

Amaria smiled and then stepped off the ledge, her wings extending. She needed to have a sense of freedom, a sense of something she was purely in control over.

And so, she would fly to the Drowning Tombs.

Amaria stood in the dank cell of Fawzia Suril, who was accused of espionage, treason, and heresy. She was thin and frail looking, likely from starvation. Amaria found herself shaking as she stared at the pathetic creature in front of her, as hatred bubbled up in her chest.

Her father's written instructions had been simple: *Limited information left to obtain. Dispose of the prisoner after the final interrogation attempt.*

Bile rose to Amaria's throat. She knew what this was and she wished she could have run away, forget about Fawzia Suril, and never come back to the Drowning Tombs. The Tombs themselves were intentionally cruel in design–Amaria had always known it–a prison that was half-underwater wasn't a pinnacle of charity or humanity to anybody with sense. But she had never evaluated, fully processed the level of abject cruelty the infrastructure was. The prisoners never were not being tortured. Even when left alone by the guards they had to fear drowning, unable to move because of the chains.

"Leave," she snapped at the guard at the cell door. "Find me irons. Bring them here." Amaria didn't want irons, she just brought them up so she could give the guards a task away from her to give her privacy.

The guard obeyed, shutting the door behind him.

"Is it my time?" Fawzia muttered.

Amaria's mouth was dry as she waded through the cell, gagging at the smell coming from the waters beyond the cell as she lit the torches on the walls. "May I sit with you?"

Fawzia's greasy dark hair fell over her eyes. "Can I say no?"

"Of course," Amaria said.

Fawzia snorted, staring at Amaria's wings. "I know of you." Her voice dripped with disdain. "Amaria Raulet. Blessed by the gods. I was warned that you would be sickeningly, falsely kind at first glance."

Amaria forced the lump down her throat as she licked her lips to force moisture back into them. "Espionage?"

"I'm not telling you anything," Fawzia said. "I've accepted my actions."

"Fine," Amaria said. "Why heresy?"

Fawzia rolled her eyes. "Do you not see? The gods are supposedly just, and yet they bless assholes like you. The Faith of the Divine is rotten to its core—the people starve and the temples are maintained with our blood."

"The temples give out tons of public aid!" Amaria said. "And we cannot fathom the gods. They are immortal and-"

"Wiser than us," Fawzia finished with a scoff. "And yet they seem to succumb to the same evil human emotions of pride, pettiness, and vanity. There is one thing in the faith I believe–it is that nobles and royalty have gods' blood."

An old belief. One that the official teachings had shifted away from.

"We are only chosen by the gods," Amaria corrected. She remembered the words of the temple's teaching better than she remembered childhood nursery rhymes. "Not descended."

"And yet you share in their pettiness." Fawzia rolled her eyes. "And wouldn't the gods choose their descendants to rule?"

Flames lit in Amaria's hands as she glared at Fawzia. "You're a heretic."

"That's why I'm here isn't it?" Fawzia said. "And I never committed treason or espionage—betraying bad leaders isn't the same as betraying Thestitiunia."

"What do you mean?" Amaria asked.

Fawzia stayed silent.

"Please," Amaria begged, letting the flames in her hands extinguish. "Tell me. I don't want to torture you."

"And what happens after I tell you?" Fawzia asked. "Heretics are executed, and I've admitted that *crime*. What would you do? Spare me? Help me escape the Drowning Tombs? Give me money to start anew in exile?" Her eyes flashed, and Amaria saw the hatred in them—a mirror to how she felt towards her own jailers.

"I don't...." Amaria trailed off, tears welling in her eyes. She couldn't breathe. She leaned against the wall, her entire body shaking as the flames dried up.

She didn't want to kill Fawzia. The only reason she wanted to hurt people was because of her father. Amaria dug her nails into her hands, the pain centering her. Was that true? She liked hurting people, she had always liked breaking people down because for a moment she wasn't the most pathetic person she knew.

Her father had honed her proclivity for cruelty, and he had made her into his weapon. He had manipulated her into coming here. He had manipulated her whole life.

And she wanted to make him proud. Even now, she craved his approval. But she shouldn't be here. She was useless in a dungeon after Rindria, how could he send her back to a dungeon? He was her father, he should care about her wellbeing.

But he didn't.

"Hold out your chains," Amaria said shakily, her hands burning with flames once more, tears freely falling down her face as she waded closer to Fawzia. She grabbed Fawzia's chains, slowly melting the chains away. Unfortunately, there was nothing she could do for the shackles.

"What're you doing?" Fawzia said, her body as still and rigid as a board.

"Helping you." Amaria glanced around, making sure they still had time. "Pretend to be chained when the guard comes."

"Why?" Fawzia asked.

Amaria said nothing. She didn't know why she was helping Fawzia. The girl was misguided, stupid in her religious beliefs, but Amaria didn't think she deserved to die. Amaria had qualms with Thestitiunian leadership, and yet, she loved her country. Despite Fawzia's heresy, Amaria understood her. Perhaps she even slightly agreed with her.

Amaria heard a rustling of metal outside the door and cut off her fire in her hands as well as all the torches except for one in the corner, forcing her hand to pin Fawzia down by her throat. "If you want to breathe again you'll tell me who you are working for," she snarled as the guard walked into the cell.

"Lady Raulet." The guard set the irons on a conclave carved into the wall by her. "The irons you asked for."

Amaria didn't turn. Instead, she focused on Fawzia. She needed her choke hold to seem realistic, but not so much that Fawzia actually passed out. "Dismissed," she said. Amaria maintained her gaze on Fawzia as she listened to the splashes and the shutting of the door in the dark cell. Amaria exhaled, bringing her hands away from Fawzia's throat. Fawzia's melted chains hadn't been discovered.

As the door shut, Fawzia leapt from her bench, grabbing the iron bar and swinging it towards Amaria. Amaria fell backwards into the water with a shout.

"I'm not stupid enough to trust a snake," Fawzia snarled, before Amaria's face was submerged in the water.

Thrashing, Amaria tried to pull herself from the water. Bubbles escaped from her mouth and nose.

I didn't survive one prison to be killed in another one. Amaria's chest felt hot, and her entire body began to glow. She grabbed onto Fawzia, her fingers digging into the prisoner's eyes as she burned. Fawzia's screams echoed throughout the cell.

Amaria sat up out of the dirty water, choking and gasping as she discarded the burnt skeleton. She stood up, leaning against the wall, spitting out water, trying not to think of what was in the cell.

The sound of slow clapping broke through the silence. "I knew you had it in you."

She turned, lighting the torches and her hands on fire with her magic as she came face to face with her father. "You manipulated me."

"I persuaded you." Aaron looked over at Fawsia's body, burned and floating at the top of the black water. "The prisoners here, they'd hurt you; do you see that now?"

Amaria's jaw locked. It was more complicated than that. However, she couldn't argue with her father on this now so she focused on his statement of persuasion instead. "And was the threat to cut me out? To reduce me to nothing more than a womb? Was inspired by our Morrian guests?"

Aaron's eye's twinkled. "Of course. I was worried I was too heavy handed."

"If it hadn't worked, perhaps." Amaria looked over at Fawzia's body. "She tried to kill me."

"Many want to," Aaron said. "You aren't well liked in certain circles."

"And the point of this is?" Amaria crossed her arms, scowling.

"What did you learn from Fawzia, intelligence wise?"

"Would it kill you to answer my question?"

"I am," Aaron replied. "What did you learn?"

Amaria sighed. Fawsia hadn't given her anything except.... *That can't be important? No.*

"A sect of heretics believe we are descended from the gods instead of being chosen by them."

"That's all?" Aaron raised his eyebrows.

Amaria still felt like she was drowning. She had almost been murdered and that was all he had to say? For the first time in her life, she saw Aaron Raulet how others saw him. How had she been such a fool to ignore his cruelty?

And how could she have been so cruel to lead an innocent girl to him. Natalya Svilas...what had Amaria done by proposing her father's marriage to her. Natalya would have been better off with the original proposal of marrying Henri.

"You'll be kind to Natalya?" Amaria blurted out, as she picked her nails, peeling back dried blood. "Please, be kind to her. Be gentle."

"I'm not going to beat her." Aaron snorted with a dismissive roll of his eyes. "You know my thoughts on men that beat their wives."

No. I know your thoughts on men who beat your daughter. Amaria thought sourly. "Treat her like Mother," Amaria said, the words feeling like glass shards.

"Your mother was infinitely more intelligent than any Morrian woman could dream–"

"Morrian women don't get the chance to be intelligent," Amaria interrupted. "Mother was Tressi. Imagine how stupid she would be if she was born in Morroek. Imagine how different I would be as a Morrian."

Amaria looked around the prison. Being in a dungeon still terrified her. She didn't like harming others now–she remembered what they did to her in the Riam dungeons and now she imagined herself in the people she tortured. "I'll do whatever you need me to do in the dungeons. I'll give you no complaint, I'll act like Rindria never happened. I'll be a better torturer and spy master than I ever was, but you need to treat Natalya like you would treat Mother, me, or Catalina."

Aaron's eyebrows rose. "And why do you care so much for her?"

"She's me if I stayed with Lyseno Vypren." Amaria had dreaded that life, and her only consolation with it was the fact that she one day would have the ability to dispose of her husband. She would have played the game, had sons, and poisoned Vypren. But she didn't want her father to die. And she didn't want Natalya to suffer. "Do we have an agreement?"

Aaron smiled. "Of course. I'll even buy her books as a wedding present. I'll give them to her after we have laid together so her father can't annul the marriage and nip her education in the bud. She'll start lessons with tudors as soon as the guests leave."

"Spend time with her in the garden," Amaria advised. "She likes it there. And thank you."

Aaron looked down at her. "I believe you have a few more prisoners to interrogate and kill tonight. I'll ensure a carriage and guards are waiting for you once you are done. You do have permission to come home early if you are not done by midnight. There's a wedding tomorrow."

"And then countless parties to celebrate new alliances." Amaria was tired at the mere thought.

"Out of all my children, I am the proudest of you."

Amaria's heart swelled and she unsuccessfully suppressed her grin as she savored her father's words. She had waited so long to hear him say that he was proud of her. It was all she had ever wanted. A few months ago she would have traded everything to have this. But now, it made her wary.

Amaria didn't need to look far to hear the unsaid warning to not disappoint him. It had been hanging over her head her entire life. As her father left the cell, she sighed, stepping over the dead body, pulling the soaked parchment from her pocket, and looking at the next name on the list, the ink running so much the names were almost indistinguishable.

Part Four

the thorns

Chapter Thirty-Four

As the morning sunrise cast a golden glow over Provincia Palancia's opulent halls, preparations for the wedding were in full swing. Blue ribbons adorned the corridors, weaving through the marble arches and ornate pillars, echoing the colors of the sea that stretched beyond the palace grounds.

Servants bustled about, arranging floral displays of white and red roses interspersed with delicate blue blooms, while artisans meticulously adorned the halls with gilded tapestries and shimmering chandeliers. Amaria pulled her robe tighter around herself as she watched the servants running around. She was grossly underdressed for the amount of visitors now in the castle, but she had spent so much time meticulously planning this wedding that stepping away, even to get dressed, was out of the question.

Juliette stepped beside Amaria, having arrived with Theodmon and the rest of the visitors from Forteresse les Blanche.

Amaria beamed as she pulled her friend into a hug. "How are you?"

"Better than you, I imagine, seeing as I'm properly dressed." Juliette laughed as she pulled away and studied Amaria's gown. "Let's get back to your chambers. I can only imagine what your father would say."

Amaria didn't want to imagine what her father would say. Her silver eyes narrowed, but she nodded curtly and walked back to her rooms without protest.

"I heard about Aloysius," Juliette said. "How is he?"

Amaria forced down bile. "Not great, but better."

"Do you know what happened?" Juliette's voice raised in pitch and Amaria could have sworn there was fear laced in her tone.

Is Juliette the traitor? Amaria forced her face to remain emotionless as she slowly shook her head. "Nothing other than he was shot with twenty-three arrows." She watched Juliette carefully from the corner of her eyes as she said this.

Juliette's eyes widened, her mouth dropping open slightly. "Is he...how is he still alive?"

"He almost wasn't," Amaria said as they passed an open window, the scent of roses drifting on the gentle sea breeze, mingling with the salty air. "We almost didn't get his message from Theo."

"Awful," Juliette said, "but neither of you cared about that message at the moment. So I ask again: How are you? You and Theodmon just lost Ophelia and the last time you were here was when your friend died."

Amaria blinked, surprised that her eyes were starting to water. "Awful," she croaked, the admission of weakness painful. Her home, previously comforting, had soon started to remind her of a graveyard.

Juliette gave her a soft smile, squeezing her arm gently. "It's alright to admit these things."

"No," Amaria protested. "It's weakness, and only suffices to get your head placed on a stake outside the palace gates."

"It's alright to feel weak," Juliette insisted as they neared Amaria's chambers. "Even if you hide your true feelings, you aren't lesser for feeling them."

If only I had that luxury. Amaria felt intensely. She felt too much, so she numbed herself. If she was hard and cold, she couldn't feel anything at all. Feeling as if the world was muted was easier than dealing with its intensity.

But she didn't want to argue with Juliette, so she smiled back. "I'll consider that."

The wedding ceremony passed with little significance. Haerdnor and Naomi exchanged vows in front of the gods of the sea, sealing their marriage in a very scenic, very pious, very boring ceremony. With that over, everyone poured back into the estate for the party--the true reason people attended weddings. Well that, and also to seem important.

Amaria held onto Theodmon's arm as they went back inside. As they made their way back into the foyer, they passed Elisa.

"Countess Redwayne," Theodmon said politely.

Amaria smiled at Elisa, trying to ignore how much the other woman tensed up at the greeting. "Are you enjoying the wedding?"

"Of course," Elisa said, meeting Amaria's eyes momentarily before her gaze drifted towards an older Riam lord. She met his eyes, smiled coyly as she played with the pendant that highlighted her plunging neckline. "One thing I enjoy about you Thestitiunians is that women can hold money. I'm charging double while I'm here."

Elisa stepped closer to Amaria. "Do you want me to dispose of some of the more fragile men?"

Amaria blinked. "What?"

"The elderly men. It'll cause chaos with their newly inherit sons, and besides, a heart attack is believable when they're seventy and fucking a girl young enough to be their granddaughter."

Amaria felt her face turning red. "My Lady," she gasped, composing herself. Elisa had a point, she had to admit. And Amaria, despite the lack of grace Elisa was showcasing, respected her ruthlessness. She swallowed, before nodding curtly to the Riam. "Be subtle."

Elisa also probably has personal reasons for wanting these men dead. Amaria thought as Elisa went over to the elderly lord, and he immediately had his hands up her skirts–in public no less.

"Are you stooping so low to whore yourself at a wedding?" A Riam woman scoffed as Elisa kissed the lord.

"It's not like Thestitiunian whores aren't already hired for this." Elisa rubbed her hands over the lord's hair. "And I can charge money here, not just barter for food and a bed." She lifted her skirts up to her thighs, the Riam woman's face turning pale. She grabbed the elderly man, leading him away from the crowd, her skirts still raised. "I'll be fucking on the second floor, Lady Minthean. Let your husband know where I am, I know how much he enjoys me."

"She knows how to make a scene," Theodmon muttered.

Amaria nodded in agreement, watching as many men–not just Riam, watched Elisa leave with hungering interest. "She'll likely be busy all night."

"A noblewoman whoring herself will always fuck more men than a common whore," Theodmon agreed. "You think she can get good information?"

Amaria nodded. "There's no reason for them not to trust her–and she's smart. Besides, we need her to keep them distracted so they're easier to drug."

Amaria moved to kiss Theodmon on the lips, speaking quickly as their lips hovered over each other. "And I've not left everything to chance. Every whore here is an agent of mine. We'll have any information shared by a man who thinks he can buy loyalty as easily as he can buy a body."

"You bought whores for a wedding?" Theodmon chuckled, before kissing her and pulling away, walking into the grand hall where dining tables lined the walls.

"Not officially," Amaria said with a smirk. "But we all know whores come to weddings–it's too much money to pass up. So instead of leaving what whores appear later tonight to chance, I've ensured they're all spies. We'll get our information, especially when successful leads tend to result in high bonuses."

Theodmon chuckled. "It'd be near impossible for someone to offer your spies a higher price than you."

"Most spies don't have strong ideological reasons for being spies," Amaria agreed. "I can buy most of my spies' loyalty."

"Is that what you are doing with Elisa?"

Amaria scoffed. "She's loyal to herself, but we have something she wants." She and Theodmon sat down at the high table, on the groom's side. "And you'll need her at the front."

"She's a field agent?" Theodmon's eyebrows rose.

"Whores have a non-suspicious reason to be at war camps," Amaria said. "She's a noblewoman in title but nothing else. Your war camp will have many rich, lonely men and if she happened to get in the commander's tent, or adjacent to it, well she's a prime double agent. She tells the Riams false plans of ours and we get true plans."

"Perfect," Theodmon said. "What if she lies to us?"

"Henri can read her mind," Amaria said, "and if he's willing, he's going to be one of the men who is sleeping with her. At least, that's what it'll appear like. He doesn't actually have to do anything with her."

Theodmon sighed. "Henri will. Damn it, he's too good."

Amaria chuckled. "Is my plan good?"

"It's clever," Theodmon said, as Naomi and Haerdnor entered the hall, cheers erupting on all sides. "Let's hope it doesn't get us killed."

The feast went on for hours. In the corridors and gardens, lovers–legitimate or elicit–roamed, caressing each other and danced as they whispered sweet nothings and secrets. When it was nearing midnight, Aaron stood up, raising a glass. "I have an announcement. Duke Svilas, would you join me in doing the honors?"

Amaria saw Durek stand up and move her way towards the great table. She looked around for Natayla and realized that she hadn't seen her since the ceremony.

"Duke Raulet," Durek greeted as he joined Aaron, turning to the crowd as Aaron continued speaking.

"Duke Svilas has given me the great honor of hosting another wedding soon," Aaron said. "I'll be wed to his daughter, Lady Natayla, within the year. And to celebrate this engagement, let us have another week of wine and food on top of the celebrations for my son's marriage."

The party goers cheered at the prospect of more debauchery. Aaron quieted them again by raising his hand "Please make way for the current bride and groom, Lord and Lady Raulet." Aaron turned his head towards Haerdnor and Naomi, indicating it was time for them to make their way through the crowd for their last appearance before retiring to their chambers.

Haerdnor stood up, and Amaria could have swore she saw him gulp. Amaria's heart ached for him, knowing how awful the wedding night could be–and how much one could dread it when you knew you could never love the person.

Naomi Brassir wasn't a Lyseno Vypren, but she still could never be a Theodmon to Haerdnor. Her eyes watering, Amaria leaned over and momentarily placed her head on Theodmon's shoulder. "I'm glad you're mine."

Theodmon kissed the top of her head. "I love you."

Amaria closed her eyes. She didn't want to be at this party anymore. She wanted to curl up in her bed, warm under several blankets, and sleep for days.

Chapter Thirty-Five

The next day, Theodmon woke up before the sun rose, pulling on his clothes with a yawn. Perivina Fluere was miserably hot, especially in comparison to the Westerlands' northern mountain and forest climate.

Theodmon massaged the calluses on his hands as he exited Provincia Palencia, pushing past a seemingly never-ending mirage of roses, shrubbery, trees, and fountains. The maze ended in grassy, sloping dunes along the stables that looked out on the seashore.

The Raulets called their training area the Grounds by the Sea. Theodmon already felt himself sweating.

Theodmon shook his head as he dropped his helmet in the sand, pulling out Winterthorne. As he went through the different sword forms, the sun rose over the training grounds by the sea, casting long shadows across the sand.

"Sorry I'm late," Lucas said, sliding down the sloping dune, Henri close behind him. "It's a labyrinth in there."

"No more than Forteresse les Blanche," Theodmon said, holding his sword upwards, counting to a hundred before he dropped the form.

"We're familiar with Forteresse les Blanche," Henri said.

Theodmon dropped his sword form as he caught sight of Henri. *I suppose this is as good of a time as any,* Theodmon told himself, his stomach knotting. Henri deserved to be told of this intelligence plan that he was instrumental too, and Henri also deserved to be told as early as possible.

"Henri," Theodmon said, "I have to talk to you—let's sit down."

"I'm a large part of an intelligence plan," Henri said calmly, sitting on the sand. "You or Amaria's idea?"

Amaria. Theodmon thought, knowing Henri would hear as he sat down next to him.

Henri chuckled. "Of course."

"Can we not do the mind-reading stuff?" Lucas asked, joining them on the ground. "I have no idea what's going on."

Henri chuckled once more, this time with a playful eye roll. "What's the plan?"

How am I supposed to tell him this? Theodmon thought, before he launched into the tale of how Elisa Redwayne was recruited by Amaria, and the plans they had for her as a field agent in Rindria.

"So who are the generals or the close confidants of the generals in Rindria?" Lucas said. "There's me, Theodmon, Aloysius, Henri–"

"Oliver Neremoux," Theodmon added, thankful that Aaron was having some Perivnians join the fight. "Michel Valrois and Samuel Beaulane," he said the Extractors name, also thankful they were helping. "Brigette Belamy." The war mage was a risk, however, he family had always been loyal and Brigette was eager to fight. Theodmon hoped this would inspire longer lasting loyalty from Brigette, more than he could have ever hoped for from her deceased brother.

"I'm not sleeping, or even appearing to sleep with a whore," Lucas said. "I'm married. I'm not disrespecting Juliette in that way."

Theodmon shook his head. "I'd never ask you too. There's unmarried men–"

"Oliver, Aloysius, and me," Henri said, his face impassive.

"I was hoping you'd agree to being the contact," Theodmon said. "If she decides to double cross us—"

"I'm the best person to know," Henri agreed. His shoulders rose slightly before he exhaled. "And I'm not injured, such as Aloysius, or a suspected ah, deviant," Henri cringed slightly, "as Oliver is suspected to be."

"It sounds unnecessarily harsh when you put it that way," Lucas muttered.

Henri shrugged. "It's true, and the plan makes sense." He looked over at Theodmon. "I'm not required to actually sleep with her, right?"

Theodmon shook his head. "Only to make it seem as if you are. Whatever you do while she's in your tent is your business."

Henri exhaled once more, his shoulders losing their tension before he curtly nodded at Theodmon, double confirming his agreement to do this plan. "When do we leave?"

"Within the end of the week." Theodmon forced himself to his feet. "We should probably start training."

"Before we cook in this armor," Lucas grumbled in agreement, stomping over to a covered basket of multi-colored ribbons. He pulled a green one and tied it around his wrist. "How do people live here?"

"Are we really doing ribbons?" Henri snorted. "We know who each of us are."

"In case others come." Lucas balled up a turquoise ribbon and threw it at Henri, before subsequently throwing a yellow ribbon at Theodmon.

Theodmon chuckled as he caught the fabric, tying it around his wrist. "You know I hate yellow."

"Why do you think I gave it to you?" Lucas said, before pulling his helmet over his head.

Theodmon pulled on his own helmet. "No training swords?"

Lucas gave him a thumbs up. Henri, chuckling as he looked in between them, did similarly.

"Who is going first?" Henri asked.

"I'll go," Theodmon offered. "Winner will rest after this fight and the loser will spar the next person. From there we will rotate in that order–but its person so not winner or loser," Theodmon sighed. "For example: I spar Henri, I win. Henri spars Lucas. Now regardless of whether Lucas wins or loses he will spar me next. And then regardless of who I win, I spar Henri next."

"Two on, one off," Lucas agreed.

"You think you'll win against me?" Henri quipped.

"Yes," Lucas said dryly. "You're not the most physical Henri."

"Strategy," Henri protested.

Lucas snorted. "We're all strategists here."

Theodmon picked up his sword and shield, nodding towards Lucas. "We'll go first." He looked over at Henri as he and Lucas both stepped into the middle of the stone circle. "Coach while waiting."

"I get to yell at you two?" Henri said dryly. "Say no more."

"I'm going to win," Lucas said, raising his sword as he faced Theodmon.

"You wish," Theodmon said with a snort, also raising his weapon.

Silently, Theodmon and Lucas watched each other, analyzing each other's stance, strengths, and weaknesses before the dance of swords began.

In the middle of the circle Theodmon and Lucas sparred, the metal of their swords shrieking, and the thuds of their shields revibrating through the morning air. "Higher!" Henri shouted at them. "Don't drop your shield, Lucas!"

Theodmon and Lucas stepped backwards from each other, as if in sync, lifting their shields higher before lunging and parrying again. Henri stood there watching, as still as a lion before it pounced on its prey. As the two men in the ring danced, the swords flashing around them as if a dangerous ribbon, Lucas pushed back against Theodmon, forcing him to the outer limits of the ring, Theodmon's feet narrowly avoiding stepping outside the boundaries.

He lept back inside the ring, slashing at Lucas with his sword. Lucas stepped back as he raised his shield, thwarting Theodmon's attempt to strike him and win the round with contract, but allowing Theodmon to amply step away from the borders of the ring.

Theodmon swung his sword up to perry, but Lucas dodged the perry at the last second, attempting to knock Theodmon from his feet with a side swept kick. Theodmon did almost a series of dance steps to avoid his feet from being swept from under him, and Lucas only managed to kick him in the shins.

"Ouch," Theodmon chuckled, half out of pain and half out of amused surprise. He steadied himself, facing his opponent. Lucas held his sword straight out in front of him with both hands, his stance wide, steady, and low to the ground.

Breathing heavily, Theodmon protected his front and sides as he lunged in for another attack, his blade swinging mere inches from Lucas' shoulder and Lucas easily brought up his sword, blocking the attack. Theodmon enjoyed this game with Lucas who was his equal in strength, stamina, dexterity, and cunning. Whatever plan Theodmon could think of to defeat Lucas, Lucas had already considered it plus one more.

It was the best challenge Theodmon could ever hope for.

Lucas swung again, and Theodmon blocked it, pushing against Lucas with his sword. Lucas stumbled a small amount, and Theodmon noticed that he wasn't exactly fully stable, Lucas weight was mainly being supported by his back leg.

Theodmon pushed his shield against Lucas with a large burst of energy, and in a risky move, threw his shield away from him, swinging his sword closer to Lucas. Lucas raised his sword to block, however, Theodmon stepped under the blow to Lucas's right side, locking his blade under Lucas's.

"Told you I'd win," Theodmon said as he pushed the weight of his blade upwards. Lucas's wrist locked and he let go of his sword, the weapon tumbling down the sandy slope.

Lucas immediately dropped to the ground, kicking Theodmon's legs from under him. Theodmon rolled out of the way, picking up his sword as he stood.

Lucas pointed to Theodmon's feet, still sitting on the ground. "I won."

"What?" Theodmon looked down at where he was standing. He had disarmed Lucas, but he hadn't landed a blow. And his left foot was squarely out of the barriers of the ring. Lucas had won. Lucas had won by being cleverer than Theodmon.

"I should be mad," Theodmon said.

"But you aren't," Lucas said, pulling off his helmet, his blond hair sticking to his scalp. "Good job. If it was a real fight, I'd be dead or at the very least, maimed." He laid back in the sand, breathing softly.

"That was a great fight," Henri agreed. "By the way, Oliver and Aloysius are coming." Sure enough, within a matter of seconds, the outline of their heads appeared.

"Aloysius should be healing," Theodmon muttered to himself, watching Oliver and Aloysius closely as they approached. He moved over towards Lucas, extending his hand to help him off of the ground. "What is he doing?"

Lucas took Theodmon's hand, and with a huff, Theodmon helped pull him off the ground.

"This is his fight too," Lucas said.

"But is he strong enough?" Theodmon muttered, seeing how pale Aloysius seemed as he made his way down the slope. His brother was about fifteen feet away now and he still looked sickly, with dark circles under his eyes and knotted, dead looking hair.

"Would it stop you?" Lucas said as Aloysius and Oliver came to a stop in front of the other three men.

"I'm training," Aloysius announced.

"Rest," Theodmon said automatically.

"When did you become a healer?" Aloysius said, crossing his arms with a scowl.

"You're injured," Theodmon said half-heartedly, knowing how pathetic of an excuse it sounded before he even said it.

"And that's why I'm starting with wooden swords," Aloysius said with an eyeroll. "Master Chironia approved me to start training, so if you want to go argue with the Raulets' healer be my guest."

"Master Chironia told me to bring him here," Oliver confirmed. "He believes it's in Aloysius' best interests to train again."

"I'm still going to the front," Aloysius said. "Right?"

Theodmon said nothing.

"Theo," Aloysius said, his voice gaining an edge. "I'm not Father. I'm not Ophelia. Stop trying to protect me. I am just as trained–just as expected as you–to fight these battles. So let me."

Theodmon gave a curt nod. "In a week. I do want you to take it easy until then so you can heal."

Aloysius rolled his eyes. "Agreed," he said. "Now give me a training sword so I can run drills while the rest of you spar."

For the next few hours, Aloysius ran drills, taking frequent breaks, while the others ran through training simulations. All five of them sat down, watching the lapping waves as they downed bags of water, the sun beating mercilessly down upon them.

They were stripping off their armor and clothes to go for a swim when another figure ran down the dunes, revealing themselves to be Haerdnor as they neared closer to them.

"Am I too late for training?" Haerdnor said easily, almost lazily, twirling his sword in his hands. Swords were often named. Theodmon named his sword Winterthorne because of the sharp, cool bite the steel gave to anyone misfortunate enough to be cut by it. To Theodmon's knowledge, Haerdnor's sword was named Eternal Flame to be reminiscent of an awful double pun. The sword caught on fire due to Haerdnor's fire magic, but Theodmon, when trying to determine what flowers to import for Amaria, learned that eternal flame was also a type of rose. Theodmon supposed it fit Haerdnor, but he still internally rolled his eyes every time he saw the blade.

"No," Henri said. "But we were just about to take a break and swim."

Haerdnor broke into an easy grin. "It's hot out here," he said, as his eyes drifted over the horizon. He paused, his entire body tensing. From his peripheral vision, Theodmon could tell that Haerdnor was looking at Oliver.

Unusual. Theodmon thought as Haerdnor's eyes narrowed. *I thought they were on good terms. Really good terms.*

"Never mind." Haerdnor sharply turned on his heel.

"Haerdnor," Oliver said softly, almost pleadingly.

"No," Haerdnor said, keeping his eyes focused anywhere but on Oliver. "Amaria needed my help in the Drowning Tombs." Without another word or glance back at the rest of them, Haerdnor Raulet trudged back up the dunes, headed inside to Provincia Palancia once more.

Chapter Thirty-Six

T hirty minutes after her husband left, Amaria was awake and was pulling a comb through her hair, yawning. She wanted nothing more than to climb back in bed, but she needed to go back to the Drowning Tombs, not to torture others, but to undergo torture training again. If she feared even stepping into a dungeon, and if she let herself get sloppy with that fear, then she was a liability.

That issue, relatively speaking, was easier to fix than the other one. Amaria had been trained to resist torture techniques since she was a child. But after Rindria, she doubted her ability to handle that. Amaria clenched her fists. She didn't have a choice but to overcome this fear, her father's expectations, and her own desires of perfection, would not allow her to do anything else.

She had asked her father to help her. Amaria had also asked Haerdnor, but whether or not he would join her was unknown. Haerdnor hated the Drowning Tombs, he much preferred honorable fighting styles, like sword play or ramming one's ship into an enemy.

Amaria looked at her fraying navy dress–the dress she always had used for torture training. She had made some alterations, lowering the back to accommodate her wings. Perhaps she should have had a new dress made instead of altering this old, raggedy one. But for some reason, Amaria couldn't throw it away. The dress, in some twisted way, brought her comfort. And she would need a lot of comfort today.

Sighing, Amaria stood up, smoothing her hands over the front of her dress, as she looked at herself in the mirror, ensuring her hair was tightly braided and pinned. Deciding her appearance was satisfactory, Amaria turned on her heels, leaving her chambers and headed downstairs to meet her father in the kitchens.

"Glad you can join us," Aaron said as Amaria stepped through the kitchen doors. Next to him, Galen stood holding a small medicine bag in one hand and toast in the other.

"Father. Master Chironia," Amaria greeted, inclining her head slightly, before turning to a servant and asking for toast with butter. Nobody said anything until the servant returned and handed Amaria her breakfast.

"Let's go," Aaron ordered as Amaria held her wrapped toast against her chest. "We've a long day ahead of us."

She forced the lump down her throat, her hands shaking as she followed her father and Galen outside to where a carriage waited for them.

"My Lady." Galen politely held his hand out to help her into the carriage.

"Thank you," Amaria told him as she stepped into the carriage. "Are you coming with us?"

Galen waited for Aaron to climb into the carriage before entering, shutting the door behind him. "Yes. I've been told my services may be needed for your training again, my Lady."

Amaria turned towards her father, her eyes widening. Galen had traditionally only accompanied her and her father to the Drowning Tombs whenever she was being tortured. "Why is Master Chironia here?"

Aaron banged on the top of the carriage, indicating for the driver to begin their travels. "A precaution."

For what? A chill went down Amaria's spine. "We are interrogating prisoners, right?"

"The last time you did that you tried to release a prisoner and almost died because of your stupidity," Aaron said. "I'm taking precautions. I trust you won't disappoint me this time."

Amaria's heart thudded against her chest as her gaze drifted towards the bundle of toast within her lap. She gently began to open it as her stomach rumbled. "I hope to make you proud."

"How are you holding up since your last trip to the Drowning Tombs?" Aaron asked.

"I'm alright. I suppose it'll be easier for me to torture others than being tortured....," she trailed off, licking her lips.

"You will have to get over that experience," Aaron said. "It's unfortunate it happened but you knew the risks of this field."

Amaria looked at her lap, staring at the stitching of her dress. "No," she whispered. "I can't."

Aaron grabbed her by the chin, forcing her to look at him. "You can." His eyes hardened. "You will remain an asset, not a liability."

"And that's why we're torturing prisoners?" Amaria jerked her face away from him.

"I have half a mind to order you to be locked up in the Tombs until you recover from this unfortunate setback," Aaron said.

Amaria crossed her arms. "Theodmon would never allow it. You wouldn't either—you care too much about appearances."

"Your Grace," Galen ventured out hesitantly. "Perhaps it is best if the Lady was granted a safe word of sorts, considering her recent experiences—"

"No," Aaron said. "She'll learn this way. Coddling does no favors in this line of work, and I believe my daughter is fully aware of how many people would love to see her head on a spike."

"Not nearly as many as those who would love to see yours," Amaria answered.

Aaron cooly stared at her for a second before he burst into a smile—Amaria was reminded vividly of a crocodile. "See Galen? Amaria understands the precarious nature of her situation."

"Master Chironia, I thank you for your concern," Amaria said emotionlessly. What more could she say? Her chest rose deeply, her eyes staring outside the carriage window as if in a trance.

I hate to admit it, but Father has a point. This is what I was good at. And this is what people expect from me. A torturer terrified of dungeons is useless. Amaria licked her lips, ignoring how much her chin was quivering. She wasn't going to cry. Not here. Not ever in front of her father. *I need to get over what happened in Rindria. For my own future.*

She looked over at her father, who was still surveying the sites outside of his window. *How are we so disconnected from each other?* She forced back the urge to reach out and hug her father. *He's my father. We used to be of one mind.*

Amaria didn't want to challenge Aaron anymore. She wanted everything to be how it was two years ago. "Father," she said, the words falling involuntarily from her mouth. "I missed you."

Cheeks flushing, Amaria stared at her lap, waiting for her Father to scold her. She felt him squeeze her hand, and she froze, waiting for the lecture.

"I miss you too," Aaron said.

As if jolted by a spark of lightning, Amaria's eyes flew open. "Father?"

"A lot has changed these past few years, and you've grown into your own." Aaron said with a heavy sigh. "I want my daughter back."

Amaria's eyes watered. "I'd never leave you, Father."

Aaron gave her a tightlipped smile. "Let's talk more after our visit. I hope you're adequately prepared."

Amaria took a bite of her toast. "Tell me about the prisoners."

Chapter Thirty-Seven

Amaria was not, in fact, adequately prepared for what was in store for her in the Drowning Tombs. She felt sick the moment she stepped into the prison, following her father though the dark, damp corridors. Her entire body shook as a shiver went down her spine. Something in the water touched her ankle and she screamed.

Aaron looked over his shoulder at her, his lip curling. "Have some decorum."

Her hands pressed against her chest, Amaria took a shaky breath, trying to compose herself. She hated it here. She didn't want to be in the Tombs–in any dungeon–ever again. Not that she could tell her father that.

"Apologies," she said.

"I don't want your apologies, I want you to conduct yourself appropriately." Aaron stopped in front of a cell door. "Don't scream in front of this one. It discredits you."

"What information am I seeking to get from this prisoner?" Amaria asked.

"None," Aaron said. "He's useless to us in that regard. His mind is gone. You're going to torture him until he dies."

Amaria took a step back, her hands shaking. What was the purpose of torturing an insane man? They could kill him simply, a dagger across the throat or poison in his water. "Why?" Her voice cracked and she sounded pathetically weak.

Aaron frowned, stepping closer to Amaria. "Because you need to become cold again. This softness is unbecoming of your station here. He'd kill you if given the chance. Remember this before you try and free this one."

Amaria recoiled at her father's verbal slap. She looked down at her feet, her face burning. Her father would never let go of her stupid decision with Fawzia Suril. He would remind her of how she had almost died as soon as she acted contrary to his teachings. It was an impulsive, stupid decision chosen only because she had a sudden burst of empathy.

Aaron unlocked the cell door, stepping away from the entrance. Amaria gulped as she forced herself to step in the dark entrance. Every muscle in her body was screaming at her for her to run in the opposite direction. She didn't want to go into the cell. She didn't want to torture this prisoner.

Fire flickered in her hand, illuminating the cell. In the shadows the prisoner sat, clutching his legs to his chest as he muttered to himself. Cutting his throat would be a kindness.

Aaron pressed a choke pear into her hand. Amaria shuddered looking at the tear shaped metal device. It was only to cause pain–how could someone talk with this in their mouths? With wide eyes, she looked over at her father.

"How long should I keep this up before I let him die?"

"Until I command you to stop," Aaron said.

"Must I use the choke pear?"

"You are free to use other methods," Aaron said. "You don't need guidance on effective ways to conduct this job."

Amaria didn't want to do this job, though. She swallowed her spit and stepped deeper into the cell, the fire flickering around her wrists. Perhaps she would burn him. Using fire magic had always been easy for her and she had no qualms or fears now regarding using her magic.

As her heart thudded loudly in her ears, Amaria reached the prisoner, grabbing his arm, the flames embracing him.

He screamed as the fire burned his skin. It was an anguished cry, one of pain, despair, and hopelessness. Amaria dropped his arm, gasping, as she stepped away from him. *I can't.* She felt bile rise to her throat. She couldn't hear the screams in a dungeon without hearing the remnants of her own.

"No," she gasped, taking a further step away from the prisoner.

Aaron stepped close to her, raising himself to his full height as he loomed over her. "No?"

She pressed her eyes shut, tears falling down her face. "I can't."

"You can," Aaron said, his voice calm. "And you will."

Amaria shook her head, her throat tightening to where she couldn't breath. "I can't."

Aaron's lip curled. "Pity." He turned to the door, summoning a guard, before stepping around her, pulling out a dagger. "You are a failure. Guard, make sure my daughter doesn't miss a moment of this."

Amaria gulped, tasting the salt of her tears. "I can do other things, I don't–"

The prisoner's screams interrupted Amaria as Aaron stabbed him. Amaria flinched, averting her eyes. A heavy gloved hand snatched her by the neck and forced her head back into place, the guard forcing her to watch her father.

"If you shut your eyes I'll make it worse for you once I'm done with him," Aaron said. "Watch."

Amaria's legs shook and if not for the guard forcefully holding her in place she likely would have collapsed. In Bria Hall they had held her in place like this, torturing her. They would have eventually killed her, she was sure of it. Clarissa wanted her dead.

Aaron summoned a briar branch, wrapping it around the prisoner. He tightened the thorny branch around the man, strangling him as it drew blood. Amaria's screams merged in the air with the prisoner's.

"Stop!" She struggled against the guard's grasp. "Stop this. Is it necessary? He's already dead."

Aaron slowly turned towards her. "You dare challenge me?"

Amaria almost apologized. She didn't want to face her father's ire, especially after they had started to reconnect. But if she apologized, she would be showing weakness, and that was intolerable. "Father, he's useless. What's the point of this?"

Aaron turned and cut the man's throat, the blood dripping into the water. "The point was for you to get over this fear you have with a low-risk prisoner. If you can't torture and kill someone like him, why should you be trusted with more serious projects?"

"I don't have to torture–"

Aaron grabbed Amaria by the arm. "Yes, you do." He pulled her towards a rack, spit foaming at his mouth. "You are to do your duty, which includes running intelligence operations."

"Father–"

Aaron slapped her across the face. Amaria gasped, bringing her hand to where he hit her. Her father had never hit her–the only time that had ever occurred was when she was undergoing torture training.

"You will obey me," Aaron snarled, pulling her hand away from her face. "You will do what I trained you to do and get over this unfortunate setback in your abilities."

Amaria struggled to pull herself from his grasp, sobbing. He had never yelled at her.

"I'm going to demonstrate what will happen to you if you don't conduct yourself appropriately."

"Father?" Amaria gasped. She pulled her arm from his grasp.

Aaron surveyed her silently before he looked over at a rotted wooden table with chains. "Get on the table."

Amaria ran. She had to get out of here. The guard grabbed her and pulled her towards the table, her thrashing against him the entire time.

"I'm sorry!" Amaria pleaded. "I'll do what you command. Please. Don't."

The guard threw her on the table and helped Aaron chain her down. "Father!" Amaria screamed, as if he would listen. As if the reminder of their familial connection would be enough for him to not hurt her.

Aaron's hand brushed over her face. "I'll be kind and ensure the water is clean." He snapped his fingers at Galen. "Render her unconscious as we make preparations."

The last thing Amaria saw before the world faded to black was Galen's face looming over her.

Chapter Thirty-Eight

A maria was pathetic. She was forced to admit that as she lay on her back, chained down as Aaron repeatedly poured water over her face.

"Please," she sputtered out, choking on the words. "Let me go."

It's not real. It's not real. Amaria tried to turn her head to the side, desperately attempting to avoid the water pouring onto her face. The water burned as it went up her nostrils. *My father is doing this to help me.*

"What's your name?" Aaron forced his hand under her chin, keeping her head in place as he poured water on her again. Nearby, in the corner, Galen watched, surveying her vitals and reactions, ready to intervene if necessary.

It's not real. My father would never hurt me. This man only looks like my father. My father wouldn't torture me.

"Amaria Raulet," she gasped out.

Aaron lifted a heavy mallet, balancing it in his hand. "And what are your failures?"

"Failures?" Amaria blinked rapidly.

"The failures you are being punished for." Aaron raised the mallet.

Amaria screamed, thrashing against the rack as if she could escape her chains. "I don't know, I don't know." Her chest hurt, she would do anything to get away from this hell. "Everything. I failed at everything. Whatever you wanted me to fail at."

Water hit her face again.

"You used to hold up better in these exercises," Aaron said. "Pity. You had real promise."

"I'll do better," Amaria sobbed. "I'm sorry."

Aaron chuckled. "I am sure you will. But until then, you will learn this lesson so as to not repeat it." He raised the mallet, throwing it down on Amaria's arm, her bones breaking. Amaria gave a wordless scream of pure agony, black dotting her vision. "What are your crimes?"

As Amaria's vision cleared, she was back in a different prison. The lack of light felt too familiar–although the water around the floor wasn't something she'd had in Rindria. Her entire body trembled as she thrashed against the rack. "No!" She screamed, frantically looking around as if she could escape. "No!"

"No, what?" Her torturer said. She couldn't focus on his face, her mind was too cloudy.

"I don't belong here," Amaria sobbed. "My husband and father will pay good money for me to be unharmed. Let me go!"

"Your Grace," the man in the corner spoke up. "Perhaps we should stop–"

"No," the torturer dismissed. "She can stop it, as long as she confesses her crimes."

"I'll do it," Amaria screamed. "Please, let me go." She sobbed, her chest constricting in pain.

"And what is your name and crimes?" The torturer said.

"I'm Amaria Raulet," Amaria sobbed. "Amaria Chauvignon. Please...." Her entire body shook as she sobbed hysterically. "I killed them. I killed the royal family."

"Your Grace," the man in the corner said sharply, moving over towards Amaria. "Stop this. Now." His hands glowed green as he moved them over her body. "She'll die if you continue." She felt her bones knitting together.

"Pity," the other man said. "Fine. Galen, knock her unconscious as you heal her. I think she's had enough pain for now."

Amaria sat, wrapped in a blanket, as she shivered upon the cot, her legs curled against her chest as she tried to not look into the water below. She had failed her father's test.

And he had failed hers. She hadn't realized this was going to be a test, but her subconscious was searching not only for reasons to trust her father, but for reasons to distrust him. He had lied to her about Vypren. What kind of parent did this to their children? Amaria couldn't imagine doing this to Lysander or Sylviana—now that she was a mother, her father's actions began to look less like clever shows of power and more like the chaotic workings of a psychopath.

"My Lady." Galen sat down next to her. "May I?"

Numbly, Amaria nodded, staring blankly at the space in front of her. *I failed.* She didn't flinch as Galen took her arm in his, extending and rotating it to check its healing. *I'm weak and a disappointment to my father.*

"If I had my way, you'd be out of this forsaken place," Galen grumbled. "Clench your fist for me."

Amaria obliged, ignoring the sheering, burning pain shooting up her arm. However, she grimaced and Galen tutted under his breath, gently supporting her arm with his own hands.

"You were in Rindria again, weren't you?" Galen ran his glowing hands over her arm. "Just nod or shake your head."

Swallowing down the lump in her throat, Amaria nodded as warm salty tears rolled down her cheeks, her eyes unblinking at the spot of the wall in front of her. "I'm broken."

"Perhaps," Galen said pensively. "However, that doesn't mean you're deficient."

"It does," Amaria said, her voice still emotionless. She barely heard herself, she was drowning but she felt at peace. She felt nothing at all.

"Show me the person who wouldn't fear dungeons after being tortured. Show me the person who wouldn't break and remember their real torture in doing this...training." Disgust dripped from Galen's voice at the last word.

"I'm a disappointment—"

"No," Galen interrupted sternly. "I've known you since you were a child, and you aren't a disappointment. Not to me, not to anybody who loves you, and definitely not to your father."

Amaria gave a small, disbelieving chuckle, pulling her legs tighter around herself. Galen meant well, but he couldn't fool her with these lies–sweet, fabricated words whose sole purpose was to comfort her.

"I'm not lying to you," Galen said.

Amaria knew Galen was loyal to her father, not to her, but still, she couldn't stop herself from confiding in the kindly healer. "Nothing ever seems to be enough for him," she said, her eyes still hazy from the tears.

"He's a bit harsh," Galen admitted. "Do you know anything about your father's childhood?"

Amaria laid her head on her knees. What did it matter?

Galen had not taken his gaze away from her. Amaria sighed, knowing she had to answer something, or else Galen would wait until she broke. The man had endless patience, something Amaria had never understood but had grown to admire.

"He was a fourth son," Amaria muttered. "He was trained to be a lawyer. All my uncles died in war. My father's leg was mangled in battle, but he was the last one standing, so he became Duke Raulet when my grandfather was assassinated." Amaria recited the family history in a monotone.

"What do you know about your grandfather?" Galen asked kindly.

"His name was Clarents, the seventh Duke Raulet of that name," Amaria said with a huff. "Married to Sabrana Descartes, from Arb–"

"Not sounding like a historical or genealogical account," Galen interrupted. "What do you know of the man?"

Amaria's head snapped around to glare at Galen. What did he mean by *what do you know of the man?* Was he daring to suggest she didn't know her own family?

"None of your business, Master Chironia," Amaria said cooly. "I assure you, I know more about my own family than you presume."

Galen chuckled, standing up. "Good." He extended his hand out to her. "The shock is wearing off."

Amaria's eyebrows rose before her eyes narrowed. "You were medically goading me?"

"That's an expression." Galen shook his head, his hand still extended to her. "Are you coming out with me?"

"Father won't–"

"Your father won't do anything to risk your health," Galen said. "I've told him not to. Now, are you coming with me willingly, or do I have to carry you out?"

Gingerly, Amaria extended her hand, grasping Galen's with it. As she stood up, she cautiously surveyed Galen, wondering, not for the first time, how a commoner rose to be so high that he dared to challenge Aaron Raulet, and furthermore, challenged him successfully and with impunity.

"How do you know my father?" Amaria asked.

"From his childhood," Galen said. "He wasn't always this harsh."

"Neither was I," Amaria said bitterly. *But nobody mourns the girl I used to be. Nobody mourns the women I could've been.*

"He sees a lot of himself in you," Galen said.

"He's always loved insulting me," Amaria said, the words clipping harshly as the echo reverberated through the underwater corridors.

"It's a compliment," Galen insisted softly.

Amaria blew air out her nose. "Spare me."

"Talk to him," Galen said. "Do you see Aaron Raulet as being the one to save a commoner from execution?"

Amaria's eyes widened as she looked at Galen. She couldn't see her father doing that, not without ulterior motives. Her eyes immediately narrowed. "If it suited him, I could see my father saving anyone from the block," Amaria said. "What price has he demanded from you?"

Amaria didn't expect a response. If it were a simple one, a normal one, he wouldn't be here. And so, she trudged silently ahead, the soaking long folds of her dress clinging to her skin as she waded through the disgusting water.

Galen ran behind her, catching up easily with his lanky legs. "He's demanded nothing," Galen said, causing Amaria to stop in her tracks.

"That doesn't sound like my father."

"No," Galen agreed. "It doesn't. But your father in his youth wasn't the same person as he is today. Your grandfather was harsh to criminals–he would kill entire families for one person's crimes. Even children." Galen looked at Amaria, the frown lines on his forehead becoming more prominent in the dimming light.

Amaria pursed her lips tightly together. "With all due respect, Master Chironia, what is your point?"

"My father stole some luxury items–perfume, silk, I can't remember," Galen sadly sighed. "Your father saved me. He argued against his father for my life. He was punished for it, in secret of course. Appearances had to be maintained, and your father was responsible for me now. Your grandfather tied my wrong doing to your father, and vice versa."

"My grandfather brought around reforms!" Amaria retorted, feeling as if her entire world was collapsing and that she was desperately trying to uphold sinking walls. "He brought forward the meritocracy of mages which strengthened the economy and the middle class in Perivina Fluere–"

"That was your father," Galen said, the two of them now walking through the dry area of the prison, the exit nearing. "Your grandfather claimed your father's work as his own."

"No." Amaria shook her head. "Why? What purpose would he have to do that?"

"He needed popularity–your grandfather was not well liked. Forgive me, my Lady, but did you ever wonder why he was assassinated?"

"I command you to stop." Amaria rose herself to her full height. "I'll not listen to further lies against my ancestors."

Galen looked at Amaria sadly as they stepped into the sunlight. "Of course, my Lady." He bowed his head in a respectful incline. "I just ask one thing, as a humble servant of your family. Please, consider asking your father about his childhood. I believe it'd benefit both of you."

Amaria's chest rose, her hands shaking as she raised them to her squinting eyes, shielding her face from the blinding sun. Galen asked a lot for a man of his position. But still–what he said, it made a sliver of sense. On why her father avoided speaking of his childhood, on why Aunt Miana avoided it too, and on why her tutors seemed to be expressly forbidden in explaining anything about the era her grandfather ruled other than base genealogical facts and positive facts–facts that were never deeply expanded on.

"Alright," she whispered. "I'll consider it."

A carriage door flew open. Haerdnor nearly jumped out of it as he jogged towards her. "Amaria!" As he neared, his nose wrinkled. "You smell like death."

"Lord Raulet," Galen interrupted. "Would you mind bringing your sister home? I see that you brought your own transportation." The healer nodded towards Haerdnor's carriage. "I will return with your father once he is finished conducting his business."

"Father isn't with you?" Haerdnor craned his head around, as if he expected Aaron to appear from behind a wall.

"Get your sister home." Galen practically pushed Amaria into the carriage. "And make sure she rests, do you understand me, Lord Raulet?"

Haerdnor's eyebrows creased together before he nodded. "Of course," he said, joining Amaria in the carriage. She was laying down on the seat, her eyes closed.

"What happened there?" Haerdnor asked as the carriage began to move.

Amaria breathed heavily. "I didn't handle being tortured well."

"Do you have to risk yourself like that?" Haerdnor challenged. "Obviously, it's not a good idea. You could do, I don't know, solely behind the scenes things. Like a puppeteer?"

"And who'll tell Father?" Amaria pushed back. "He's made it clear disappointing him isn't an option, and me letting my experience in Rindria continue to be a hindrance—"

"Tell him to kick rocks."

Amaria blew air out her nose, scoffing.

"I'm serious," Haerdnor insisted. "How do you think I got out of this bullshit?"

"You had a better capacity for naval warfare—"

"And you have a better capacity for running things behind the scenes and using flashy magic."

"He puts us where he needs us—"

"And if you got captured again, you'd be doing a prison break," Haerdnor said. "Let's not lie to ourselves. It doesn't benefit anyone, not even Father."

Amaria sighed, bringing her hands up to her forehead, rubbing her temples. "What do you know about our paternal grandfather?"

"Why?" Haerdnor asked, his voice lifting slightly.

"Galen said something about Father's childhood and our grandfather...I was just, it's nothing." Amaria sat up and studied her brother's face, tracing the familiar lines of it to see if there was something he knew.

"Father told me about grandfather's ruling methods," Haerdnor said, "in warning perhaps, or truly maybe it was to prepare me for my future role."

"And?" Amaria questioned.

"He wasn't the best person," Haerdnor said with a dry chuckle. "Aunt Miana was married off at thirteen—far too young by even the most archaic nations' notions. He'd cut off hands for minor offenses, such as a singular speck of dust. He'd take away titles and inflict heavy fines on a whim. There were whispers of uprisings against his entire rule— you know he was assassinated." Haerdnor leaned back in his seat. "Father had to undo a lot of the damage done for years to gain a semblance of stability. Since then, Perivina Fluere has prospered."

"Father's seen as a tyrant."

"No, he's seen as cruel," Haerdnor corrected. "But he's fair, has consistent rules, and awards merit and loyalty."

"So a competent tyrant." Amaria leaned her face against the window, closing her eyes as the city whirled past. "I wish he wasn't so hard on us."

"Me too," Haerdnor agreed. "But I understand it."

He is strengthening a near dying empire. Amaria's eyes fluttered open and close, as the exhaustion finally washed over her, now that her heart wasn't thudding loudly against her chest. She hadn't even noticed how wired she had been until she relaxed in this carriage.

"I understand it too," Amaria admitted in a fraught whisper. "But it still hurts."

Chapter Thirty-Nine

"Cheater!" Lucas shouted at Henri as Henri playfully kicked his coquet ball out of the pit.

"It's only cheating if you lose," Henri said, picking up his ball with a smirk, walking to the hoop and placing the ball through it.

Lucas barreled towards Henri, the two of them wrestling; Theodmon laughed as he watched from the bench with Aloysius before catching sight of Amaria and Haerdnor entering through the gates. Theodmon immediately noticed that her shoulders slouched and her skin was sallow.

His brows knitting together, Theodmon jogged over to them. "Amaria, what's wrong?"

Her eyes were red and puffy and her skin was sallow. As she gripped her cloak, shaking, Theodmon noticed the red welts around her hands.

"She went to the Drowning Tombs," Haerdnor said. "Not for prisoners."

Theodmon's blood turned to ice as his features contorted into a glare, his knuckles cracking together. "You didn't," he said towards Amaria, his voice aghast.

"Yes." Amaria's voice was barely a whisper. "It needed to be done. I didn't have a choice."

"No," Theodmon snapped. "It didn't."

If Aaron keeps this up, I may consider assassinating him. Theodmon pulled Amaria to his chest, in part to comfort her, and in part to hide his glare. *What purpose could he hope to achieve from this?*

"She doesn't need to do that anymore," Theodmon told Haerdnor, his voice as cold as ice.

Haerdnor held up his hands. "I told her that."

"Did you tell your father?"

Haerdnor's eyes narrowed. "You think me fighting her battles is going to save her from our father? She has to tell him herself." He took a deep breath as he looked around the yard. "Get her inside."

"I'm alright," Amaria protested, her body shaking.

Theodmon put his hands on Amaria's shoulders, steering her towards the palace. The feathers of her wings brushed against his hands and he wanted to pick her up and carry her. *Perhaps trying to readjust how you carry her with those things when she looks like she's about to meet Sadthos isn't the best timing,* Theodmon reminded himself.

"You, over here," Theodmon shouted to a nearby steward. The steward's posture straightened, and he ran towards Theodmon.

"Yes, my Lord?"

"Go find maids and tell them to prepare my wife's bath," Theodmon directed. "And tell them to find nannies to prepare the children for an outdoor picnic for dinner."

"Yes, my Lord," the steward said before rushing off.

"Thank you." Amaria softly smiled, her eyes sparkling. Theodmon would never admit it to her, but he didn't do the bath completely for her benefit. She reeked from the prison and it was all he could do to keep breathing through his mouth instead of his nose.

"Of course, my love," he said.

As the afternoon sea breeze wafted through his hair, Theodmon sat on a blanket on the beach, watching as Amaria held both Lysander and Sylviana's hands as she waded into the ocean, the bottom folds of her lilac and pink dress floating around her ankles. Lysander was trying to make a break for the ocean, waiting for his mother to be distracted with his little sister. Sylviana had just recently learned how to take her first steps and as such, was unsteady on them.

"No," Amaria said as Lysander ran into the water. Despite it being late May in one of the hottest geographic areas in Cesmassia, she froze the water in front of him into ice. "You'll drown. Stay close to me."

"No!" Lysander stomped his foot.

"Lysander," Amaria warned sternly. Theodmon stood up from his spot to go and help her with their strong-willed child.

"No!" Lysander said again.

Amaria sighed, plucking up Sylviana before the incoming waves could knock her wobbly legs out from under her.

"Then I guess we won't get to see the turtles later," Amaria said. Immediately, Lysander's eyes widened, and Theodmon saw his chance to rush into the waves, scooping up the distracted toddler.

"Turtles?" Lysander questioned, clapping his hands with a wide grin.

"In the gardens," Theodmon said. "We'll see them after supper–look, the food has arrived." He pointed to the maids coming from over the sandy hill, bringing a basket that Theodmon knew was filled to the brim with meats, cheeses, fruits, and drinks.

Lysander laughed as he wriggled out of Theodmon's grasp. Theodmon set him down on the dry sand, allowing Lysander to break free and run towards the dunes, excitedly waving his hands to the bringers of food.

Next to him, Sylviana also started wiggling out of her mother's grasp. "Alright," Amaria laughed. "Be patient, Sylvie, I'm putting you down."

As soon as Syvliana's feet hit the sand, she followed her brother, falling down on her butt after only ten steps. Amaria reached out to her, as if she were about to run to her, but pulled her hand back, staying in place as Sylviana happily stood up and continued wobbling after Lysander.

Amaria moved closer to Theodmon, slipping her hand into hers, her wings prodding against his shoulders. He moved forward slightly, allowing her wing to extend fully behind him, as he wrapped his arm around her waist.

"Perhaps more public affection than what is conventionally appropriate," he said under his breath, unable to stop the smirk from appearing. "But, who will chastise us for it?"

"My father," Amaria said, rolling her eyes.

"Aaron can keep his opinions to himself," Theodmon said. "He needs us, and he knows it."

"He wants us to lead a coup. Not now but soon enough," Amaria whispered, "that's a bit different than he needi–"

She cut herself off as the maids were within earshot and were laying out the food. "Lysander, Sylviana," Amaria called out. "Come here."

"You know they're not going to do that," Theodmon chuckled, Amaria joining in, her eyes sparkling in the sun.

"Perhaps I had hope they'd surprise me."

"With how loud they can scream, maybe," Theodmon joked. However, Lysander and Sylviana both came towards them. "Let's meet them at the blanket," he told Amaria, already moving forward with his hand wrapped around her waist.

Amaria nodded in agreement, already walking with him, sand particles sticking to the wet drapes of her dress. Theodmon brushed some sand off his sleeve, hoping that it didn't get in his food.

The Émeraudes Sea was beautiful, with its blue-green water that was so crystalline it was almost clear. But Theodmon had long ago determined that he preferred the mountains, with a part of that decision coming from the fact that sand was nowhere to be found in the Westerlands.

Home. Theodmon sighed, his chest sinking inwards. He wouldn't be seeing home for a long while–and he didn't count the march through the Westerlands as being home because he couldn't enjoy it. He couldn't feel peaceful, not when he was about to instigate a war. And not just any war, but a war for complete conquest.

"You may go," Amaria directed the maids, who were placing the plates on the blanket.

The maids looked at their uncompleted work, back at Amaria, and then gave shallow curtsies, one slipping on the sand, and departed.

Amaria sat down on the blanket, Lysander immediately running to her lap. Sylviana looked over at Theodmon, met his eyes, and then fell down in the most dramatic fashion. He chuckled, going over to her and picking her up, holding her upside down as her shrieking giggles pierced the air.

"I'm hungry," Lysander said, eyeing the skewered chicken and peppers.

Amaria was already loading up two plates with the chicken, as well as grapes, dried dates and cold cheeses. "Here," she maneuvered around Lysander to place one plate beside him. "Sit down and eat."

Lysander didn't move from her lap, reaching over to eat a grape from the plate next to him. Amaria kissed the top of Lysanders head, hugging him tightly. "I suppose you can stay."

Theodmon looked into Sylviana's eyes as he set her down on the blanket and knew that he too, was going to be holding a child in his lap the entire dinner. And, as he sat down with his and his daughter's food, and she placed a small hand against his cheek, her deep brown eyes unblinkingly looking at him, Theodmon decided that he didn't mind at all.

They had a peaceful meal, and at the end of it, Amaria gave Lysander and Sylviana bowls and cups, allowing them to play in the sand and make mounds with their newfound tools.

"As I was saying earlier." Amaria leaned against Theodmon with her feet tucked underneath her, extending her wings to be behind them both. "My father wants us to lead a coup. That's different than needing us."

"Is it?" Theodmon challenged. "He needs me because a Chauvignon has the best claim to the throne–and a Chauvignon who is respected and proven militarily is another asset. He needs you because you have more sway over the mages than Aion, and with recent developments you may have more sway with the Faith."

"He doesn't need to have his daughter, or his grandson, on the imperial throne," Amaria said. "He already runs the nation."

"And his grip on Aion is slipping. It has to be if he's considering this," Theodmon said. "And your father cares about legacy–it's why he's marrying a girl younger than all his children. Because he can't have the line end with Haerdnor. Having his child and grandchild on the throne is the best thing for his legacy."

Amaria sighed, snuggling closer to Theodmon. "What do you think?"

"About the coup?"

Theodmon stared ahead of him, taking in the sunset over the waves–the pinks, golds, and violets of the sky seemed to melt down into the turquoise of the sea, feeling as if he were pulling a knife out of a wound. He was loyal to Thestitiunia, and planning anything to harm its leader, especially as one of her top ranking military leaders, was treason. But Aion was incompetent, and Theodmon truly wished that Aion would fight his own battles for one.

"We'll have to be careful and we'll have to be patient," Theodmon said. "We have a war soon and I can't put my men through a civil war after that. A war against magical atrocities, a war against Rindria, and a war against their countrymen is too much in such a short span of time."

Amaria's soft palm touched his cheek, sliding down to cup her hand under his jaw. She kissed him on the mouth, her smooth lips covering his chapped ones like a balm. Theodmon placed his hand under her jaw, cupping it as well as he pulled her into the kiss.

"Mama!" Sylviana pulled at Amaria's sleeves. Once Amaria broke away from the kiss to look at her daughter, Sylviana pointed her pudgy hand towards the Émeraudes Sea. Amaria and Theodmon locked eyes, and he felt himself smiling at her. She was radiant, and not just physically. Amaria was smart, ruthless, and unconditional in her love. He loved how she wrinkled her nose as she smiled at the children. He loved how soft her voice was and that she always smelled of roses, oranges, or jasmine.

And he loved how she saw him as he truly was and didn't hide from him. And he saw her and loved her even more for it.

"Theo?" Amaria questioned, her head in a slight tilt as she stood above him.

He smiled at her. "I love you."

"I love you too," she replied, holding Sylviana's hand in her own. "Will you watch Lysander? I think he's determined to make the world's largest sand mound."

"Of course." Theodmon watched as Amaria and Sylviana went back down to the shore and as Lysander shoveled sand nearly ten feet away from him.

It would be nice to just be husband and wife and nothing else for once. Theodmon thought. And, as he sat on the beach, with the tranquility needed to have thoughts about something other than war or backstabbing politics, Theodmon realized something that made him pause.

As he sat on the beach, watching his family enjoy the sunset, Theodmon wished that Amaria and Theodmon could stay here forever, as loving parents, who had no worries or concerns for how to lead a nation and preserve their power—they only had to worry about themselves and their children. And Amaria and Theodmon were those people; until Amaria and Theodmon had to change into Marquis and Marchioness Chauvignon.

How much of my true self exists and how much of it died to make way for a role, a title that was forced upon me? Theodmon leaned his head against Amaria's, who had it laying on his shoulder as she held their sleeping daughter in her arms. Beside him, Lysander was stacking buckets of sand on each other, seemingly unbothered as the mounds of sand collapsed under the weight of the new sand.

And, as he looked at his son, Theodmon despised that Lysander was being raised to be thrown into the same title that was slowly killing Theodmon, and had been killing Theodmon since the day he obtained it.

All he could truly have hope for is that Lysander became Marquis Chauvignon through more peaceful ways–when Theodmon died of old age, in his bed, and not in war. He prayed that Lysander never had to be fighting at the same time, the same battle when Theodmon died. Theodmon prayed that the future for his children would be better than the world he grew up in, and the world that they were living in now, although he doubted Vathar would hear his prayer.

Of course, he couldn't fully look at his sleeping daughter–an infant and already engaged to an immortal being. He had saved his wife but condemned his daughter. And while Theodmon didn't regret the choice to make a deal with the faeries to save Amaria's life, he did regret the repercussions Sylviana would have for the rest of her life–a life that was likely to be long lasting with Oberon.

He leaned forward, jostling Amaria off of his shoulder. She looked at him questioningly, and he smiled, kissing the top of her head, before turning to kiss the top of Sylviana's head.

"She's turning one in a few months," Amaria said. "In August."

Theodmon sighed heavily. "And I'll be at war."

"I wish you weren't," Amaria said hoarsely. "I understand we've to, but I wish–"

"That we were just Theodmon and Amaria–a couple, with our son and daughter," Theodmon finished. "And that Marquis and Marchioness Chauvignon could die and resign themselves to let them and their simple family live."

"Yes," Amaria chuckled. "In this fantasy, we'd keep our wealth, I am rather comfortable in silk and velvet wool." She leaned down and kissed the top of Sylviana's head. "Would you hold her or better yet, try to wake her so she can join us? I think I'm going to see if Lysander wants to wade in the sea–look, he's about to eat sand."

Chapter Forty

U nfortunately, Amaria and Theodmon had to make way for Marquis and Marchioness Chauvignon as the sun rose the next day.

And besides, she had other duties outside of being Marchioness Chauvignon or a Raulet. The time had finally come to quit putting off her Princepsia Magia Exia duties and finally act like the head of the Extractors.

She pulled on her gold and cream overcoat–the traditional outfit worn by female extractors for non-combative and no-Extraction duties, pulling out the long strands of red fabric from her under dress to better frame the outfit. Extractor uniforms usually had high necks, but Amaria's draped off her shoulders, with a deep cut in her back, allowing her wings to comfortably spring from it. However, Amaria hated how exposed she felt.

Amaria picked up a large, heavy necklace–a giant golden seal of a dragon and a hydra intertwined in the middle. Nearly fifty smaller golden bulbs covered the link of the chain, each bulb with its own seal, showcasing the types of known magic–a purely ceremonial item only worn by Princepsia Magia Exia. Adair had worn it for years. And now, it was her burden.

"You look beautiful," Theodmon said from his tangle of blankets in bed, watching her look into the mirror again.

Amaria fixed a crease in her dress. "Are you coming to breakfast with me?"

"We can't have breakfast here?" Theodmon lounged back on the pillows.

"Father doesn't like it," Amaria said.

Theodmon groaned, but still sat up and swung his legs out of the bed. "I guess I'll respect the man's rules in his home."

It's a stupid rule. Amaria thought, a small chuckle escaping her. *And I prefer private breakfasts more.* She hadn't really had private breakfasts until she married Theodmon. Now, almost every breakfast was private. Theodmon seemed to despise dealing with court before eating a hearty meal and at least two cups of coffee.

He never seemed to be short or impatient with her before eating though, something she deeply appreciated. "After you come back we won't have a public breakfast for months, years even," Amaria promised, moving to sit next to him on the edge of the bed.

"Yeah?" Theodmon smirked. "How can you know that?"

"I fully intend to not leave Forteresse les Blanche for a long while," Amaria laid her head against his shoulder, closing her eyes. "I want every breakfast to be just us and perhaps the children."

"Perhaps," Theodmon said, an eyebrow raising.

Amaria shook her head playfully. "Perhaps," she repeated, unable to hide her laughter. "Now get ready. I'm hungry."

Theodmon grudgingly stood up, stretching as his feet hit the floor. "Can we at least go to the kitchens?" He asked as he pulled a black tunic over his head, followed by a deep red shirt. "Everyone from every corner of the continent is here."

"No objections here," Amaria said. She shook her head, clearing her thoughts as she draped her arm over Theodmon's, both of them walking together through the crowded corridors.

"Thank you for visiting us, Lady Extractor," the headmaster of the Teplia Street Magic School of Raulle said.

This school was one of five in the city—sans the private tutors the wealthy had. These magic schools were funded by the dukes of each province by imperial degree. Magic was volatile if not trained, and so, if any mage did not have the means to be trained privately they could attend school, free of charge. While villages might not have a school, there was a town within three days riding of most villages, and every town had a school. Major cities, like Raulle, had more.

"It is my honor, Headmaster Daedulae," Amaria replied politely. "I've a personal interest in not only mages' education as a whole, but the education of Raullians."

"Of course Lady Extra—my apologies." Headmaster Daedulae looked at Amaria's heavy necklace. "Do you prefer to be called Princepsia Magia Exia?"

"It is the formal name, so for the sake of these young mages' education, yes," Amaria said. "However, in private, I would prefer Lady Extractor–or better yet, Marchioness, or a simple 'my Lady.'"

"Of course, my Lady," Daedulae said as they ascended the stone stairs. "Our education is primarily practical at Teplia Street, but there is a theoretical element all students must study." Daedulae entered into a long winded explanation of the teaching philosophy of the school and Amaria smiled politely, allowing the academic to ramble on, not truly listening as he showed her around the facilities.

"May I observe the lessons?" Amaria asked once Daedulae stopped speaking.

"Of course," Daedulae said with a small bow. "Perfect timing, we have an elemental magic class starting in a few minutes."

"Delightful." Amaria grinned. "All elements or a specific one?"

"Fire and water," Daedulae said. "We find that classes with water and earth mages can be counterproductive and classes with fire and air mages destructive."

Yes, that does sound like a disaster. Amaria laughed as she imagined the unintentionally increased or vanquished flames due to a wind mage wayward accidents in learning magic. She used to do that with Haerdnor, although it wasn't always unintentional.

"I look forward to observing," Amaria inclined her head as he led her into a classroom, the desks pushed against the wall, the chairs stacked on top of them.

"I can get you a chair, Princepsia Magia Exia," Daedulae offered, the door staying open behind him as a few students walked in, their eyes widening at the sight of Amaria.

"No need," she told him. "I'm not going to be sitting in one place during a practical training session." She turned to the three students. She noted their plain blue dresses, all embroidered with the school seal over their heart. The embroidery was frayed, and Amaria wondered how often they wore their uniform.

She gave a short nod of her head in greeting. "I hope you don't mind that I am observing your class today."

"No, I mean none at all–not at all," a small boy with wild golden curls stammered. "My Lady Extractor," he added hastily.

"She's not Lady Extractor, she's Princepsia Magia Exia," Daedulae scolded. "Mister Pêcheuse, I have half a mind–"

Amaria held up a hand, cutting the headmaster off. "It's alright," she sternly told the older man before turning back to the student. "In truth, I'm not quite used to the title yet, myself. What's your name?"

"Jonathan Pêcheuse," the boy said so softly it was almost a whisper. He kept his eyes averted from Amaria.

Amaria's heart twisted. She didn't want children to fear her–why did children fear her? Was it her role as an Extractor, her role as Princepsia Magia Exia, her wings, her position as Aaron Raulet's daughter, or her reputation? As if she could have a premonition, Amaria sensed that she would one day need all of these titles; but titles wouldn't be enough. She needed goodwill.

She smiled kindly as she crouched down to the eye level of the two other students, a boy and girl who looked younger than Jonathan. "And you two?"

"Bella Mircares," the girl said with a clumsy curtsy.

"Edward Alignes," the boy said, giving a more polished bow than his classmate's curtsy.

"It's a pleasure to meet you," Amaria said. "What is your magic?"

"Fire, Princepsia Magia Exia," Edward said.

"Water," Jonathan said, his voice small. "So is Bella."

"Princepsia Magia Exia," Bella said cautiously. "You're a water mage too?"

"Yes." Amaria smiled. "And fire, wind, and earth." She held her hand out, summoning a small piece of each element at the tips of her fingers. "May I see what each of you can do?"

The students hesitantly looked at each other before shuffling to their positions, maintaining their training forms as they summoned their elements. Slowly, they became more confident, and Amaria walked around the classroom, watching their forms. Bella was methodic, Edward was confident, perhaps leaning towards recklessness, and Jonathan was cautious. Over the next hour, Amaria watched, and gave a few notes to the students when appropriate.

"Good job," Daedulae said, once the class had ended and the students were slurping down water. "Princepsia Magia Exia." He turned to Amaria respectfully, walking towards the door. "Would you want to see another class? Perhaps a theoretical lesson?" Amaria could hear the longing in his voice.

I'd rather do anything else than listen to a dry professor explain the theoretics of magic; I suffered those lessons for years. Amaria gave Daedulae a warm smile as they stepped outside of the classroom and into the corridor. "Of course, Headmaster. Please, lead the way."

Daedulae beamed, humming slightly as he walked through the halls of the school, seemingly more vibrant in his steps than he was before.

Amaria chuckled behind him. She might have thought magical theory was dry, but it seemed to be the most interesting, and the most beloved, thing in the world to the headmaster. She had her own interests that people found dull, or perhaps disturbing, she was sure. Who was she to critique others' passion?

Doors burst open, students emerging from them. Amaria moved to the side, her palms flat on the wall.

The students milled pass, but paused in their tracks as they passed her.

"Hello, all," Amaria said. "I'm visiting your school to ensure you have the best magical education possible. Please, don't mind me."

Like they're going to listen to that. Amaria sarcastically thought. *What a stupid request.*

"Get to class!" Daedulae said loudly. "Princepsia Magia Exia I apologize for my students' impolite beh–"

"They're not being impolite," Amaria interrupted.

She smiled at the students as she moved away from the wall, deciding to just walk through the crowd and let them clear up and go to class after she departed. "Pleasure meeting you all," she told them.

A small boy, likely around seven, grabbed the folds of her dress as she passed, his eyes glowing a brilliant gold. "You are not Princepsia Magia Exia," he said, his voice sounding like a million echoes.

"Excuse me?" Amaria's hands shook. *Last time a seer said something to me—*

Amaria pressed her eyes shut momentarily, trying to force out the memory of the High Priestess of Dandar. She didn't particularly like those who followed Dandar, and those who were blessed by the god of seers scared her. But this was a little boy. She couldn't tear her dress out of his hands and flee. What kind of leader of all Thestitiunian mages would she be?

She opened her eyes, keeping the gasp building in her throat suppressed, as she forced herself to look at the seer-mage. Although, she looked at his forehead instead of the golden eyes. She had never seen another mage with metallic eyes. Is this how others saw her?

"You're closer to having unprecedented power, and you fear being despised," the boy chanted. "Be more sure in yourself or face death."

Amaria took a step backwards, nearly stumbling away from the boy. She barely noticed his eyes were no longer glowing, and he collapsed on the floor until it occurred. *You will be a queen among mortals, and you will be despised.* The words of the high priestess, from that time long ago, rang in Amaria's mind.

This boy, while as unnerving as her, was not the high priestess. He was just a boy. And so, Amaria crouched down and supported his head as the boy woke up, Daedulae cleared the hallways of students.

"What happened?" The boy blinked slowly.

"You had a vision," Amaria whispered. "Do you remember it?"

The boy blinked again, as if he couldn't fully understand her. "What did I say? Was it bad? The others say my prophecies don't make sense, but they don't sound good."

"No," Amaria lied, brushing her hand through the student's hair. "Nothing like that."

What in all the gods' names does 'be more sure of yourself or face death' mean? Amaria bit her lip. This student, whoever he was, did predict doom and death–as all good servants of Dandar did. Amaria would have to watch his education closely, and when she wasn't in Raulle have her father or Haerdnor watch him in her stead.

Still, she was shaking as much as the boy on the ground in her arms.

Chapter Forty-One

T he last thing Theodmon wanted to do during a party was to go to a secret strategy meeting. However, as they were into the fourth day of the party, it was determined that nobody would miss the hosts.

Still, Theodmon and Amaria held champagne in their hands, laughing loudly in their bright dresses and garments as they made their way through the decedent halls of Provincia Palencia–it made Theodmon uncomfortable. In the south, especially with the Raulets, everything felt more garish than it felt in the Westerlands.

Theodmon missed home. He sighed deeply. He wished he was going back to Forteresse les Blanche instead of Rindria when the celebrations were over.

"Look." Amaria squeezed his hand. He slowly averted his gaze to where she was looking, seeing two Riam men enhancing furtive glances as money changed their hands. "Kiss me," she commanded. "I'm conducting magic to eavesdrop but they cannot know."

"Why kissing?" Theodmon laughed, moving her towards the wall.

"Public displays of affection make others uncomfortable," Amaria said before their lips met.

Through the kiss, Theodmon heard the amplified voices drifting to them.

"....instability, pay for my upholding of power." A greasy voice said.

"What are your ties to the former Riam nobility we can exploit?" A second voice questioned.

"Make something up," the first voice said. "But my wealth and access to military force matter more."

Rindria is in the beginning stages of a civil war. Theodmon thought, a smile breaking across his face as he kissed Amaria. *They're unstable, more than we thought.* He almost felt giddy. *This is going to be more efficient than I thought if we can play our cards correctly.*

Amaria broke away from Theodmon, staring at him with widened eyes as Theodmon downed the rest of his champagne, setting the flute down on a nearby bench.

Together, without saying a word, the two of them made their way to Aaron's study. Stopping only once they reached it, and with a nod to the guards, Theodmon opened the double doors to reveal a polished mahogany room with an ornate writing table surrounded by similarly decorated bookshelves and filing cabinets. Once the doors were fully opened, he and Amaria stepped inside, revealing that Haerdnor, Celestine, Aloysius, Henri, and Aaron were already waiting. His chest raising, Theodmon made his way over to sit on the couch with Amaria, watching Aaron carefully, as he shifted through papers on his desk.

Nobody said a word, the atmosphere as tight as a coiled violin string. Haerdnor cleared his throat, shifting uncomfortably on his chair, as if he would rather be anywhere else but here. Theodmon saw Amaria throw him a few concerned looks and Haerdnor quickly shook his head. Theodmon shifted to look at Henri and Aloysius, who met his eyes and gave a small shrug.

After a few painful minutes, the door creaked open. Lucas and Juliette stepped inside the room. "Sorry we're late," Lucas said.

"Bar the door," Aaron directed without looking up. "Nothing said here will be discussed outside this room without my permission. Understood?"

Lucas curtly nodded, bolting the door, before he and Juliette came to sit on the couches with the rest of them.

"Get on with it," Aloysius said. "There's a plant. What else?"

Celestine picked at her nails as she kicked her feet under the sofa. Theodmon placed a hand on her shoulder, in part to comfort her, and in part to warn her of the danger of the situation.

Theodmon forced himself to stay as rigid as a statue, hiding his surprise that Aloysius dared to be so discourteous to Aaron Raulet. And he had to hide the pride swelling in his chest at his brother's daring.

"Are you aware of the dire circumstances this spy may put us in?" Aaron hissed.

"I was shot with arrows. Twenty-three times," Aloysius said dully. "I understand how dangerous this spy is, probably better than anybody else in this room."

"Your Grace," Henri said diplomatically. "We are short on time with the invasion mobilizing within the next few days, perhaps we can revisit this?"

Aaron coolly scanned the room, and Theodmon swore that his eyes seemed to bore into Aloysius for longer than anyone else. "Alright," he finally said, looking between Theodmon, Amaria, and Haerdnor. "Theodmon, you're leading this conquest, why don't you direct this meeting."

"Gladly," Theodmon said. "We've three locations we need to cover. Let's start with the simplest." He looked over at his sister. "Celestine, you are going to be at Forteresse les Blanche, ruling in not only mine, but Amaria's stead. Don't let our mother know what's occurring, she'll be...." He sighed, trailing off as he struggled to find the diplomatic words.

"She'll be a raging bitch," Celestine finished, shocking Theodmon with her coarse language. Celestine had always been the most polite, the most gentle of all his siblings. "She never approved of Thestitiunian expansion," Celestine finished. "Where will Amaria be?"

"Here, in Raulle," Theodmon said. "She, Aaron, and Juliette will be conducting intelligence activities from here–it'll be our home base instead of Forteresse les Blanche."

"I'll fly to Forteresse les Blanche periodically to exchange intelligence and get help to Rindria more easily," Amaria added.

Celestine gave a small nod. "Alright."

"I'm helping with intelligence?" Juliette asked, her voice a mixture of pride and surprise.

"Of course," Theodmon said. "You aren't a fighter, but you have a stake in this, we trust you, and Amaria believes you have a skill set needed to be effective at this."

"You're warm. People trust you," Amaria added. "They might say something to or around you that's helpful. Raulle is the City of Spies, I need someone unassuming to listen out for us."

"Of course," Juliette agreed.

"Speaking of spies," Aaron interjected. "Amaria, how is your...ah, recovery, going?"

"Father!" Amaria hissed.

"You're needed," Aaron said coolly. "How will you do your job if you hyperventilate every time you step into the Drowning Tombs? You're so worried about losing control you are willingly giving it away."

"I don't think this is appropriate–" Amaria began, her cheeks flushing.

"Alright," Theodmon said, clearing his throat. "Moving on to Rindria. Henri, Lucas, Haerdnor, Aloysius, and I are going to lead the siege."

"I'll be joining after the others," Henri added. "After they leave to mobilize their forces, I'm staying here and redirecting any Riams thoughts if they have an inkling of maybe returning home with a sudden and unshakable desire to continue drinking, whoring, and partying. I am having Juliette and Elisa help spike their drinks—the rest of you are a bit too conspicuous."

"Let's talk about Elisa," Aaron said. "Why are we trusting this Riam?"

"She hates them," Amaria said. "She hates us too, but she gets a benefit from working with us. She's proud–how do you think a noblewoman reduced to whoring feels? Riam rule prohibits her from owning money. Thestitiunian rule changes that. And she will be rewarded, moved to the top of society."

"Self interest?" Aaron raised an eyebrow.

"It's a powerful motivator," Amaria said. "And Henri is her contract on our side. If she betrays us, we'll know immediately."

"Give her a powerful negative motivator as well," Aaron told Amaria. Amaria paled, her hands starting to shake.

"What?" Theodmon sharply questioned.

"Amaria, you should find one of your other spies for torture training, you aa the torturer. And without Elisa knowing what truly is occurring, let her witness it."

"I...." Amaria whispered.

"It'll help you feel in control," Aaron said. "You control the situation. You control the narrative. It'll help you, ah, heal."

"I don't enjoy it," Amaria whispered.

"You do," Aaron said. "Don't lie to me, Amaria."

"Let's finish discussing our plans," Lucas said. "With Elisa, she'll be whoring between the two sides, Henri as her contact to receive assignments and deliver information. We are planning a siege at Forteresse les Blanche."

"We are burning the countryside as we invade," Aloysius added. "They'll have no food."

"Which is where I come in," Haerdnor said. "I bring food and provisions, along with more men from Perivina Fluere. I should be arriving between a week and a fortnight after the rest of you reach Wéorren City."

And to give the Raulets a visible claim in assisting expand the empire. Everyone knows Amaria and Aaron do things behind the scenes, but the citizens have a more favorable view of soldiers than they do of spies.

"Eighty percent of our forces will siege the city," Theodmon said. "Lucas and Brigitte Belamy will go with the other twenty percent, going in opposite directions to burn the rest of Rindria. Wéorren City will be the only stronghold and once it falls, then the country is ours."

"That's diabolical," Aloysius said.

"But it works," Theodmon said.

"Keep a few pockets on the outskirts unburned for the civilians to flee too," Henri added. "Avondra is in the middle of their own civil war–they won't aid or harm them. Tressidil is more our ally than Rindria, they won't like it but they'll remain neutral. And for Morroek...well, one of the attackers future step-mother is the daughter of the future Morrian king. They'll not risk that marriage, it's too profitable."

"Mercy will go a long way," Amaria agreed. "These people, they're Riam now, but they'll be Thestitiunian eventually."

"Wise decision," Theodmon said approvingly. "Only burn farmland, mills, barracks, and places suspected of holding munitions. Leave temples and residential buildings alone." He looked severely at everyone in the room. "And if anybody intentionally harms a hospital I will kill you myself."

Theodmon felt Amaria squeeze his hand. He turned, meeting her silver eyes. *"Thank you,"* she silently mouthed, giving him a smile.

He squeezed her hand in return. *We aren't heartless. Despite what it seems, we don't want to commit senseless war crimes.*

"When do we depart?" Lucas broke the silence that was quickly encompassing the room.

"In two days," Theodmon said. "Pack quietly. We're leaving before daybreak."

Chapter Forty-Two

Amaria stood in the foyer, trying her best to look as haughty as possible. *Neck elongated. Keep your nose slightly downturned. No smiling–in fact have the slightest curl of your lip. Shoulders back. I am above everyone here. I am perfect. Indestructible.*

I'm not terrified.

She wasn't haughty. She wanted to cry. She wished she had told her father no to this absurd request–she couldn't go back to the Drowning Tombs. And bringing Elisa? Amaria didn't know why, but the idea made her stomach turn.

I am in control. Amaria reminded herself of the conversation she had with her father only a day previously. *I hold all the cards–I know what is happening, Elisa doesn't. Elisa doesn't even know this trip is to the Drowning Tombs.*

Amaria had even worn a normal, nice, dress for this occasion so Elisa wouldn't know anything until the last possible moment. Amaria controlled this day, not Elisa. She was choosing to do this. She wasn't letting her father do this to her. She was in control. She wasn't terrified. She was calm.

Her heart still thudded against her chest as if it were about to burst free from her body. Her mouth was dry, and her palms were clammy. She was terrified, and no matter how much she tried to deny it.

Her only hope was to suppress the fear, ignore it, become numb to it, and hope that her suppressed emotions didn't burst forth, overwhelming her and causing as much damage as a volcano.

Elisa approached Amaria with a curtsy. "You asked to see me?"

Amaria clasped her hands tightly together to hide their trembles. "We're going to the city."

"Why?"

"You mentioned needing clothes and I wanted to ensure you had a wardrobe to your liking, as a show of good faith," Amaria said. "We will pick the fabrics you like, buy them, measure you here, and we will have them crafted and mailed to Henri."

Elisa's brown eyes narrowed. "Why?"

"As I said, it's a show of good faith. In this partnership we gain benefits from you earlier than you gain benefits from us."

Elisa bit her lip, her eyes shifting over Amaria, as if she were analyzing her and her motives.

Amaria smiled warmly, trying to pretend as if she weren't manipulating Elisa and leading her like a lamb to slaughter.

The atmosphere in the carriage was almost stifling. Amaria wanted to fan herself, but that seemed too dramatic. Would using magic to cool herself startle this Riam when she needed her nerves to be calm?

"My Lady," Elisa said, causing Amaria to jump in her seat slightly.

Amaria looked over towards her, arching an eyebrow as if to say *"yes?"* as if that could make up for the absolute lack of composure she just displayed.

Elisa wet her lips. "You may find that Rindria isn't as unified as you believe. Many, especially in the lower classes, may be sympathetic to Thestitiunian occupation if they knew it could better their lives."

"What are you saying?" Amaria asked, already knowing the answer.

"You have allies. Leverage it," Elisa said. "The Thestitiunian middle class is amazing, I've seen it here–it is what Rindria needs. The middle class—they have hope here. Riam peasants need hope, but instead they have rage. Use that."

"And you're an expert on war now?" Amaria's eyebrows arched. Secretly, however, she was impressed with Elisa's insight and her strategy.

"No," Elisa said. "Merely comfortable with desperation."

"Where're we going?" Elisa peered outside the carriage window, the bag of folded spools of velvet, silk, and cotton at her feet. "This isn't the road back to Provincia Palencia….are those slums?!" Elisa's head whipped over towards Amaria, her eyes blazing. "Where are you taking me?"

"The Drowning Tombs," Amaria answered, deciding to come clean. Elisa was smart, she would be insulted if Amaria continued to pretend as if she wasn't.

"The Drowning…," Elisa's face paled drastically, quickly morphing into a panicked anger. "Why should I go with you?"

Amaria scowled, despite the small flicker of approval she felt. "You're joining the intelligence community. I rather you get acquainted with the ugly now instead of later when your reactions matter infinitely more than you can imagine."

Elisa's eyes narrowed, but she said nothing as she curtly nodded. Amaria sighed, leaning back against her seat, feeling the tension momentarily escape her body. She didn't want to argue now. Amaria was trying to keep her hands from shaking.

Why am I so terrified? Amaria scolded herself. She shouldn't be terrified, this wasn't Rindria, and she wasn't a prisoner. *Why does Rindria bother me so much anyways?* She wasn't a fragile summer rose, ready to wilt at the slightest discomfort. Despite being a Raulet, a rose didn't describe her anymore–she was aconite, oleander, and wisteria.

Amaria kept her gaze locked outside her window, keeping her face away from Elisa as she watched the slums pass.

As Amaria saw the looming lighthouse above them, the carriage rolled to a stop. Amaria wiped her hands over her dress. "Get out," Amaria commanded Elisa, the door already swinging open.

Hesitantly, Elisa exited the carriage, the two women passing the lighthouse, guards running by, a few casting sharp glances towards them but making no effort to approach as they approached a stone bridge, two guards on either side of it.

"Move." Amaria held out her right hand, the sapphire of her insignia ring flashing in the sunlight. The guards surveyed the ring, immediately bowing upon realizing that the wearer was who she claimed to be. Amaria raised her hand, and the guards rose.

"Boat," Amaria directed towards the guards.

"Yes, my Lady," a guard said, his head still bowed. Amaria nodded curtly, then started walking briskly across the bridge, hoping she seemed self-assured. In truth, she wished that she was almost anywhere else but here. She looked back towards the city, momentarily wondering what would happen if she just left Elisa here, or if she and Elisa left together.

I'm not weak. Amaria told herself as she turned back to face the direction of the prison, exhaling softly. *I can do this.* Numbly, Amaria walked across the stone and sand, barely processing that Elisa was beside her. And as they approached the other side of the island, a small boat prepared for them, Amaria looked across the small channel trying not to vomit at the sight of the prison.

"Get in the boat," Amaria muttered under her breath to Elisa.

Elisa cast her a questioning glance but then shrugged, climbing into the boat. Taking a deep breath, Amaria followed, keeping her eyes shut as the boat began moving.

"Nervous?" Elisa asked, a mocking lift in her voice.

"I get sea sick," Amaria lied.

Elisa scoffed under her breath. "In a boat this small?"

"Aren't you from a land-locked country?" Amaria snapped.

Elisa shook her head. "Of course," she said, the mocking tone still there. "Fortunately for you, it seems as if land is approaching."

Amaria stopped herself from scowling, looking as if she was grimacing instead. *Clever.* She thought scathingly. *If I'm sea sick I should be thrilled to be on land. Even if that land is the Drowning Tombs.* The boat hit the shore, and she forced her eyes open.

Amaria stood up and stepped on shore. "Let's go."

"After you." Elisa smirked as she stepped on the grainy sand. "After all, I'm just a visitor."

Amaria's nostrils flared and she debated drowning Elisa. *No. She's intentionally provoking you.*

Silence smothered them like a blanket as they walked into the prison; Amaria felt a chill run down her spine, her skin covered with bumps as she wrapped her arms around herself. *I am in control.*

The metallic scent of blood filled Amaria's nostrils as she braced herself to step through the portcullis gate down to the dungeons below. Even without stepping down the stairs she could smell the sweat, urine, feces, and decomposing flesh.

I'm in control. Amaria repeated those four words, almost as if they were a mantra as they descended deeper into the prison, picking the skin around her fingernails. Amaria's dress hit spots of water on the floor, and she flinched as the wet fabric clung to her ankles. Behind her Elisa screamed.

Amaria turned around, her eyes wide. "What?" She gasped, her heart beating fast.

"Is...." Elisa caught her breath. "Is there anything in the water?"

Immediately, Amaria had horrific thoughts of drowned rats chewing on dismembered fingers and an octopus eating both. "Please," Amaria choked out. "Don't. Not now."

Elisa and Amaria met eyes, and Amaria feared that Elisa would use this moment of weakness to dig her knife in deeper—to twist it to obtain power over her. Amaria would have done it to her.

Elisa's eyes dropped and she swallowed hard. "Let's keep going," Elisa whispered. "Quickly?"

Her mouth dropped open, her eyes unblinking. Elisa didn't strike. *She's waiting for later,* Amaria told herself, *she's building up an arsenal.* Still, she curtly nodded her agreement and the two waded through the prison until they reached a cell.

"What's this?" Elisa asked.

"Prisoner's name is Aratus Beaufort - he is Perivinan born, from a small village called Hyllasi on the island Euodia. He came to Raulle in search of work around six years ago, where he was a low-ranking sailor on merchant ships. We suspect he has been relaying information to our enemies for four years," Amaria stated.

"Which enemies?"

Amaria smiled crudely as the cell door opened. "That's the question, isn't it."

The two women stepped into a dingy cell; Amaria gagged at the overwhelming smell of rotting fish, salt, and urine. Beside her, Elisa retched, pinching her nose in a desperate attempt to compose herself. Unfortunately, Elisa failed and she squarely vomited into the grimey water.

Shaking, Amaria picked up a torch, bringing it over to her spy, Louis. "Hello Aratus," she said. "Who are you working for?"

I'm in control. I'm in control. I'm in control. Amaria screamed this mantra in her mind as she forced her eyes shut as she slowly burned Louis. He would get the best medical treatment after this. *I'm in control.*

She didn't process what she was doing, drowning herself in the mantra, suppressing her emotions. *I'm in control. I'm in control. I need to leave.*

She sharply turned towards Elisa. "You," she said, her voice husky and cracking. "You give this a try."

"No." Elisa stepped away from them, her back now against the door.

"This is part of it," Amaria said, her voice almost pleading.

"Not to me," Elisa spat. "Maybe it's all tied together for you, but I'll not stoop this low."

I am in control. Maybe if Amaria lied to herself enough times she would finally believe it. "It's under the same—"

"Then I won't help you," Elisa snarled. "All I have left is my humanity. I already sacrificed my morals. You ask too much."

"If you are caught, this is likely what you will face," Amaria said, trying to stop her voice from shaking.

"I'm sure you know better than most how they treat spies and murderers beneath Bria Hall," Elisa spat.

Amaria blinked and she was back in the dungeons of the Riam castle, tied upon the rack instead of Elisa. Her chest was constructed and she dug her nails into her hands as she felt a wave of nausea rise to her chest. *I'm in control.*

I'm hurt. I'm losing control. I need to be in control!

A roar rushing in her ears, Amaria grabbed Elisa's arm, twisting it. "If you betray me in Rindria," Amaria hissed in Elisa's ear, "you will wish for this pain."

Elisa stared at Amaria intensely. "And if I'm loyal?"

"Then you are rewarded handsomely, as we discussed," Amaria said. "I'm a better friend than an enemy."

"So am I," Elisa said.

Amaria had to force back her smile. Loyalty was only tested in adversity. Serpents often produced deadly venoms, but from those same venoms, medicine could be procured. Elisa couldn't know that Amaria might have an inkling of respect, perhaps even admiration for her. Not yet anyways.

For the serpent would lie in the grass, waiting for weakness and an opportunity to strike.

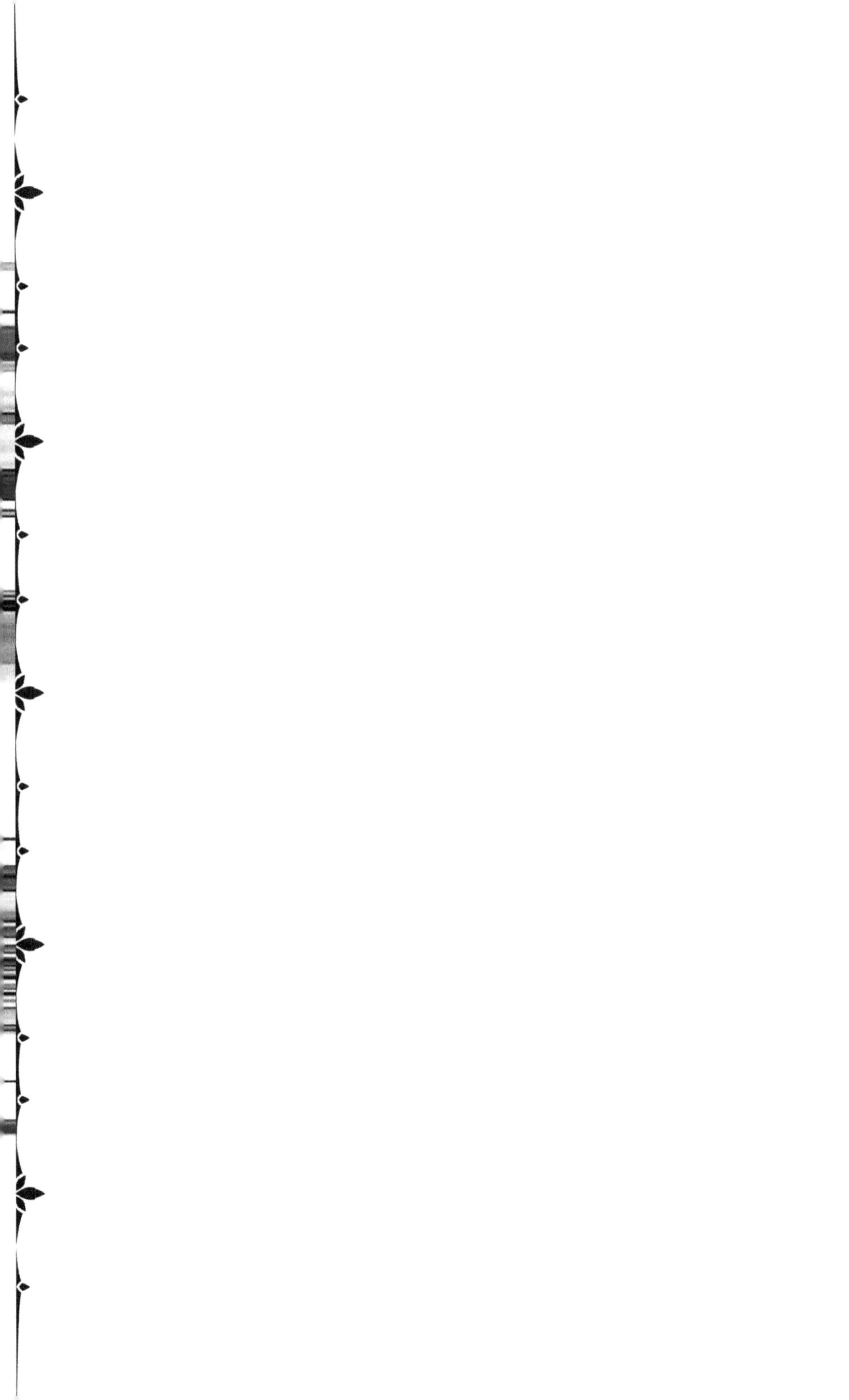

Part Five

the traitors

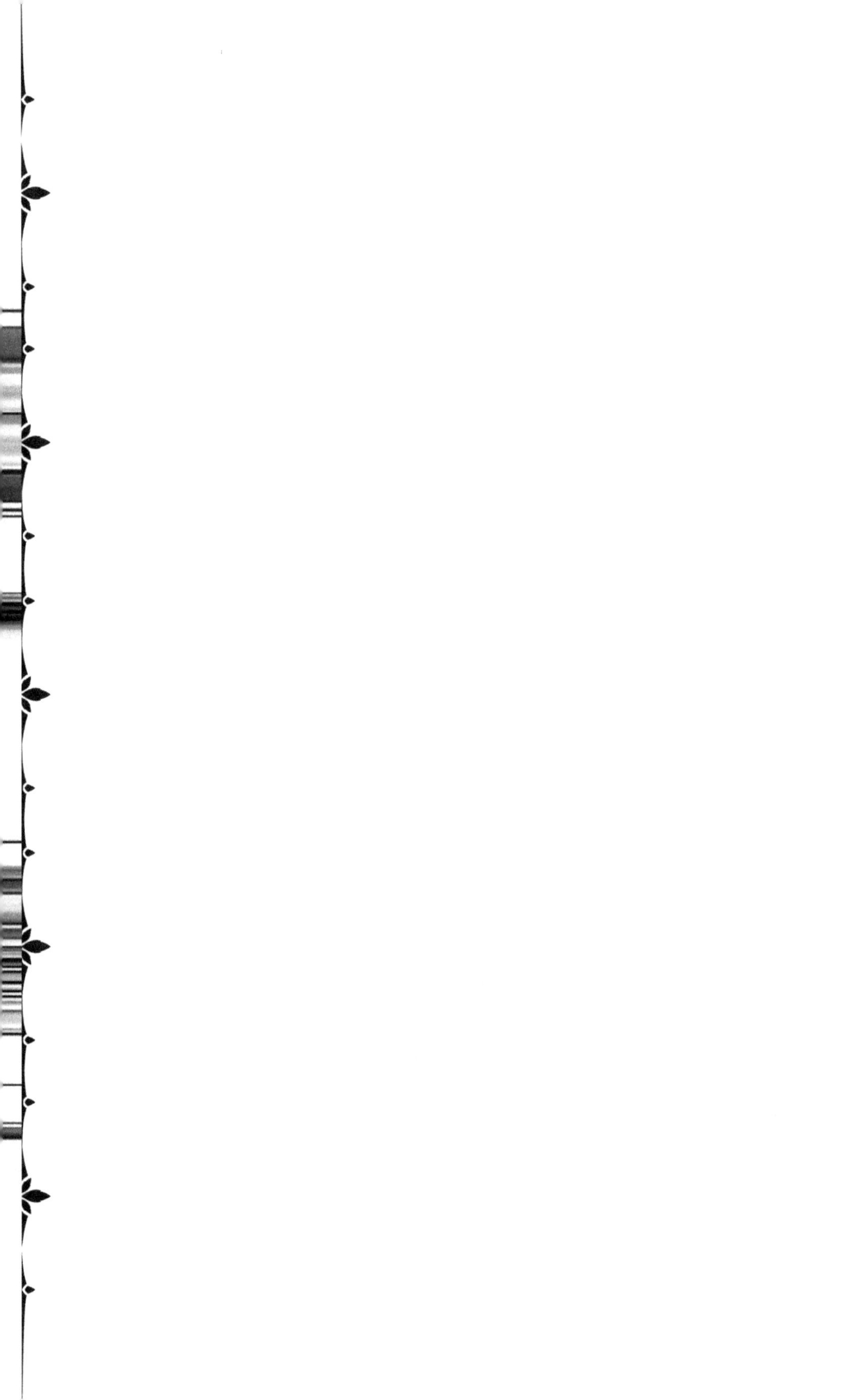

Chapter Forty-Three

R indria smelled of burning grass. Even the strongest mages would have struggled to stop the wildfires that consumed the plains. Theodmon tried not to inhale the constant smoke, adjusting the wet rag tied around the lower part of his face. He and his army had long passed the mountains, but were still a long ways away from Wéorren City.

"The horrors of war," Lucas muttered from atop his horse beside Theodmon. "The poets will find a way to romanticize this."

Screams followed Theo and his men as they trudged across the land. They'd started up the moment they entered Rindria and hadn't stopped since. Theo wondered if they were real any more or the discant of angry ghosts hunting him down for their vengeance. War was hell. It was destructive. And the soot and blood of it tore apart the soul. If an idealistic poet wanted to tell the world about the glories of war, he should first live it.

Lucas clenched the reins of his horse, his hands shaking and white knuckled.

"Are you alright?" Theodmon asked under his breath.

Lucas looked around tightly, his shoulders tense. "This reminds me..." he paused, taking a deep breath. "It reminds me of when I found Tesden Nalaeny."

"What happened?" Theodmon asked softly. He hadn't asked for specifics before, deciding that however Lucas accomplished his assignment was Lucas's business–Theodmon wasn't about to ask for the gory details when Lucas presented a decapitated head to the

Westanni court. Afterwards, Lucas had seemed haunted, staying tight-lipped about the ordeal Theodmon trusted and respected Lucas enough to pry, but now--watching sweat line Lucas's brow and noting how he jumped at every sound and shift of movements, which triggered violent shifts in his mood--Theodmon knew he had to ask. Not only because he cared for Lucas as a friend, but because he could be blindsided without this knowledge. A lack of planning could kill innocent men.

Lucas's face twitched as he stared ahead; the only sound was the marching of the army.

And the screams. Always the screams.

"Tesden Nalaeny was popular. Resourceful," Lucas finally said. "Nothing like his sister. And because of that, people hid him. They would fight for him even...They sent me on so many false trails that I didn't know what was real after a while."

Theodmon nodded, giving his silence over to Lucas like a stage.

"I found him across the border, in Skeletosa," Lucas continued. "His loyalists...they were unskilled fighters. It was almost too easy to cut them down." He lowered his head, breathing deeply. "And then Tesden and I fought. I killed him. I cut off his head, crossed the border once more, and returned home through Avondra."

Theodmon felt himself wanting to tell Lucas that he should have never asked that of him. It had been a cruel thing to ask of a friend, but Theodmon could never only be someone's friend--he was cursed to be their Marquis as well, and that came with large asks.

"I hate having to ask you to do these things," Theodmon said.

"I know that," Lucas said. "It doesn't make it easier."

The sun hung low on the horizon as Lucas and Theodmon rode side by side, their armor clinking with the rhythm of their horses' hooves, the silence between them somber. How had life turned them both into harsh, stern, sometimes cruel people. Theodmon remembered how they had once gone to Lake Holimeda, and seeing the boats, had decided to craft their own.

"Remember the time we tried to build a raft to sail across the lake?" Theodmon asked, his rough parched with scorched air and exhaustion.

Lucas softly chuckled, shaking his head at the memory. "How could I forget? We spent the whole day scavenging for wood and tying it all together with bits of string. The moment we set foot on it, the whole thing fell apart."

"One side of the boat was already capsizing before we stepped on it," Theodmon remembered. "Aloysius teased us for weeks."

"Henri kept giving me nautical books," Lucas said. "And Ophelia asked if I could swim constantly."

"Didn't you fall in the lake?"

"And I pulled myself out of the water," Lucas said indignantly.

"After you splashed around dramatically." Theodmon snorted. "You looked as if you were drowning."

"I was merely surprised," Lucas countered.

"The water was shallow." Theodmon laughed, feeling some of the stress melt away from his shoulders.

"Remember the tournaments your father used to host?" Lucas said with a smile.

"I enjoyed them more than my tournaments," Theodmon said.

"Mhmm. It's much more fun when you're a child. There's a certain thrill of watching the knights joust and watching the reenacted battle that can't be replicated once you've seen...." He trailed off, staring ahead of him. The crackling of flames and the distant cries of distress echoed through the coming night, a haunting symphony of destruction.

"We used to pretend we were champions ourselves, wielding wooden swords and donning makeshift armor," Theodmon softly agreed, his heart feeling as if it were breaking as he looked out over the blackened land. "I suppose people want to believe in stories that give them purpose."

"People want to believe they can be more than they are. They want to be remembered as lords and kings. Hell, they want to be gods," Lucas corrected with a harsh glare. A burning wooden cottage collapsed in on itself nearby, causing its flames to grow and roar, casting long shadows across the two rode away from the destruction that had wrought. "And the best way to do that is war."

Theodmon looked at the once vibrant fields that now laid in ruins, the crops reduced to smoldering husks that crumbled in the hot breeze. The crackling of flames sounded like a mournful lament, a symphony of death that echoed through the night. The sighed as he surveyed the damage of his handiwork, knowing he couldn't argue with Lucas--war made heroes out of paupers and ghosts out of kings.

"The tournaments didn't prepare us for reality," Theodmon sighed.

"I'd disagree," Lucas said. "They teach one lesson that we all learned and enforced early, and we always will live by that rule."

Theodmon's head snapped up and he blinked at Lucas. "And what lesson is that?"

A pyre that had once been a stable crumbled, casting a bright, menacing glow across Lucas' face. Theodmon could see the fire reflected in his eyes as he said, "Violence is the most honest form of power."

Chapter Forty-Four

Not even a week later, the army broke into its three battalions, splitting like the heads of a hydra that burned every inch of Harréow Fields and beyond.

With no one to properly lead them, the military on the outskirts of Rindria crumbled. A murder of ravens could trace the path of Theodmon's men from above thanks to the scorched land and ash as they went.

And some murders did follow, lured by the promise of ripe bodies mowed down by the battalions like a scythe cutting wheat.

The burning crops and field felt like a pyre for Raphael Chauvignon, giving his son a chance to release all the grief he'd never been allowed to release. He'd tried to let it go in battle, watering the earth with blood in hopes that the sacrifice would make him a ruler his father could be proud of.

But war wasn't ruling. And Theodmon had been drowning in the weight of the expectations placed upon him. He suppressed his grief, he couldn't show weakness—he was a sixteen year old without a regent. If he was weak the Westerlands would fall to war.

I wish you hadn't died. He thought up in the skies. *I wish this war didn't exist. I wish I didn't see you die. I wish I was better so I could have prevented it. I wish you were better so you could have prevented it.*

Brigitte Belamy led one of the legions, her armor shining in the reflection of the flames, grinning widely. Michel Valrois accompanied her. And Lucas, more somber than Brigitte, departed with another branch by himself.

With the last of the army with him–Henri, Aloysius , and Samuel Beaulane flanking him on either side, Theodmon marched towards the Riam capital. The last time he had been in Rindria was another siege on this city—a war that ended due to instability within the ranks of their allies. The Morrians had grown discontented, suspicious of what was occurring. And when Amaria killed the Riam Royal Family, they had to end the siege prematurely.

But this time there would be no retreat. The Riam capital, and therefore Rindria itself, would fall to Thestitiunia. Theodmon's eyes lifted towards the sky. *Father,* he thought, *I'm avenging your death.*

"I can't wait to see some real action," Aloysius muttered to Henri. "You have to hold back so much in training when you have war magic."

The immature whine in his voice grated against Theodmon's ears. "Would you shut up?" he snapped. "We're marching on a city, not out on a bender."

Aloysius scowled at his brother. "What crawled up your ass?"

"Your ignorance, that's what." Theodmon glared back. "Only an idiot would actually *want* war."

"Says the man who is known first and foremost for being good at war," Aloysius scoffed. "Stop being a hypocrite."

"Being good at something isn't the same as liking it–"

"Could have fooled me, Archangel of Harréow Field—"

A roar rushed in Theodmon's ears and his vision flashed red. Before he could say or do anything, a numbing wall of peace enveloped him. He whirled on Henri with a glare. "Get out of my mind," he snarled.

"Then stop." Henri stared harshly at the two of them. "Do you want to explain yourselves or will I have to tell both of you what the other was thinking?"

"Neither," Aloysius scoffed.

"It'll be one or the other, because I'm not going to war with you two acting like this," Henri said. "Choose."

"I'm sorry for snapping at you." Theodmon grumbled, hoping that words alone would placate Henri.

"Not going to work," Henri said. "Are you two going to talk to each other or am I going to have to story-tell?"

"We'll talk," Aloysius groaned.

Several lieutenants shouted in the background as one of their horses stumbled and fell. Theodmon gave Aloysius and Henri a curt nod, studying the chaos of the fallen horse in the distance.

"I'll take care of it." Henri kicked his horse forward before he turned around and trotted towards the band of lieutenants.

Sighing, Theodmon turned to face Aloysius. "Are you actually excited?"

"Of course n–," Aloysius began, then stopped short.

Theodmon's eyebrows bunched together, his frown lines deepening on his forehead. "Aloy, talk to me."

"So you can scream at me again?" Aloysius scoffed.

"I already apologized," Theodmon said sternly, yet not unkindly. "Talk to me."

"Are *you* going to talk to *me*?" Aloysius asked.

Theodmon's first instinct was to tell his brother to stop deflecting. However, as he watched Aloysius focusing intently ahead of him, his hands quivering slightly over the reins of his horse, Theodmon realized he owed his brother a bit of honesty. Aloysius was right--like it or not, there was a reason he had that nickname.

He drifted his eyes downwards towards his left to see his intricately etched gold and silver hilt, a golden griffin encased in a circle at the top of it, gleaming at his hip, the blade sheathed in weathered red leather. *Winterthorne.* A blade made specifically for Theodmon from his grandfather's blade. Lysander would use the metal from Raphael's blade, Silver Storm, unless of course he chose to use that blade as it was. Winterthorne had previously been Heartsbane, and it was unwieldy, awkward in Theodmon's hands.

The metal was special, breathed on by the Hydras and the Dragons, if the stories were true. It was stronger than any substance, unless the wielder hesitated in their fight, and it would become as brittle as ice. Nobody knew how to recreate it, and so the metal was more precious than gold.

And Aloysius, as a second son, would never get a family heirloom such as this. Despite being a war mage. Despite being a Chauvignon. Theodmon's stomach clenched as he realized what this truly meant. Aloysius had never had anything of their father other than his looks and his surname. And he never would.

Theodmon set his hand on Winterthorne's hilt. "This was the country where Father died." The words felt like boulders falling from Theodmon's tongue. "This is where I almost lost Amaria and we both lost Ophelia because I got her dragged into battle from an entire nation away."

His shoulders slumped as he traced the design of the hilt. "I'm tired of war."

"And yet here we are, instigating another," Aloysius said.

"Yes," Theodmon said somberly. "We are."

"How can you hate war and keep going back?"

"It's expected of me." Theodmon sat up taller in his saddle. "When is the last time there's ever been a non-militaristic Marquis Chauvignon?"

Aloysius shrugged as their horses' hooves clipped beneath them. "I never paid attention to family history. I wasn't carrying on the family legacy, so why bother?"

"It was the first Marquis Chauvignon." Theodmon ignored Aloysius's self-pitying jab. "He lost the imperial crown to the Marions and he was knocked all the way down to the office of a marquis--not even a duke."

"We don't have an imperial crown to lose," Aloysius argued. "So, why bother?"

"We can lose the Westerlands." Theodmon's voice cracked. "Our home."

"Your home," Aloysius said. "Nobody has wanted me around since Lysander was born."

Theodmon paused as he played back the way his brother had protested his engagement to Amaria, despite the way they got on so well from day one.

She hadn't been the problem--she and the child she would bear meant Aloysius wouldn't be needed anymore.

Theodmon tried to calculate the right words to ask his question delicately. "Do you want some part of the family legacy?"

Aloysius huffed. "Don't pity me--"

"I'm serious," Theodmon said. "You're my brother and you deserve to have an heirloom."

Aloysius studied his brother with a shrewd glare. "Give me a chest of jewels and I'll knock you out of the highest tower in the keep once we're home."

Theodmon laughed. It was a fair worry on Aloysius's part--family jewels were the most common thing to pass along to non-heirs, which most often meant daughters. Theodmon studied his brother in earnest and, for the first time, saw the hurt behind his falls.

"I used to be jealous of you," Theodmon admitted.

Aloysius snorted.

"I'm serious," Theodmon said. "I resented all of the responsibility that I suddenly had. Meanwhile, you seemed to be having so much fun, but you were drowning, the same as I was. And neither of us could help the other."

"Everyone seemed to only care about you. Sometimes Ophelia and Celestine." Aloysius avoided Theodmon's eyes. "But nobody cared about me."

"That's why you agreed to marry Liara Nalaeny without more of a fight," Theodmon realized.

"I wanted to be useful." Aloysius' expression soured in disgust. "Look where that got me."

Theodmon rolled his eyes. "You don't have to be useful, you dolt."

Aloysius flinched at the words, making Theo regret them. He scrambled for a way to actually say what he'd meant, but he wasn't a man of words--that was why he had Amaria. What he understood was action. Motion.

"I have extra steel." Theodmon said. "You can forge your own sword with it."

Aloysius's eyes narrowed suspiciously. "Why?"

"Because it's your family too. And you're a war mage, and by the time my grandson forges his own sword, we'll be dead or too old to fight. "And who knows– you may be Marquis Chauvignon."

"That's impossible," Aloysius said. "You and Lysander would have to be dead."

"Not if I'm emperor."

Aloysius's eyebrows shot up. "You're planning a second war?" He snorted. "Hypocrite."

"Aion can't even be here for his own conquest. It's all Westannis and Perivinans," Theodmon pointed out.

"And a Westanni and Perivinan would sit upon the throne," Aloysius chuckled. "Clever. I'll give you that."

Silence fell between the two, the looming gray walls of Wéorren City coming closer as they rode. "Alright," Aloysius said. "But if I take over the Westerlands, there won't be a Marquis Chauvignon anymore."

"What do you mean?" Theodmon pulled his horses' reins in surprise.

"Duke Chauvignon," Aloysius said. "And make the Marions marquis's as a symbol of their ineffectiveness as rulers."

Theodmon gave a hearty laugh, as he pulled out Winterthorne. "Deal, if you can convince Amaria."

Aloysius snorted, pulling out his sword as the city wall loomed large. "Easy. She's more vengeful than you." He turned to look at the Riam guards fighting the onslaught of Thestitiunian men, desperately trying to flee to sound the alarms. "Shall we go help them?"

"As good leaders do," Theodmon said dryly. The two of them kicked their horses, charging into battle.

The foot soldiers put up a good fight, but the Riam guards were talented warriors once they had recovered from their surprise at the sudden attack. But they were faltering, and the fight was getting close.

Aloysius commanded a cavalry archer, pointing his sword towards a Riam guard who almost reached the warning bell for Wéorren City. Immediately, the archer fired, the Riam guard falling off the steps of the walls.

Theodmon spotted a Riam moving towards one of his men as the Thestitiunians' back was facing him. He yelled, kicking his stirrups harder. The Riam killed his man, but Winterthorne clashed against the Riam's bone and flesh, and his head fell into the dirt, a horse's hooves immediately crushing it underfoot.

Theodmon swung himself off his horse, the long, blood-stained grass reaching up to the middle of his thighs. "Set up here," he commanded the lieutenants around him, as he wiped the blood off his blade. "Don't kill anyone unless they attack you first, but don't let them into the city."

"Why, General?" a brave lieutenant asked.

Theodmon remembered what Amaria had said to him before he left. "*The Riams are familiar with desperation—there's no love for their rulers. If you can show that we have something to offer, but can leave their culture and traditions intact, the peasants may help.*"

And she had a point. Pent up rage made a good tinder pile. And desperation for survival and a better life could turn the people they were conquering into allies.

"Build the siege towers," Theodmon told another lieutenant as he handed his horse to a squire. "Have my tent set up and leadership brought to it." He pointed to another squire. "You, come with me. Bring a quill–you're taking notes."

The squire rummaged in his saddle bags, pulling out parchment, a clipboard, quill, and ink. As he did so, Theodmon surveyed the land around him as he waited for the rest of the leaders to join him. The city was circular, surrounded by a wall. Outside the walls, there were farm fields and villages. They were unsecured, but that could be fixed.

"You called?" Henri said as he approached Aloysius and Samuel.

"Once we are set up we first need to take the villages," Theodmon said. "Nobody burns the farms. It'll be a mercy to these people."

"Mercy?" Henri scoffed.

"Yes. A mercy that also helps us," Theodmon said. "Survey the walls with me. I'll need your insight on Wéorren's defenses and how to make her fall."

Chapter Forty-Five

E arly the following morning, Theodmon stood upon one of the siege towers, surveying the village below. It was small, but there seemed to be ample food supplies. And miraculously, perhaps because the nobles had sheltered inside the city, the villages surrounding Wéorren were easily occupied.

Recruiting spies as Amaria suggested might be difficult when the food was being confiscated and ration cards were being given out, as most of the food would be used for soldiers. If Theodmon was a Riam peasant, he would be bitter about the situation himself.

"Beautiful day," Aloysius said with a false chipper, as he climbed the siege tower, standing next to Theodmon.

Theodmon's eyes flickered over towards Aloysius darkly. "Yes, seizing assets is always beautiful."

"Some conquerors are worse," Aloysius shrugged.

"I doubt the Riam people share that sentiment."

"Of course not," Aloysius snorted. "But it doesn't make the sentiment less true. And I said some are worse than you—not that you're good."

"A mediocre conqueror?" Theodmon chucked. Aloysius gave a short laugh in return, almost like a bark. As quickly as it began, the laughter died out as the two brothers watched the scene below. Theodmon in particular watched the peasants.

Some of the peasants were glaring, clearly unhappy. Theodmon made note of them. Others were shying away, as if they feared the soldiers would turn and harm them. A valid sentimen; not one Theodmon liked but one that he understood. Some seemed to hang on to the soldiers, whether it was opportunism, hope, or blind stupidity. Those were also ones Theodmon would watch. This final group might be useful in Amaria's plan.

"I think that's enough for now, unless you're intending on watching this all day," Aloysius said. "Don't we have war plans to finalize?"

Theodmon exhaled. "Yes. Let's go to the tent—I need to get the—"

"I already commanded them to come," Aloysius interrupted.

"And what if I didn't agree to come with you?"

"Then we would have proceeded without you until you decided to come." Aloysius shrugged. "Thankfully, you decided to not be difficult."

"Hey," Theodmon protested.

Aloysius rolled his eyes, saying nothing more as they descended from the siege towers. As Aloysius walked in front of him, his hands lightly brushed over the railing, but not as a crutch, or even for support. Aloysius walked with an easy confidence, and with that came the poise needed to not fall down a siege tower, or at least to believe you wouldn't fall down a siege tower.

Theodmon had always seen Aloysius as a scared eleven year old, much as he saw himself as a scared sixteen year-old. But Aloysius was nearing twenty-three and Theodmon was twenty-seven. They had grown up, moved past their scared teenage selves. Theodmon should have acknowledged this before, in how Aloysius accepted marrying Liara, in how he was always a gentleman to her, and how he was always willing to go to battle for their family.

I'm a brilliant strategist. How could I overlook my own brother?

"Do you think we're doing the right thing?" Aloysius asked, interrupting Theodmon's thoughts.

Theodmon blinked rapidly. "What?"

"With this war," Aloysius said as they strode through the labyrinth of tents and makeshift towers. "Do you think we are doing the right thing?"

Theodmon turned his sharp gaze towards the preparations as they walked through the camp, appearing as if he were surveying his troops as his thoughts were a whirlwind inside his head. *What a question,* he thought sourly.

But still, he thought about it. Was there any moral right they had to invade another country? This country hung magic users, and their intolerance and inefficiency made life worse for the rest of the continent. But Morroek was no different from Rindria in these regards, and yet, Thestitiunia didn't invade Morroek.

Rindria was weak, an easier target. Pretending that was not a consideration or motivation was disingenuous. And Thestitiunia–Theodmon–wasn't only mounting a siege; they were also using civil discord to cause more friction between the Riams when they were already vulnerable.

So many people would be hurt. And could that harm actually be justified away with the belief that the future would be better? Did the end justify the means?

Of course it does. Theodmon scowled. *Or else we're all depraved fools.*

Still, Aloysius was waiting for an answer, and Theodmon knew no amount of silence or an attempt to change the subject would distract him from getting one. Theodmon could snap at Aloysius, deliver a biting remark about their father's death and how Aloysius couldn't understand. Once, Theodmon held that bitterness close to him, using it to protect himself. But, he had also harmed those closest to him in doing so.

"Does it matter?" Theodmon asked as they stopped in front of his tent. "If the answers to all these questions were answered would it change a thing about this conquest?"

Aloysius silently stared at Theodmon, the two of them staring at each other in challenge.

"Perhaps not," Aloysius said. "But it's something to consider afterwards."

Theodmon exhaled. "Perhaps. And if we survive, we will have all the time in the world to contemplate it."

"But not now," Aloysius said with a wry grin.

"No." Theodmon pushed open to the entrance of his flap, stepping inside to where a few lieutenants, Samuel, and Henri were waiting. "Now we plan for the conquest of Rindria."

Theodmon laid on his cot, looking up at the fabric of his tent, relaxing after the long hours spent in finalizing the strategy for tomorrow. Finally, the siege's leaders had all left his tent, allowing him to be alone. Outside his tent he heard chatter from the troops, enjoying the afternoon—perhaps the last peaceful afternoon they would have for a while.

He closed his eyes, exhaling. It would be the last time he had peace for a while.

There was a rustling at the entrance of his tent. He frowned, crossly wondering why the sentry's were disturbing him in spite of their direct orders not to. He sat up, intending to tell them off when he saw a hooded figure burst into his tent.

They were fast, but he was faster, his reflexes more trained for a fight. He threw the figure against the floor, and pointed his sword against their neck. "Who are you?"

The intruder extended their hands further away from their body, writhing on the floor slightly. "I'm not here to hurt you."

Theodmon faltered slightly. The voice was female. However, he quickly recovered, pressing the point of Winterthorne more tightly against her throat. "Remove your hood. State your name."

The figure, her palms still upturned, slowly moved her hands to her hood, lowering it. "Charlotte Petersdaughter, though I would prefer if we ignored that last name."

"Why?" Theodmon asked suspiciously, not lowering his sword. However, he did stand up away from her, allowing Charlotte to sit up.

"Because he let me burn when I was suspected of witchcraft. Because even after my name was cleared, he didn't claim me," Charlotte spat bitterly, rubbing her neck.

"And why are you here?" Theodmon asked.

"Don't you remember?" Charlotte said with a slight smile as she rubbed her neck. "You and your wife saved me around two years ago. I was about to go to the pyre and Lady Chauvignon intervened, claiming she was the mage. Luckily we had similar enough physical descriptions to fool the guards."

Theodmon blinked. Last he remembered of Rindria was Amaria getting herself thrown in a prison while war waged on—and Theodmon remembered the stench of blood, dirt, sweat, piss, and fear. He'll never forget the unique smell of war.

But the time before that—had anything occurred other than Amaria throwing herself onto an exploding gemstone? He racked his memory, knowing that Charlotte and her story sounded familiar.

An illusionist. Theodmon lowered his sword. "That's how you got past the guards. You're an illusionist."

Charlotte bowed her head slightly. "Yes, my Lord. Let me help you."

"With what?" Theodmon asked, curious to see what she'll propose.

"I can distort reality," Charlotte said. "And that's a skill that'll be helpful in this siege. I've heard the news. The rest of the country is burning, isn't it?"

Theodmon gave a curt nod.

"And Thestitiunia doesn't kill mages?"

"Not for being mages," Theodmon agreed. "Magic alone isn't an offense under the law."

"And we're not shunned by your culture?" Charlotte asked.

"Of course not," Theodmon said shortly. "Mages are integral to Thestitiunian culture."

Charlotte gave a small laugh. "Perfect. My Lord, would you hire me to help you with this siege?"

"You know—"

"That Rindria will no longer be a country?" Charlotte interrupted, the mask of deference momentarily gone, replaced with raw defiance and desperation. "Why do you think I'm offering?"

"How much money?" Theodmon asked, knowing this offer was too good to refuse. He cast a glance towards the flap of his tent. Nightfall was coming, and he didn't want to risk Charlotte staying here longer. War camps weren't safe for women at night and Theodmon didn't delude himself of that reality. "You should leave before the night sets—"

"You misunderstood me, my Lord."

Theodmon stared at Charlotte, surprised at her boldness.

Charlotte bowed her head slightly. "I'm never going back to Rindria, there's nothing for me there. My father left me to die. Perhaps he reported me to the guards, I don't know. I don't care to know." Her fists clenched. "My price is to offer me a job, safety, and Thestitiunian citizenship–regardless of the result of this siege."

She has a contingency plan. Theodmon suppressed his smile, grudgingly admitting that this Riam peasant was smart; even though she was clearly desperate, Charlotte was able to keep a logical head. *She'll be a good asset. Even without her magic.*

Theodmon's skin prickled. Good assets weren't always trustworthy. Even if he accepted her into his ranks, Theodmon would have Henri read her thoughts to determine how much of a threat she may be.

And for now, he would have to confirm she has no ties that may become a liability later on.

"Nothing?" Theodmon asked. "No family outside of your father?"

"They left me to die," Charlotte repeated. "And even afterwards, they whispered rumors about me. I was marked, either by magic or being spared, favored, whatever you would prefer to call it, by an enemy."

Theodmon sighed, taking in Charlotte's story and the steely determination in her eyes. "Alright. But I'm dressing you as a noblewoman, I'll find the clothes from somewhere. A war camp isn't safe for a woman, especially at night. And you'll have guards and a private tent. Is that acceptable to you?"

"Of course, my Lord." Charlotte gave a small smile. "How could I refuse?"

Theodmon watched her carefully. "Welcome to being a traitor."

"I'm not a traitor," Charlotte said. "To be a traitor, there had to be something for me to be loyal to."

Theodmon chuckled, impressed with Charlotte's fire. "Alright." He tilted his head respectfully. "A revolutionist then."

"A loyalist," Charlotte proposed. "I'm loyal to my ideals. You need my magic, and I need a better world."

"A guard will lead you to your tent. You won't be allowed to leave until I've done further investigation," Theodmon directed. "I need to introduce you to Lord Henri Delaluna."

Charlotte paled, her lip quivering. "What? I heard he can cause insanity."

"You'll be working with him as a mage," Theodmon said. "And if you were honest with me, you have nothing to worry about. Were you hiding anything from me?"

"Of course not," she whispered.

Theodmon motioned for her to follow him. "Then you have no reason to worry he'll turn on you."

Chapter Forty-Six

The crackling torches cast flickering light upon the tents, their canvas walls rippling in the night breeze like ghostly apparitions. Shadows prowled the edges of the camp, lurking in the darkness like silent sentinels, ever watchful for signs of danger. The distant hoot of an owl echoed through the trees, and amidst the camp, the soldiers' armor clinked softly as they tended to their weapons. Women from the nearby villages lurked. Theodmon surveyed where they came from, noting the camp's weak areas. And he listened, hoping to hear a woman say she came from inside the city.

Theodmon walked through the camp, hearing the men loudly drinking in their tents. They hadn't suffered losses from fighting yet. The war hadn't properly begun--it was so easy to be jaunty about the whole thing right now. Theodmon knew that morale would fade fast. Once they watched a friend die. Once food started running low. Once the whores started looking at them with hatred. Once they started missing their wives and children—that's when danger would engulf the camp like a choking smoke.

A few gasps and grunts from women came from the tents—Riam women from the villages desperate for coin or food to hoard before the siege began. Or perhaps some were like Charlotte, planning on staying in the camp full time. But unless they shared Charlotte's rare magical power, they were in for a nasty surprise.

High above, the stars glittered like diamonds scattered across a velvet canvas, and Theodmon saw a figure slink through the camp. Theodmon pulled out his sword, ready to strike when he saw Henri approach the figure.

Henri pulled off the hood of this figure, kissing them. Blinking, his eyes adjusting to the darkness, Theodmon saw that it was a woman, her breasts almost popping out of her dress. Elisa Redwayne.

I don't trust her. Theodmon knew Amaria had decent judgment and that Henri was more than capable of protecting himself, but someone so willing to turn on their countrymen wasn't someone Theodmon could trust. Slowly, Theodmon followed them, stopping once he was outside their tent.

"...put your clothes back on," Henri said.

"You don't want–"

"I'm here for intelligence. Your other services are a cover," Henri interrupted. "What do you have for me?"

"You should know about the sewage system," Elisa said. "It's a weak spot of Wéorren that nobody bothers to learn as only the poor deal with it."

"Mark where the entrance is," Henri said, and Theodmon knew he was pulling out a map.

"Thank you," Henri said after a while. "One last thing, who're you sleeping with in Wéorren?"

"Anyone who gives me food or shelter," Elisa said defensively.

"But is there a common lord?" Henri pressed. "Someone who would be interested in weaponizing you if he knew you were sleeping with Thestitiunians?"

Elisa sighed. "Lord Stuart Rockwood. He's one of the governors of Wéorren that have been ruling since the Royal Family died. I've been in his bed weekly since we've returned. His wife is heavily pregnant but he already has five daughters—it's his way of punishing her, especially since the doctors are predicting the baby is another daughter."

"Get him to exchange your Thestitiunian coin for Riam coin," Henri said. "Make up an excuse, that it's safer for you to only hold Riam coins, especially as you'll steal intelligence for him."

"It's illegal for women to hold money," Elisa reminded him.

"Then ask him to hold it safely for you," Henri said. "As a favor to you, leverage your intelligence services. Get him to trust you. Do you think you could become an official mistress?"

"This is a terrible plan."

"Do you have a better one?" Henri said, and Theodmon flinched at how cold his friend sounded.

"Thestitiunia is a disease." Elisa's voice dripped with disdain.

"And you're now part of it," Henri said evenly.

Elisa was silent for a while. "Alright. I'll propose becoming Rockwood's mistress."

"You will," Henri said.

"I should go."

"Stay a bit longer," Henri said. "Just to convince others that you actually were in here....whoring."

"I do actually have to whore. I need money," Elisa said darkly. "I'm nobody's mistress yet. It's a bit suspicious if I was, let me offer my services here for a few more weeks before you officially offer."

There was a rustling of coins and then a thud. "Here. Take five gold coins from that."

There was a long silence.

"Thank you," Elisa muttered.

"Stay," Henri repeated. "Do you need food? I have some wine and bread."

For a while, Theodmon heard nothing. He debated if he should move, inspect other parts of the camp as he was supposed to be doing. However, for some unknown reason, he was compelled to stay standing there, as if he was a sentry assigned to guard Henri.

"Look, you need an alibi for how you obtained the false intel you're feeding them," Henri said. "You could get it...," Henri trailed off, sighing deeply. "It's not as likely as...be my mistress."

"What?" Elisa asked incredulously.

"If you're a major's mistress," Henri said slowly, as if he was trying to decipher what he was saying, "then you'd be in more of a position to secretly see war plans. The types of war plans the Riams would want. It would protect you, the Riams won't be as likely to hurt you as they need that information, the men here won't touch you as touching my mistress would be a sentence of several lashes, and you can be safe here. I'll pay you fifteen gold coins a night."

"Why would you be so kind to me? I know I'm not that essential. As the war goes one you'll find more and more desperate—"

"I don't want you to be hurt," Henri said. "I can feel your hurt. I can feel everyone's horrible, pained thoughts. And considering how much time we are spending together—you having less pain makes everything easier."

"How am I to be both yours and Lord Rockwood's mistress?"

"Make sure you're an exceptionally good lay," Henri said. "But don't return until you have proof that he trusts you."

Elisa snorted. "What do you mean by good lay?"

A goblet clattered to the floor. "Uh...uh...," Henri stuttered. "Just make sure he can't live without you?"

"What if I do that to you? Will you ever recover?" Elisa said.

Theodmon heard the rustling of a cloak. "Take this wine. Wet your legs with it to make you sticky."

A few more minutes passed. Theodmon saw Elisa leave the tent, and stroll over to a group of soldiers sitting near a fire, immediately sitting on one's lap. Theodmon looked away, needing no imagination to know what would happen next.

"I know you heard that." Henri stepped outside his tent.

"I didn't mean to," Theodmon said.

"I know that too," Henri said tiredly. "Come inside, I know you want to discuss that intel."

"We can wait," Theodmon offered half-heartedly.

Henri scoffed lightly. "Let's skip the niceties. Just lean your sword against the bed, I don't want you swinging it in here."

Theodmon chuckled as he followed Henri back into his tent. The space was brutally practically--a singular table and chair and a singular bed was all there was inside. Henri's armor was on the table, near an open bottle of white wine, and his sword leaned against the bed.

Theodmon's eyebrows rose slightly. High ranking leaders usually had a few more pieces of furniture than just this.

"You can sit on the chair." Henri moved the armor so Theodmon could sit.

"I'm shocked at how you spoke–" Theodmon began.

"I feel awful," Henri interrupted. "I know that after this siege, it will be better for everyone, including the ordinary, non-ruling Riams, but it feels so shitty to manipulate people." Henri looked at Theodmon, a tear rolling down his cheek. Henri's chest heaved momentarily, and Theodmon sat silently waiting for him to speak again when he was ready. "She's been through a lot already and she despises Rockwood."

"We all have to do things we don't like in war," Theodmon said.

"It still feels wrong to ask that of somebody," Henri countered.

Theodmon didn't disagree. But he couldn't focus too much on the individual morality of each decision. He had to focus on the morality of the greater good. War was hell. War was inherently immoral. But war was alright when the end result stemming from it was bringing a better world. If people were better off after the results of a war, was the war really that bad?

Theodmon felt Henri looking at him, and when he turned to meet his friend's eyes, they were laced with sadness. Theodmon knew that Henri read his thoughts, and based on his expression, Theodmon wasn't sure that Henri fully agreed with him.

Please don't say anything. Theodmon begged. *I don't want to fight.*

"It's been a long journey." Henri stood up from his bed with a groan.

"I need you to do one more thing for me," Theodmon said. "There's a Riam peasant, Charlotte—"

"I can hear her thoughts from here. I know," Henri said. "From what I've heard she has no ill intentions towards us, but I'll do a more thorough search in the morning." He yawned, laying on his bed. "Now, we should both get some sleep."

"Thank you." Theodmon's voice cracked as he departed from Henri's tent and headed towards his own, ready to take the heavy armor off and sleep.

"My Lord." A sentry entered Theodmon's tent as he finished undressing from his armor. Startled, Theodmon lunged for his sword.

"My apologies," the sentry said. "I just received letters from Raulle and was told they should immediately come to you."

Slowly, Theodmon lowered his sword, breathing heavily. "Thank you. Leave them on the table."

The sentry followed his command, leaving two sealed envelopes on the large wooden table, nearly knocking over one of the wooden horses used to showcase the calvary. The sentry adjusted the horse and then bowed before leaving the tent.

Theodmon watched him depart, before picking up the letters. Sighing, he broke the seal off the smallest one.

> **I XWJV YSZMZEHY ST**
> **NEBXVXE LEK A**
> **TDFIMBIX YMGCW. LA**
> **MVB LWSX IPWVX.**

Cipher. Theodmon cursed under his breath. Amaria's cipher's were notoriously diffi-cult to crack, but he could remember some of her codes. For the next few hours he went through every system he could recall.

All resulted in gibberish.

"Damn you," he said. "Fucking damn you, Amaria."

Theodmon understood the need for secrecy. He really did, but what use was this level of secrecy if he couldn't understand the messages? There was important information in there. Amaria wouldn't have gone through all this trouble if it wasn't. but he wasn't good with ciphers and she knew that.

I love her. He reminded himself. *This is part of the reason I love her.* Taking a deep breath, he grabbed her other letter, breaking open the griffin seal. There, in clear and readable Thestitiunian, was a letter written in her curling script.

My love,

I miss you. It has only been a few months and yet, it feels like years. I miss seeing the orange trees and the turquoise waves with youu. Our children are fine. Lysander has found ways to escape his nannies and terrorize the kitchens for cookies. And Sylviana, she grows every day. They miss you as much as I do, but they will learn of what you did for Thestitiunia and be proud.

I am proud of you.

I have spent a lot of time reading philosophy books since you've left and I've been pondering some things. Perhaps you can help me answer them: What is the code to a healthy marriage? Is it love? Is it trust? I know you will never let me down, and I too try to do the same. Without thread, without conditions, I love you. And together, we will be able to decipher anything.

I wish I could say more, but for now, I hope you are healthy and doing well.

Your loving wife,
Amaria

Theodmon held the letter to his heart, closing his eyes as he imagined Amaria writing it. Perhaps if he let his imagination run, he could almost believe he smelled the roses and oranges of her perfume. If Amaria was here she could decipher this mess, or simply tell him what she knew.

But she wasn't here. Theodmon sighed, looking down at the letter and reading it once more. *I miss her.* He thought as he read the last lines of the letter. *And together, we will be able to decipher anything. I wish I could say more, but for now, I hope you are healthy and doing well.* He placed the letter down, rubbing his temples. He had to break this cipher—*Wait.*

Feeling as if he was struck by lightning, Theodmon re-read the last lines of the letter once more. *Decipher. The code is here. She placed it in the letter.* Feeling suddenly energized, Theodmon pulled out a blank sheet of parchment, the ciphered note laying on top of it. Which sentence could be the code?

He tried *"what is the code to a healthy marriage?"* first, and it too was gibberish. Perhaps it was a singular line? But *"I am proud of you,"* and *"I wish I could say more, but for now, I hope you are healthy and doing well,"* yielded similar useless results.

Owls hooted in the distance and Theodmon knew he should sleep soon so he could be prepared for when battle began. But he needed to know what this letter was. It may be crucial for tomorrow.

How many letters are in this cipher? Theodmon rubbed his eyes before he counted the letters in the cipher. *Fifty-four. What sentence here has fifty-four letters?* Theodmon lowered his head, counting the letters of each sentence. "...turquoise waves with yo–" Theodmon trailed off in his mutterings, seeing that the final word of that sentence, "you," seemed to have an extra swirl, as if it were spelled "youu" instead. *Fifty-four letters with that misspelling.*

Theodmon broke into a grin, shouting momentarily in elation. This was it. That was the code. And Amaria gave another clue when she said "algebraic," so much that Theodmon knew how to decode her message–it was like graphing on an x and y axis. He had never enjoyed his mathematics class as a child, but he could appreciate the complexity of this code now that he knew how to break it.

It was so complex that only highly educated people who spoke Thestitiunian could speak it–narrowing the possibility of it being cracked by adversaries. And if it was cracked, it gave immediate suspicions of who may be involved in espionage.

If I survive this, I promise to the gods I'll tell her she's a genius. I'll buy her whatever jewels she wants. We can take a two month vacation by the sea–whatever she wants.

Still beaming, Theodmon drafted out the graph, and then placed the cipher letters on top of the sentence. After several minutes of work, he knew what Amaria had said.

A Lord Governor of Wéorren has a gambling issue. He may take bribe.

Rough grammar, but that was to be expected with these messages. And Amaria's intel was useless for the siege, but invaluable in developing more intelligence activities. Henri, tonight, unintentionally set the stage for more complex intelligence and framing with Elisa. And in sieges, brute force was helpful but traitors were the true reason nations fell.

Chapter Forty-Seven

T he sun hadn't even risen when the first attack on Wéorren City occurred, the troops assailing the walls in the dark, as deadly as snakes in the grass. As the Thestitunians attacked the walls and the Riams defended their home with arrows, the sunrise turned the sky red as blood splattered the brown fields and gray walls.

Theodmon watched from above the hill.

"How long do you think it'll take to overrun?" Aloysius asked.

"At least a year," Theodmon muttered. "They have to know this is their last stand for their home country. They'll hold out as long as they can."

"We burned their food," Aloysius said. "How much food is stored in Wéorren?"

"We'll find out." Theodmon looked at Henri. "Any word from Elisa?"

"We won't see her for a while," Henri said. "She's gaining the trust of the enemy; we can't engage in counter-intelligence until she is secured."

"And you think he'll trust her?" Aloysius questioned.

"He thinks Elisa is loyal and is in the perfect position to steal information that can help save his power—he's a ruler now, he won't give that up," Theodmon said. He hadn't always felt the most comfortable with this plan, but tactically, it did have its strengths. He just hoped its severe weaknesses wouldn't cause the rest of it to implode.

"Wéorren is Rindria's last stand," Aloysius noted, inhaling deeply.

"And our job is to divide the people defending it early." Theodmon nodded towards Charlotte, who silently stood next to Henri.

"I'll make it seem as if there is infighting, friendly fire, stealing food, all to divide the guards from each other. Word will eventually reach the people...." Charlotte trailed off, staring ahead at the fighting below.

"And Elisa will help spread the rumors when it's time," Henri added. "How far is your range?" This last part was specifically directed towards Charlotte.

She bit her lip. "Perhaps five hundred feet at most?"

"Are you trained?" Henri asked.

"I trained myself," Charlotte said, her chest puffed out.

Henri frowned. "I can tell."

Charlotte turned red, averting her eyes towards the ground.

"You need formalized training for this." Henri began walking towards the tents. "Let's go."

"Where are you going?" Theodmon asked.

"I'm not going to fight today, and you and Aloysius are more military-minded than I," Henri said. "But if you're relying on her magic, you will lose. I can change that by training her. Sam will help."

Theodmon frowned, remembering how exhausted mages seemed after their training. Amaria had once slept for two days straight after a particularly nasty fire training that had resulted in the entire courtyard catching fire. He wasn't sure exhausting Charlotte to that capacity, if not worse, was wise.

"She needs it," Henri said sternly, looking at Theodmon directly. "And I can pull rank—she's a Thestitiunian citizen now–you granted it in every way but the official papers and we all know she is getting those as soon as we cross the border. And as an Extractor, I have the authority to train, discipline, and reward Thestitiunian mages for their magic. Don't make me stoop there. It's better for everyone if you don't set an untrained mage loose on an entire city."

Slowly, Theodmon exhaled. Henri was right. Even Theodmon, a non-mage, knew untrained mages could be volatile. And her range only being five hundred feet was problematic. If Henri and Sam, both powerful Extractors, could train Charlotte and expand upon her powers, it would be better for everyone.

"I can train her while I handle the intelligence and oversee the mages," Henri said. "Play to your strengths, hide from your weaknesses, right?"

Theodmon snorted. "Alright. Do what you have to do."

Henri curtly nodded to Theodmon and then to Charlotte, the two mages departing from the Chauvignons and towards the camp's metal forge, likely to collect Sam to help train her.

"Should I leave too?" Aloysius ran his hand through his hair as he leaned against a post.

A smile crept over Theodmon's lips. "You can't join the secret mage club."

"You're just mad you aren't invited."

Theodmon turned his full attention to the scene below. "I need you here."

Monstrous siege towers inched towards the walls, like slow-moving behemoths amidst a cacophony of shouts and the rhythmic thud of machinery. The battering ram, a colossal wooden ram's head, swung back and forth with methodical precision, each strike against the gate reverberating through the earth like a heartbeat of war.

Soldiers scaled the walls, only to meet showers of arrows, streaking the stone with blood as their limp bodies tumbled to the ground below. They had to know they would die, and yet they still charged. People acted as if the calvary, sitting upon their horses above it all, were the epitomes of bravery and heroism. Theodmon disagreed—it was those who led the front line, the simple soldier who would never see home again.

"I can't believe we're training our secret weapon on the job," Aloysius muttered, shaking his head. "Do you trust her?" Aloysius asked.

"Yes," Theodmon answered without hesitation. "I normally don't trust anyone who can easily turn loyalties like that, but Charlotte...any rational person would want an escape."

"It must be awful to be hunted and killed for how you were born," Aloysius said. "I'm not as attached to my magic as most but...it'd be a cruel punishment to have to suppress it or die."

"Why don't you like your magic as much?" Theodmon asked. It was true, Aloysius always seemed to be less attached to his powers than Henri, Amaria, Juliette, or Katerina were—but Theodmon had always assumed it was because Aloysius was less powerful.

"It's the only memory I have of Father," Aloysius whispered. "He taught me how to use my magic, and I don't want to corrupt that memory by doing something he'd disapprove of."

Their father had been a war mage, and only Aloysius had inherited the gift. "He'd want you to use it," Theodmon said confidently. "He wouldn't want you to suppress your talents."

"He was talented at war," Aloysius said. "And look where it got him, look where it got us."

Theodmon focused on the siege, the rising sun illuminating the burning stones flying through the air, crashing into the walls of the city. The Riams were strong, but over time these defenses would falter and Theodmon would be able to anticipate the weaker points in the Riams defenses, solely from using today and the coming weeks as a control.

"I'm not good at war. I don't have clever strategies or use tricks in my fighting," Aloysius continued. "All I can do is withstand attacks for a time. Turning my body into a shield until my energy runs out."

"Don't minimize yourself," Theodmon said. "That talent will come in handy. I don't know when, but it will."

You're so much more than you see yourself. And in part I'm to blame for this. Theodmon had spent so long minimizing Aloysius, looking for the worst in him—hating that he didn't use war magic, seeing it only as a tool, a connection to their father that Aloysius was wasting.

He looked over at Aloysius. *I was wrong. And I'll have years to make this up to you.* Blinking rapidly, Theodmon refocused his attention on the siege below. But that too was painful. He saw his men fall in the first attack and he had to wonder if they believed they had years to live before they were conscripted into this war.

It's for the empire, Theodmon reminded himself. *It is part of Thestitiunia. It is an honor to fight and die for our country. And the dead feel no more pain, it is the living who anguish for them.*

Chapter Forty-Eight

Four months of the siege had passed when Lucas, Brigitte, and Michel, along with their troops, rejoined the rest of the Westanni army. It had been nine months since Theodmon had seen home, and he found himself thinking fondly of it more and more each day.

"It's done," Lucas told Theodmon as he rode into camp early in the morning, before trudging himself into a tent and onto a cot.

Brigitte said nothing when she returned, but her eyes no longer shined. Lucas and Brigitte, along with their men were granted leave for two days before they were expected to join the siege. It was needed, they had lost a lot of men in the initial waves of the siege.

There was no way to bury and mark each grave. The dead soldiers' identities were accounted for if they weren't so disfigured from the fire to be rendered unidentifiable, and a letter was sent to their family. After that they were thrown into mass graves. However, the rites were followed, the three priests of Sadthos that always accompanied the army in wartime were haggard.

Theodmon did his best to ensure that the dead were honored, but there were too many of them to properly follow tradition. The night was falling fast, and he walked around the edges of the camp, taking his turn on watch. In truth, he needed something to do other than move figures around an infernal war table, imagining hypotheticals that truly couldn't account for the horrors that occurred.

And by inspecting the borders of camp, he could pretend that they had made more progress than they truly had. Theodmon now could tell that the south of Wéorren was the weakest point—it consistently had less men defending it–not so much that it was easily identifiable. Theodmon had been searching for small discrepancies, for any sign of what to do next.

Charlotte, according to Henri, had just recently reached a level of control where she could start minor illusions in the city from the camp. She caused minor discontent in Wéorren, a missing piece of bread, a rotted fruit. She practiced with small things, nothing to give any cause for alarm, but could give her adequate practice for when she would be needed during the fall of the city.

Theodmon noted that the village outside Wéorren was a ghost town. There seemed to be two schools of thought among the Riams-- some were willing to abandon and flee, and some stood their ground and refused to let anyone get close to their home. But the village outside was a ghost town, all of its survivors had fled to the walled city long ago.

And yet, the whores still managed to come in and out of the city. However, Theodmon hadn't seen Elisa in a while. Henri informed him of what Elisa had to do before she returned, and Theodmon had to grind his teeth and accept this asinine plan because he had no better option. He just hoped that she could get Rockwood to trust her more easily.

He also waited for Haerdnor. Where was he with the reinforcements? More importantly, where was he with the food? Perivina Fluere had some of the most fertile land in Thestitiunia. Theodmon needed it to deliver with its half of the alliance.

Patience. Theodmon reminded himself. *Sieges are an exercise in patience.*

He wasn't a hasty strategist. He could play the long game, but he still longed for home, missing the comforts of sleeping in a castle, seeing his wife and children, and not living on rations of stale bread and ale. There was always ale. Even running low on food, there was somehow always an excess of alcohol. And the men were always drinking. Truly, it was a miracle of the gods.

Perhaps it was the only miracle they'd have for a while. Theodmon's eyes flickered across the stone walls, watching the sun set behind them.

Theodmon found sieges difficult—he wanted to do something substantial. And relying on a Riam peasant while he was unable to do anything was maddening. He trusted Charlotte to do her part, and he had full confidence in the Extractors' training, but he didn't like waiting for others to fight his battles for him. He needed to be in control of something, anything, but instead he was at the mercy of time.

Exhaling, Theodmon cast one last look towards the walls as the sun set, the sky turning dark and filling up with stars as he trudged back into the center of camp. Near his tent, there was a bonfire roaring. Henri, Lucas, Sam, and Aloysius had already started drinking. Aloysius was singing a folk song, his voice thin, raspy, and out of pitch.

Theodmon sat down next to them, rubbing his hands together to create friction as he held his hands close to the flames.

"How was the watch?" Lucas asked.

"Boring," Theodmon said. "Hand me something to drink."

"...and bring the lass home!" Aloysius finished his song, the words slurred together.

"I'm not drunk enough to tolerate his singing yet," Theodmon said as Lucas handed him some ale.

"Hey!" Aloysius protested. "I can sing."

Lucas rolled his eyes. "And lions can fly."

Aloysius started sputtering, trying to stand.

"Language," Henri said. "And no you won't do that, you can barely walk."

Everyone but Aloysius burst into laughter. Aloysius looked around the group with narrowed eyebrows, his face flickering in the firelight, shadows dancing across his face before he broke into a grin, joining in the laughter.

"What did the bartender say to the soldier?" Aloysius asked.

Theodmon took a swig of his drink. "What?"

Aloysius's eyes glazed over. "I forgot the rest of the joke."

Lucas clapped Aloysius on the shoulders with a hearty chortle. "I think you're too drunk."

"Elisa is coming," Henri said, his voice sounding as if an echo, his eyes a glowing blue.

"What?" Theodmon stood up, throwing his glass in the dirt. His hand rested on the hilt of his sword as he silently scanned the dark camp, watching to see if anything moved in the shadows.

"She's not a threat," Henri whispered to him.

"I view everyone as threats," Theodmon replied.

"And that's why you're an uptight ass," Lucas snorted.

Once again, the group laughed, barely stopping when a woman stepped beside them, pulling down the hood of her cloak to reveal long honey-brown hair as she sat on Henri's lap. "My Lord," she almost purred. "Have a coin for me?"

"Elisa," Henri whispered, his shoulders tensing.

Aloysius scrunched his nose. "You smell of sewage."

"Probably because I came through the sewage," Elisa dismissed, adjusting the hemline of her dress. "Couldn't be bothered to change. Forgive me."

"Are you saying all the women that our men are sleeping with—" Aloysius paled.

Elisa gave an almost jeering laugh. "Who knows what sort of diseases and infections they have."

"And Rockwood let you out the city?" Lucas questioned.

"Rockwood thinks I'm loyal to him and that I am a wonderful intelligence asset." Elisa pulled out a key from under her dress, twirling the chain of the necklace in her fingers. "The key to his chambers."

"Thank you for doing this," Henri said.

"Rockwood is ambitious." Elisa ignored Henri's thanks as she tucked the key back under her dress. "He wants to see if he can use me to get information to make him a hero in this siege." She put her hands on top of Henri, leaning forward to whisper in his ear in a way where her breasts pressed against his face. "Put your hands up my skirt."

Henri turned red, slightly turning his head so Elisa wasn't covering his entire line of vision. He whispered something unintelligible to her, in which Elisa threw her head back as she laughed. She placed her hand on top of Henri's, guiding him up her skirt.

"I'm sorry," Aloysius said, his words slurred.

"Don't be," Elisa said, kissing Henri on the lips. "Anyways, I have information. So Henri, if you wouldn't mind bringing us to a private place." She stood up, extending her hand to Henri, looking very much the part she was playing for any bystanders.

"Wait a few moments and join us," Henri muttered under his breath to Theodmon as he stood up. "I can tell you don't want to wait for information. You're itching for something to do."

He knows me too well. Theodmon gave Henri a curt nod. *Thank you.* He thought, knowing Henri would hear.

Theodmon waited for around ten minutes before he left to join Henri and Elisa in his tent. He moved through the camp, silently surveying the night until he stopped in front of the tent.

"Henri," Theodmon said, pushing open the flaps.

"What the hell?" Elisa jumped to her feet.

"Elisa," Henri said soothingly, his hands outstretched as if she were a wounded animal. "He's here to listen to what you–"

"You didn't think to warn me?" Elisa asked, a red rash appearing on her chest.

"Let's sit down," Henri said, as calm as ever. "Elisa, you have a lot to discuss with us, right?"

Elisa looked between Henri and Theodmon, her eyes wide and unblinking. Theodmon was sure she was going to bolt, that they would have to chase her through the camp. However, Elisa gulped, and gave a short nod before she sat down on Henri's cot.

"Food storage is running low. The lower classes have been rationing, but even now in Bria Hall people worry. The nobles are hoarding food in their apartments," Elisa said.

"So tensions are high," Theodmon remarked.

"Yes," Elisa said. "But there's solidarity. The entire city knows they are Rindria's last stand. They are willing to withstand the siege as long as they can as a matter of pride."

"For now," Henri muttered.

"I told Rockwood I'd get him information that can help him win this war for Rindria," Elisa said. "What sort of lies do you have that I can feed him?"

"Haerdnor Raulet is coming with provisions," Theodmon clipped.

"Obviously," Elisa said. "Everyone expects Raulet aid, considering who is leading the siege and who he's married to. Do you have something that's not common knowledge?"

Theodmon found it disconcerting how blunt Elisa was about everything. She was raised in polite society and yet she decided to eschew it all. Perhaps she was molded that way, as they all were molded into themselves. But still, Theodmon couldn't stand her.

But he needed her and she unfortunately had a point. He gritted his teeth, pacing around the tent, trying to come up with anything that sounded believable but wasn't true, or at the least not critical information.

After a few minutes of this, Elisa cleared her throat.

"I'm thinking," Theodmon snapped.

"I didn't say anything," Elisa replied.

"Come up with a new plan," Henri suggested. "One just for this."

"We'll attack the north wall when Haerdnor Raulet comes." Theodmon gritted his teeth. They couldn't attack the south wall. Not yet. But he hated that he had to sacrifice more men in a futile exercise. "I'll scribble out a plan you can steal from Henri."

"Yes, you wouldn't tell me your plans, that'd be stupid," Elisa agreed.

"Plant Thestitiunian coins on Rockwood," Henri instructed Elisa.

"Of course," she said. "All the money I get tonight is going to be confiscated by him. And you're giving me a lot, as I've agreed to be your official mistress."

"How much did we agree on? Fifteen gold coins?"

"For most nights," Elisa said. "But for tonight, make it thirty. I am another man's official mistress—it seems as if I'm high in demand."

Theodmon cleared his throat. "I'll let you discuss these specifics in private. Henri, come to my tent after this."

Henri wouldn't have to do anything, but Theodmon preferred to keep the appearance of him going into Henri's tent with a command as opposed to, gods' forbid, that he was participating with Henri and a whore.

"I'll be there in thirty," Henri told him as he departed.

And as he left, Theodmon realized that he had something to do other than sit. He had what was essentially a suicide mission to plan. Haerdnor Raulet was coming with his men from his province. It was cruel that the Perivinans would come to give aid only to be rewarded with death.

But how many lives would they eventually save because of that? And did that matter at all?

Chapter Forty-Nine

"**G**eneral!" Men burst into Theodmon's tent early the next morning. Crossly, he sat up, rubbing his eyes. *This better be important, or else I am going to flay them for waking me at this ungodly time.*

"What?" Theodmon snapped.

"Apologies sir," one said. "There's been a fight."

"Why can't you take care of it?" Theodmon growled. "Are you this incompetent–"

"It was a riot over rations," the man hastily added.

Theodmon ground his teeth, standing up from his cot. "Wait outside."

Theodmon had expected something like this to occur once rations were dangerously low.

This wouldn't be an issue if Haerdnor Raulet was already here. He was supposed to be here with food and more men. Where was he? *Fucking Raulets. You can't trust any of them.*

Except Amaria. Theodmon pulled a shirt over his head, pulling on his boots sharply afterwards. He grabbed Winterthorne, leaving his armor behind.

He arrived at the brig, where seven men were bruised, bleeding, and tied to posts. As he arrived, the officers in charge launched into an account of what had happened.

Theodmon would have been happy with the summary, the details were unnecessary. Still, he said nothing, letting the officers explain.

It would postpone him having to decide what to do with men, whose crime almost boiled down to being hungry. Theodmon didn't want to punish them–he himself was hungry and cross. Still, he couldn't let food riots go unpunished–if it seemed as if they were permitted the entire camp would be in chaos before nightfall.

The officers stopped talking, looking at Theodmon, waiting for his decree.

"You," he said, directing his words towards the men in the brig. "Explain yourselves."

A horn drowned out Theodmon's voice. Sharply, he turned towards the noise, the music accompanied by the rumble of griffins, horses, and thousands of marching men. "Steady," he muttered, more to himself than anyone else, as he pulled out his sword.

In the breeze, a blue banner with a golden money scale and red roses fluttered. The Raulets sigil. The Riams, they wouldn't have that. Theodmon felt his shoulders slump, and he sheathed his sword. "Don't attack!" He shouted.

"It's food," he said softly, almost in disbelief. Reinforcements had finally come. He looked towards one of the officers. "A week in the brig for all involved," he directed. "Handle with discretion."

Without another look back, Theodmon went to meet the army brought to him. Haerdnor Raulet sat at the head of the reinforcements, with Oliver Neremoux at his right. Both of them looked tired but still put-together. The Perivinans men didn't look gaunt. Haerdnor had delayed, taken his sweet time, all at Theodmon's men's expense.

Theodmon wanted to drag Haerdnor from his horse and beat him to a pulp. He could imagine his hands around Haerdnor, squeezing his neck, snapping it once all the air had left him. It would be one life to make up for the hundreds lost by his delay. How could Haerdnor let his allies suffer?

"What took you so long?" Theodmon demanded.

"We had to gather the griffins and you burned the entirety of Rindria–"

"You want me to believe animals and peasants held you up?" Theodmon growled.

"If you let me finish," Haerdnor said. "Mages made and maintained ice boxes for the food. Amaria's idea. She didn't want any food to spoil."

Involuntarily, Theodmon's chin dipped, his posture slumping. He felt himself raging. How was he supposed to know that? "I wish you told me."

"Amaria didn't want to risk our movements being intercepted."

Theodmon scowled. She could send other intelligence information with a gods' damned cipher but not this?

"She couldn't tell you. How could she explain the magically made ice boxes in vague terms?"

Theodmon's arms crossed. Haerdnor had a point, unfortunately. "Who came up with the ice boxes?" He asked, purely to defect.

Haerdnor raised an eyebrow. "Amaria, as I already said. There's no need to be an ass."

"I'm not apologizing," Theodmon said. "My men died."

"I'm not expecting you to," Haerdnor said. "But we're allies, you're married to my sister, and I would appreciate it if we could at least act as if we respect each other."

Theodmon swallowed hard. Haerdnor Raulet had always been irresponsible. He still almost frolicked around with his life—Theodmon had to make decisions that Haerdnor shied away from at twenty-three when Theodmon was only sixteen.

He opened his mouth slightly to speak, but found that his mouth was dry. His mouth shut and he licked his lips, desperately trying to bring moisture back somehow so he could swallow a smidge of saliva.

"Amaria trusts me," Haerdnor said with a sigh. "And you trust her judgment right?"

"She's loyal to a fault," Theodmon said.

Haerdnor smirked. "So you admit your wife has flaws."

"She's your sister–"

"Which is why I know her faults. I was tortured by some of them–she's very vindictive, you know," Haerdnor said. "Anyways, you trust her judgment? You trust my father's judgment with military and political things, right? They trusted me here–give me a chance or else this entire conquest will fail."

Theodmon stared off into the distance, looking at the ash blowing in the wind. Why was he so bitter towards Haerdnor? He knew he had to work with him, it would be stupid to not work with him. And Haerdnor was his wife's twin brother–he knew that it would break Amaria's heart to know that he was so antagonistic towards her brother.

But he hated how carefree Haerdnor got to be. Theodmon had never gotten that luxury—oh. *I'm treating him how I treat Aloysius.*

Theodmon exhaled, balling his hands into fists. "You're right," he said, the words sharp as glass. "Let's work together."

"I've no issue with you," Haerdnor said. "I wish you didn't have a giant stick up your ass, but I respect you as a leader, military strategist, and I might even like you as a relative–you make my sister happy. You don't hurt her." He shrugged. "I wish I knew you could say the same for me."

Theodmon grimaced, turning his face away from Haerdnor.

"I need to talk to you about something." Theodmon moved Haerdnor towards a post leaning against a tent. Theodmon, his eyes alert, scanned for any bypassers. There was none, everyone seemed to be rushing towards the arrival of food.

"What?" Haerdnor lowered his voice to match Theodmon's.

Theodmon relayed the plan he had made with Henri and Elisa and the specifics of attacking the northern wall. He told Haerdnor of Elisa and how she was needed, and how they had Charlotte–she wasn't in this plan but the fact there was an illusionist in Theodmon's payroll made him feel as if his entire siege wasn't falling apart. As if he wasn't a fraud and a failure.

Because Theodmon also had to tell Haerdnor that this attack would fail.

"Why are we attacking the northern wall then?" Haerdnor questioned. "This is supposed to be a siege, not a suicide mission."

"To get our counterintelligence assets secured," Theodmon said. If a sailor knew this was suicide then the plan was worse than any of them anticipated. "Look, I know it's an insane strategy–"

"I expected better," Haerdnor interrupted. "You're well known for being a brilliant strategist. Where is that strategy?"

"War is messy," Theodmon said, his voice raising. "We're just leaning into that."

"By sending men to die," Haerdnor said. "They just arrived, I don't want to send them to their deaths. Part of a siege is waiting. Why can't we do that?"

"We need to destabilize the city from within."

"You can win a siege without clever tactics," Haerdnor said. "Sometimes the most obvious solution is the best one."

It's not only about the siege. It's about the years of colonization that would need to happen. Theodmon's jaw locked as he looked at Haerdnor, meeting his unblinking brown eyes. "Riam culture needs to be in disarray for us to change it after the fact."

"Then we can–"

"Do you know what they do to fire mages?" Theodmon interrupted, knowing that perhaps this would help Haerdnor see what he was trying to do. Mages always seemed fiercely protective of their own and Raulets had their own special flavor of tribalism. "You can't burn. So they have you mauled by lions instead. It's a game—they watch them die for fun. They bet on which arm would be mauled off first—"

"And I hate them for it," Haerdnor growled, his eyes turning red. Theodmon noticed the flames flickering up and down Haerdnor's lower arms and took a step forward. They were in a cloth tent, surrounded by other cloth tents. In hindsight, perhaps provoking a fire mage was a stupid idea.

None of his ideas were going well in this siege.

"Trust me," Theodmon said softly, not knowing how he could ask that from anybody when he didn't even trust himself anymore. "Please, I need your help."

The flames died out from Haerdnor's body, leaving his clothes singed but his skin unharmed. His eyebrows bunched together, Haerdnor turned towards Theodmon. "You told me once I should act like an heir. My father told me the same thing. And none of you trust me to do it."

Theodmon crossed his arms. That was a rash oversimplification from Haerdnor; there were more reasons that they viewed him as a struggling heir. Theodmon wanted to tell Haerdnor that he was jumping to conclusions, but he couldn't truly explain how he was. "That's not-"

"Don't," Haerdnor interrupted. "You'll only embarrass yourself. You're an awful liar."

Theodmon was taken aback. "What?"

"I am too," Haerdnor said. "We're too easy to read. You're smart, Theodmon, smarter than most. But you're an open book when it comes to politics and emotions—it's why you have Amaria handle those matters for you. It's why I'm a disappointment to my father. And it's why we both prefer either a battleground or a naval battle rather than being in court."

This little shit is more insightful than he let on. Theodmon looked at Haerdnor, actively trying to hide his expressions from his face. Theodmon hated court-he was good at navigating it-it was essentially a strategy game: war games and chess weren't so different from each other. However, he didn't find joy in the mind games and the alliances that were essential for navigating court that Amaria did. Amaria could lie as easily as she breathed-he had seen it in not only Court but in the dungeons of Mortensia Labyrinths.

That sort of thing exhausted him. Being at war—as much as Theodmon hated to admit it, it energized him. He could plan strategies and it was almost purely intellectual. There were limited emotions involved with clever tactics needed in killing your enemy before they killed you. His main worry was about how his enemy thought, not about how his enemy felt.

"Let's say you're right," Theodmon said.

"I am," Haerdnor said.

"Regardless," Theodmon said, thankful that Haerdnor said something, as now he could move forward without acknowledging the truth of what Haerdnor said—at least he knew how to better evade the conversation now. "I need your help. You care about your men; I care about mine too. And this isn't clever just to be clever, it'll save more lives in the long-run."

For a long while, Haerdnor looked at Theodmon, his eyes narrowing. Haerdnor's chest heaved, and he turned his back away from Theodmon, facing the wall. Theodmon's heart began to pound. He couldn't do anything if Haerdnor refused—he was here as an emissary for Aaron Raulet. Theodmon and Haerdnor were of equal rank, and one leader of a province could not command another leader.

If Haerdnor refused, Theodmon had no recourse. His clever plan would crumble and he would either lose the siege or risk losing the colony in a few years. If Riam culture wasn't in disrepair and also beginning to be distrusted by the Riam people, Thestitiunia could never fully integrate them.

"Convince me," Haerdnor said, still facing the exit of the tent. Theodmon blinked, a jolt of electricity running through him.

"What?" He croaked, barely daring to believe the chance he had.

"Convince me that this isn't a suicide mission," Haerdnor said. "If you do that, then I'm in. I'll listen to you. I'm more of a seafarer warrior—you're better at ground attacks. But, I can't lead my men to slaughter. And I had hoped that I was correct in viewing you as a man with similar morals."

I tried to be. Theodmon didn't always believe his facade of honor. What was the point? Everything you loved would eventually be taken away. In his darkest moments, he screamed these things in his head. But he didn't want to be as cruel as the world wanted him to be. Honor was his way of reclaiming what was lost of himself when everyone he ever loved seemed to die.

Theodmon nodded in agreement, pushing back the thoughts of perhaps he was wrong about Haerdnor and that they were more similar than he ever admitted. *Not now. Compartmentalize.*

Theodmon told Haerdnor the plan once again, except this time he went more into depth of what was expected of Elisa and what Elisa had already done for them. As he explained her double agent status with Rockwood, Haerdnor cursed. Theodmon wondered if he had also judged Elisa too harshly.

Not now. He reminded himself. *You can't afford it.*

Theodmon's currency wasn't money--it was time, mental fortitude, and alliances. He thought others put too much stock in money. But now, as he realized what he could and could not afford with his own currency, he understood why.

"And with this, we will have Elisa in place to further spread rumors of Charlotte's illusions," Theodmon finished explaining his plans. "It's a catalyst to end this siege early and to break the Riams so much they may welcome Thestitiunian changes."

Haerdnor leaned forward, his elbows resting on his knees. "I agree," he said slowly. "With conditions."

Theodmon's fingers drummed against his leg. "Which are?"

"Charlotte uses her magic to make it seem as if we breached the city. If I'm sending men to die, I think we should at least ensure the Riams are demoralized."

Theodmon gave a shaky laugh, his hands going still. "That's all?"

Haerdnor shrugged. "You've done more sieges than I have. And my men won't be unnecessarily dying with this. I'm convinced."

"Thank you," Theodmon breathed.

"Give my men two days to rest," Haerdnor nodded towards Theodmon, turning to head back to the Perivinans, likely to help set up their part of camp. "Then we'll attack."

Chapter Fifty

It took four days to finalize the plan. Still, the Thestitiunians were on top of the hill before the sun even rose, waiting for the horn to blow. Theodmon sat atop Phantagero, the horse's black tail swishing as Theodmon lightly pulled on the reins, surveying the city and fields below.

This attack was going to be a colossal disaster. And although it would save lives in the long-run, Theodmon was dreading the end of it. He would despise seeing all of the dead and dying, knowing that it was his decisions that put them there.

Beside him, Henri, Lucas, Aloysius, Brigitte, Haerdnor, Sam, Michel, and Charlotte were beside him, Charlotte being the only one not on a horse.

"Are you ready for this?" Henri, who was the closest to Charlotte, asked.

She gave a curt nod, wringing her hands together. Theodmon understood the feeling. He was trained and forged in war and he couldn't even fully say he was ready for every attack. He felt nauseous, nervous, perhaps even scared until the horn blew and he began fighting. Then, swinging a sword and cutting through people felt as easy as breathing.

"And you know when to make it look like we breached?" Henri said as he discussed the plan with Charlotte. "We need you to cause a panic."

"Not too early, not too late." Charlotte's voice quivered.

"You've got this," Henri told her. "And I'll be helping on the ground, jumbling their thoughts together."

"This is good practice for the real thing," Aloysius told Charlotte with a bright smile. "You'll do great."

"And if I don't?" Charlotte whispered.

"Then we can figure out what went wrong," Theodmon said. "And we can fix what happened. Aloysius said it best–this is practice." He looked directly at her. "We all trust you and your abilities. That's why you're here. You'll be fine, whatever happens. Alright?"

Charlotte gave a hard swallow as she nodded. "Alright," she whispered. She looked over at the city, her former home, and then started climbing the stairs of the nearby siege tower. This tower wouldn't be joining the fray--its sole purpose was to give Charlotte a safe vantage point to see the city without being near the archers. They wanted her away from people in case her magic went haywire. Henri said it was a minimal risk, that despite having minimal formal training, Charlotte was a remarkably well-controlled and powerful mage. Still, having illusions fuck with your mind was the last thing that needed to happen to anyone firing a weapon, so they made arrangements to minimize the risk.

"It's insane that we are fighting," Lucas said.

"We have to act like we aren't knowingly sending our men into a suicide mission." Theodmon's shoulders slumped. "Good leaders always fight with their men."

I always fight with my men. Theodmon's hand tightly gripped the hilt of his sword. *How would it seem for me to stop now?*

"Mine and Charlotte's magic will help minimize the losses," Henri said. "This is an unfortunate necessity for this war."

"We can mourn later, not before," Brigitte agreed. "We need to focus."

Beside them, Haerdnor lit his sword on fire. Not a moment later, the horn blew and the infantry ran to the northern wall as arrows and catapults flew towards Wéorren. As the projectiles from the catapults hit the walls with a thud, arrows rained down from the city, striking the Thestitiunian soldiers.

Theodmon flinched watching man after man fall. It seemed to go on for days, although Theodmon knew it likely was only around an hour. It was a slaughter. He looked over at Henri and Lucas, giving them a short nod before turning his head slightly to look at Charlotte above them in the tower.

"Charlotte," he called out. "Around ten minutes after we join, do your part!"

Without waiting for response, Theodmon spurred his horse forward, his sword in hand. Lucas, Aloysius, Henri, Haerdnor, and Brigitte followed him into the chaos below, the stench of sweat and blood overpowering everything except for the primal urge to survive.

"Get off your horses!" Aloysius screamed, his body glowing a rust red as his war magic kicked in. "Enemy arrows can't hurt me. You lot aren't so lucky."

Theodmon gritted his teeth. The Riams hadn't left the city, nor would they. Horses were a liability. Grudgingly, he swung off Phantagero, hitting the horse on his back to make him run back up the hill. Hopefully the stallion would survive, Theodmon rather liked him.

"Come on Charlotte," he grunted under his breath. "Breach the city."

Men fell around him as arrows struck, their flights disappearing in the light of the rising sun until they struck their target. Theodmon raised his shield, cowering behind it as a volley came overhead, almost every man around him falling to the ground.

Around him, catapults launched their deadly payloads, hurling massive stones toward the walls with thunderous force. Theodmon wished this was the southern wall–then this attack might actually amount to something. It just seemed as if they were losing man after man. He hoped securing Elisa as an asset was worth it.

"Come on, Charlotte," Theodmon repeated, as if it were a mantra. If Charlotte and Henri could cause the Riams to lose morale, then perhaps he could swallow the losses today easier.

As if Charlotte could read his thoughts, as if on cue, screams came from the walls.

"The wall is breached!" Theodmon could have sworn he heard that, although that could have been wishful thinking as words were hard to decipher in the middle of battle.

"Protect me," Henri ran up to Theodmon, glowing blue. "Charlotte's illusion is wor—"

An arrow flew past Theodmon, striking Henri behind him. Immediately, the blue glow died, and Henri fell to the ground, clutching his chest. He coughed, and blood came out of his mouth.

"Move," Aloysius's horse galloped from behind them as he pushed Theodmon out of the way and onto the ground, dismounting and standing in front of him and Henri. Aloysius's rust aura seemed to be smoking. As a series of arrows volleyed towards them, Aloysius protected them with his body, the arrows bouncing off of him.

Theodmon could smell his flesh burning. He glanced over at Henri on the ground, an arrow protruding from his chest, but still, Henri was alive. Coughing up blood and growing paler by the moment, but alive. Perhaps a healer could save him. But if Henri stayed here a second longer, nothing could ever be done.

I'm not losing anybody else. Fuck Sadthos and his kingdom. Not today.

"Go!" Theodmon commanded Aloysius, running to Henri. "Get on your horse and get Henri out of here!"

"You're going to survive," He hissed to Henri, helping hoist him up, ignoring Henri's screams of pain. "A healer is going to help you."

Aloysius came, holding his horse's reins as he and Theodmon both helped Henri onto the horse. A part of the arrow shaft snapped as they did it, and Henri gave a ghoulish scream.

"Save him," Theodmon felt tears falling from his eyes as Aloysius mounted his horse. "And take care of yourself too."

Aloysius nodded. "You should call the retreat."

Theodmon gave him a curt nod. "Call it when you return. Have them sound the horn."

Aloysius nodded, kicking his horse and galloping away. As he did so, Theodmon started screaming for his men to retreat. The cry caught on. By the time the horn blew, have the men had already fled back towards the hill.

Theodmon prayed to the gods that ensuring Elisa was a trusted asset in Wéorren was worth it. Because if this counterintelligence never came to fruition and Henri died, Theodmon would hang the Riam noblewoman himself.

Chapter Fifty-One

B *lood.* Theodmon's hands shook as he pushed open the flap to the field medicine tent. That was all he could smell as he walked in. He walked past the rows of men, many with amputated limbs or covered in gauze that filled with blood within a few minutes. *This is where people come to die. They won't survive. The healers are too overworked, their magic and energy are draining quickly.*

Nobody stood or bowed as he passed. He was irrelevant here. There was more important work, here staving off Sadthos, if only for just one day more. Theodmon couldn't bear to look at them—not when he was the reason they were dying. Not when Henri was facing Sadthos's cold, dark kingdom.

Theodmon reached Henri's cot, a healer moving her magic over him. "How is he?"

"He's receptive to our healing magic." The healer's voice was almost monotone. "We'll easily be able to repair the clavicle and ribs."

"Organ damage? Internal bleeding?" Theodmon questioned, barking out the words.

"Yes," the healer said. "In the lungs. He'll live, though. Please move, General—you're an impediment to my work."

Theodmon stepped to the side and the healer bustled around him, moving his hand under Henri's back, placing his other hand over Henri's chest. Theodmon tensely watched as the healer maintained the soft green glow surrounding himself and Henri, wondering what was happening.

It was miraculous that healers could exist, and perhaps Theodmon feared them. His skillset took life away, but healers could snatch death away from the gods or, Theodmon suspected, give Sadthos more subjects than any soldier ever could and never be suspected of such an act.

Henri coughed, a horrible gasping and retching noise. He coughed again, this time spitting up blood. Immediately, Theodmon moved closer to cot, kneeling next to his friend, staring at the healer on the other side. The healer had no reaction, blandly and monotonously pulling the blood from Henri's mouth in a continuous stream.

"What are you doing?" Theodmon asked.

"Removing the blood from his lungs," the healer said, turning to Henri as he brought his hands down, and the blood splashed onto a mat. "Your lungs will have scars, and you may have issues breathing for the rest of your life. I've set your bones, you'll be ready to leave here and report either back home or back to war."

"I'm not going home," Henri said.

"Most soldiers would jump at the chance," the healer muttered, walking away.

Henri glared at the healers back as he left. "Impetuous shit."

"He saved your life," Theodmon said.

"Which is probably the only reason you've not called him out on being an impetuous shit." Henri attempted to sit up with a loud grunt.

"And I need him to save others." Theodmon gently grabbed Henri's arm. "Lay back down."

"I'm not staying here."

"You have to heal."

"I'm meeting Elisa tonight," Henri argued. "You know there's spies in our camp. Her cover will risk being blown if I'm not there. We still need her."

"Are you really having sex tonight?" Theodmon stared at Henri whose entire body was shaking from the labor of attempting to sit up and fail. He knew that Henri wasn't doing anything with Elisa, or so Henri insisted. Still, to others watching, Henri having a whore in his tent in this state would raise eyebrows.

"Of course not." Henri beckoned Theodmon closer to him. "I've never even touched her in that way. And she can comfort me in other ways if I need to spin that cover. Don't worry about it." He seemed almost insistent, desperate to have Elisa be with him tonight.

Theodmon's eyebrows rose. There weren't many who would refuse a woman coming into their bed in wartime–even one as arguably plain as Elisa. She truly was no beauty, but she was desperate and so Theodmon saw the appeal she had to other men—a quick fuck that would do anything and could be discarded. She didn't need anything else.

"Don't." Henri's voice laced with anger. "She's not."

Theodmon blinked, taken aback. "You...you don't actually like her?"

"And if I do?" Henri shot back. "So what?"

I don't want to see Henri get hurt. Theodmon's heart thumped. *Whores had their place, they could be fun to single men, but loving one was almost insane. They don't care about anything other than money. It's transactional. And Elisa's more transactional than most.*

"I can read minds," Henri said. "And her intentions aren't as black and white as you pretend."

"It feels perverse."

"Imagine Amaria wasn't a Raulet," Henri said. "Or even if she was, imagine that Aaron wouldn't help her, house her, anything after marriage. And now imagine your house lost all its wealth and you died. There's no estate–it was sold to pay debt. Imagine Thestitiunia had Riam laws on women owning property and now she's destitute. What do you think your wife would do to survive in that situation?"

"She has magic." Theodmon looked away from Henri, understanding the point he was making, but still not wanting to hear it.

"And imagine she didn't. Imagine if she was just some noblewoman. You call mine plain, and I supposed she is by most people's standards. If a woman as plain as her is as great a whore as everyone says, imagine what a woman with Amaria's look would be in her situation."

Theodmon's hand crashed down upon the ground. "Stop." He commanded. "She is the wife of your liege lord and you'll respect her as such."

"I respect Amaria," Henri said. "And I respect you." He forced himself up into a sitting position. "And we both know that Amaria will never be in her situation. But if she was, could we blame her?"

Theodmon tried to block out the images of Amaria lying with other men. But it came through, the men faceless. He tried to deny it, but Amaria was practical, hell bent on thriving. If she were in a situation like Elisa was, Theodmon knew Amaria would do whatever she needed to do.

It made him uncomfortable, angry, but not at her. In this situation it would be Theodmon's fault for losing everything and also Aaron and Haerdnor's for not supporting their relative. In this situation, Theodmon knew his ghost would be restless, seeking revenge.

But it wouldn't be against his wife. As the realization hit, Theodmon felt as if he had been struck by lighting. Elisa was a victim.

"No," Theodmon said. "I suppose I've been a bit harsh."

"I like her. There's just something about her. I'm being cautious, I know my job," Henri said, almost breathlessly. "But can you fault me for liking her? She's not perfect, she isn't well liked by everyone, but neither am I. Neither are you. Neither is Amaria. If being perfect was a requirement for love, nobody on this planet would be deserving."

Theodmon exhaled, placing his head in his hands. He despised when Henri was more logical than he was. "I've been an ass, haven't I?"

"You're always an ass," Henri said. "But I'm one too and we're growing from it. Now, can you help me get to my tent?"

"And I'm going to tell the healers?" Theodmon placed his hand on Henri's back and arm, slowly supporting him as he shakily stood up.

"You outrank them," Henri said nonchalantly. "And it's how you can make up for being an absolute jackass to the women I might like. Your thoughts are vile."

Theodmon cast him a dark look. "You're going to use that as a sword and shield?"

"Until I can't anymore," Henri took a small step forward. "You might have to bribe a healer to administer medicine to me in my tent. I'm not coming back here."

Theodmon wished that Katerina was here–he could trust her with that. He sighed, looking around the room. "Which one?" He asked Henri. "Who is the most trustworthy?"

Henri closed his eyes, swaying dangerously, blue fog coming from his arms.

"Don't use magic–"

"That one," Henri nodded towards a mousy looking woman.

Henri stumbled, and Theodmon tightened his grip around him, preventing Henri from falling face first onto the ground.

"Don't use magic," Theodmon told him. "I'll order her to let us go, just as I'm ordering you to rest."

"I appreciate that," Henri said with a chuckle that turned into a wheezing cough.

"Shut up," Theodmon muttered. "You'll choke before I get you to your tent."

Chapter Fifty-Two

The Thestitiunians spent another ten months camping outside Wéorren City. Food dwindled, even with the ice boxes. Haerdnor had already written home for supply reinforcements. They had been away for a year and a half now, and the fatigue of holding a siege was setting in.

The camp was dead except for those on post, or those preparing to pass out the morning rations. Theodmon walked through the camp silently, noting the somberness that had fallen over it as compared to the first night when the tents were pitched. The toll of war hadn't set in then, but now everyone knew it too well.

Theodmon wondered how the city was holding beyond the walls. Perhaps it was time to attack–Henri would get the information from Elisa whenever she appeared again. Apparently, Elisa had gotten accidentally pregnant and it was suspected to be a boy. Ever since then, they'd seen her less and less. It seemed as if Rockwood was less eager to risk someone who was pregnant with a son–perhaps she had even delivered, the timing seemed close. Rockwood probably was filling her up with more bastards as they spoke, favoring them over his trueborn daughters. Theodmon scowled; the man was despicable for many things, but despising his children for something so petty might have been his worst crime.

Theodmon missed Lysander and Sylviana. He wanted this endless war to be won so he could see them again. He had been gone for so long. would they recognize him? He paced through the camp, the sun rising above him, looking as if he was a collected commander inspecting the troops. In truth, he was doing anything to remain active, as to banish his fears from accumulating in his mind.

Theodmon's gaze set over the hill, looking at the dug mounds. The mass graves. They would haunt him until he joined those souls in Sadthos's kingdom. And maybe, he would still be haunted even in his death.

A wave of fatigue washed over Theodmon as the sun rose. Nothing was prepared for the day, and nothing would be prepared for a while. Perhaps Theodmon should sleep. Shrugging off the thoughts that he was being lazy, and that laziness was the sign of an ineffective and foolish leader, Theodmon trudged back to his tent.

As he neared his tent, he saw a woman slip out of Henri's, rushing towards Wéorren before the camp would know she was there. It seemed as if Elisa had been able to make a visit. Theodmon did not move towards her, letting her flee. It was not useful for either of them to interact.

Theodmon should really show Henri more appreciation. If not for him, this whole thing might have been a disaster a million times over. However, he did need to talk to Henri, see what information Elisa might have brought them. Sighing, he trudged towards Henri's tent, nodding to the sentry's who thankfully let him in without a word.

"Elisa visited." Theodmon announced himself as he brushed past the flaps to the entrance of Henri's tent.

"Sit down," Henri said tiredly, half undressed on the bed. He yawned, pulling the blankets over himself. It was chilly, even in the tents. The Riam autumn wasn't as unforgiving as the Westanni version, but it still wasn't comfortable.

Theodmon was cold, too, now that he thought about it. He sighed, sitting down at the chair, watching Henri from across the small tent.

"Rindria is ready to fall." Henri threw a spare blanket at Theodmon. "There's fighting within the classes in the city. Food is worth more than diamonds, prostitution is at an all time high, and infants, the elderly, and the sick are being abandoned in the streets."

And the south wall is weak. Theodmon frowned, looking around Henri's tent. He seemed attached to Elisa, so if the city was ready to fall, why did he send her back? Theodmon couldn't imagine sending Amaria into danger like that.

"Why did Elisa leave? What assignment does she have?" Theodmon asked.

Henri sighed. "Remember Rockwood's gambling issue?"

Theodmon racked his brain, trying to remember what Henri was speaking about. It seemed vaguely familiar but everything had been so mind numbing during this siege that his memories seemed to blur together.

"No," he admitted.

"Elisa has been giving him her Thestitiunian coins from sleeping with me," Henri said. "And he has a gambling issue, but he doesn't want to be a traitor, so only Riam coins can be used."

"And?" Theodmon was unsure of where Henri was going with this.

"We did discuss this a year ago," Henri chuckled. "I suppose you've had other issues you've focused on."

"It's why you are in charge of intelligence here," Theodmon said.

"According to Elisa, Rockwood has no more Riam coins," Henri said. "But he has a store of Thestitiunian coins. I gave her a few fruits to place with the coins, and Charlotte will be able to change people's perceptions of this to make it look as if he's hoarding food."

"He'll be a traitor," Theodmon noted.

"And he'll be sure to be discovered as his wife has written a letter before she commits suicide."

"Elisa?" Amaria had told him of her blatant refusal to commit torture in the Drowning Tombs, and based off that information alone, murdering an innocent women didn't seem to be something Elisa would be willing to engage in.

"I've given her a poison to slip in Lady Rockwood's food," Henri said. "It's painless, tasteless, and impossible to trace. Lucas was helpful in suggesting and drafting it for me."

Lucas had studied medicine and poisons at the Westanni Regional University for a few years. He'd always enjoyed learning, whether he had been expected to continue his education or not. Especially if the skill in question was particularly unnerving.

"Thank the gods for Lucas," Theodmon said. *And thank the gods he's not my enemy.*

"As Lady Rockwood's dead body and Lord Rockwood's treason is discovered, we'll be breaching the city walls," Henri continued. "Charlotte will stage riots, the townspeople will learn that Rockwood committed treason early, hearing the screams of random bystanders announcing it."

"It will be chaos once the wall falls," Theodmon noted.

"And we offer amnesty to calm the chaos. No looting. No rapes. No killing," Henri said.

"Of course not," Theodmon said sharply. "Once that wall falls they are Thestitiunian citizens. If any of our men commit a crime they will be tried not as a conqueror committing an atrocity but as a citizen harming a fellow citizen in the worst way possible."

"It'll still happen—"

"And I'll ensure they are all publicly punished." Theodmon wasn't stupid—he knew war crimes would still occur, but he would hang every man who committed them. This wasn't an enemy nation—Rindria was soon to be a colony, and within twenty years it would be a full blown Thestitiunian province. Harming fellow citizens was the last thing they needed to do to a conquered people.

"Next time she comes she's not going back," Henri said, his voice cracking. "The next time she comes we attack the next day."

"I wouldn't expect anything else," Theodmon said.

"And she's staying at camp and I'm protecting her," Henri said. "If she can somehow smuggle her child away from the city, I'm protecting him too."

Theodmon looked at Henri sadly. He loved this woman, and she would be hated and hunted—by both sides. He sighed. Henri would be overwhelmed in battle anyways, it was the greatest weakness his magic seemed to have. And Henri had already done so much.

"Alright," Theodmon agreed. "Keep her safe."

"Thank you," Henri told him.

Theodmon shook his head, waving away the thanks.

"I have one more thing to ask." Theodmon slumped in the uncomfortable wooden chair. "Rindria will need a governor, I know you are in line for your father's title—"

"I'll be the governor," Henri interrupted. "I'll revoke my claims to my father's title—my younger brother will be thrilled."

"You'll be a Duke in twenty years," Theodmon said.

"Who will I marry?" Henri sighed. "I'm assuming I'll need to marry a Riam girl immediately."

Theodmon sighed, leaning forward to rest his arms on his knees. Marriage was always a requirement for nobles. Yet, Theodmon felt awkward asking this of Henri. Henri was technically a Westanni subject—but if he accepted, Henri would no longer be Westanni, not in anything but blood. Henri would be Riam, and Theodmon would have no right to command him.

Even now, he was a noble from another house. Westanni or not, marriage was an intimate family discussion, not to be interfered with by outsiders. Even liege lords.

"My father will be thrilled," Henri said with a snort. "And I get it. I don't mind."

"That's creepy," Theodmon said. *I hate when he reads my mind. I know he can't help it but gods....*

"Sorry," Henri said with a sheepish shrug. "It's harder to manage when I'm exhausted. I do usually try to block you out."

"I know," Theodmon said. "We were discussing your inevitable marriage." He shook his head, trying to remember if he spoke last or if Henri did.

"Who am I marrying?" Henri prompted. "Do you know yet?"

Theodmon didn't know; he didn't know that Riam nobles were still alive. "Watch for a year," Theodmon said. "Then give me candidates."

"Elisa," Henri said immediately. "Let me marry Elisa."

Theodmon had hoped for a Riam noblewoman without an untarnished reputation. Theodmon groaned, his head pulling back as his chest pushed forward. "Are you sure that's wise?"

"Her reputation is already going to be tied to me. Everyone already thinks she's my mistress."

"You'll actually have to sleep with her if she's your wife. She'll have to bear child*ren*," Theodmon said, emphasizing the multiple. "She doesn't seem happy to be a mother."

"Let me try to convince her," Henri pleaded. "If she doesn't agree within a year, I'll pick another."

Theodmon sighed. He could give Henri recommendations, but he couldn't force a match. Hopefully Elisa would refuse, she was stubborn and difficult—qualities that Theodmon appreciated for the first time.

"Alright," he said. "You have a year from the date Wéorren falls. If Elisa doesn't agree, marry a Riam lord's virgin daughter."

"You had to specify that didn't you?" Henri said sourly. "But deal."

Theodmon gave a hard swallow, hoping he wasn't making a horrible decision. However, this matter couldn't concern him now—for this issue to become a reality, they first had to conquer Rindria.

And now Theodmon had to finalize the preparations for it. Wéorren would fall and he would be going home. He would see Amaria again. He would see Lysander and Sylviana again. He would see Celestine again.

He had missed his family. And he had missed the smoky mountains and vibrant forests of the Westerlands. Soon he would be returning. He would be with those he loved.

And Henri would stay behind, with only Elisa for comfort.

Theodmon stood up. "I'll see you later."

"I'll let you know when Elisa returns." Henri yawned, laying back down, pulling his blankets over him. "And give me my blanket back."

Chapter Fifty-Three

Theodmon gnawed at the tip of his quill, impatiently waiting for the day the war would end. Soon they'd be breaching Wéorren City, and he didn't know if he would survive. He wasn't Dandar—Theodmon couldn't see into the future or control its outcome.

His quill scratched against the parchment, writing what may be his last letter to his wife. If he survived this, he would send a detailed second letter. Theodmon chuckled as he wrote, imagining Amaria receiving his letters within a fortnight of each other.

My Love,

This siege will have ended by the time you receive this and I will either be returning home to you or waiting for you in Sadthos's kingdom. I have missed you during this—but I am forgetting the sound of your voice, and sometimes it's hard to envision your face. It hurts to think I'm forgetting the small details.

I never want to be parted from you again. War is hell—we both know this. We've both experienced our own share of Vathar's unique horrors and I wish we hadn't. I want to experience everything with you—swim in the ocean, climb the mountains, skate on a frozen lake, dance at a million balls—Amaria, I have missed you.

I could write it a million times and still not get my point across. I have missed you that much. And I have missed our children. I hate that I haven't been able to see them grow.

I hope to come back, but in case I don't I have to tell you these things. Amaria, you're the best thing that ever happened to me. I would be lost without you. You will be a wonderful regent for Lysander until he comes of age—do not let him rule until he is twenty. Give him the childhood I never had.

Lysander, I am sorry I failed you. But you are so loved, and I am so proud of you. Sylviana, I wish I could see you. I believe you'll be a powerful mage one day. I don't know why you haven't shown signs of magic yet, but I feel it in my soul.

I love all of you.

Theodmon

Sighing, Theodmon set down his quill, burying his face in his hands as he began to weep. He was breaking from the siege. He wanted to be home, back in Amaria's arms. He was exhausted and likely needed to sleep in his bed for a week straight, but if she could stay up all night, he wanted to be with her, talking, playing cards, sex, anything when he got home. They missed out on so much of their lives being apart because of this conquest. Sleep would only be a distraction from being with his wife.

"Amaria," he muttered, saying her name as if it were an invocation and the sound of it could protect him from harm.

Suddenly, a scream came from outside his tent, causing his eyes to open, the hairs on the back of his neck standing up on end. "Marquis Chauvignon!" a familiar female voice screamed. Theodmon stood up, running outside his tent to see his sentry's holding Elisa, pushing her down towards the dirt.

"Stop!" Theodmon commanded.

The sentry pulled Elisa upright, but still kept a firm grip on her.

"What are you doing here?" he demanded.

"Lord Delaluna told me I should go straight to you. He said the sooner you can work my intel into your plans, the better."

Theodmon paused. Henri was handling intelligence and he seemed eager to shield Elisa away from him.

"May I speak with you?" Elisa sounded breathless, her eyes widening. "It's important. Please."

Theodmon's initial response was to tell her to wait until she saw Henri. But he had never seen her look so desperate. Her protective wall was gone, and for some reason she was asking for his help.

He nodded to the sentry, turning to go back into his tent. "Release her."

She ran towards a second sentry, grabbing an infant from him. Theodmon hadn't even noticed the baby before, he had been so focused on Elisa.

"Lady Redwayne," Theodmon motioned for her to follow him into the tent.

"Thank you, my Lord." Elisa gave a curtsy.

Theodmon's eyes narrowed. *She wants something.* Elisa wasn't the groveling type.

"Spare me," he said. "What do you want?"

"Take my son as a ward," Elisa said.

Theodmon glanced down at the bundle, then frowned. "He's probably better off with his mother–"

"I'll not stay with him. I'll abandon him on the streets," Elisa said. "I don't want him to die, but I cannot be in his life. Please. I'm not asking for much. A ward won't be a drain on your resources."

Theodmon looked at the squirming infant in her arms. Elisa was clearly uncomfortable in holding him, and she seemed to almost be holding the baby away from her, instead of pulling him closer to her as Theodmon had seen Amaria do with their children.

This child wasn't better off with Elisa, with a mother who despised him. And Elisa's words cut him deep–he would never notice any change in his household with a ward. And he couldn't protest against a baby–it was a baby. An infant. Innocent.

"Why?" Theodmon questioned.

"I don't want much," Elisa said. "And think about this position you'll be in, your new governor will be in with this baby."

Theodmon massaged his temples. "What do you mean?"

"Did your wife not tell you the terms of my services? The price I am owed at the end of this?"

Amaria had. Theodmon had just not considered it during the siege. He closed his eyes, trying to remember what Amaria had told him. He could barely remember her face, and he felt his throat constrict, a well of emotion threatening to explode.

"You received Thestitiunian citizenship."

"Same as any Riam, yes," Elisa affirmed.

"You gain land, money, and a husband, correct?" Theodmon asked. He remembered Amaria telling him that; there had to be more specifics, but he couldn't remember. Perhaps Amaria would deal with Elisa's reward once they returned. "What does this have to do with the governor of Rindria?"

"I marry the governor of Rindria," Elisa said, "With the title of Lady Governor until Rindria moves from a colony to a duchy."

Theodmon's jaw dropped. Amaria had promised that? "The governor?"

"Ask your wife." Elisa blinked back tears. "I promised I'd bear him sons–I know that I'm... *used*... and I wanted to give my new husband some consolation so that my only children were his at least." Elisa was crying, all her vulnerabilities bare. "I want what I'm due. I gave up my autonomy, had a baby for that man," she spat this out like it was a curse. "I did it for you. I can't kill an innocent baby, but I want nothing to do with him."

Theodmon gave a short laugh. The gods had a twisted sense of fate. "Fine," he said, reaching his arms out for the baby. "What's the boy's name?"

"Why are you laughing?" Elisa asked, her voice wavering.

"Your husband won't care," Theodmon told her.

"You don't know that—"

"Henri is the governor," Theodmon said. "And when I asked him to choose his wife, he asked for you specifically."

Elisa blinked rapidly, her chest heaving as she began to sob.

"Give me the boy," Theodmon said, hastily reaching for the child, fearing he would be harmed. "Do you need a moment?"

Elisa shook her head, handing the baby over.

"Tell me the baby's name," Theodmon said.

Elisa hugged herself. "Erik."

Theodmon looked down at the infant taking in the boy's blonde curls and bright green eyes. "Erik Rockwood or Erik Redwayne?"

"Erik Yearwood," Elisa muttered, her voice cracking. "If possible, I'd prefer that. But if you could, please, give him a Thestitiunian name. I want his life to be easier than mine. And please, never tell him who his father is."

"I won't," Theodmon promised her. "Do you want to help choose the Thestitiunian name?"

Elisa shook her head. "I trust that you'll not break your word. You're many things, Marquis Chauvignon, but you never striked me as an oathbreaker."

Theodmon swallowed hard, as he looked at the sweet face of his new ward, thinking of a name for him. He breathed, his finger brushing against the baby's smooth cheek. "I'll ensure he has every privilege and opportunity my children have," Theodmon promised to Elisa. However, she was already gone, her presence a whisper in the breeze.

Theodmon looked at the infant once more, smiling and bubbly as if he wasn't just abandoned. "Helioson." The baby smiled, as if he understood this was his name. "Helioson Erik Yearwood."

Theodmon and Henri walked through the camp together, the soldiers hurrying for the attack. The siege was ending, and everyone knew it.

"Henri, I need you to also protect Charlotte and Helioson during the breaching of the city," Theodmon whispered.

"You don't need to ask," Henri said. "I always planned to have Charlotte with me–she'll be exerting a lot of magical energy, I want to be able to funnel mine to her. And I'm not condemning a baby–and I am sure Elisa can tolerate being around him knowing it ends after the siege." Henri sighed. "Thank you for taking him from her."

"Has she told you yet?" Theodmon asked.

"What?" Henri questioned.

"That she is to be your wife," Theodmon said. "Amaria promised she'd be the Lady Governor and I forgot about it."

Henri's face broke into a wide smile. "She hadn't, but I heard her thoughts. I'm not bringing it up until she does."

"Is she...?" Theodmon cringed, hating that he was asking Henri for this intimate information–it would have to be painful if Elisa didn't want him. She'd been emotional, but that could mean so many things.

"She's happy, mostly," Henri said. "She just feels....almost embarrassed around me. She fears that she's not what I want in a wife."

"You asked specifically for her," Theodmon reminded him. "I told her that when she was worried about her husband caring about Helioson."

Henri shrugged. "Emotions are complicated. I'm sure she'll feel better in a year."

"A year?" Theodmon expected that Henri would marry Elisa sooner, especially considering she was promised to her.

"I want her to have a Thestitiunian wedding," Henri said. "As expensive and grand as a future duchess deserves. But it'd be in poor taste to do that so soon after a siege." He gave a short laugh. "Besides, I want her to process what has happened to her, and I want to get to know her as her fiancée."

"People will be cruel."

"I'm going to set the tone of how she will be treated as my wife," Henri said somberly. "Usually men are less protective over fiancées than they are of their wives; and I'll make these Riam fucks keep their mouth shut and use their manners around her." Henri's eyes darkened. "I've seen their worst fears, and I can make them all come true."

Chapter Fifty-Four

The next few days were a flurry of hectic preparation; swords were sharpened, shields were counted, new arrows were hastily forged, armor was shined, and the commanders had bolted themselves inside Theodmon's tent, moving the figures on the war board one last time.

And now, as the day finally arrived. The horizon was veiled in the eerie glow of dawn with long shadows being cast over the desolate landscape. Theodmon surveyed the scene from atop his griffin, his gaze piercing through the morning mist that clung to the ground like a shroud. Behind him, a multitude of banners fluttered in the wind: the red banners adorned with trees and a griffin from the Westerlands; the gold banners with a ship and hydrangea to showcase Perivina Fluere; the purple banners with green hydras and red dragons to represent Thestitiunia as a whole; the red banners stitched with golden griffins of the Chauvignons; the blue banners, a golden scale and red roses upon it to showcase the Raulets; and all the other houses that had nobles in attendance.

The catapult corps prepared their weapons, lighting nearby braziers on fire, and a supply of torches. Those with siege towers and ladders prepared to move them. The archers moved to the more permanent towers, preparing what seemed to be an endless supply of arrows. Soldiers, clad in shining armor, either stood at attention or upon their horses in silence, awaiting the signal that would spur them into war.

Theodmon sat tensely upon his griffin, Bluequill, his hands shaking over the animal's blue-grey feathers. Feeling nauseated, Theodmon's eyes frantically surveyed Wéorren's walls, taking in its battered southern gate. He looked over at Haerdnor, whose sword was already burning, a lump forming at his throat. "You're sure you and your fire mages can get us an entrance?"

"Eventually," Haerdnor said somberly. "There'll be losses, but it's more effective than a battering ram. It's wood, it'll burn."

Theodmon's jaw locked, trapping any words he might have said as he gave Haerdnor a nod in acknowledgment. He closed his eyes, tilting his head upwards towards the rising sun. *Let me survive this,* he prayed to Vathar, the god of war. *Let me get home alive, let me be victorious, and I'll give your temples a hundred pieces of gold a month.*

It seemed as if every war Theodmon was in he upped the amount of pieces. It started with ten with the wars over Perpives Pass when he was sixteen, and by the end of that war it was twenty five. He had upped it to forty during the skirmishes along the Morrian-Westanni border. Last time they were in Rindria, he had upped it to sixty, praying for Amaria's return. And now, he was giving Vathar a hundred. If he survived, the god would be very rich at Theodmon's expense.

He opened his eyes, scanning the horizon once more before he raised his hand, bringing it down hard, giving the sign for the horns to blow. And they did, a deep rich sound reverberating through the empty fields. The infantry and cavalry charged, thousands of feet and hooves sounding as if they formed a living avalanche.

Fiery masses hit the walls from the catapults, and those with the towers and ladders scaled the walls, meeting a torrent of arrows that sent their bodies tumbling to the ground. All the while, Haerdnor, and his fire mages—all on horses, galloped to the southern gate. They dismounted and set themselves ablaze, storming the gates, consuming the wood of the doors with the inferno. The Riams pelted them out, putting out the mages with death from above. The mages raised their shields, but it still wasn't enough. More of them fell, one by one.

They're not going to make it. Theodmon turned to Lucas. "Get battering rams ready."

"No need," Aloysius said. "They breached the gate."

Theodmon turned his head to look back at the southern gate, and sure enough, the gate was on fire, burning quicker than he'd thought possible, the fire mages retreating in a red glow.

Haerdnor did it. Theodmon breathed a sigh of relief. He looked over at the calvary that had stayed behind with him, raising Winterthorne to the sky. He bellowed for his men to follow, spurring Bluequill into action, flying down the hill and towards the burning walls of Wéorren.

The thunderous sound of hooves and the terrifying screech of griffins crying echoed across the battlefield as the cavalry charged into the heart of the siege, descending upon the walls of Wéorren City like a tempest unleashed.

At the walls, the first few Thestitiunians were successful in climbing the ladders and reaching the top of the battements of Wéorren, stabbing an archer in the stomach before they were riddled with arrows. The Riams poured out of the city and into the surrounding fields, meeting the Thestitiunians in open battle for a first time since this siege had started. It had been nearly a year, and now everyone knew without denial that this was the final stand. Rindria would fall, but her defenders weren't going to let it be an easy win for her invaders.

It was still too early to take the griffins over the walls--too many would die. With a shout, Theodmon landed his griffin on the ground, directing him to run, but not fly, into the battle. For hours, Theodmon fought and cut down Riams, focusing only on the movement of his sword and the armor the soldiers around him wore, as to avoid cutting down an ally.

He focused only on war, on killing those who crossed him until he saw Aloysius fighting in the distance, perhaps fifty feet away from him.

Aloysius's griffin, Lightcrest, was dead, laying on the battleground, his red feathers turned to rust with his own blood. Aloysius used his magic as an additional shield of protection as he fought. But he was fighting almost ten adversaries, and he was quickly faltering.

His heart pounding, Theodmon fought off a calvary member from the Riam side, stabbing him through the heart, determined to make his way to his brother. *I'm not losing a person to war.* Theodmon swung his sword, cutting the jugular of a nearby Riam soldier, blood pouring from his neck. *I'm not losing my brother to this gods' forsaken shithole country the way I lost my father.*

He dug his spurs into his griffin, directing it to fly and then dive at breakneck speeds towards Aloysius as Aloysius nearly missed blocking a blow that could've cut off his arm. Still, Aloysius hadn't blocked the blow fully. Even from where he was, Theodmon knew it struck the limited area the chainmail didn't fully cover. Theodmon knew that Aloysius was bleeding profusely.

And as he rode closer, Theodmon saw Aloysius's aura flickering. His brother's back was turned to a Riam soldier who was injured, but not dead. The Riam stumbled to his feet, entrails hanging from his stomach, but moved faster than what should have been possible towards Aloysius. The soldier raised his sword in the hand that wasn't holding his stomach as he advanced towards Aloysius.

Theodmon kicked his griffin harder. "No!" He galloped down the hill, screaming for Aloysius to turn, but his brother didn't hear him—not until the last second when turned, meeting Theodmon's eyes for the last time, as he was stabbed through the throat.

Theodmon gave a primal, inhuman scream, his griffin landing on the ground as Theodmon cut off Aloysius's killer's head with one fell swoop. Theodmon had seen Aloysius's death happen before it occurred, and he had tried to stop it. He had tried to stop it and he had failed.

His brother was dead.

He's not going to stay here. It was stupid and unjustifiably risky, but Theodmon didn't care. His father was buried in this country. Ophelia was buried in Morroek. Aloysius is going to be buried at home, in the crypts, where he belonged. Theodmon ran towards his brother's body, almost blind from tears.

He slashed through the Riam soldiers in front of him, not processing how many he killed, or that he was even killing at all. The ground around him was stained red as he reached Aloysius, quickly sheathing his sword. He pulled out a whistle that was on a string around his neck, whistling it, praying Bluequill heard it through the chaos.

He looked down at his brother, a sob racking his body. Perhaps Aloysius wasn't dead. He was injured. He couldn't move because he was injured. But as he looked at his brother and saw the deep gash in his neck, Theodmon knew he was delusional. Aloysius was gone, his soul undergoing judgment in Sadthos's silent kingdom. Unsuccessfully trying to blink back tears, Theodmon crouched down, lifting Aloysius body the best he could, his knees buckling under the weight. He trudged along, making his way to Bluequill, who was landing near Theodmon.

Theodmon threw Aloysius's body over the griffin's back. Swallowing the lump in his throat, Theodmon mounted Bluequill, Aloysius's body laying in front of him.

As he adjusted himself on Bluequill, he saw a group of Thestitiunians and Riams in a deadly battle. *No more of my men will die today.* Theodmon felt a well of rage overcome him, drawing his grief. He spurred Bluequill into a gallop, and then into flight, recklessly charging the group of men. He slashed through Riam men from above, Bluequill lowering himself enough to give Theodmon range, but not enough to stop flying. Inspired, the Thestitiunians gained a burst of energy, and they helped Theodmon kill their foes.

What was the point of this? Theodmon shook as he killed one of the last Riam men. *We all die in war and for what? Am I better off after any war? My brother is dead.* He swung his sword at the last Riam, who was charging at him. As Winterthorne made contact with the Riam's arm, Theodmon's sword shattered in his hand.

Theodmon sat there, looking at the hilt in his hand. Winterthorne was supposed to be unbreakable. *What?* He stupidly didn't move, looking at his destroyed sword, the fragments of steel scattered across the grass.

If not for his men killing the last Riam, he'd be dead.

"Retreat," the slayer of Theodmon's attacker advised. "Get a new sword and come back!"

His voice sounded fuzzy, so much that Theodmon couldn't understand him. But Theodmon looked at his broken sword, realized he was without a weapon, and his battle instincts and self-preservation kicked in.

He fled from the siege and back to camp, bringing Aloysius's body with him, barely processing those swarming around him once he had dismounted in the Thestitiunian camp. He left his brother with the healers; they would soon realize they were useless and give Aloysius's body to the priests of Sadthos to perform rites.

His brother was dead, but it was Theodmon who was drowning.

Chapter Fifty-Five

Theodmon felt as if he had been plunged into an icy abyss, one where the cold seeped into his bones and chilled him to the core. It was as if he had fallen through a thin sheet of ice when skating on the lake in winter and he was drowning. He couldn't come up for air, every breath hurt and was obstructed with an impenetrable wall of grief.

He's dead. He's dead.

His body shook as he pushed his way into his tent. Grief descended like a thick, unmovable fog. *He's dead.* Theodmon threw the hilt of his shattered sword at the ground.

"Useless!" He screamed, unsure if he was directing the words towards Winterthorne or himself.

He's gone. All we talked about...he's gone. He died here, in a war just like Father. And his death will mean nothing, just like Father's because the world keeps demanding more blood and nothing ever changes.

And then, like a tidal wave crashing over the shore, he felt as if he couldn't breath. It was a visceral, physical sensation, like a punch to the gut, one that would leave even the strongest of men doubling over in agony. Tears stung Theodmon's eyes, hot and bitter against his cheeks, as the reality of the loss washed over him in relentless waves.

Theodmon's heart clenched, his breath catching in his throat, time stopping for a moment. *Aloysius isn't coming back.*

Gulping for air between the sobs, Theodmon leaned against the post in the tent, leaning his back against it as he slid down to the floor. A dull ache spread through his chest, a heavy, crushing sensation that threatened to consume him whole.

Theodmon's mind raced, searching desperately for some semblance of understanding: *Why Aloysius? Could I have prevented this? Why did my sword shatter after his death? Should I continue on with this siege?*

The answers eluded him, slipping through his fingers like grains of sand. Theodmon needed to hold onto something, anything, to anchor himself in this storm, but there was nothing to grasp onto. He was adrift in a sea of grief, tossed about by currents beyond his control.

Aloysius is dead.

He could do something about it. He couldn't bring Aloysius back to life. But Theodmon could avenge him by destroying those that killed him. Theodmon screamed, doubling over on himself as he crouched on the ground. At that moment, he knew what he had to do. In that moment, it was as if the world had been reduced to a singular moment, to a singular point of pain.

He needed a sword.

His body still being racked by sobs, Theodmon forced himself to stand up. He could get a sword from Sam–there were tons to spare. They wouldn't be the same quality as Winterthorne–but even the best swords broke.

His unbreakable, undullable sword broke. The magic infused into the steel had broken when his convictions had swayed. In the moments of battle following Aloysius's death, Theodmon wavered long enough for his sword, the metal carried by generations of his ancestors, to shatter into a multitude of shards so small that it would be impossible to recover them.

He had wavered for only a moment. And the magic had failed because of that hesitation. It was the cruelest punishment, made only by those who valued strength and power above all else. And perhaps Theodmon's ancestors were right—he would show Rindria a merciless strength. He would no longer be a mediocre conquer; he would become as ruthless as they believed him to be, and as ruthless as he would need to be to become an avenger.

Vathar Ultoris, Theodmon prayed silently to the war god, invoking his more unforgiving side. *Help me be as righteous in rage as you were. Let the streets be so soaked with Riam blood that every stone will have to be pulled out if they ever want to be free of the stains.*

Theodmon was fully on his feet, pushing his way out of the tent. As he stepped outside, he was immediately flanked by Lucas, Henri, and Sam, the three of them blocking his way.

"Move," Theodmon barked.

"Where are you going?" Lucas said, his eyes bloodshot. He crossed his arms, but Theodmon could tell he was on the verge of breaking down himself.

"I need a new sword." Theodmon said.

"I can forge one for you," Sam said. An Extractor forging a sword for someone was a great honor but Theodmon didn't care. He couldn't wait for a new sword to be forged, not when Aloysius's killers lived.

Theodmon gripped his wrist with his hand, using the pain of the pressure to focus. "I need one now."

"No," Henri said. "Not now, rest."

"I'm killing them." Theodmon moved to push past them. "You can't stop me. I outrank you."

"And we care for you!" Lucas said. "Are you so eager to join Aloysius that you'll leave everybody else behind? What about Celestine? Should she lose all her siblings? What about Amaria? Who do you think will have to tell her she's now a widow? Your children?"

"You can kill them later," Henri said. "There's still time left in this siege. But right now you're tired. You aren't thinking straight. You need rest, Theodmon."

"I need a sword."

Lucas sighed. "You have a point there." He looked over and met Henri's eyes, slowly exhaling before turning back to Theodmon. "We are going to the blacksmith to get you a sword. And then you are coming back here and sleeping."

"I don't think I can," Theodmon croaked.

"I can numb the pain," Henri said. "It's a placebo—I'm only pushing the harmful thoughts away for a time, but it should be enough to help you sleep." He looked at Theodmon sadly, the frown lines protruding on his forehead. "Or we could get a healer to make a sleep potion. Whatever you prefer."

Henri is about to pass out, he's in so much pain from this. Theodmon realized with a jolt. *He has to hear our pain, our thoughts, but Aloysius was his friend too.*

"Go," Theodmon ordered. "Take a sleep potion, drink, do whatever you need to do."

A tear rolled down Henri's cheek. "Thank you." And then he departed, almost running back to his tent.

"I can't believe he's gone," Theodmon whispered to Lucas, the two of them standing alone in the forest of tents, yet feeling as if they were an island unto themselves. "We had just started mending our relationship...."

Gone. Aloysius was gone.

"I'm sure he'll liven up Sadthos's kingdom." Lucas almost choked on his own words. "There will be more parties than the somber god will know what to do with."

Sadthos's kingdom was so far away from the land of the living. Perhaps war was the closest thing to it on this side of the veil. Half of the men were half-alive, traumatized with what they had seen and what they had done. They were all dead men walking, and so, Theodmon should have felt a stronger conviction in his religion and the god of the dead.

But he didn't. He still believed in the gods– only idiots tempted fate by willfully ignoring their existence. But Theodmon didn't like the gods very much and even at what was the curtain between death and life, Theodmon could only bitterly think that Sadthos kingdom was a palliation for the chaos of life. Perhaps there was no afterlife kingdom and that was a story humans made up to give themselves false comfort.

Because Aloysius's death did not feel temporary; Theodmon did not feel as if he would see Aloysius again when Theodmon's time on earth ended. It felt final. Theodmon didn't know how perdurable the afterlife was–he wasn't a philosopher, scholar, or cleric.

But Theodmon's rage was eternal. The rage and the bloodlust was real, it was tangible. Theodmon could feel it, he could describe it. And he could do something about his helplessness. Death and War both took from their participants, but War allowed its followers to reclaim their agony.

And that was why Theodmon prayed to Vathar. And why he now invoked Vathar's more draconian form. He needed to become an avenger, and so he would.

For all those who had already died. For those who hadn't died yet. For those who didn't need to die yet.

For Aloysius.

Chapter Fifty-Six

Avengers didn't wait for the war to lull. Sam had made Theodmon a new sword; it wasn't a great sword, but it was balanced and sharp. Nighttime was falling quickly, but Theodmon didn't want to give Rindria a chance to breathe. This city, this country would fall before the sun rose. He swore to all the gods that he would succeed in making Rindria bleed for what they had done.

Wéorren City was already in chaos. He passed by Charlotte, a warm pink glow covering her entire body, her eyes closed as she swayed back and forth, her lips silently muttering something. She was making the already chaotic siege worse, and Theodmon would capitalize on that.

The men were retreating, pausing the siege with honor as the night fell. Theodmon didn't know what fool told them to retreat, but he would strip him of all ranks and honors. He grabbed a shield, moving towards the stables, quickly mounting Bluequill when he arrived.

Theodmon's heart pounded like a drum, his fists clenching around the griffin's reins as they flew. Henri and Lucas had warned him to not do anything rash—but what did they know? He wasn't being rash, he was ending the war.

He would have liked Aloysius's counsel, but Aloysius was gone. Heat rushed up Theodmon's neck. His brother was dead, and some idiots wanted to pause the siege.

They would suffer more losses until Wéorren fell. And neither side would fight with honor—the Riams were barbaric, desperate, and civilization would beat them until they complied.

Theodmon slashed and hacked enemy forces down like they were stalks of grass as he rode through the fields outside the city, his breathing fast and shallow. The retreating forces paused, neither moving forward or continuing their retreat as Theodmon rode past them. His heart beat so fast it threatened to explode from his chest.

None of these men mattered. Why should they matter, why should they live when Aloysius was dead? A sudden urge to scream overtook Theodmon, and he didn't fight it, releasing a blood curdling yell as he cut off a Riam soldier's head.

"Are you cowards?" He screamed at his men, tears falling down his face as he continued to cut down soldiers from on top of his griffin. "Fight and destroy this city!"

His entire body was hot, he could feel the sweat on his brow. How could they retreat? They were giving up at the eleventh hour. If his men couldn't be relied on, Theodmon would take the city himself. He directed his griffin to fly to the gates, and as Bluequill glided over the fields, Theodmon jumped, landing in front of the gates, the fighting thick around him.

He caught the blow of a Riam soldier with the hilt of his sword, kicking the soldier away from him and pulling his sword away, a Thestitiunian thrusting their sword through his neck, the blade nearly touching Theodmon as blood sputtered into his face. Theodmon turned, killing another foe. He killed and killed, not processing his actions as the adrenaline coursed through his veins.

As Theodmon cut his way through Riams, his body began to glow a deep bronze red. He was aware he was killing, every sense he had was in overdrive–he could hear the slice of human flesh as it connected with his sword, the roar of previously retreating men following him into battle, and the screams of those in the city.

Aloysius died for this, Theodmon should make his death worthwhile. His heart pounded in his chest as he listened to the cries of the dying, those that he killed, those that were trapped under rubble, those that were killed by others, and those that were being burned alive. Theodmon heard the clash of steel, sounding like the sweetest symphony as the roar of flames consumed everything in his path.

His lungs burned from the smoke filling the air, but as soon as he realized that he felt discomfort from it, the feeling vanished. He was made to kill, and he would not give into minor human discomforts until he had avenged Aloysius. He couldn't rest until those who had hurt him were awaiting judgment in the afterlife.

Around him, civilians screamed, cowering as they were pulled from their hiding spots. Once, Theodmon had wanted to prohibit this type of behavior. Now, he didn't give a shit—they, by association, had killed his brother. And they deserved Thestitiunia's vengeance and fury for it.

Arrows, spears, and swords seemed to bounce off Theodmon's body, as if he were suddenly invincible as he raged against the Riams. His sword glinted in the firelight as he laid waste to everything in his path, a band of soldiers following him as he forced his way to the center of Wéorren. He was going to take Bria Hall. If he had to take it by himself, he would. He was pure rage, the crescendo of a never ending nightmare to the people living within Wéorren.

"It's the blessing of Vathar Ultoris," one of the Thestitiunian soldiers shouted from behind Theodmon. "Look! The god's symbol is above his head."

Theodmon finished pulling his sword from out of a Riam soldier's chest, briefly looking up above him. Sure enough, there was a bronze double sword with blood dripping from the blades hovered over him, his body still glowing a deed red, only to alternate with bronze. His blood was rushing to his head, he had to take the city. This wasn't important.

He continued slaying everyone in his path, dismounting his horse when he neared Bria Hall. This place should be turned to rubble, its windows shattered, and its tapestries burned. This place hadn't only killed Aloysius, it was the force behind his father's death. And below this castle, Amaria had been imprisoned and tortured. Theodmon wanted those pristine halls to be permanently stained with blood, that Rindria would have to tear Bria Hall apart stone by stone if they ever wanted to be free from the horrors.

At least a building could be replaced.

His eyes felt scratchy and stiff, and he realized they felt this way without it bothering him. All he could truly feel, at the front and center of everything, was rage. Everything else was secondary, as if it didn't truly matter.

It was easier than Theodmon anticipated to breach Bria Hall. And somehow, he knew exactly where to go—where the governors had fled too. He shouldn't have known this, he had no experience with Bria Hall or its passageways, but, as if someone had taken over his body, he tore down a tapestry, and pushed against the wall, a latch turning. Without even a torch, Theodmon rushed into the passageway, only stopping when he had run for a while, feeling as if this was where he needed to exit. On his left, there was a clear doorway. Theodmon opened it, stepping into a bedroom, where the three Riam governors cowered.

He killed the first one easily, stabbing the old man through his chest.

The other two, more spry, ran toward the balcony. Theodmon easily reached them, killing the second by stabbing him through the back, his body falling one story below to the public square below, his head cracking open on the stairs.

"Please." The last governor fell to his knees, holding his clasped hands up above his chest. "I surrender."

Theodmon didn't care. A peaceful surrender wasn't vengeance, and Aloysius deserved to be avenged. He chopped off the governor's head, throwing it over the balcony to the crowd below. He glowed with the red and bronze colors of war as griffins flew overhead. In front of Theodmon, people kneeled, their heads bowed.

"Rindria has fallen!"

The Thestitiunian soldiers cheered. The Riam civilians sobbed.

Slowly his senses dulled, the glow dissipating. And then, everything in his body hurt and black spots dotted his vision. He stepped back inside the castle, slamming the door behind him as he moved towards an interior wall away from a window. He made it far enough that nobody could see him, and then he promptly sunk to the floor, blood pounding in his head as he vomited.

Rindria had fallen. And with that, so had Theodmon's honor.

Chapter Fifty-Seven

The throne room in Bria Hall was the one place in the entire city that felt untouched by war, so Theodmon spent a large majority of his time there, alone, pretending that war had never happened. Pretending that he had never essentially slaughtered an entire city.

He had engaged in a massacre once before–earning him the nickname Archangel of Harréow Field. Theodmon cracked his knuckles. He'd never wanted that nickname, but drowning in his grief, he took it out in the only way he had been taught how—combat.

This episode of slaughter, with the blessing of Vathar Ultoris, felt different. He didn't fully remember everything he did, but he hadn't blacked out. He'd been a lot more controlled on the streets of Wéorren City than he had been on Harréow Field.

Now that the waves of vengeance had passed, Theodmon only felt shame. He despised himself for what he did, and he feared knowing what nicknames were being bestowed upon him. If cutting down fifty or so men by himself at once when he was sixteen earned him the name Archangel of Harréow Field, what would they call the conqueror who slaughtered a city and with that, destroyed a country?

As Theodmon sat silently in his own thoughts, the door opened to the throne room. Numbly, Theodmon looked up to see who had entered, intending to banish them from the room so he could be left alone.

However, it wasn't a sentry or some officer who was coming to bother him; Henri silently walked through the throne room. Theodmon said nothing, his shoulders slumped and heavy.

Henri sat down next to Theodmon on the stone stairs before the throne. "How are you feeling?"

"Like hell," Theodmon said. "It doesn't feel real that Aloysius is gone."

Henri gave a pensive nod. "And how are you feeling after..." he took a deep breath, trailing off as he looked into the distance. "The blessing of Vathar Ultoris. I thought it was a myth."

Theodmon's chest sank. He pulled out a dagger, cleaning the dirt from beneath his finger tips.He hadn't been aware he had the blessing until he had finished cutting down every person in his path. He hadn't wanted to be that violent towards the Riams, knowing that they were now Thestitiunians. But he had. He had the sneaking suspicion he might have killed civilians, non-combatants. He wasn't sure, and frankly, as long as it was unconfirmed he could avoid processing that act.

"I did too," Theodmon said.

"Are you prepared for how it'll be taken back home?" Henri asked.

Theodmon bowed his head, closing his eyes. He had always commanded respect in areas of war, and even respect and deference in his role as the leader of a province in the empire. But how the soldiers had treated him after this felt different, as if he had ascended to a level of untouchability as if he were a god among mortals.

"They're saying you're god-blessed," Henri said.

"I didn't ask to be," Theodmon said.

The corners of Henri's eyes dropped. "But you were. You were god blessed by Vathar, no less. That is going to have serious implications, whether you like it or not."

Theodmon sighed, knowing that Henri was right. He looked down upon his arms, as if to see if he was still glowing red and bronze. There was no reason for anybody to be treating him differently. He gained Vathar Ultoris' blessing once, but that didn't change anything now. It didn't mean that he would ever receive the blessing again.

But Vathar Ultoris' was one of Thestitiunia's most revered gods; what a surprise that a militaristic empire would value a war god. Theodmon looked at his knife and brought it to the edge of his tunic, wiping the dirt off of it.

"What are people thinking about it?" Theodmon sheathed the dagger. Maybe if he had this insight he could prepare for the future implications.

"Some fear you. Some admire you. Some have started whispering that the gods favor you more than any other human–including the emperor. Some are taking this blessing and Amaria's wings–remember, people think the gods' blessed her, not the faeries–"

"Which is inaccurate," Theodmon interrupted.

"Is it?" Henri raised an eyebrow. "Ghagyn is the mother of all magical things, including faeries. It's not illogical to conclude that a powerful mage was blessed by the goddess of magic."

"The faeries changed her," Theodmon repeated. "It was a bargain. A deal we couldn't refuse, no matter how much we may regret the consequences. Not a blessing."

Henri held up his hands. "Alright. Just keep in mind that's what most Thestitiunians think–Amaria is goddess blessed, and blessed by one of the most important deities in our pantheon."

"Like I am." Theodmon slumped forward to lean on his knees, his hair hanging in front of his face.

"Whether or not this is an accurate perception is besides the point," Henri said. "It'll exist and Aion will view you as a threat—"

"You know what I think of Aion," Theodmon stated.

"And what Amaria thinks," Henri said. "And what Aaron Raulet thinks. And potential plans you have floated. Don't worry, I won't tell a soul. And here's a secret of mine—I agree. Aion is lazy, ineffective, and pathetic. And if you decided to go that route, you'd have my full support."

"We just got through a war," Theodmon sighed.

"I'm not suggesting you do it now," Henri said. "I'm not suggesting that you do it at all, actually. I'm just letting you know, you'd have my support if you made that decision."

Theodmon sat up, leaning towards Henri and clapping him on the shoulders as tears welled in his eyes. "Thank you."

"No problem," Henri replied as they broke apart.

"This city needs to heal," Theodmon said softly, fully aware that he was the reason for so much damage. "This country–colony now–needs to heal. Are you ready for that as governor?"

Henri snorted. "No, but I'll figure it out as I go. It's going to take a while before healing, we have to integrate Rindria into Thestitiunia first."

"Second sons and minor lords looking to rise should be arriving soon," Theodmon said. It was a common tactic, at least from what his war history books had told him, for conquerors to marry in with the population. And as there hadn't been a conquest to receive ambitious young nobles in over six hundred years.

"You're ready to handle the marriage arrangements for an entire colony?" Theodmon asked.

Henri shook his head, giving off a harsh chuckle. "Everyone will be vultures."

"If anybody could effectively handle that, it's you," Theodmon told him sincerely. Henri was calm, patient, empathetic, and intelligent. Even without accounting for his special skill set of magic, he had the qualities needed for a new governor of a colony, and the future duke as well. "I'll miss having you around."

"I always thought I'd be in your court," Henri admitted. "Thank you for trusting me with this."

"You are one of my dearest friends," Theodmon told him, tears welling in his eyes again, falling down in hot, angry droplets. "I wouldn't leave it with anybody else."

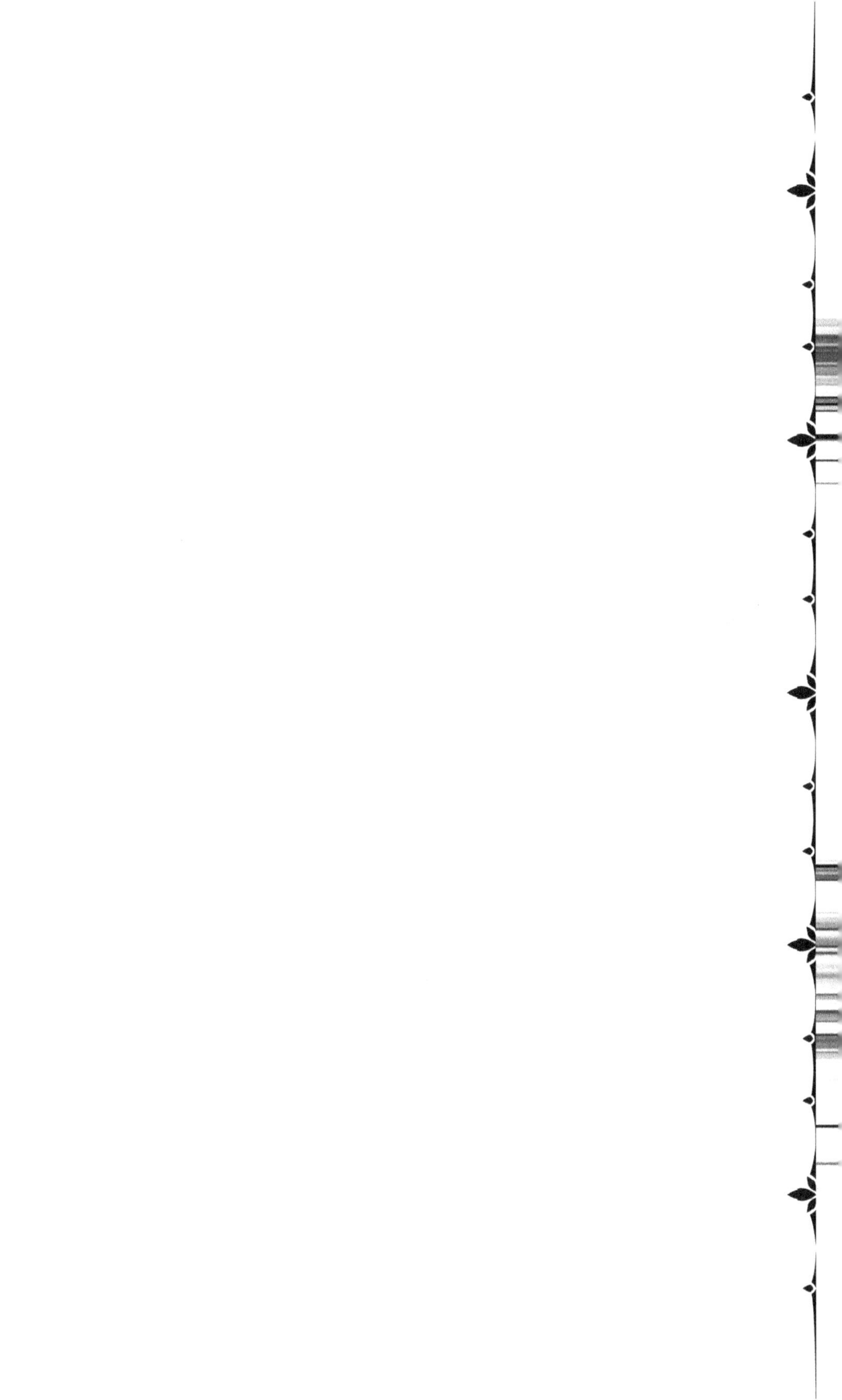

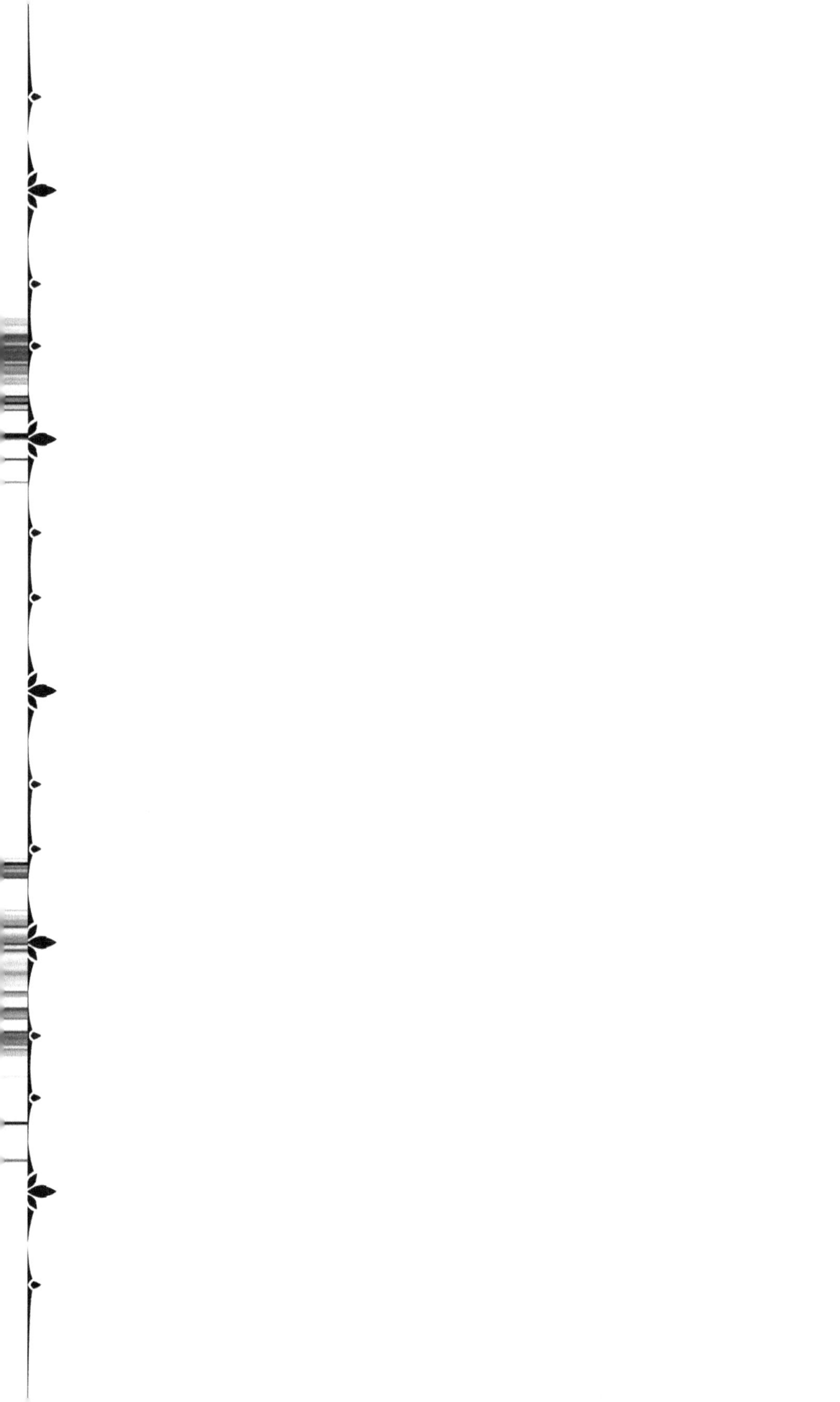

Part Six

the laurels

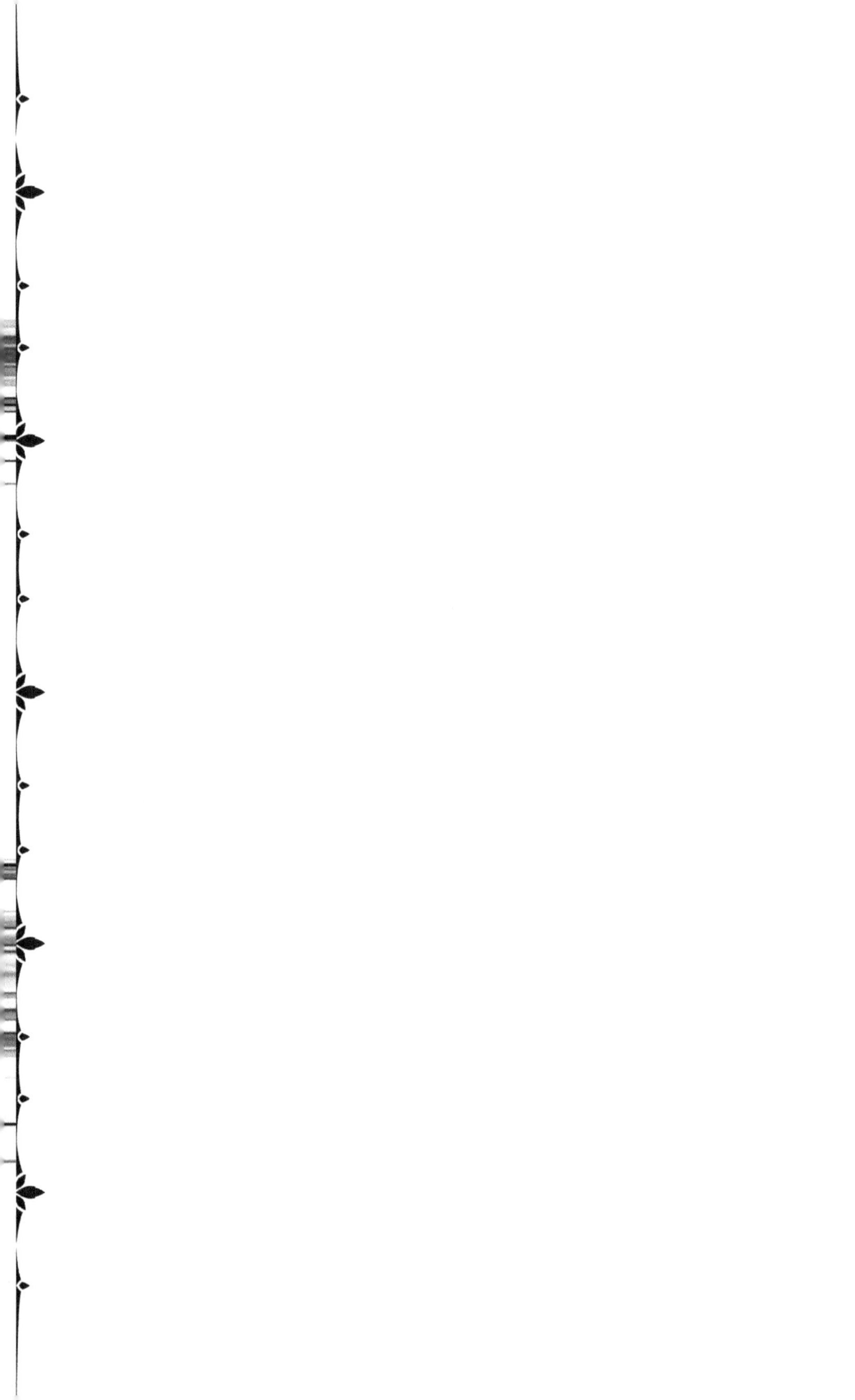

Chapter Fifty-Eight

A maria's knife scraped across the plate as she cut into her eggs.

"Any news?" her father asked.

It'd been almost two years since Theodmon had departed Raulle. She and Theodmon had only communicated with letters, never saying fully what they longed to say, not wanting anything to be used against them in case the letters were intercepted. They had married almost six years ago. When she was nineteen, terrified of leaving home permanently, terrified of marriage itself, she could never fantom that she would be twenty-five, back at Provincia Palencia, and longing to be back with her husband in their home. He would be turning thirty soon, and she had wanted to throw him a party. That wasn't going to happen, and while it was a stupid thing to mourn, she did.

She wished she had news of this infernal war ending.

"No." Amaria took a sip of her drink to avoid further conversation–not that she knew what to say anyways. Last thing she had heard about the war was a letter from Theodmon before Rindria fell, and later that week, a short letter that confirmed that he was alive, Aloysius was dead, and that he had taken on Elisa's son as a ward.

"Hopefully they'll win soon," Aaron said.

"We've a lot to plan for when that occurs," Amaria replied. "Funerals, economic recovery for the new province–"

"Another war?"

"Not now, Father," Amaria said. "We need time before starting that again."

"Amari–"

"Wait for Theodmon, at least," Amaria interrupted. "This is just as much his war as ours and he needs to be involved in these discussions."

"Why are you so deferential–"

"Didn't seem to be an issue when I was deferential to you." Amaria glowered. "Besides, it's not being deferential, it's avoiding talking about war over breakfast. It ruins my appetite."

"It's unfortunate–"

"And you need to marry Natalya to secure that alliance before we actively move against Aion. I'm not sure Durek Svilas will be eager for his daughter to marry a traitor."

"When we win, he'll be more eager."

"*If*," Amaria corrected. "And we'll need his troops. I guarantee it."

"Do you have the gift of foresight now?"

"Only the one you gave me," Amaria answered. "Let me focus on planning this wedding for now. What better time for than on the tails of a grand victory?"

Aaron paused. He leaned forward, surveying Amaria with narrowed eyes before he leaned back in his chair with a scoff.

A smile crept over Aaron's face. "I should be angry.".

"But you aren't," Amaria replied tentatively.

"No," Aaron chuckled. "You are everything I had hoped for in a daughter and more."

She had waited so long to hear an affirmation like that. Once, she would have been jubilant, grateful for a shred of his approval. Aaron's accolades were the one thing she could never have, and it became more tantalizing to her as he withheld praise. Aaron's approval had been an effective motivator until Amaria realized that she could live without it.

"You made me," Amaria said. "For better or worse I was your creature."

"Was," Aaron noted.

"Was," Amaria confirmed the past tense. "I'll always do what's best for my family–I'm a Raulet through and through. But don't mistake that for doing what's best for you, Father."

For a long moment, Aaron looked at her. Amaria, against all her better instincts, did not turn or flinch away. Years could have passed before Aaron sighed, taking a long gulp of his drink. "I can respect that."

"Good," Amaria said, proud that she didn't sound surprised. Instead her voice was unshakable. "I do want to speak to you about something though."

Aaron silently looked at her. Amaria wet her lips, forcing herself to not avert her gaze away from her father's eyes. "Tell me about Grandfather."

"What's to tell? He was your grandfather–"

"Not a base summary. The truth. Galen told me that he took credit for your achievements. That he was crueler than I was taught."

"He didn't take credit for my achievements," Aaron said. "I gave them to him. And yes, your grandfather was a horrible person. It's why he was assassinated and why nobody mourned him when he died. The citizens were about to revolt against him, so I made reforms. And over time, I rewrote history to make it seem as if he was the reformer."

Amaria's brow furrowed. "Why?"

"Stability." Aaron paused for a drink of wine. "I was a third-born son. There were whispers that we were losing favor with the gods due to our family's personal tragedies. And the people were angry—I was avoiding us being slaughtered." Aaron pinched the bridge of his nose as he slumped forward. "Your grandfather was monstrous. He raped women on their wedding nights–viewing it as his right as a ruler. He killed entire families because a child stole something. He taxed our people into poverty—peasants in Rindria were doing better than even our most skilled tradesmen and merchants."

"I always thought he was a great reformer," Amaria whispered. "It doesn't bother you that you'll never get credit for what you did?"

"I was willing to sacrifice my reputation for stability," Aaron said coldly. "And I leaned into it. I am stern, but fair in my justice—some might say the Drowning Tombs are cruel but notice how we're not on the brink of revolution because of it. I keep taxes low, our citizens prosper. And I am clever–why should it bother me that people view me as a cruel snake when that's the truth?"

"You're not cruel," Amaria breathed. "You did what was necessary."

"You should remember that," Aaron told her pointedly. "Now, do you want to write to Durek while I write to Aion?" Aaron asked, effectively ending the conversation.

Amaria smirked. "Shouldn't you talk with your future father-in-law?"

"Planning dates seems to be more of a woman's sphere," Aaron said. "Durek will expect these letters from you."

Amaria narrowed her eyes as Aaron waved for a servant to bring parchment, ink and quills, then went back to cutting his sausage. Was this a test? He had already lost faith in her, was this another way to prove she was a failure? Would she fail, not seeing the trap she fell into until it was too late?

"I figured we'd co-author our letters–although one will be in my hands and the other in yours," Aaron continued.

"Are we finishing breakfast before working?" Amaria had wanted to enjoy breakfast in peace. Perhaps if she and her father were able to have one normal breakfast together, perhaps...Amaria didn't know what she wanted exactly. Proof that they were good, or at least not horribly dysfunctional people? Even that seemed too much for them to accomplish.

Ambitious people tended to be the worst at achieving and appreciating the small goals and the small acts that made up most of life. Amaria too, was horrible at slowing down and appreciating the simplicities of life. She didn't think she'd be incapable of doing so—but she had a thrill with scheming over breakfast, and that thrill masked the fatigue she felt. Sighing, she bit into her eggs once more. How could she achieve breathtaking things but not a simple, politic free, breakfast with her father.

Aaron chuckled, as if he could read her intent as easily as a scholar of literature could recite poetry. "Naturally. I find that working after breakfast helps with my indigestion."

Amaria's lips pursed, which she quickly hid by dapping her mouth with a napkin. Was her father mocking her? All of his comments, and even his compliments seemed to have a level of backhanded mockery.

Her father was her greatest blindspot and so he was her greatest weakness. She praised the gods that he valued family and that was what made her safe. Amaria suddenly felt as if she were choking, remembering what Delphina had said once ago. The memory threw itself against the barricade of her mind, intent on breaking it. Amaria could see the bathhouse, see Delphina's smirk, and almost smell the soap as she remembered what Delphina had once told her.

"Your father runs the country," Delphina had said. Amaria could see the wet hair clinging to her. Amaria wanted to cling to her as if a hug could make this ghostly image that only existed in her mind real.

"We have to let the emperor think he's doing it," Amaria had said.

Delphina's eyebrows didn't drop as she stared at Amaria sadly. "I think you trust your father too much."

"He's my father," Amaria had said. "He wouldn't hurt me."

"Amaria?" Aaron said, jolting her back to the present.

Amaria furiously blinked back tears. "Yes, Father?"

"Are you alright?" Aaron peered down at Amaria in concern.

"Yes," Amaria said. "Just thinking."

"On what?"

I'm not sure I trust you. Amaria knew she couldn't tell her father this. She didn't know how he'd react if she told him that–at least not the specifics of his reaction–but she knew that she would likely suffer the consequences of his wrath. Amaria loved her father, despite everything. And while she still wanted to cling to the notion that her father would never hurt her because she was his daughter and she understood him, she couldn't. She knew her father would always be inclined to hurt her because that was her first instinct too. In the end, she was the same as him.

"I just remembered how Delphina and I used to eat here," Amaria lied. "It seems as if her death is still impacting me more than I know."

Mixing a truth with a lie was always the most effective way to be dishonest. She placed her napkin down upon her plate. "I'm finished with my meal whenever you're ready to begin writing, Father."

Aaron set down his food, motioning for servants to clear the table and to bring them ink and parchment.

"What else have you heard from Rindria?" Aaron asked once the servants had departed. "Any notable deaths?"

"Aloysius Chauvignon...." Amaria's mouth dried and her eyes watered as her lips quivered over the words. "Aloysius...."

Aaron silently watched her, prompting her to speak with his silence.

By a miracle, Amaria choked out: "he's dead."

"That's a shame," Aaron said. "How's Theodmon handling that?"

"Personally or strategically?" Rage bubbled beneath Amaria's calm exterior at such a crude question.

"Strategically," Aaron said. "I know personally he's a wreck–as anybody would be when a sibling dies. I was horrible when my brothers died and I'd be even worse if I lost Miana."

I suppose he's not completely heartless. Amaria grumpily thought to herself. *Just brutally practical. Still, it couldn't kill him to be nicer, right?* She looked at her father, keeping her expression neutral. "I heard he killed hundreds by his own hand afterwards with the blessing of Vathar Ultoris. The capital city was on the brink of falling–likely it's already fallen and we just haven't received the letter yet."

Aaron leaned back in his chair, stretching out his leg. "Rindria is a Thestitiunian colony now."

Amaria frowned. "Theodmon didn't mention that."

Aaron shrugged.

Amaria's eyes narrowed as the hairs on her skin prickled. "How'd you know that?"

Aaron paused, licking his lips. "I received a letter from my spies this morning. Your husband must have been beside himself with grief." Aaron took a long drink of wine. "Your brother is alive, in case you were wondering. We're departing for Aionstown for the celebrations within the week."

Amaria frowned. Her father was being dubious. She turned her head away from him, staring at the roses resting on the mantle. Or perhaps she was being overly paranoid.

"We'll discuss this later." Aaron picked up a piece of parchment. He began writing and Amaria heard the frantic scratching of a quill as she stared at the empty piece of parchment in front of her.

How exactly was she supposed to discuss wedding dates with Durek Silvas? If this was a note in which she needed to threaten him, this would have been an easy task. Sickly polite threats were her specialty. But being genuinely nice to him wasn't a skill she had honed.

Duke Svilas, it is in our— Amaria shook her head. Even with the sentence unfinished she knew it wouldn't end right. Sighing, she lifted up her quill. She could always edit whatever she wrote to make it sound better afterwards.

Amaria brought her quill down, and her temples throbbing, she wrote. Multiple drafts and crumpled up parchments later, as her father watched her impatiently, she was finished. Inhaling deeply, Amaria looked at her handiwork.

Duke Svilas,

I write to you on behalf of my Father, Duke Aaron Raulet of Perima Fluere, Thestitiunia, Lord Protector of Raulle, Lord Guardian of the Treasury, and the advisor to Emperor Aion Marion II.

We are anxious to share the wealth and power between our families—and as Thestitunia has conquered Rindria, we wish for us to showcase this bond closely after the conquest celebrations. Please let me know so I may complete wedding preparations for my father's wedding as a dutiful daughter.

Amaria Raulet Chauvignon
Marchioness of the Westerlands

She supposed it would have to do. She sealed the letter with wax, pressing the seal of her ring against it.

"I suppose we should prepare the laurels." Amaria looked up towards her father and beckoned for the page to come to take her letter.

Aaron chuckled, his hand outstretched to take Amaria's letter from her. She obliged without protest and Aaron gave the page the letters.

Once the page was gone, Aaron stood up, Amaria following his lead.

"Who do you think will be appointed governor?" Aaron said as they made their way out of the dining hall.

Amaria knew exactly who would be appointed governor—if he was still alive of course.

"I have a few ideas of good candidates," Amaria said neutrally, letting her magic spike and thread over towards her father's magical energy, allowing them to speak privately and securely through the mage link.

"You know," Aaron immediately said as the mage link opened.

"Henri Delaluna," Amaria admitted. *"He's loyal to us, but Aion will have a hard time denying him a governance position, all things considered."*

"And is Lord Delaluna alright with being governor of a place that despises him?"

"Better than to hear the screams of a civil war." Amaria pointedly looked at her father. *"Besides, Henri is necessary there—it's unstable. He'll do what needs to be done."*

"Laurels with mistletoe for the living," Amaria said out loud to maintain the illusion of normal conversation. It was unnecessary. He didn't do anything with planning grand gestures–although he was an earth mage and he could greatly help with growing some out of season plants. But he wouldn't. He would delegate and then criticize those who actually did the work. Amaria clasped her hands together, forcing her annoyance down. "Lillies and laurels for the deceased as a base and add flowers with house colors for nobility."

"Do you need help?" Aaron asked.

Amaria's eyebrows arched.

"We're both earth mages," Aaron said and Amaria wasn't certain her father hadn't read her thoughts. She thought she closed the mage link, perhaps she hadn't?

"I'd like that," Amaria said stiffly. Still, her smile was genuine. "There's a lot of laurels needed to prepare for."

"And flowers for my upcoming wedding," Aaron added dryly.

"Will the wedding be held here?" Amaria asked, knowing that the answer would be yes. Aaron was much too traditional and much too proud to have it anywhere but his ancestral home.

"It'll have to be more extravagant than the one with your mother," Aaron said softly, almost a whisper lost in the wind. Amaria tensed, wondering why he would say that. "Let's go to the courtyard, I'll tell the gardeners and earth mages to bring seedlings for us to start with."

"Where are the ones helping us?" Amaria asked.

"Other earth mages over the city and empire will have notices sent out. For what we do, we will give to servants to craft–they only need the living plants to shape them," Aaron replied.

"Alright," Amaria agreed. She chewed on her bottom lip for a moment. "What did you mean before? About Mother."

Amaria missed her mother. She missed her in how a fish missed water and hearing her mentioned in such a nonchalant way hurt Amaria the same way a fish was hurt by air.

"What do you mean?"

"About the extravagance of the wedding."

Aaron's shoulders slumped. "Illyana wasn't marrying Duke Raulet–she wasn't even marrying the future Duke Raulet. I was the youngest son. Our wedding was more subdued than my older brothers."

"Subdued?" Amaria narrowed her eyes, disbelievingly.

"For a Raulet wedding," Aaron amended.

"What happened to my uncles?" Amaria asked. She had known they had died. However, out of respect, or perhaps fear of her father, she had never dug further into the story. But she had never pressed for information about her grandfather either.

"Avondra and Thestitiunia were at war–it was how Lynette ascended the throne. She killed her brother and a Thestitiunian princess–Aion's sister–to do so." Aaron paused in front of a tapestry, appearing as if he was studying every strand. "Thestitiunians fought in this war because of Stellaria Marion's death." Aaron's fists clenched. "I saw every sibling but my sister die."

Aaron grabbed Amaria by her shoulders, his nails digging into her. "I saw my mother commit suicide at their deaths, and my father died alongside my brothers because of Lynette!"

Amaria tensed, taking a step backwards from her father. She had never seen him angry—not like this. Aaron's anger was cold and calculated, not explosive.

Aaron's knuckles cracked before he breathed in deeply.

Amaria looked at her father, her eyes scanning his face, when she realized he was crying.

"Father." Amaria placed a hand on his arm.

Aaron's hands dropped limply to his side. "I don't take pleasure in death and I have spent my entire life devoted to strengthening my family and my country." He gripped his cane as he began walking down the corridor once more.

"I know," Amaria whispered.

"Do you?" Aaron said. "You've been different. As if you don't trust me."

Amaria swallowed. "I'm sorry. When I learned the truth about Vypren....When I learned what you did..." Amaria wrung her hands. "Things changed." She forced herself to lift her eyes to her father, desperate for his remorse, for an apology. She needed him to show remorse. How could she have been so blind to how her own father had hurt her?

"I should have told you earlier."

Amaria moved her hands closer together, using her long, willowy sleeves to hide her balled up fists. Was that all her father was going to say about this? She would never receive an apology for this, this paltry crumb was all she could hope for.

"It doesn't change anything," Amaria said sharply. "You won't ever actually apologize so let's just discuss the flowers for the soldiers–"

Aaron grabbed her by her shoulders. "Don't avoid this conversation."

"I don't want to have this conversation anymore." Amaria took a step back from him. Her father would never give her what she needed, and forcing this conversation wouldn't change that. It would only hurt her. She needed an apology, yes, but these half-hearted apologies in which her father seemed more focused on avoiding fault than acknowledging how he had hurt her was more harmful than his silence. "I'd rather you not give me hope."

Aaron looked at her sadly. "I regret every day you had to spend with him. I regret not cutting him open when I came to rescue you."

Amaria's fists uncurled as she looked up at her father, tears forming in her eyes. "Why didn't you?"

"You were bleeding." Aaron's voice cracked. "He cut you deep–I could see an organ, or it was tissues, I'm not sure—but you were so cold, so pale. I chose to focus on getting you to a doctor."

"Why?" Amaria asked.

"What use was revenge if revenge caused you to die?" Aaron said. "I chose to focus on saving your life, and I don't regret that."

Amaria stood there silently, her mind whirling.

"I do regret lying to you," Aaron said. "I know you've been wanting me to say that–"

"So you're only saying it to appease me," Amaria crossed her arms.

"No," Aaron said. "Admitting fault is difficult for us. But I mean it. And aside from Vypren, I haven't lied to you."

"Don't lie to me again." Amaria's eyes narrowed. She wasn't sure how true it was that Aaron hadn't lied to her. He was like her. And she lied as easily as she breathed. But Aaron's assertion would have to do for now.

"I underestimated you, and that was my mistake," Aaron said. "You are far more capable than anybody has ever given you credit for, including me."

Theodmon never questioned my capabilities. Amaria thought as thick angry tears fell down her face. She turned her face away from her father, furiously trying to wipe the tears away with her sleeves.

"You should go," Aaron said as they entered the castle. He paused, then began to make his way down the opposite corridor. "I'll see you at dinner."

Amaria didn't respond. Instead, she made her way to her chambers, attempting to appear elegant despite the tears staining her face. She would be left alone to think of her father's revelation, the war, and everything to come until Theodmon returned. Amaria would, of course, spend time with her children–more time than what was socially acceptable–but she would burn the world if anybody took that from her.

And Amaria would have parades and banquets to plan for all the victorious return of all the men, but that was truly idle work. And planning for a wedding was even more extravagant, and yet more mind numbing than the laurels of war. However, it was enough to momentarily distract her during the day but did nothing to dull the raging anxiety she felt at night.

Chapter Fifty-Nine

Since news of Theodmon's conquest reached Amaria, her life had been a blur of travel. Aion insisted on the Parade of Conquest being in Aionstown, despite the soldiers and leaders hailing from the Westerlands and Perivina Fluere. Amaria scowled. How apt of Aion to force these people to further spurn the comforts of home for his ego.

Now she stood on the balcony of a shopkeeper's store in Aionstown, the merchant easily bribed with a bag of gold. Her deep blue silk dress clung to her, the cape coming from her shoulders lightly fluttering in the breeze, causing goosebumps on her bare arms.

"We should have waited for the procession at the Imperial Palace," Nicoletta grumbled beside her.

"I prefer this," Juliette said from Amaria's other side, discreetly squeezing her hand. "I want to see if I can spot Lucas."

Amaria gave Juliette a small smile before averting her gaze to the freshly washed cobblestone streets below. The golden brown buildings of Aionstown basked in the late afternoon sunlight and the air was filled with the sounds of music, children playing, and the excited jubilations of the citizens. Streamers of crimson, purple, and gold adorned every corner, replacing the hanging wash for one day.

They heard the parade before they saw it—trumpets blaring as the drums and marching soldiers made a rhythmic thudding noise. "Oh gods," Amaria breathed, her heart skipping.

"Lucas, Theodmon, and Haerdnor will be at the front," Juliette said, craning her neck.

"This is quite the spectacle," Nicoletta remarked.

"Mhmm," Amaria replied absentmindedly, her attention drifting as she scanned the crowd for any sign of her husband. As the parade drew nearer, Amaria's heart quickened, almost feeling like a palpitation. She longed to catch a glimpse of Theodmon, to see his proud stature amidst the triumphant procession. Yet, beneath her anticipation, there lingered a deep sense of worry for her husband's well-being. Aloysius had died. Theodmon had lost his father in war and recently he had watched his sister's decapitation on a battlefield; his brother dying in war had to be tearing open those wounds.

And he was being celebrated instead of comforted. Amaria's hands clenched into fists, her nails digging into her palms.

"He should be here any moment," Nicoletta said, her voice laced with a hint of excitement that seemed almost too eager.

Amaria's eyes drifted towards Nicoletta, momentarily narrowing. There was something in her friend's demeanor, a subtle shift in her gaze, that set Amaria on edge.

"Look!" Juliette exclaimed, pointing to the nearing procession. Amaria almost didn't hear her because of the cheers that erupted from the crowd below as Theodmon rode into view. His golden armor gleamed in the sunset, his sword hanging from his side. One hand waved at the crowd as the other gently guided his horse's reins, navigating the animal through the winding streets.

He didn't smile. *Thank the gods a stoic warrior is an acceptable image*, Amaria thought dryly, her mouth curling in distaste as she looked around the street below as the citizens threw flowers, blessing the gods and Theodmon too. *If he had to smile at this, I think he would finally break.*

Next to Theodmon, Lucas and Haerdnor rode, looking equally stoic. "They're safe." Juilette clutched Amaria's arm as tears poured down her face. "They're alive."

"We heard reports–" Amaria started.

"Oh, but it's not the same as seeing it!" Juliette hugged Amaria so tightly she thought her ribs could break. "They're safe. They're home."

Amaria hugged Juliette back, tears welling in her eyes. There was no logic to it–she knew Theodmon had been safe–but Juliette was correct; Amaria felt almost lighter now that she saw Theodmon alive with her own eyes.

"Isn't it magnificent?" Nicoletta's eyes sparkled with excitement as she gestured towards the colorful procession. "I never imagined I would live to see such a grand celebration."

Amaria bristled. "People died."

"And that's stopped you before?" Nicoletta scoffed. "You can eat at a state dinner mere hours after torturing and killing people but a parade is too much?"

"Nicoletta," Juliette gasped lightly. "Don't."

"We should be celebrating," Nicoletta said. "Thestitiunia has a new colony. If all goes well, it'll be a province before our grandchildren are born."

Amaria forced a smile, focusing on Theodmon, Lucas, and Haerdnor as they rode their horses directly below.

"Lucas!" Juliette waved feverishly towards her husband. Amaria stretched her wings, flapping them upwards, to hopefully draw his attention.

Lucas did a double take at the sight of the wings and broke into a genuine smile. Amaria wasn't paying attention, she met Theodmon's eyes. Silently, they stared at each other.

Amaria's heart ached, knowing all too well the depth of pain that lay beneath Theodmon's stoic facade. With each shortwave he gave, even from here, she could sense the weight of his burdens pressing down upon him, the invisible scars of war etched into his soul. She longed to reach out to him, to offer him solace for what he had seen and done–for his loss of Aloysius, but she knew that his wounds ran deeper than any physical embrace could heal.

A physical embrace won't hurt though. He shouldn't be doing this alone.

Amaria broke her gaze away from Theodmon, looking at the parade behind him. "I'll see you at the Imperial Palace," she whispered to Juliette.

Juliette reached for Amaria's arm as Amaria stepped towards the railing. "What are you doing?"

"He needs me," Amaria said. "And it's not exactly easy to deny I helped with the war effort."

"It seems more unbelievable if you didn't," Nicoletta agreed. "Also nobody is going to argue about the person with wings joining a parade."

Amaria couldn't place it, but it felt as if there was a slight sneer in Nicoletta's voice. Amaria sighed, both of them had been tense with each other recently. It had been difficult—everything in their lives had changed so quickly once Delphina died. *I'll need to spend more time with Nicoletta. Just us two.*

She laughed, smiling at Nicoletta. "They might try to pluck a feather to see if it's real."

Nicoletta's eyes flickered before she gave Amaria a tentative smile of her own.

Juliette pushed an embroidered handkerchief into Amaria's hands. "Give this to Lucas, then." Amaria felt the lump rising in her throat as she took the handkerchief from Juliette, nodding.

Jumping into the middle of a parade is the exact type of behavior ladies don't engage in. Amaria heard her father's lecturing voice in her mind as her hands gripped the railing.

It'll embarrass Aion, Amaria justified, not knowing why she was justifying herself to her subconscious. *A show of strength by national heroes before they commit treason.*

Amaria jumped off the railing, her wings extending to carry her down to Theodmon. *I am ready to commit treason.* Amaria's stomach lurched as she landed near Theodmon and Lucas, their eyes widening in surprise as they pulled their horses to a stop.

"That's an entrance," Lucas said.

"Wow, rebellious," Haerdnor snorted. "Is Father dead?"

"Don't stop," Amaria told them. She reached up towards Theodmon. "Help me up."

"Amaria," Theodmon murmured, his voice tinged with a hint of surprise. Now that Amaria was closer, she could see that his eyes were bloodshot, with dark circles underneath them. "Why aren't you at the palace?"

"Avoiding someone," Amaria answered, already climbing onto the back of his horse. She looked over at Lucas, handing him the handkerchief as the horses began to trot once more. "From your wife."

Amaria's hands brushed against Theodmon's back, his touch a silent reassurance to her.

"You always know how to find me, even in the midst of chaos," Theodmon murmured, a ghost of a smile playing at the corners of his lips.

"How's Juliette?" Lucas asked.

"She misses you. How are you two?" Amaria put more pressure against where she was holding Theodmon. "I'm sorry about Aloysius."

She felt him tense. "I'm not done avenging his death." Theodmon's voice broke. "I'm ready to do what your father asked."

"Me too," Amaria whispered. She wanted to fully embrace Theodmon, take him away from this public space and protect him from prying eyes as he did whatever he needed to do to heal from the loss of Aloysius.

"We haven't even buried and honored our dead," Theodmon's voice broke, as if he were fighting back tears. "Their corpses are laying in salt at home and we couldn't stop to burn and bury them."

Amaria's heart clenched at Theodmon's words, his anguish clear in the tremor of his voice. She reached out to him, her hand gently caressing his cheek, wishing she wasn't sitting behind him on a horse so she could do more for him. "The salt will preserve them, and when we get home, we'll do the rites together," Amaria said firmly, trying to keep her own voice from cracking. "We'll honor their memory, together."

"We had mass graves." Theodmon's voice barely carried a sound. "It was impossible to mark all the graves...so none were marked." His chest started to shake.

"Don't give Aion the satisfaction of having you cry," Haerdnor hissed, the Imperial Palace looming closer.

Amaria turned towards Lucas, her eyes widening, as she rubbed Theodmon's back. "We can build them memorials," Amaria told Theodmon. "In the Westerlands. We will honor them and their families there. We will have the priests and priestesses of Sadthos do all the rites–I'm sure temples from other provinces will send people to help." She was breathless, and her hands shook. She didn't know what to do, but Lucas was correct–Theodmon couldn't cry. Not so close to Aion. Not as they reached the gates of the Imperial Palace and were dismounting their horses to walk up the stairs.

Not as a girl handed Theodmon a bouquet.

"Marquis Chauvignon," she said. "For your gallant victory."

"Gallant," Theodmon scoffed under his breath, anger flashing like fire in his eyes. "There's nothing gallant in starving and murdering civilians."

"Thank you," Amaria quickly interceded, taking the bouquet from the girl. "They're lovely."

She firmly gripped Theodmon's shoulders, guiding him up the stairs. "You can do this. I'll make an excuse to get you out of dinner."

"And the ball?" Theodmon glowered.

"You'll be with me." Amaria batted away a golden streamer; they were thicker near the Imperial Palace. "We can easily sneak away after a short appearance. We haven't seen each other in months, everyone will have their assumptions of what's happening–they're just too polite to say it."

She gripped him tightly, using her touch on him as an anchor to the present. "We can do this. Together."

Theodmon gave a shaky nod, pulling her in close to his chest. He hugged her tightly, and Amaria heard the fast beating of his heart. She closed her eyes, breathing in deeply through her nose. Theodmon had always been her source of stability and strength. And now, she would have to be his.

"I love you," she breathed.

"I love you too." Theodmon cupped his hand around her face before kissing her on the lips on the steps of the Imperial Palace for all to see.

Chapter Sixty

Theodmon felt as if his entire body was tied to the bottom of a lake with an anchor as he dragged himself up to the Imperial Palace. His head throbbed as the streamers brushed against him, large strips of paper folded to appear as if they were griffins, soldiers, or dragons. This whole affair was perverse–the colors were too bright, the songs too cheerful for what should be a solemn affair. How many had died? How many funerals were left to plan? How many funerals had been had already?

How many soldiers laid in an unmarked mass grave? Their families would never know where they rested. Perhaps they didn't know if they died–a few might assume some fled to never return. Theodmon had to admit to himself that perhaps they would have been dishonorable. Cowardly.

What was honor to a dead man?

Theodmon sighed, wishing he could sit down and place his head on his knees. This parade was not the place to have philosophical musings. Yet, without these out-of-place thoughts, the whole affair was uncomfortably shallow. Women and children in the streets shouted thanks and blessings to the brave Thestitiunian saviors.

Saviors.

The word was ash in Theodmon's mouth. Nobody was a savior in Rindria when they sacked the city–nobody was a hero in war. He couldn't blame the civilian women and children for not knowing that. However, Theodmon still didn't need to hear the ignorant screeching of misplaced gratitude.

His fists clenched.

"Stop," Amaria whispered in his ear, holding the bouquet of flowers in her hands. "We must maintain the façade."

Theodmon saw her grinding her teeth from his peripheral vision, disguising her discomfort behind a radiant smile. She was his small kernel of solace in this storm of grief and anger.

"How can you bear it?"

"They're ignorant," Amaria said. "The things we do, it 's so others don't have too. A baker is needed for his bread, not his ability to break bones in a dungeon."

"They don't know the cost!" Theodmon screamed, his words lost in the music and cheers from the parade.

A few citizens turned their heads towards them, their eyes widening. Theodmon took a shaky breath, composing himself. He had to maintain the façade of celebratory stoicism, regardless of the cost to himself.

Amaria rubbed his arm, pausing for a moment. "I know."

"I'd trade all my gold for Ophelia and Aloysius," Theodmon said. "Gods, I'd do anything to prevent them from dying on a battlefield."

His father. Ophelia. Aloysius. Who was next?

"The ability to control life and death isn't a luxury we are afforded." A small tear fell down Amaria's cheek. "Theo...it's hypocritical coming from me, I know, but this path–it's dangerous."

"You killed the entire Riam royal family–"

"And the nation is gone. Who else is to blame for Aloysius' death?"

Theodmon looked at the emperor, glowering at him. "You know."

As if Aion had heard them and had made his life goal to further agitate and insult the Chauvignons, he stepped towards them, his voice magically amplified for the crowd. "Thank you for your service to the empire as General and Princepsia Magia Exia." Aion reached to pull Amaria and Theodmon towards him.

Amaria stepped away from Aion. "I'm not an Extractor for *your* benefit."

"I didn't do this service for you," Theodmon said at the same time.

"Must you be difficult?" Aion hissed, his face fracturing from its happy and pleasant facade momentarily. He turned towards the cheering crowd once more, waving to what he believed to be adoring subjects.

All it would take was one arrow. One expert archer who was willing to die as an assassin. Theodmon wished he had hired an assassin now–perhaps this gilded nightmare under Aion's reign would be over.

"My empire flourishes!" Aion announced. "And through my generosity we will have public feasts, dancing, and coins gifted!" At this, coins from the Rindria coffers were thrown into the streets, the common folk scrambling over each other to reach it. Aion chuckled under his breath. "My reign has been prosperous and peaceful."

Theodmon saw red. Peaceful? How could Aion say that when the country had been in constant war.

That wasn't quite true—he and the Westerlands had been in constant war. Perivina Fluere had often assisted the Westerlands, even before the marriage alliance, but the Raulets lands had long stretches of peacetime. Aion's land—his cozy little bubble he had built for himself, that knew peace.

He was so detached as a ruler he couldn't fathom what a fifth of his subjects, at minimum, had suffered for years.

"The gods are proving my strength as a ruler," Aion continued telling the crowd.

He would take the glory for nothing. Theodmon's rage boiled beneath the surface, threatening to explode as magna in a volcano did. *After this useless emperor did nothing. He had no losses. None of his family or men died–would he care if his men died?-- none of them died in expanding the empire.*

"The gods blessed me," Theodmon snarled, low enough only Aion and Amaria could hear. "I received the blessing of Vathar Ultoris, not you."

"Theo," Amaria muttered.

Theodmon stared at Aion with hardened eyes. "The gods blessed her."

"And the gods bless my empire through it." Aion's jaw locking before he turned back to the crowd, waving to them.

"Strength tested by blood," Theodmon muttered the Chauvignons family motto under his breath as Aion continued boasting to all those around him about his victory.

Aion hadn't shed any blood. Aloysius. Ophelia–they had paid the ultimate price. Theodmon had paid a heavy cost as well–he wasn't dead but he would see the dead every night until he joined them.

Amaria stepped forward, standing so close to Theodmon that not only was she she under his armpit, but he was also under her wings. Her silver eyes narrowed severely towards Aion as her wings adjusted themselves over Theodmon as if they were a feathered protective blanket.

Theodmon pulled her tighter against his chest, as if he too, would be protecting her. Perhaps they protected each other.

"Your Imperial Majesty," Amaria said chillingly, the title in itself a subtle warning in her mouth. "We thank you for your bravery on the battlefield."

Aion's mouth narrowed. Theodmon resisted a smile–Amaria was clever. Aion couldn't publicly rebuke her–not without admitting he had never seen battle. Still, anybody around would perceive Amaria's words for the scathing jab they were, and Theodmon saw the smirks of the few bystanders that heard it.

"Thank you," Aion reached out for the bouquet of flowers Amaria was holding, seemingly unaware of the danger he was in. Glowering, she pulled the roses closer to her chest. Theodmon felt her back tense against him, as if she were a spring ready to burst from its box.

"These are for my husband," Amaria said.

"Not your emperor?" Aion's nostrils flared.

"I'm sure you'll have many more accolades than the simple one of a wife being glad her husband returned from war." Amaria's eyes sparked, her wings extending.

Aion reached for the flowers again and Amaria moved them further away from him. "Do not presume to make a scene, Your Imperial Majesty," she said, disdain dripping from her tone. "I will burn these flowers for all to see."

"For your pyre?"

"For all the brave Thestitiunian men who died." Amaria's fists clenched around the stems of the roses. "Kill me for honoring our soldiers and lose your empire; both the nobles and peasants alike will riot."

Aion stepped closer to Amaria as he grabbed her arm. "You've shown great insubordination since you've returned from the faeries."

Amaria grabbed his hand in her own, beaming for onlookers. Theodmon stepped closer, glowering, not bothering with pretense.

"Let go of her," he snarled at Aion.

"Who are you to command an emperor?" Aion responded.

Who are you to command me? Theodmon glared at Aion. "A man who has done something other than preen his ill-earned jewels."

"I could revoke titles, take lands–"

"Do it," Theodmon challenged. "Give me a reason to destroy the façade you've built."

"You'd harm the empire?"

"The empire would do it to you," Theodmon said. "I'm the one who won you a country—nobles won't take kindly to me receiving punishment, I am the reason they have more wealth, a way for their second sons to do as well as their first ones."

"Your success makes you arrogant," Aion snarled.

"It's not arrogance if it's earned," Amaria responded back just as viciously. "Now smile, Your Imperial Majesty. It's a public event—I'd hate for all of us to lose our image."

"Clever little Amaria." Aion eyed her with disdain. "You once were so polite, so docile. Where is she?"

"She never existed." Amaria turned to beam and wave towards the cheering citizens. "I was always as dangerous as I am today—the only difference is now I'm not pretending to be harmless. Who would believe it now?"

"You're both traitors," Aion said.

Traitors? After countless sacrifices to the empire, the mummers of dissatisfaction due to the wretches of the unbounded trauma seen in war was enough to be a traitor. Theodmon debated if he should punch Aion in front of the world and see how traitorous he could be.

"Not now." Amaria clutched Theodmon's hand. "Not here."

Sighing, Theodmon nodded, walking away from Aion, holding Amaria's hand as he shot hateful glares towards everybody around him. What were they going to do? Chastise the war hero? Most people were not as arrogant as Aion to do such things.

"We need to find your father at the party," Theodmon said. "It's time we let him know we're ready."

Amaria looked upwards at him, her eyes shining. "Shouldn't you rest first, you just came back from war—"

"And there will be more wars; wars Aion never has any stake in. We cannot be good subjects to a ruler who is incapable of being a competent leader. I cannot in good conscience send more of my men to fight and die for that man."

"They'll die fighting him for you," Amaria said. "Let them rest with their families, for a while–"

"I will," Theodmon promised. "Once Thestitiunia is ours. Admit it, you're ready to dispose of Aion–you're ready to rule."

Amaria sighed. "Yes. I don't think Aion is the best, but the men don't need to celebrate the end of a war by reentering one!"

"Would Aion care?" Theodmon gripped Amaria by the shoulders. "The fact we ask these questions shows we will be better rulers than him—how many citizens does Aion care for?"

"I," Amaria paused, wetting her lips. "Civil wars are bloody."

"Giving the façade of peace does no favors except for those who benefit from complicity," Theodmon said. "We've suffered under Aion–commoner and noble alike. Thestitiunia deserves better."

"You'll be a good ruler."

"We," Theodmon corrected.

"I'll be a consort."

"No," Theodmon said. "We'll both be rulers in our own right. No consorts."

"That's never been done—"

"And there's never been an emperor and empress who took the empire with blood as active participants. There's never been an empress like you. Ammy, I need you for this."

Amaria swallowed. "Alright. We'll start making plans after tonight. Let's finish the parade and mourn the dead?"

Theodmon hoped they could reach Aaron at the ball in the imperial palace; there was a sweet irony that excited Theodmon in which future historians would write Aion's undoing started its plans at a party in his honor—an honor he had stolen from the one who then stole his country from him.

Chapter Sixty-One

Aaron watched the brightly colored gowns twirl across the marble floor. His leg would bother him if he joined, but besides, Aaron had never enjoyed being in the thick of the action–he preferred orchestrating from behind the scenes.

He had power. True power. He controlled the finances of the empire. However, as rich as he may be, one day the money would trickle in less and less. They needed more to secure the position of remaining the most powerful family on the continent.

Having an empress come from their House would ensure security.

And security would also come from his upcoming marriage. Despite his earlier misgivings, Aaron was looking forward to marrying his new wife. He had loved Illyana, but this should have occurred years ago. Natalya Svilas was young, she would be eager to produce children. She was functionally illiterate–Morroek had never bothered to teach its women anything beyond sewing, music, and how to be an appropriate wife for their social class. He had promised Amaria to educate Natayla, and he would follow through the promise. However, Aaron doubted Natalya would stay with her education for long—learning was difficult, especially to an untrained mind.

Not that Aaron minded. His pretty bride would be easier to control. Aaron would keep her entertained with jewels and balls and would use the children she bore him to bolster relations with her father. Durek Svilas was no longer a duke; he had recently been crowned Morroek's King.

Aaron turned his head to watch his son dance with his wife. They were stiff with each other, unnatural almost. Shaking his head, Aaron averted his attention to his eldest daughter, who was dancing with her husband. Unlike Haerdnor and Naomi, Aaron noted Theodmon and Amaria had almost the opposite problem—they were almost too enamored with each other, staring lovingly into each other's eyes as they twirled around the dancefloor. At least their devotion seemed to be successful in their marital duties—Amaria had always taken her responsibilities seriously, and one of those was to further her family's power.

Aaron noted that whenever Amaria and Theodmon had their third child—and Aaron expected it to be soon—they would have already provided as many heirs for the empire in the early years of their marriage than Aion did in his entire reign. Hopefully, those two would soon start overthrowing that incompetent idiot—they had given Aaron an indication they would, but even then, it was crucial the coup started when everybody was unequivocally ready.

He blinked, noticing that Amaria and Theodmon had left the dancefloor. It wasn't until they were thirty feet away that he saw them. Aaron exhaled, forcing himself to remain stern. Amaria was his favorite child—she was smart without being difficult, she was eager to please those who needed to be pleased and dismissive of those who weren't worth the effort. Haerdnor was too challenging, and Catalina too soft—it was best she spent her days in a temple. Amaria, however, was his creature.

But Aaron wasn't one to show favoritism, so he maintained his icy demeanor as Amaria and Theodmon approached on either side of his chair.

"Aaron." Theodmon stood beside him. On the other side of Aaron, Amaria kneeled, giving the appearance of a caring daughter as she asked Aaron if his leg was troubling him and if he needed

"Father," Amaria whispered, so low strained to hear her. "The sun rises over the prosperity of the empire every day."

"And griffins are as gold as the morning," Theodmon continued.

A slight smile broke across Aaron's face. It was time—they'd finally admitted they were to take their true places as Emperor and Empress, with Aaron as a most trusted royal advisor.

"A rose may smell as sweet as perfume," Aaron replied. "But its thorns will draw blood more painful than a thousand knives."

"I'll bring you medicine." Amaria hugged him, hastily whispering when and where she would meet him before breaking away from their embrace.

"Let's give a toast." Aaron groaned as he stood up, "to the longevity of the empire's rulers." He made his way through the crowd, Amaria and Theodmon following behind him, as he went to the front of the hall.

A toast to Aion's health would be appropriate for a loyal subject. Aaron had advised Aion, had been a confidant, a friend–all while hiding how much he despised him. Aaron wished for Aion's health as much as his son wished for a woman's embrace. But they all had a part to play, and the more they inflate Aion's ego, the less likely he was to notice the dagger plunging into his back.

The sheep would welcome the wolves eating him.

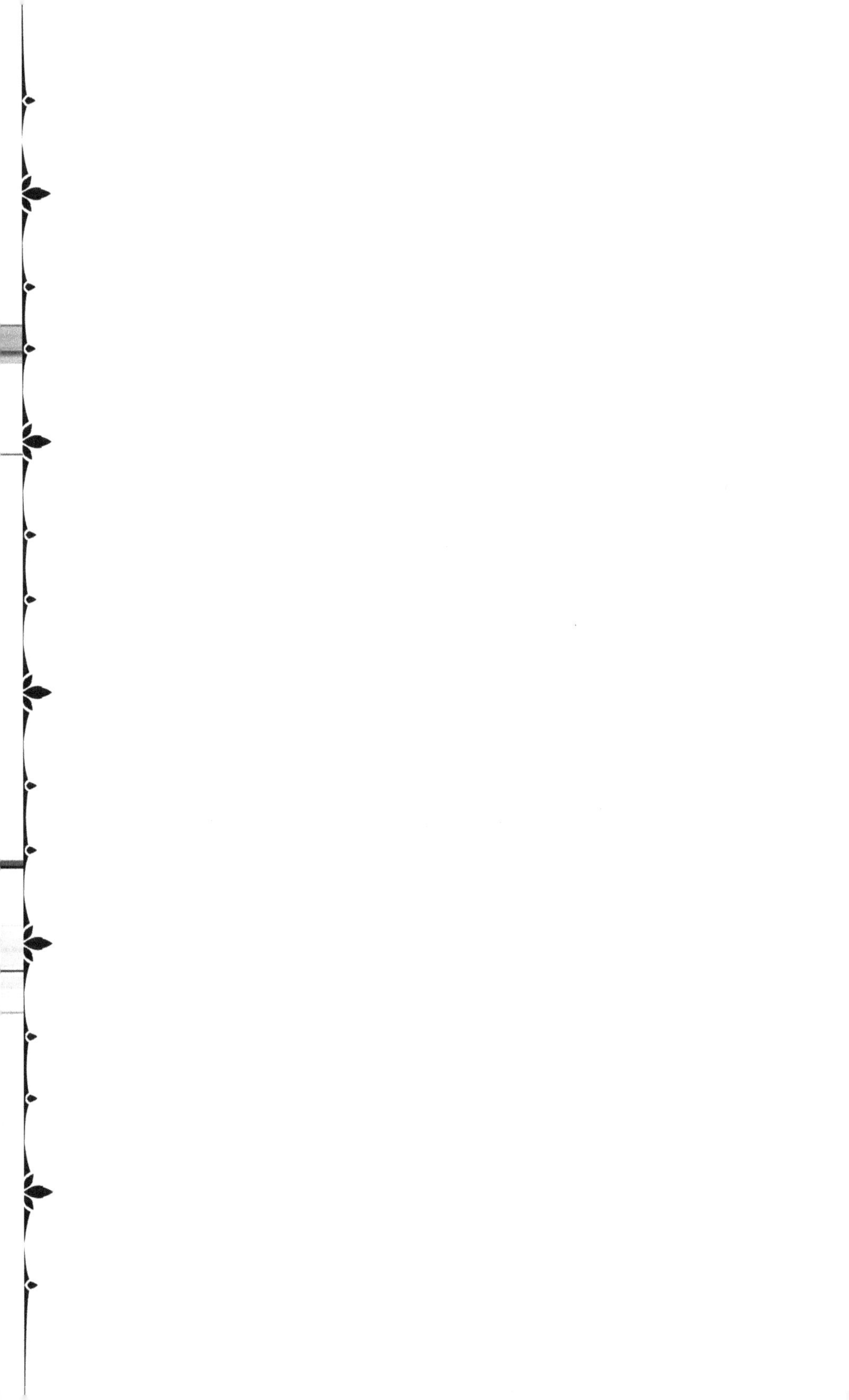

Laurents Alexandre (Loh-hanh Alex-ann-dray): The Duke of the province of Dalia in the kingdom of Avondra. He is ambitious and influential. He is married to Miana Alexandre, née Raulet.

Miana Alexandre (Me-anna Alex-ann-dray): Also known as Miana Raulet. She is Aaron's sister and the wife of Laurents Alexandre. She has seven children and is clever, ambitious, and vindictive. The Duchess of Dalia, Avondra.

Edward Alignes (Edward Al-line-ees): A Raullian fire mage studying at Teplia Street Magic School.

Nicoletta Astasuel (Nicoletta As-tas-u-elle): A Countess. Previously Nicoletta Lemaire. She was born in Raulle, in Perivina Fluere, Thestitiunia. She has been a lady-in-waiting and friend to Amaria Raulet since she was a child. Her husband is a Westanni Earl. They don't speak much.

Stephan Belamy (Stef-fan Bell-am-me): Deceased. An Earl from the Westerlands, Thestitiunia. A war mage with the ability of precognition regarding the opponent's battle plans. He is an Extractor.

Brigitte Belamy (Bridge-et Bell-am-me): A female war mage and Westanni noblewoman. She is the sister of Stephan Belamy.

Juliette Bécharil (Juliette Beh-char-ill): She is originally from Minelle, Avondra. She married Lucas Bécharil and is lady-in-waiting and friend to Amaria Raulet. She is a water and earth mage, commonly called "Hydra Blessed."

Lucas Bécharil (Lucas Beh-char-ill): Currently an untitled Lord. Will be a Marquis once his father dies. He is one of Theodmon Chauvignon's closest friends and bannermen. He is talented with a sword, torture, and tracking.

Ophelia Belegines (Oh-feel-ee-ah Bel-lee-ginny): Deceased. Previously Ophelia Chauvignon. Eldest daughter of Agatha and Raphael Chauvignon. She is married to Duke Lancelin Belegines of Skeletosa, Avondra.

Samuel Beaulane (Samuel Buu–lane): A commoner from Raulle. He is a talented blacksmith and powerful metal manipulation mage. He is an Extractor.

Naomi Brassir (Nay-ome-e Brass-seer): A noblewoman from Tressidil. She is married to Haerdnor Raulet.

Adair Cassidae (A-dare Cass-ee-day): Deceased. The elderly head of the Extractors. His magic is invisibility and shield protection. He is a Thestitiunian Viscount.

Agatha Chauvignon (Agatha Chauv-ing-non): Widow of Marquis Rapheal Chauvignon. Mother of Aloysius, Celestine, Ophelia, and Theodmon. She is from Morroek, and she hates magic and Thestitiunia to a degree.

Aloysius Chauvignon (A-lee-soy-us Chauv-ing-non): Deceased. Youngest son of Agatha and Raphael Chauvignon. A war mage who can harden his body into a shield.

Amaria Chauvignon: Marchioness of the Westerlands of Thestitiunia. Also known as Amaria Raulet. She is an Extractor, a powerful elemental mage, able to control the elements of water and earth ("Hydra Blessed") as well as fire and air ("Dragon Blessed"). She is the Head of the Extractors. She was turned into ulzania by the fae, and has large silver wings. She is the wife of Theodmon Chauvignon and mother of Lysander Chauvignon and Sylviana Chauvignon. She is Aaron and Illyana Raulet's oldest child and the twin of Haerdnor.

Celestine Chauvignon (Sell-est-tine Chauv-ing-non): Youngest daughter and child of Agatha and Raphael Chauvignon.

Lysander Chauvignon (Lie-sand-der Chauv-ing-non): The firstborn son of Theodmon and Amaria Chauvignon.

Sylviana Chauvignon (Sil-vee-aan-na Chauv-ing-non): The second child, but first born daughter of Theodmon and Amaria Chauvignon. She is engaged to the faerie Oberon.

Theodmon Chauvignon (They-od-mon Chauv-ing-non): Marquis of the Westerlands of Thestitiunia. He is the equivalent of a Duke for all intents and purposes, however, due to the Faerielands on his lands; his acreage is shy of what's needed for the legal title of 'Duke'. He is a liaison for the humans and Faeries as his father was before him, and his father was, and so forth. He is married to Amaria Raulet. A talented military strategist and swordsman.

Galen Chironia (Gay-len Ky-ron-nee-ah): The resident healing mage of the Raulets and Provinica Palacina.

Archille Desmond (Des-mon): Deceased. A Westanni Lord, knight, and military lieutenant. Killed by Lucas Bécharil.

Henri Delaluna (Henry De-la-luna): An Extractor. He can read minds, control and alter thoughts, and change memories. He is from the Westerlands, Thestitiunia, and while currently an untitled Lord, once his father passes he will be a Marquis.

Marisa Dubois (Marisa Do-Boys): Deceased. A war mage Extractor. She has enhanced speed and durability as well as advanced reflexes. She is a Thestitiunian commoner who has become comfortable in her wealth due to her magic.

Lynette Edrion (Lynn-et Ed-ree-on): Deceased. The Queen of Avondra. Years ago, she killed her brother in a coup. She is a dark mage, set on bringing chaos into this world.

Faelyn Laurellanza (Fae-lynn Laurel-lan-zaa): Duke of Lirerre Fidelles, Thestitiunia. An Extractor. A powerful healing mage.

Aion Marion (A-On Mare-ree-on): The Emperor of Thestitiuinia.

Cedric Marion (Cedric Mare-ree-on): Deceased. The former Crown Prince of Thestitiunia. He is Aion's firstborn son.

Elena Marion (Elena Mare-ree-on): Deceased. A Princess of Thestitiunia. She is Aion's sister. She is an Extractor. She is blind. A powerful mage who can manipulate others energies and emotions.

Bella Mircares (Bella Mer-care-ees): A Raullian water mage studying at Teplia Street Magic School.

Liara Nalaeny (Lee-are-ah Nale-aah-len-knee): Deceased. A political prisoner to Thestititiunia after she ran away from home from her mother, Clarissa Nalaeny. Married to Aloysius Chauvignon. At the start of the story was the heir to the Riam throne after her brother, Tesden.

Tesden Nalaeny (Tes-den Nale-aah-len-knee): Deceased. At the start of the story was the heir to the Riam throne.

Oliver Neremoux (Oliver Nare-aah-Moo): A minor noble from Perivina Fluere, Thestitiunia. He is in a secret relationship with Haerdnor Raulet.

Oberon (Obb-ber-on): A male Faerie.

Jonathan Pêcheuse (Jonathan Fish-shoes): A Raullian water mage studying at Teplia Street Magic School.

Charlotte Petersdaughter: A Riam peasant with illusion magic. She was saved by Amaria for having magic previously. Charlotte turns against her country and helps the Thestitiunians bring down the capital city.

Aaron Raulet (Aaron Raul-lay): The Duke of the Perivina Fluere Province of Thestitiunia. Cold, ruthless, and cunning, he is efficient in getting his political goals accomplished.

Catalina Raulet (Cat-ah-lein-ah Raul-lay): The youngest daughter of Aaron and Illyana Raulet. She survived a deathly childhood illness that left her with golden scars over her face and throat. She is training to enter a Temple of Ignoia (the healing goddess).

Haerdnor Raulet (Hair-den-noir Raul-lay): The oldest son of Aaron and Illyana Raulet. A hot headed fire mage, he is brave and arrogant. The younger twin of Amaria. In a secret relationship with Oliver Neremoux.

Elisa Redwayne (Elle-Lis-saa Redwayne): Former Lady-in-Waiting to deceased Riam Princess Karissa Riarl. Her husband went bankrupt and died and she is destitute, selling herself as a way to survive. She turned traitor against her country out of self-preservation. Also known as Elisa Yearwood.

Stuart Rockwood: Deceased. A Riam nobleman and one of three governor's ruling Wéorren City and Rindria since the death of the Royal Family. Hung as a traitor by the Riams before Rindria fell.

Fawzia Suril (Faaw-zee-ah Suur-ee-elle): Deceased. A Raullian prisoner in the Drowning Tombs accused of espionage, treason, and heresy.

Svilas (Dur-rek Civ-vil-az): A Morrian Duke. He married the eldest daughter of the Morrian King. Due to the Morrian King having no sons, he is the presumptive heir. Amaria Raulet, Aaron Raulet, and he have engaged in business relations. Talented with a bow and arrow.

Natalya Svilas (Nat-taa-ll-ee-ah Civ-vil-az): Durek Svilas' daughter. She is engaged to Aaron Raulet.

Michel Valrois (Mic-chel Val-roy): An Extractor. A power mage who can transform into other people, a bear, an eagle, and a dolphin. He is an untitled minor Thestitiunian Lord.

Lyseno Vypren (Lis-sen-no Vie-pren): Deceased. The Duke of Darcassa, Avondra. Amaria Raulet's ex-husband. Their marriage was annulled, and he is an angry, bitter man, feeling as if he were embarrassed internationally because of it.

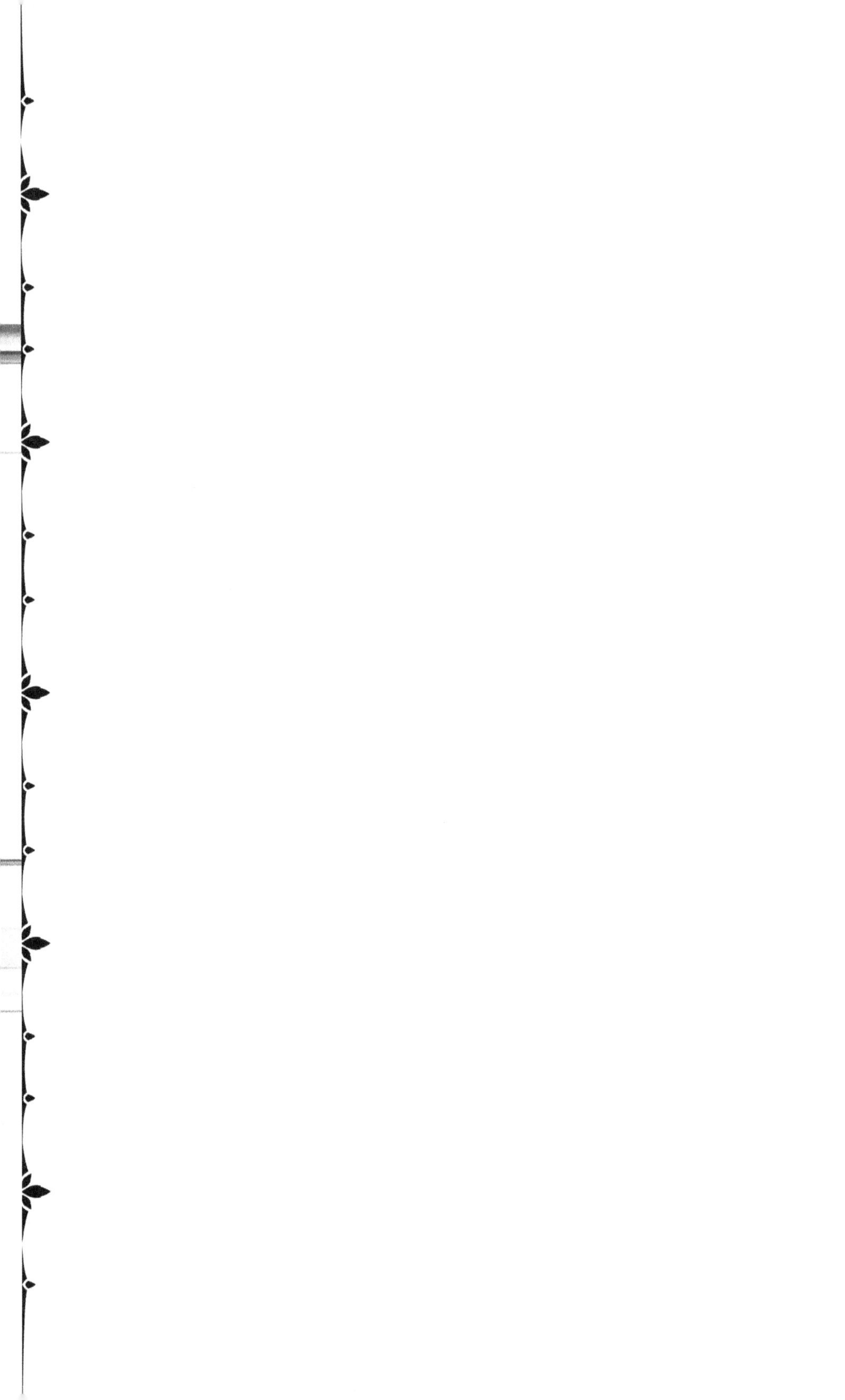

<u>Thestitiunia (Thes-tit-tune-ee-ah)</u>

Thestitiunia is an empire comprising of five provinces: Perivina Fluere, the Westerlands, Lierre Fideles, Arbres Dorés, and Sauvegarde Corolline. Each province is ruled by a Duke (or in the Westerlands' case, a Marquis). These provinces are almost like "mini-kingdoms" within the empire, each province is larger than both the sovereign nations of Rindria and Tressidil. Perivina Fluere is larger than the sovereign of Morroek. Thestitiunia is the richest nation, as well as the most aggressive militarily. Magic is highly valued here.

<u>Perivina Fluere (Per-ee-veen-aah Flu-er-ree)</u>

Perivina Fluere is a wealthy province in the south of Thestitiunia. It borders the sea, with Arbres Dorés to its east, Sauvegarde Corolline to the north, and Avondra to the west. Many fertile plains, islands, a mountainous border with Avondra, and a small desert near Avondra. Perivina Fluere's ruling family is the Raulets. Perivina Fluere is seen as a cornucopia of agriculture, fishing, magical herbs, and a developer of luxury items such as perfume. There is a strong Navy and arts and trade thrive. The inhabitants are called Perivinans and/or Thestitiunians, depending on the regional or imperial context.

Raulle (Raawl): The capital city of Perivina Fluere and the seat of power for the Raulets.

Provincia Palancia (Prov-enn-cee-aah Pal-enn-cee-aah): The Raulet's palace, located in Raulle.

Drowning Tombs: Known as one of the worst prisons in the world. The Drowning Tombs is located on a small island directly off the coast of Raulle. It is incredibly fortified, and half of it is sinking underwater.

Émeraudes Sea (Ay-mer-aude-ays Cee): The ocean to the south of Perivina Fluere.

Calmeanis Harbor (Cal-may-nee-iis Harbor): A major harbor in Raulle. A center of international trade and intelligence networks.

Euodia (Ee-oh-dee-ah): A small island in Perivina Fluere. The village of Hyllasi is here.

The Westerlands

The Westerlands is the north-west province in Thestitiunia with Morroek to the north, Rindria to the west, Lierre Fideles to the east, Sauvegarde Corolline to the south, and in the eastern southernmost part of the Westerlands there is shared border with Arbres Dorés. Many forests, farms, and mines, and weapons industry. The ruling family is the Chauvignon. The Westerlands ruling family is a Marquis as due to the faerielands they are just shy of the acreage needed for Thestitiunian Dukehood.

The entrance to the faeries' lands is located here, with the ruling family acting as liaisons between humans and faeries. A wild place, it is blessed with the highest percentage of mages per capita in the empire, as well as the rest of the world. However, wild and magical animals roam free and it can be a dangerous place if you are not careful. The people are called Westannis and/or Thestitiunians, depending on the regional or imperial context. Westannis can be stern and militaristic, however, they tend to be community-oriented. The Westerands host the strongest standing Army in the empire.

Chauvi (Chauv-vee): The capital city of the Westerlands and the seat of power for the Chauvignons.

Lake Holimeda (Lake Hal-ee-me-dah): The large body of water by Chauvi.

Mount Mortensia (Mount Moort-tiin-cee-aah): The Mountain on which Forteresse les Blanche is carved from. It also hosts the Mortensia Labyrinths carved deep on the inside of the mountain.

Forteresse les Blanche (Fort-eer-esse les Blan-ch-ay): The castle of the Chauvignons. It is carved from Mount Mortensia. It is incredibly fortified with a pulley system designed to bring in supplies.

Mortensia Labyrinths (Moort-tiin-cee-aah Laa-bre-inths): The Chauvignon maintained dungeons and prisons. Tends to be harsh and dark—the only light comes from torches, there are no windows and there is only one entrance and exit into the prison.

Perpives Pass (Per-pii-vees Pass): A natural gap in the mountains between Rindria and the Westerlands. Heavily armored and fortified on both sides of the border due to the Riam-Thestitiunian distrust of each other.

Valemont Tunnels (Valemont Tunnels): The maintained entrance between the Westerlands and Morroek. The mountains were carved to allow this wide tunnel between the nations for travel and trade. It it heavily fortified on both sides of the border, due to Morrian-Thestitiunian distrust of each other.

Lierre Fideles (Lee-err-ree Fii-dell-lees)

Lierre Fideles is a province in the northwest of Thestitiunia. It borders Morroek to the north, sharing Retilisk Cove with the sovereign nation, the Westerlands to the west, the Escada Sea to the east, and Arbres Dorés to the south—sharing the Cove of Ghagyn. The Laurellanzas are the ruling family. Arts, forestry, livestock, medicine, and universities are the main industries. There are more temples per capita in Lierre Fideles than anywhere else in Thestitiunia. The people are called Lierrians and/or Thestitiunians, depending on the regional or imperial context.

Laurelle (Laur-elle): The capital city of Lierre Fideles and the seat of power for the Laurellanzas.

Bracenora Harbor (Braay-ce-nora Harbor): A large body of water that flows out to the Escada Sea and which Laurelle is located near.

Retilisk Cove (Ret-til-iss-ck Cove): A body of water bordering Lierre Fideles and Morroek. Retilisk Cove goes to the Escada Sea.

Escada Sea (S-caa-daah Cee): The ocean to the east of Lierre Fideles.

Cove of Ghagyn (Cove of Gah-gen): A body of water that borders both Arbres Dorés and Lierre Fideles.

Arbres Dorés (Arr-brey-ees Door-ay-es)

Arbres Dorés is a province in the southeast of Thestitiunia. It borders the Escada Sea to the east, the Émeraudes Sea to the south, and is the only Thestitiunian province to share a border with each of the other four provinces. Arbres Dorés ruling family is the Marions, and while there are Dukes that officially run the day-to-day of the province, in reality, Arbres Dorés is ruled by the Imperial Family (still the Marions). The citizens of Arbres

Dorés are called Arbrians and/or Thestitiunians, depending on the regional or imperial context. There is a strong fishing, winemaking, and artisan market as well as arts, religion, and universities.

Aionstown (Ay-ons-town): The capitol city of not only Arbres Dorés, but of Thestitiunia as a whole. The city's name changes depending on who is the currently ruling emperor.

Cove of Ghagyn (Cove of Gah-gen): A body of water that borders both Arbres Dorés and Lierre Fideles.

Escada Sea (S-caa-daah Cee): The ocean to the east of Arbres Dorés.

Émeraudes Sea (Ay-mer-aude-ays Cee): The ocean to the south of Arbres Dorés.

Imperial Palace: Where the emperor and his court live. Located in Aionstown.

Le Golfe Lontaine (le gulf lon-taay-ne): The body of water outside Aionstown. The Imperial Palace overlooks part of it.

Mariisope (Mar-ee-soope-pay): A major city in Arbres Dorés. It is the seat of power for the Duke/Duchess side of the Marions.

Sauvegarde Coroline (Sauve-ee-gaurd Cor-oo-lee-nee)

Sauvegarde Coroline is a province in the center of Thestitiunia, bordering Avondra, the Westerlands, Perivina Fluere, and Arbres Dorés. Heavy winemaking region. The ruling family is the Archambeaus. The citizens are called Corolinés and/or Thestitiunians, depending on the regional or imperial context.

Archama (Arr-chaa-aa-ma): The capital city of Sauvegarde Coroline and the seat of power for the Archambeaus.

Rindria (Rin-dree-ahh)

Rindria is a landlocked country filled with tundra grasslands and sparse pockets of trees (mainly to their eastern border with Morroek and Thestitiunia). It is a relatively poor country, but it's proud. Most of their industry comes from the horse trade. Its economy and political structure are unstable, and its issues have been exacerbated by foreign interference. The Riarls used to be the ruling family, but the country is currently experiencing a power vacuum. The people, called Riams, are very suspicious and guarded, hating magic—having magic is a crime punishable by death to the Riams.

Wéorren City (Wee-oor-en City): The capital city of Rindria.

Wéorren Fields (Wee-oor-en Fields): The villages and farmland outside of Wéorren City. Is often destroyed in times of war/sieges.

Bria Hall: The castle of Riam Royalty, located within Wéorren City.

Perps Pass: The Riam version of the Thestitiunian Perpives Pass.

Harréow Field (Haar-e-row Field): A battleground near Perps Pass.

Morroek (Moor-oh-ack)

A mountainous, tundra country with very little fertile land but many natural resources such as iron, gemstones, gold, silver, coal, and lumber. There's a heavy fishing industry in the easternmost part of the country. The citizens are called Morrians. Most Morrians live within fifty miles of the Thestitiunan or southernmost Riam borders, or a hundred miles of the Retilisk Cove or Escada Sea. A few Morrians live on the surrounding islands in the Escada Sea. Morroek nobility and royalty are rich and powerful, however, their citizens tend to be extremely poor. An extremely patriarchal culture. They have a strong Navy and a decent Army. Morroek borders the Badlands, and it has the longest border with the Badlands out of other nations; as such, it has been plagued with dark magic escaping from its prison. As such, Morrians despise magic and are deeply superstitious people. Magic is an offense punishable by death. However, they are practical people and were willing to overlook magical differences with their allies in the war against the Badlands.

Retilisk Cove (Ret-til-iss-ck Cove): A body of water bordering Lierre Fideles and Morroek. Retilisk Cove goes to the Escada Sea.

Escada Sea (S-caa-daah Cee): The ocean to the east of Morroek.

Sielvahella (Cee-eell-vah-elle-aah): The field and village that borders the Badlands. Considered cursed.

Avondra (Av-onn-dra-ah)

A large kingdom with several disjointed duchies. There is no shared economic system, however, there is a shared culture, language, and religion. The duchies elect one king to rule over them in terms of wartime. However, there is no central government although some wish to change that. There are several ecosystems in Avondra, as it is the largest nation aside from Thestitiunia. It borders Rindria, Tressidil, Thestitiunia, the Pentaine Ocean (to the south), and the Hasenfort Ocean (to the west).

Dalia (Dah-lee-ahh): One of the wealthiest provinces in the Kingdom of Avondra. Ruled by Duke Laurents Alexandre and Duchess Miana (nee Raulet) Alexandre.

Raeria (Ray-ree-ah): A wealthy province in the Kingdom of Avondra. Was the former capital of the nation as the Edrion Family was from there. Queen Lynette Edrion was the last ruler of this province.

Skeletosa (Skel-elle-toe-saah): A province in the Kingdom of Avondra. Ruled by the Belegines family. Ophelia Chauvignon was married to Duke Lancelin Belegines before her, Lancelin, and their children's deaths. While not the wealthiest in Avondra, they are strong politically due to a standing army and an abundance of powerful allies.

Darcassa (Dar-caass-saah): A wealthy province in the Kingdom of Avondra. Ruled by the Vypren Family.

Cowaneles (Cow-anne-elle-lees): A wealthy province in the Kingdom of Avondra. The current Empresses of Thestitiunia come from here.

Angora (Anne-gore-ah): A wealthy province in the Kingdom of Avondra.

Jassini (Jass-sin-nee): A province in the Kingdom of Avondra.

Frisca (Fris-caah): A province in the Kingdom of Avondra.

Hirane (Hii-ran-ee): A province in the Kingdom of Avondra.

Dalia City: The Capital of Dalia.

Carcalet: The Capital of Skeletosa.

Raeria City: The capital of Raeria.

Poigenoux: A major port city in the south of Dalia.

Milcaires: The capital of Darcassa.

Pentaine Ocean (Pent-tayne Ocean): The ocean to the south of Avondra. It eventually meets and becomes the Émeraudes Sea.

Hasenfort Ocean (Has-en-fort Ocean]: The ocean to the west of Avondra.

Cowlany Harbor (Cow-lane-ee Harbor): A major natural harbor in Cowaneles, Dalia, and Raeria.

Lake Navitiva (Lake Nave-ee-tee-vaah): A major lake in Dalia, near Dalia City.

Musgrove Basin (Muss-grove Basin): A large and deep natural port that borders Angora and Raeria, giving those provinces protected trade and naval cities.

Otterflow Reservoir (Otter-flow Reservoir): A natural body of fresh water between Minelle, Jassini, and Tressidil. Home to lots of wildlife, such as river otters.

<u>Tressidil (Tres-saa-dill)</u>

The singular democratic nation in Cesmassia, strictly speaking, they are a constitutional monarchy. The citizens of Tressidil are called Tressis. Tressis are an industrious people, highly skilled artisans and tradespeople, merchants, academics, fishermen, shepherds, and farmers. They border the Badlands, however, they have commissioned their mages to control and monitor dark threats. Magic is seen as commonplace. It is a relatively well-off nation.

Otterflow Reservoir (Otter-flow Reservoir): A natural body of fresh water between Minelle, Jassini, and Tressidil. Home to lots of wildlife, such as river otters.

Hasenfort Ocean (Has-en-fort Ocean): The ocean to the west of Avondra.

Freedom Gulf: The body of water near Kratos.

Kratos (Cray-toos): The capital of Tressidil.

Sherril (Share-ill): A major and wealthy city in Tressidil ruled by the Brassirs. They are an inland city, relying heavily on agriculture. Haerdnor Raulet's wife, Naomi Brassir, is from here.

Baymore (Bay-more): A major port city in Tressidil ruled by the Montagnons. The current Lord Prime Minister is a Montagnon. Aaron Raulet's first wife, Illyana Montagnon was from here.

<u>N'angora Desert (Nah-Ann-gore-aah Desert)</u>

A Sahara-like desert that is not governed by any common system of monarchy found in the other nations. Instead, the N'angora is uncharted territory sparsely populated with various tribes of desert people. It is referred to as *Nagalia Aride* by the Thestitunians, *Vastus Nangoli* by the Avonnians, and *Nagore* by the Riams.

<u>The Badlands</u>

A wild, unhabitable place where dark magic resides. It is a prison made by the goddess Ghagyn to cast her rejected creations. However, it is not an impenetrable prison, and every so often its prisoners will escape or an innocent person will wander in.

Hello, and thank you for reading. If you read in the About the Author Section from *The Guileful Rose* that *The Topaz Crown* was the second book in The Curoria Chronicles, you may be wondering why this book is instead titled *Winterthorne's Shards*. In writing this book I realized that the events planned were so vast that I needed to split up this book as well as move a few plot points around. That being said, *The Topaz Crown* will be the third book in The Curoria Chronicles series.

To my son and husband, you guys are the true MVPS. I do it for you.

And for those who read as betas, as ARCS, street team members, or as regular readers, thank you most of all.

Books Written By E.A. Almanza

The Curoria Chronicles

The Guileful Rose

Winterthorne's Shards

The Griffin and the Rose: A Curoria Chronicles Novella *(November 26, 2024)*

The Topaz Crown *(TBD)*

9 7 9 8 9 9 0 5 1 9 7 0 1